Inter**

THE KING PIN

James Hanford

Published in 2013 by Puissance Publications

ISBN: 0957643802
ISBN-13: 978-0-9576438-0-2

In loving memory of my father,
John Hanford (1932–2013),
and with immense gratitude to my
family for their encouragement whilst
I was writing Intervention: The King Pin.

Intervention
The King Pin

James Hanford

1

Rob emerged from the ensuite shower room at the guesthouse where he was staying and pulled his long-sleeved T-shirt over his head before opening the curtains with a flourish. The room was spartan, furnished only with the bare essentials, but it was perfectly adequate for his purposes.

"Damn, that's bright," he muttered, crinkling his eyes into a squint.

The blackout curtains had certainly done their job. That, coupled with the poor lighting in the room, made the morning sun breaking through the clouds appear very bright. Instinctively, Rob suddenly stepped to one side of the battered, loose-fitting window. Without looking, he brushed off the blistering paint that had caught on his shirt and continued to look down to the street below.

"What is it with this place?" he thought aloud to himself as he noted yet another twenty-something man wandering along the street. The man was as equally out of place as himself in the small town. But there was a distinct difference; Rob was a legitimate tourist, and these guys did not give that appearance.

Despite himself, Rob Krane tensed as the adrenalin rush of butterflies hit his stomach. It was exactly the same feeling he got before going into a meeting with a senior executive. Well, that had been until a few weeks ago, when he had lost his job. Of course, it was also the same feeling he had prior to a bout in one of the many championship fights he entered as he anticipated an unknown combatant's moves. Shaking these thoughts away, he recalled how uncomfortable he had felt the previous evening and during his morning's exercise when he saw these characters wandering the streets of Postojna.

Everyone he had spoken to and all he had read in the guidebooks and on the official websites had clearly indicated the general safety of travelling around Slovenia. However, the number of walk-past encounters he had experienced with these out-of-place, twenty-something, lone men was distinctly disconcerting. The similarities were evident. Their dress-sense, swagger, and expressionless faces all resembled those of the guy who was currently disappearing from Rob's sight. They were certainly not locals, so who were they? And why were they here in such numbers?

Okay, there had been similar men in some of the villages he had passed through en route to Postojna following his visit to Predjama Castle the day before. But this was different. Something was up. He knew it. Regardless, why should he be bothered? Rob was on holiday and having a great time, courtesy of both his redundancy and his fight winnings two weeks before at Wembley Conference Centre in London. Rob recalled standing on the podium to collect the gold medal for the European Combined Martial Arts and Unarmed Combat Championships.

A sufficiently loud gurgle from his belly reminded him that he was hungry. "Breakfast," he said aloud, reaching down to pick up his iPhone off the bedside table. "Damn it," he cursed as he scanned the screen, looking at the time and to see if he had received any texts.

The low-battery indicator was flashing. Rob pulled a small day sack from a far larger backpack, smiling as he rubbed a thumb over the flexible solar panels on the face of the bag. It was a new toy for him—one that he had been unable to resist for this holiday because he was planning a few days of camping. After looking out of the window again at the weather, Rob decided he would go out for breakfast. It was warm enough and certainly bright enough for him to test his new purchase. He could also check e-mail instead of having an ingratiatingly painful conversation with his hosts.

Lightly jogging down the stairs, Rob waved to the unconvincingly jovial owners of the guesthouse. "No breakfast today, thank you. I ate too much last night."

Whilst that was partially true, the pleasant weather gave him the opportunity to avoid the unnecessarily large and unhealthy breakfast Madam Kos insisted upon rustling up, and of course, he would avoid having to converse with the elderly couple.

Closing the door gently behind him, Rob turned down the street and headed towards the Kras Hotel. He had noted the previous night that breakfast was served outside in the square, and since it was the only four-star hotel in town, he hoped he would get reasonable fare. Unlike at most places he visited, he didn't bother looking around at the buildings and the general environment. He had seen enough during his exercises. The area in which he was staying was really rather bland, the house frontages having very limited architectural appeal.

Few of the exterior tables were occupied, and those that were all clearly contained tourists. Schools had restarted after the summer holidays, so the number of tourists was dwindling, which was by far Rob's preference. There was little movement inside the hotel foyer. All he could see was an attractive woman with a fidgety young girl sitting down and looking out into the square. The mother, he presumed, appeared a few years older than he was and had pleasant but not striking features, shoulder-length, straight blond hair, and the tired looks of a concerned, caring mother. Rob recognised the signs from his sister-in-law. He settled himself at a non-shady table not far from the hotel door, set up his solar-panelled backpack, and plugged in his iPhone, iPad, and other gadgets to recharge.

The pretty waitress who served Rob gave him more attention than he really wanted, distracting him from his e-mails and catching up on the day's news from the BBC website. Not that Rob really minded. The girl was possibly a few years younger than him, and engaging her with some idle banter and reciprocating her playful flirtations was fun. Rob felt good as he noted her name, Irina Vidmar, and ensured he used it as they chatted. He made a mental note to come here more frequently, particularly after he returned from his planned hike in the hills and mountains to the south and east of Postojna.

Half an hour later, Rob was relaxing as he read the news headlines from the BBC website and drinking his coffee when, from outward appearances, a distinguished, well-built man in a dark tailored suit and open-neck shirt walked into the square and straight into the foyer of the hotel. Only the tanned face and purposeful, almost-cold demeanour suggested something entirely different. Rob chose to ignore him and continued to read the ridiculous intrigue and implications of the latest political sex scandal involving one of the government's ministers. Shaking his head slightly Rob wondered, *Why do they always dice with the illicit? Eventually the press always finds out.*

A few minutes later, the same man left the hotel, holding the young girl's hand, with the mother walking along beside them. The girl was smiling, half-skipping, and happily chatting away to the man, whose demeanour had softened markedly. Rob followed their progress across the paved, pedestrianised square. Their direction suggested they were headed for either the Karst Museum or transportation for the Postojna Caves. Rob presumed the latter, as a museum of predominantly archaeological collections was unlikely to be of interest to the young girl, who did not have the grumpy air of a child going somewhere that in her mind would be dull and boring. Well, that would have been his attitude at that age. Instead, her demeanour exuded excitement and joy. As they approached halfway, one of the young men Rob had noted appeared at a far corner, talking on a mobile phone. Moments later a black saloon followed by a red four-door Nissan four-by-four pickup with white cover over the rear charged into the square, tyres squealing.

The man froze, with his spare hand inching into his jacket. He also glanced at the woman and young girl beside him, at which point his hand dropped to his side and he became a spectator to the impending horror in which he would play a central role. The black saloon raced over towards him whilst the Nissan screeched to a halt adjacent to the hotel. Young hooded men jumped from all doors of both vehicles, each wearing the same uniform of dark jeans and shirts of all those lone men Rob had noticed over the past couple of days. In their hands they held a variety of machine pistols. Those from the saloon approached the man, woman, and girl whilst the others turned their attention towards Rob and the others having breakfast. There was no hesitation. Grabbing his belongings, Rob flipped his and a neighbouring table over to provide a semblance of cover. As the other hotel guests looked on with bemused, uncomprehending expressions the square was filled with bursts of gunfire and bullets slamming into walls and pinging off the metal tables.

The realisation that his cover was decidedly limited was rapidly reinforced as bullets started piercing other nearby tables. Quickly assessing his position, Rob glanced over his shoulder towards the hotel lobby and the relative safety that being behind its walls would bring. Screams from the others who had been sitting outside with him punctuated the racket hammering in his ears, making thinking hard.

As more bullets whined overhead, ripping through the windows and glazed doors, Rob rolled over to the next table behind him, drawing closer to the hotel entrance and the hoped-for shelter. With a whooshing, chinking sound, all of the glass of the doors collapsed in a myriad of glistening beads and gleaming shards, spraying across Rob's back.

With his heart thumping, he shuffled on hands and knees behind the next table, scrunching painfully over the pieces of glass. Groans from the injured hotel guests gave a constant, disconcerting background sound reminding him that each and every move could determine his fate. Looking around the edge of a table to check the route for his next dash, Rob recoiled as he came eye to eye with Irina, whose lifeless body was surrounded by pieces of broken crockery and food from her tray. Summoning all of his willpower, Rob shook his head to remove this nightmarish vision to focus on his next move. Then, with a final roll and dive, Rob made it through the door, into the hotel lobby, and behind a wall, followed by a volley of bullets.

Rob watched, mesmerised, in horror as the apparent terrorists went about their business, spraying bullets in all directions. The smell of cordite floated into the lobby on the gentle breeze, making him shudder.

One of those from the Nissan flung the tailgate open, hauled out a couple of large sacks, and ran over to his accomplices in the centre of the square, who had surrounded the man, woman, and girl. As the man was unceremoniously punched to the ground and gagged and a handgun removed from his jacket, the girl was shoved into one of the sacks, kicking and screaming, before also being gagged and the sack firmly tied. The mother, standing in a frozen and dazed state, was grabbed roughly by one of the men and brought face-to-face with another who, after the briefest of looks, summarily shot her twice in the chest. The man holding her then thrust the body away to flop onto the stone slabs, where a pool of blood began to form around her. The man in the suit reached out a hand from where he was lying and caressed her face. He was then bundled, struggling, into the second sack, and both writhing sacks were dragged slowly back across the square towards the Nissan truck.

The other terrorists meanwhile fanned out across the square, firing in all directions, at passing cars and the windows to all of the surrounding buildings, including the hotel. Two were headed towards the hotel as they fired. Calmly walking between the carnage of the upturned tables and chairs, the two periodically lowered their guns and took single shots aimed at the heads of those lying helpless on the ground, whether apparently already dead or not.

These guys don't want witnesses, Rob thought as he once again slid across the hotel's floor. All the others there were momentarily frozen in disbelief. Milliseconds later, however, they were screaming and running in all directions as the two men from the Nissan came walking into the lobby, calmly spraying bullets all over and cutting people down. Rob had no choice but to jump up and dive through one of the broken windows to head back outside.

Rolling over, Rob came to a halt behind a table and some chairs, his back sack cradled in his arms.

Once outside, Rob wormed his way quietly through the morass of up-turned furniture, seeking an escape because he had no doubt the area would be thoroughly checked for survivors. Looking about it became obvious that there was no opportunity to make a run for it down the street, and not far away was the open tailgate of the Nissan, which was between him and the men dragging the sacks his way, their intention obvious. It might well have been suicide, but Rob sprinted to the rear of the vehicle and leapt in, relief flooding through him as he saw a cluttered interior. It didn't take long to slide a large toolbox out slightly from the rear and duck behind it, covering himself with other sacks and cloths that were lying around.

Every sinew was tensed virtually to the point of snapping, if that were possible, as Rob tried to control his breathing and listened to the approaching footsteps.

For the first time, Rob heard voices.

"Well?"

"All taken care of in there." came the response and Rob surmised that the speaker had referred to the hotel.

"No survivors, then?" said the first voice again brusquely.

A third voice replied, "We think not. We thought one jumped through the window but didn't see anyone when we got to look."

"Idiots!" the first voice yelled. "Boss will deal with you later if that turns out to be correct and details reported. Orders were no witnesses!" After a momentary pause, he continued, "Get those two into the truck, and let's get moving before we get company. Stephane! You're in the back to watch over the packages!"

They had all spoken in rough English but with varying accents, suggesting differing nationalities.

There were grunts of exertion followed by two soft thuds as the sacks were heaved into the rear, and the truck jiggled slightly in the process. Rob heard the sound of sackcloth being pushed over the bare metal of the truck floor before he was squeezed by the large toolbox as the man and girl were shoved as far in as possible. Rob barely suppressed a groan. A third jiggle signalled that Stephane had climbed in before the tailgate slammed shut with an eerie finality.

Doors slammed, engines started, and they moved off quickly. The sound of the tyres thrumming upon the road surfaces acknowledged that. Hard braking compressed the heavy toolbox against Rob, alerting him to either a road junction or corner, and he braced himself against the sides to avoid slipping and potentially giving himself away. After a while, there was no hard cornering, which suggested they had joined one of the nearby main roads. It was also telling that judging by the steady thrumming of the tyres, they were not travelling at breakneck speed anymore. He could

11

only presume the kidnappers were hoping that no one had survived to describe the vehicles to the local police, or *policija*, and therefore did not want to draw attention to themselves by travelling too fast.

There was no way of knowing in which direction they were travelling, but judging by the periodic slowing down followed by gentle acceleration, Rob decided they were going through other small towns or villages. That suggested he was not on the A10 highway between Italy and the capital, Ljubljana. Instead, from his recollection of the maps, they were travelling either north, further into the heart of Slovenia, or south towards Croatia.

From time to time the thug, who Rob presumed was Stephane, shifted his weight and asked, "You still alive in there?" as he thumped the larger of the two sacks, soliciting a grunt or moan, and subsequently chuckling to himself. Occasionally there was a gentle whimper from the young girl.

Rob's limbs started to ache from his cramped position, but he dared not stretch, let alone move to try to alleviate his discomfort. This was a trifle compared to whatever would befall him were he to be found.

2

The emergency services arrived rapidly at the scene, and the medical workers ran from victim to victim, searching in vain for any sign of life. The local policija initially stood around in undisguised disbelief and horror at the scene. A radioed message from one of them brought their chief racing to the square, by which time the officers had started to corral the remaining hotel guests around the corner into the neighbouring park. It didn't take the chief long to cast his eyes over the devastation before he radioed for expert support from Ljubljana.

Chief Horvat then set about ordering and directing his men to knock on all the doors of the buildings surrounding the town square, first to determine if there were any other casualties and second to determine if there were any witnesses prepared to come forward and describe what on earth had happened.

"Don't forget," he yelled after his men through the radio, "make sure that everyone understands they're not to touch or move anything." Then, after a short pause, he followed up with, "However small! It must not be touched! Locate all bullets! Seal off the entire square, including the roads. I don't care how inconvenient. Just do it! Report everything back to me and write it down. I'll be in my car," which he had parked at the opposite side of the square from the hotel. With that, he stomped away.

◆

An unexpected, sharp jerk indicated that the truck had clearly turned off whichever main road they were on. Stephane, or whoever it was, cursed loudly as he slid about, not having expected the sudden change of direction. They had only been going for maybe fifteen minutes, but it seemed like an eternity for Rob cooped up where he was. The cornering now became more frequent and more pronounced as time ticked past. Only rarely was there any respite when there was a straight road along the route, but that was short-lived. Stephane's curses came thicker and faster in a language that Rob did not recognise.

The girl was whimpering far more regularly now as she slid around the floor of the truck, crunching into the metal sides. Barely a sound came from the man, except for when he was unexpectedly punched by Stephane, who alternated using his fists with the gun that he carefully kept below the level of the tailgate. The road soon became steeply inclined, so the toolbox would frequently slide away from Rob slightly. Again, this was short lived as Stephane became cramped for space, and as he was able to do something about it, he rammed the toolbox back hard against Rob as far as the large box would go. The journey went on for an indeterminate amount of time, and the oily rags and rugs coupled with the violent motion started to make Rob feel queasy. He swallowed hard a few times as bile rose in his throat, almost gagging in the process.

Oh man, how much longer? Rob wondered. *Okay, I'm currently better off than those slaughtered back in the square and the two poor souls in those sacks, but even so. Urgh, that hurt,* he thought as his head once more thudded into the metal side of the truck. It was proving a challenge to keep himself constantly braced against both sides to reduce the impacts of each corner turned.

This section of the journey was clearly the longest. *And the tyres are still thrumming along a metalled road surface,* Rob thought to himself. *A way to go* then, he reasoned as he braced against yet another sharp corner. *What's this going to be like if they turn off on to a dirt track?* he wondered. He had a long wait, but to his relief, he was proved wrong. There was to be no journey up a dirt track.

The truck eventually slowed to a halt, and doors started to open and clunk closed. There were no bumps, no scrunching of gravel or other surface that could be expected from a lay-by or from pulling off to the side of the road. Rob held his breath, every muscle taut and every sense straining to work out what was about to occur.

"Quick about it!" Rob recognised the first voice from the town square in Postojna.

"Unwrap the packages away from the road and remove the gags so they can breathe for the walk," the voice continued.

Moments later the tailgate squeaked open, and the two sacks were manhandled out of the rear of the truck. To Rob's relief, the tailgate was slammed shut again.

"Ali, Gustov!" the apparent leader barked. "You buffoons will guard the base of the path just back from the road. You'll hear what the boss says about your idiocy later. You two," the leader continued, pointing to the two drivers, "dispose of the vehicles while the rest of us take KP and the girl to the house. Make sure you're not followed."

The engines started, and the two vehicles laboriously manoeuvred to make a U-turn. As the truck started to move, so did Rob. *Damn, should I bail here or later?* thought Rob. An image of the girl's terrified face flashed into his consciousness, so as the truck reversed once more, practically

16

backing into the bushes at the side of the road, Rob gathered his belongings plus the rug he had been lying under and leap-frogged from the tailgate, landing in the midst of some tall grass and bushes. There was no reaction from anyone, so he assumed he had not been noticed.

The two vehicles raced off back down the hill and disappeared around a bend less than fifty metres away. For the first time, Rob noticed just how steep the landscape was. He had been fortunate that the bushes had prevented him from rolling further and creating a greater commotion. He crept as close to the edge of the road as he dared to watch and listen.

"Ali, Gustov! You're staying here. Beware you don't stray, and don't set off any of the alarms we set along the way. Stephane here will bring down some food later. It would be bullets if I had my way, but there are no reports of cars following us, and the policija appear to be in disarray, so if someone escaped, you appear to have gotten away with it so far.

"Right, you idiots," the leader continued to yell as he turned his attention to the others. "Why are you standing around gawping? We're hardly going to carry these two, are we? Get them out of the bags! Now!" The leader was yelling, almost screaming at the remaining three men, clearly confident that they were in a very isolated area where there would be no one else around to hear.

That also means that there's no chance for me to find help easily, thought Rob dejectedly.

They were clearly all distracted, and Rob realised he had to move and move quickly. *I can't afford to lose these guys, particularly if they're setting alarms*, he thought to himself.

Rob wormed his way back into the forest a little way and then scampered downhill to the bend in the road where he could hopefully cross without being seen. The road was narrow, barely sufficient for two cars to pass, so after a quick check, a sprint across the road saw him arrive safely on the other side and ready to make his way back uphill towards the terrorists or thugs or whoever they were. All six were still standing around, albeit well back from the roadside, when Rob approached. The man and girl, both well bound with their hands behind their backs, were slumped on the ground among the damp leaves and earth.

Rob looked at himself and considered his surroundings for the first time. He was filthy. The fresh, damp, earthy smell of the forest filled his lungs, which was immensely gratifying after the oily rags in the truck. He was also underdressed. *Okay, I've got my waterproofs, this smelly rug, and some semi-decent footwear, but that's it*, Rob mulled.

Whilst he knew he should scarper, when he saw the young girl, who couldn't have been more than ten or eleven, he could not leave. She was leaning against the man, snuggling up as close as she could, terror clearly displayed in her wide eyes, her thin dress a mess and her hair all awry. The man, whilst outwardly composed, was clearly weighing up the situation. He gently leaned his head against the top of hers and quietly whispered to the little girl, presumably trying to give some level of comfort through his proximity and words. *There is clearly a relationship there. Very possibly he's the girl's father,* Rob thought. His suit was also a complete mess and as equally unsuitable for this environment as the girl's dress.

There's nothing I can do here. It's too dangerous, but at the very least I have to see where they are going. Then possibly I can go for help, Rob thought to himself. *Be careful of twigs,* he warned himself as he moved to a new vantage point. *This is for the girl. That dad looks as dodgy as you can get, so tough on him.*

Glancing at his watch, he saw it was already 11:40. They had been travelling for over two and a half hours.

———◆———

Chief Horvat of the Postojna Policija was soon trudging disconsolately back across the square from his car. He had just taken a call from Franc Kovač, a revered inspector at the Slovenian Intelligence and Security Agency in Ljubljana, and had come out at the end feeling rather dim witted.

"What are you doing just sitting in your car? Go commandeer some conference rooms in the hotel. I will need a base to conduct operations, won't I? I hope you weren't expecting me to shuttle back and forth from your station. And make sure there's a side entrance available for use so the crime scene is not disturbed."

However, Chief Horvat did receive an, "Okay, you made some reasonable decisions so far," as a consolation.

That was two hours ago. Now Kovač, who did not make use of his inspector title, had arrived with a small team by helicopter, landing in the nearby park. More were to arrive by road. Mercifully for Chief Horvat, Kovač and his team had swung into action immediately and taken charge. Kovač had also praised Chief Horvat for what had been accomplished in a relatively short time. Even so, Chief Horvat still felt a little raw from the earlier call but was pleased to be still very much involved and learning, although he really hoped he would never have such an experience again. Petty theft, speeding, the occasional burglary, and the odd alcohol-related bust-up were sufficient for his wife and himself.

They were in one of the hotel's conference rooms, a number of tables rearranged throughout the space, each with fewer chairs encircling the table than the annoying hemmed-in arrangement hotels typically adopt. In one corner, to provide a little isolation, Kovač had set up his own station, together with a couple of flip charts and an outlying desk for his assistant to act as gatekeeper.

Chief Horvat, Janez Potočnik, the hotel's manager, who was looking haggard and shell-shocked, and a couple of others were gathered together with Kovač, peering through a scribbled list of names.

One of the local policija approached and nervously cleared his throat. Addressing no one in particular, he announced, "We've been through all receipts and tables-in-service records." Almost as an afterthought, he added, "As Chief Horvat requested." He immediately continued in an effort to avert any comment. "All paperwork can be accounted for and associated with either a body or a guest." He hesitated briefly and then, taking on a serious expression, continued with, "Except one, that is. A single person, male and not resident at the hotel. We know this because the kitchen staff told of how Irina Vidmar, the waitress covering the outside area, kept talking about this non-guest guy who she rather fancied and on the face of it was reciprocating through their conversation. The kitchen staff were all encouraging her on because she, well, was feeling—"

"Enough!" barked Kovač. "That's great work and very helpful, but we don't need the unfortunate girl's life story and romances, at least not yet. Please go back and find out if there's any description of this man. Did the waitress say anything, whether descriptive or anecdotal, like nationality or where he's staying and for how long? Did any of the kitchen staff take a peek out of interested curiosity for the girl? Put a message out across town for anyone who had breakfast here to come forward and check the hospital. I don't suppose there's CCTV there?"

"No, sir. No CCTV. I will go and start those enquiries, sir." And with that, he turned on his heels and headed off, and from the expression on his face, he was greatly relieved to be doing so.

"Now that was interesting and helpful intel," Kovač commented, emphasising the word *was*.

"So we now have fifteen people dead, including seven who were eating breakfast outside between three tables, two ladies and one man on reception, four who had been sitting in reception, and crucially, a mother whose daughter has disappeared, presumed kidnapped. I understand that Chief Horvat has initiated a search just in case the girl escaped, but at this stage, I consider that unlikely considering the location of the murdered mother and the tyre tracks. Almost certainly the girl would have been with her, but such a search is required to discount that option. Remarkably, no one else was injured, just more than a few irate motorists with bullet holes in their cars presumably designed to dissuade them from paying attention to the activities in the square. This was clearly a well-planned and efficiently executed operation, so we are dealing with an organised group. We now also have a missing man who had been eating breakfast outside the hotel.

"The unmarried mother and daughter were staying by themselves. They arrived last night in time for dinner and were not due to leave for another two days. Killing the mother and kidnapping the girl, leaving no one against whom she can be used as leverage, is not rational.

"The missing and unidentified man may be pivotal to this or a mystery man in the wrong place at the wrong time. Whatever, I don't like coincidences. He may have been a spotter for this gang, or he may have been taken as well. I want to know who he is and why he was here. At this stage, for whatever reason, the girl appears to be central and the reason for this carnage, and I want to know why.

"Have I missed anything, or does anyone have something more to add? If not, get working!"

"Guv," said a member of his team from Ljubljana who was reviewing a paper on the desk, "the mother, her name is down here as Evelyne Dupois. She was a French national. The daughter's name was registered as Anja. Shall I contact our counterparts at the DSGE?"[1]

"Glad someone's alert. But no thanks, please ask my assistant to get a message through to Henri Simmonet, my opposite number. I owe him a call anyway."

With that and after a momentary silence, everyone started to drift off to their own business, leaving Kovač pouring over the various papers and sketches of where the dead had fallen. After a few minutes, his mobile phone buzzed and vibrated on the table beside him. Kovač snatched it up as he recognised the name flashing on the display.

---

1 The Direction Générale de la Sécurité Extérieure or the French intelligence service.

"Henri, *bonjour. Comment va-tu?* Many thanks for calling me back."

"You are always welcome, *mon ami*. I am well, and how are both you and your good wife?"

"We're both well, thank you, Henri."

"Good, good. I'm pleased. Now tell me, how can I help? A call in work hours is a sign of activity, *n'est pas?*"

"Exactly, and sadly, in this case you're right. A French woman, Evelyne Dupois, has been shot dead in Postojna, where I am now leading the investigation." Despite the pause, Henri did not interject, and Kovač continued. "Her daughter, Anja, aged nine, is presumed taken. Fourteen other people are also dead. One person, male, remains unaccounted for. The possible hypotheses for his identity are a spotter, also taken, or that he disappeared and was simply in the wrong place at the wrong time. We doubt the latter. Tyre tracks suggest two vehicles, and from the clusters of cartridges, up to eight hostile participants, so a large group for just one young girl." Following another pause for breath, Kovač finished with, "Motive unknown."

"Mon ami," Simmonet whistled, "you have certainly been an unwilling host to a most horrific and strange situation. I assume you wish checks on this Dupois woman?"

"Absolutely, together with anything on the girl's father if he is known."

"I shall do so with pleasure. Presumably you can send copies of the documents lodged upon her arrival."

"Yes, they are ready and will be e-mailed very soon. Thank you for agreeing to help and speak soon."

"*Au revoir.*" And with that, Kovač hung up and put his phone back down on the table.

Rob kept his distance from the group and watched cautiously from behind a clump of bushes. *Muppet!* Rob cursed himself suddenly. He shrugged out of his back sack, opened it, and pulled out his iPhone. *Bother, no signal.*

He started to drop it back into his bag when a thought struck him, so he slipped the iPhone back out. Holding the gadget between the branches and leaves of a bush, Rob fiddled a bit and zoomed into the man's and then the girl's faces, taking a photo of each separately and then together. Flipping through the menus, Rob opened another app. The words "Media Face Recognition" flashed across the screen, followed by a command to upload the desired photo. Rob navigated through yet more menus, found the man's photo, and pressed "OK." Ignoring the options to refine the search, Rob set the app running. *Yes! Now you're thinking. E-mail—let's do an e-mail. Who to?* he asked himself, pondering for a moment.

Just then the group of terrorists or gangsters—Rob had still not made up his mind as to which—broke up as the apparent leader handed a small radio to Ali and Gustov, the two men nominated to stay behind as lookouts. They moved away, inserting an earpiece as they did, each in his own direction to find a place of shelter that would provide a view of the road and Rob presumed, the route along which the rest were about to walk.

Rob stuffed his iPhone back from where it came without composing any e-mail whilst trying to note where the two went, but he lost sight of both quite early on. *I'm going to have to move carefully,* he thought as he eased deeper into the wood whilst still keeping an eye on the remaining four, who were in the process of separating and pulling the hostages to their feet. Rob cursed as they headed off directly away from him. He was going to have a game of catch up on his hands and knees whilst also having to avoid the two spotters or guards, wherever they may be. Keeping as low as possible and scanning the ground for potentially noisy materials, Rob followed as rapidly as he could. The thick foliage proved a huge hindrance as he zigzagged around trees, stumps, bushes, and other clumps of plants. At least the dampness prevented any scrunching from the thick mat of leaves upon which he was forced to scamper, often on all fours.

Soon it became clear that the group had found their intended path because their progress speeded up significantly, leaving Rob in the precarious position of potentially losing them and becoming desperately lost with two armed thugs not far beyond spitting distance.

Periodically Rob lost sight of his quarry behind a mass of trees or bushes, but he plunged on regardless, trying to parallel track whatever path the group was taking. The going became harder as the ground started to slope upward more steeply. Gradually, he moved closer to their trajectory to pinpoint the path. Thankfully, it was not long before he spotted, by now quite a long way ahead of him, that two of the group had stopped and were bending over their back sacks. The other two were still guiding the hostages forward, holding their bound hands, which were strapped behind their backs. The girl was in front of the man, with her guide clearly holding a gun close to the girl's head. The display was obviously for the man's benefit. Possibly, and very gratifyingly if it were the case, the girl may have been unaware of the proximity of the gun.

Damn, they are setting alarms or traps, Rob muttered under his breath. At least he had been able to watch and avoid this set. Rob kept weaving his way along, trying to gain ground, but he was losing the battle. The two men finished their work, one on either side of the path, and promptly jogged up the path at quite a pace after their colleagues. Rob eased up close to the path's edge beyond where the alarms had been set and scanned both ways. Clear. However, he hesitated to scramble up onto the path. First, he would potentially leave a trace, and second, he would not know when he could either happen upon a member of the gang or trip one of their alarms. Both were risks he did not want to face, so he gently slid back down some five metres from the path and set off once more.

After one hundred metres or so, Rob paused. Trying to ignore his hunger as time had now ticked to nearly 1:30 in the afternoon, Rob sat down to assess his situation. *I'm going to have to keep creeping up to the path to check for changes of direction or turn-offs.* Rob maintained this pattern of progress for nearly five hours and had donned his waterproofs sometime earlier as it had started getting cooler the higher he climbed. The path had changed direction a number of times as it weaved up a narrow valley, so by the time Rob moved up to check on the path, it was not where he expected. Consequently, he had to re-trace his steps carefully to recover his intended direction. As he progressed, the ground became increasingly rocky, and he had not once seen those he had followed since the two had set that first set of alarms. At least he could see the recent marks on the path of feet scuffing the surface of the earth.

Easing back from the path once again, Rob identified a small area suitable for a breather. Taking his iPhone from his bag once more, he checked for a signal. *Bother!* No signal again. *Oh well, e-mail.* He tapped in his password and was welcomed by a flashing icon indicating that his face recognition app had returned a result. At some point during his ascent, he must have picked up a signal. Forgetting his intention of sending an e-mail, he went straight to the app and stared in disbelief as he found himself looking at a mug shot of precisely the same man associated to a report from the *Independent* nearly two years earlier entitled "Legitimate Face of Corruption?" The article read:

Burak Demir walked free from a Parisian court yesterday after the spectacular collapse of the trial into his involvement, or otherwise, with criminal activities. The secretive, fifty-one-year-old Turkish billionaire was the alleged indirect owner of and more importantly, the "instructing director of operations" for three businesses domiciled in France. Each business, under express direction and knowledge of Mr Demir, was alleged to have laundered millions of Euros over at least five years, avoiding tax on the associated activities and being fronts for an array of other criminal activities. The trial was expected to run for at least a further five weeks when it collapsed suddenly today as the prosecution failed for the fourth consecutive day to either introduce any evidence or substantiate any of the allegations. Papers and other apparently incriminating evidence were mysteriously lost in the police and the court's evidence lock-ups. Witnesses for the prosecution have variously recanted their testimonies, failed to turn up at court, or outright contradicted the prosecution's allegations, and in one unsettling instance, one witness was found dead two nights ago following an apparent suicide. Prosecution lawyers were unavailable for comment on how a case three years in the making and involving the police and intelligence services of many countries could collapse quite so spectacularly.

Burak Demir left the court building rapidly, refusing to answer questions, and disappeared in a waiting car. A source has suggested that, frustratingly for the UK authorities, the current whereabouts of Burak Demir are not known as they were expecting to interview him about a raft of similar matters across Britain during the course of his confinement here in Paris, a fact Burak Demir was apparently acutely aware of.

A voice of someone talking alerted him to someone heading his way. "Okay, guys, I'm heading your way with some currently warm food and clothes. Boss is still not happy, so you're parked down there for the long haul."

With that, Stephane appeared from around a corner on the path, his attention focused on a small two-way radio in his right hand. Rob slipped further behind a tree for greater cover, once again stuffing his technology back into his bag, index finger fumbling for the off switch so no sounds could give him away.

"Bad news is that police are talking about an unaccounted person, so you did miss someone.

Good news is that they don't appear to have anything to go on." Stephane continued on his way and disappeared down the path.

Rob settled back against the tree to think and give his heart time to stop racing and the thumping in his ears quieten down. *That was too close for comfort,* he thought as he took a series of deep breaths. He must be close to the gang's destination and hideout.

◆

Kovač was sitting at his desk with a dry sandwich, a half-eaten bar of chocolate, the skin of a banana, and a large, freshly brewed cup of coffee. He was becoming increasingly frustrated as the day slipped past. Government ministers were understandably on his back for updates, but so were the multitude of news reporters who scented something big. It had been necessary to make a statement that a large number of people had been gunned down, many of whom were foreign nationals—Australian, Belgian, British, and French. Unfortunately, it had also been necessary to make public that a nine-year-old French girl appeared to have been abducted, the reasons for which the police were keeping an open mind about. That piece of news had sent the reporters wild with excitement and speculation, at times bordering on the ludicrous. He had not heard back from Henri Simmonet yet, but that was to be expected, even though he was impatient to know about this Dubois woman as quickly as possible.

The only piece of remotely good news had followed the 5:00 p.m. radio broadcast repeating the request for any information on the still unaccounted for man. Kovač's assistant had just announced the arrival of a Madam Kos, who ran a guesthouse located not far from the hotel and had telephoned about her only current guest. She was promptly invited for an interview. It was now approaching 6:00 p.m.

Kovač stood up, stretched, and headed off to a smaller meeting room that had been requisitioned and in which Madam Kos had been settled. He walked briskly to get the blood flowing and to clear his head. Chief Horvat followed, as did his assistant to take notes.

"Let's hope that this leads somewhere," he called over his shoulder. "If only all people were as forthcoming as this lady, even if it comes to nothing, but I have that feeling it will." Kovač smiled as he approached the room, determined to put the elderly lady at her ease.

Opening the door, Kovač smiled broadly at the lady and extended his hand in welcome. His lean, two-metre-tall figure in a smart, plain, light grey suit, white shirt and blue tie and neat haircut made an impressive figure beside Chief Horvat. The now slightly crumpled appearance of Kovač's suit and shirt from his journey and lengthy day did not detract at all from his appearance. Chief

Horvat, on the other hand, was simply wearing his ill-fitting police-issue uniform, belly protruding slightly, forcing a small corner of his shirt to dangle down over the front of his trousers.

"Inspector Franc Kovač from the Slovenian Intelligence and Security Agency in Ljubljana. Madam Kos, I presume?" Upon receiving the nodded, nervous confirmation, he continued, "You know, I am sure, your local chief of police, Chief Horvat, and this is my assistant, Nina Lah, who is here to take notes so Chief Horvat and I can concentrate on your good self instead of on my handwriting."

Kovač paused to allow space for the humour to take effect. "Please, have a seat. I see you already have a drink, but please, if you require anything else, do let me know. I am extremely grateful that you came. Your thoughtfulness is a compliment to your family and society."

He knew that he was laying it on thick, but he had to get people on his side, and this lady would almost certainly talk once she left. He wanted positive messages to permeate through the town to both give confidence to others so they would come forward with information and also to start the process of putting people at ease with their own personal security and safety.

After they were all seated, Kovač launched in to avoid any embarrassing silence. This was not an interrogation. This was different, and he was at pains to put the elderly lady at ease and make her feel important.

"Now, I understand that having heard our broadcast message about an unaccounted man following today's atrocity, you are concerned about someone who is staying at your guesthouse. Please, we would be most grateful to hear why you are concerned and who the young man is. I can assure you that no one will be visiting to look at your accounts for at least six weeks."

And with that, Kovač gave Chief Horvat a fleeting but meaningful look. This lady was not to be hassled over any failure to declare all of the income from running her guesthouse, a practice the authorities knew well.

Madam Kos was wearing what was possibly her best dress saved for special occasions. Not surprisingly from her conservative attitudes and approach to running her business, it was medium-weight, cotton, modest, and plain, falling to midway down her calf and sufficiently full to not cling to her now slightly sagging body but still close enough to accentuate her overall slim build. Over the top, she wore a matching jacket. The pale blue reflected her eyes and set off the grey, arguably silver shoulder-length straight hair.

She briefly fidgeted and shuffled her behind slightly to make herself more comfortable before saying, "I really do not want to insinuate anything because he is such a pleasant young man. He arrived two days ago and intends to stay for another five days."

Such a long stay visibly made both Kovač's and Chief Horvat's eyebrows raise, so Madam Kos hastily added, "He's been to Predjama Castle and the caves there twice. He's an amateur photographer, you see, and has taken some lovely photographs. Such clever things cameras these days. Do you know that you can replay the photographs back on a small television-type screen on the back of the camera? Very clever. He showed my husband and me. Today he decided to stay here and visit our castle and caves. Tomorrow he is planning to go hiking in the hills and mountains for a few days." At this point, Madam Kos paused, partly for breath, partly for a drink.

Kovač filled the silence, having been listening intently, nodding occasionally and starting now with another of his smiles. "That's very helpful background into this person, Madam Kos, so thank you. Please could you tell us his name and also why it is that you are concerned? Presumably you saw him this morning."

"Absolutely, Robert, although he likes to be called Rob, was as cheerful as always this morning. He went for his daily run. I really don't understand why young people these days like running around so much. Anyway, he didn't stay for breakfast today, simply waved and said hello as he went out. I can't really remember the time. He did say that sometimes he wouldn't have breakfast with us and would take a coffee elsewhere. Well, out he went, and I presumed he would come back because he was not as fully dressed or prepared as he usually is when he leaves for the day. Then, when I went up to his room to make the bed, the guide for the castle and caves was still laid out on the table with his camera and notes for what he wanted to take photographs of. Also, he had said it was possible that he would dine with us tonight and show us more photographs. He was good at telling us his plans. A charming and considerate young man."

Here she paused again but was not interrupted. Kovač recognised that whilst Madam Kos liked to talk, she was also perfectly switched-on and would not miss a beat. "Now, where was I? Yes, his name is Robert Krane. As I say, he likes Rob. He's English and says he's from London. Lost his job a little time back. I can't remember what it was that he did, something at a bank, but he always stressed not banking, which is all terribly confusing. The first thing he asked when he arrived was where he could register his arrival. He said he'd do it himself and did not want to inconvenience us. Had time on his hands since he'd lost his job and said his habit was always to take care of the paperwork, at work and for himself. But he did show me the confirmation of registration so I could relax about that."

Kovač noticed that both his assistant and now Chief Horvat had both started scribbling since the man's name and nationality had been revealed. It would be easy to trace. The woman's nattering was testing his patience, but he knew she would clam up if he interrupted, and allowing her to talk in her own way was the best way to get information from this particular lady.

"I haven't touched anything in Robert's room, of course," continued Madam Kos. "That would be improper. Other than cleaning and making his bed, that is. I'll be pleased to show you around if that would help."

"That would, indeed," confirmed Kovač. "If you could leave your address and telephone number with my assistant here, someone will be in touch. It may be later this evening, if not too inconvenient. But please do call back straight away if Robert has arrived back or if you hear from him. If he does return, we will want to speak to him anyway, just to discount him from our enquiries."

"Yes, of course. I will do that. I do hope he is okay. Such a nice young man."

Kovač stood and extended his hand. "Many thanks once again, madam. Most helpful. Now, if you'll excuse us, we will leave you with my assistant."

With that, Kovač and Chief Horvat left the room and hurried back to the main conference room. "Chief, I presume you will pull this Robert Krane's registration papers immediately. I will contact MI5 in London. Whatever you do, please do not speak to anyone else. I really do not want the reporters hounding us more than they already are."

———◆———

There was nothing else for it but to press ahead.

Rob ran his fingers through his hair and sighed. He had been wondering what challenge he should seek next now that he had no job, and if the truth be told, he was greatly relieved to be out of that place. Doing something to challenge himself physically had been appealing, but he had not envisioned anything quite as extreme as this. And ideally he would have been better prepared with clothing, equipment, and stuff. *Stuff?* he thought to himself. "Come on, Krane, what sort of comment is that?" he muttered with a shake of his head and stood up, stiff from his huddled position on the cold, damp ground.

It was now ticking on towards 5:00 p.m., and if he wasn't careful, Stephane would be returning. Rob wanted to have moved on by then and found some cover since it appeared he would be camping. Stepping forward, avoiding sticks and loose stones on the rocky areas, Rob came to the edge of an area where the trees became more spaced out and the going became easier. Some two hundred metres ahead a rocky outcrop materialised from between the trees and towered above a small timber cabin. "Shit!" he whispered to himself in alarm.

Rob immediately froze and then very slowly, very cautiously, and watching very intently eased backwards to the cover of some bushes and waited. Had anyone seen him? Could he have set any alarms off?

Idiot! he thought as he chastised himself for letting his attention lapse. Scanning the area, he mouthed "very clever" to himself. Trees had been cleared in a planned way, providing sight lines to the two paths leading into the not-quite-a-clearing yet also still providing a near-seamless canopy over the entire area. There were also two traditionally built timber Alpine-style stable-type structures, mimicking the design of the cabin, just smaller.

I doubt any but the most thorough fly past would notice this place, he thought to himself. Sinking back to the ground, he checked reception on his phone. Nothing. Rob glanced at the rock face. *Maybe at the top of that.* He started working his way round the not-quite-a-clearing and to where the rock face merged into the forest floor.

Making his way up, careful not to dislodge any loose rocks or stones, it soon became clear that he was in the absolute middle of nowhere. Tree-covered hills and the occasional rock face were all he could see. His hair had become matted to his scalp, and Rob scrubbed his fingers vigorously back and forth across his scalp before once again checking for a signal and scanning for alternative networks. Still nothing.

Dusk was approaching. It was getting dramatically colder, and he had to find cover. Optimism spurred him on as he thought about the area he was convinced he had been brought to and the fact that the Notranjska region of Slovenia was famed for its networks of caves carved out of the generally limestone rock by rivers and the elements. A search for a cave in which to spend the night was a feature for his planned trekking that he had keenly anticipated. His incurable sense of adventure and fantasy distracted him from his perils and lack of suitable equipment, instead providing a valuable fillip as he thought of discovering a previously unknown network of caves glittering with crystals and majestic stalactites and stalagmites. He knew the prospect of crystals was a pipe dream as the region was not known for crystals, but so what?

Once back down and having found a new vantage point, Rob systematically scanned the rock face and identified a couple of possible opportunities for shelter a little way up the rock face and with access routes that provided cover. Once again skirting around the not-quite-a-clearing to reach the rock face, he heard a rustling sound as he approached one of the two sheds, and to his amazement, he saw the rear end of a young wolf reversing out of a hole in the stable wall. In its mouth it was carrying food of some sort, but Rob could not work out what. It then proceeded to wriggle back in and come out with some more food, at which point Rob had an idea.

Lifting a large branch that he could use as a club and a couple of fist-sized rocks, Rob positioned himself, out of the cabin's line of sight, so he could launch an attack upon the unsuspecting creature when it next emerged, which it soon did. So startled by the onslaught of flying stones and Rob's manic charge, waving a large branch over his head wildly like some over-excited sports fan during a tense match, the wolf turned tail and fled. Rob hastily glanced at the food left behind. There was a smelly joint of some sort and a variety of other unrecognisable items. He left them there and carefully peered through the gap in the wall, gagging at the nearly overpowering combination of smells.

Eyes smarting, he leant in further. Spying a number of bags of food, he grasped a couple, pulled them through the hole, and rapidly transferred as many of the contents into his back sack as possible, scattering other contents around himself in a haphazard manner. He was acutely aware both that he was exposed and that the wolf might return imminently, and he wanted out of there fast. Doing another quick grab and pull through the hole, he realised he had more than a full bag and could also carry at least one of the strong carrier bags in which the food was contained. He slipped quickly to the rock face and started to climb. His spirits were now about as high as he could ever think possible given the circumstances.

Not surprisingly, as he looked down, he saw the wolf was soon back at the scene sniffing around the scattered food.

As Rob inched closer to the first of his chosen openings, two men came out of the cabin, lighting cigarettes. Rob pressed himself into the rock, wishing it would absorb him to avoid any possible sighting by the two men. His blood turned to ice, and shivers spread through him, the high of a few moments before evaporating like liquid oxygen in a furnace. He held his breath as the men turned, raised their arms to point, and started to yell. To his immense relief, they had seen the wolf, not him. The two bent down to pick up and then throw stones at the animal, which promptly turned tail and fled once more. All the other men came pouring out of the cabin, guns at the ready.

Rob recognised the boss-man as he demanded sharply, "Hey, what's going on?"

One of the men pointed to the rear of the shed and explained, "A bloody wolf was taking our food, that's what."

The group of men walked over to the scattered food, and the boss-man said, "Fix that hole and clean the mess up. I don't want more animals." With that, he sauntered back to the cabin.

The remaining men set about their boss' orders in a leisurely manner so when, nearly twenty minutes later, they had finished, Rob was sweating profusely and his fingers and arms shaking with the exertion of holding himself so close against the rock for so long. Only once the men were safely back inside the cabin did Rob gingerly climb the last couple of metres into a small cave and collapse in a heap, exhausted, on the rock floor.

After a while, Rob sat up and tried to scan the cave but to no avail. The light was approaching negligible, so all he could do was to sit in the mouth of the cave to inspect some of the food he had captured and start eating. He was famished. Once the light had faded completely, Rob had no choice but to wrap up in the smelly rug he had brought from the truck and settle down to sleep. He did not want to risk turning any of his gadgets on in case their light alerted someone. At one point, the night's peace was shattered with the roar of some quad bikes.

"More people arriving," Rob groaned. He had just started to settle after the heart-thumping shock of the latest arrivals who had disturbed his light sleep when rain started to hammer down hard. However, after a while its hypnotic rhythm helped Rob to drift back to sleep.

3

Dawn broke over the hilly, almost mountainous region of Notranjska in Slovenia, and a cold, tired Rob Krane started massaging life back into his limbs. He was sore and stiff after an uncomfortable and disrupted night trying to sleep on the cold, hard, bumpy, and mainly rocky floor of the cave in which he found himself. Rob tried as many of his daily stretching exercises as he could in the confined space. It was still raining and with such intensity that Rob immediately decided upon staying put. From the cave mouth, he could just make out the area immediately in front of the cabin, so he would be able to witness any comings or goings.

Following a light, jumbled breakfast from some of the food he had purloined, all there was to do was to take an inventory of what he had. The range and quantity of food was a pleasant surprise. *At least this will last for a while,* he thought as he looked down at the other contents of his sack: iPhone, iPad, various cables, a Gerber multi-tool, a lock knife, a Maglite torch, and a pocket tripod for his camera back at the guesthouse. *Hmmm. I wonder how Madam Kos has reacted to my absence. She's probably informed the police. Oh joy! Oh well, not much I can do about that, and not much else to do other than to explore this cave I've found myself in.*

━━━

At the same time as Rob was starting to eat some of the cold food he had captured the evening before, people wearing various uniforms and civilian clothes started materialising in dribs and drabs at the Kras Hotel. They made their way to the main conference room, where Inspector Kovač had established his base for the investigation into the events of the previous day. Most of the arrivals had their hands curled around steaming cups of coffee as they made their way to designated desks or tables to start work.

Shortly after 8:00 a.m., Kovač's mobile phone buzzed. Henri Simmonet's name flashed on the screen. "Hopefully with helpful news," muttered Kovač.

"Ah, Inspector," his French counterpart started with that singing French accent that attracts so many. "Evelyne Dubois. Not much I can say. I'm sorry. Thirty-eight years old and from Vichy. That's in central France in the Auvergne region. Most people skip the Auvergne on the way south, but it's worth a stop. I digress, apologies. Both parents died whilst she was young, and she was raised by her grandmother, who is also now dead. No siblings. Registered occupation is florist and lives above the shop. Was reasonably successful by all accounts, but she is not the proprietor. No record of the daughter's father.

"On the face of it, yet another baby conceived without realising and the woman not keeping a trace of the men in her life to chase for support. No record of any trouble with any of the authorities, but she was flagged by her bank shortly after her daughter was born because a regular, second source of income started filtering in. Nothing substantial, simply unexplained. It was declared and tax paid. Too small to register as a priority for investigation, so appears to have been forgotten and never looked into.

"They travelled to Ljubljana two days ago, as you said, using a variety of modes of transport. No indication from her bank account that she paid. Passports were issued for the first time six years ago. It appears she's visited other countries, always with her daughter, and some quite a few times. This was their first trip to Slovenia. The other countries were Austria, Belgium, Germany, Italy, Spain, Switzerland, and Turkey. I'd suggest that the latter together with your own country are the unexpected destinations out of that list. There were two visits to Turkey.

"On no occasion does it appear that she paid from her known bank account. Her lifestyle and the apartment's contents suggest that she was not extravagant. The photo albums contained nothing of interest from our perspective (i.e., no one special), although if I may say so, it does appear coincidental that once the little girl was born Mme Dubois started receiving financial assistance and when the girl reached a reasonable age to travel, they did so quite a lot. That's all we've found so far, but I intend to keep looking because there are a number of intriguing elements in all this that have caught my attention. I'll stay in touch, but please also let me know how you progress."

"Well, that is most interesting, especially the countries and timing for matters surrounding the daughter. Many thanks indeed," said Kovač who had been listening intently and scribbling notes in a pad as he propped the phone between ear and shoulder. He had also waved at his assistant, Nina, who had trotted over obediently and stood beside him, listening and waiting for instructions.

"My news carries a certain amount of intrigue as well. A young English man appears to have disappeared. The guesthouse where he'd been staying has not heard from him since yesterday morning." Kovač continued looking intently at his assistant, who nodded in confirmation, indicating that Madam Kos had not reported Robert Krane's reappearance.

"We are working on the presumption that he is the unaccounted for person according to the meals in service records from the hotel. Name is Robert Krane, had been chatting the waitress up and according to his guesthouse hostess was into fitness and photography and had recently lost his job. The meals in service record indicates the person had been sitting close to the hotel door so could have been a spotter for when the mother and daughter left. Alternatively, he could have been in the wrong place at the wrong time, but like you, I don't like unexplained coincidences. A team is gathering to go search his room at the guesthouse. We were waiting to see if he would return and didn't want to alert him at all. I'm waiting for the English to wake up before I call MI5. I want to speak to my contact to ensure appropriate attention is given to this, so I will be able to call soon. I will most certainly keep in touch."

"Many thanks, mon ami."

"My pleasure. Let's speak again soon, although if I'm moving about I may ask my assistant, Nina Lah, to update you."

"That won't be a problem. I perfectly understand. Well, au revoir and good luck."

Kovač stabbed at the red disconnect call button on his phone and looked intently at his assistant. "Green light to the search team for Mr Robert Krane's room please, and then type up these notes and circulate both to our team and also to the authorities of the countries this Dubois woman travelled to. We want to know anything they've got on her, if anything. A long shot, I know, but worth the question."

Kovač was on a roll, his adrenalin pumping. Scrolling through his phone's contacts list, he soon found who he was looking for and punched the green call button.

"Gurning." Kovač was taken by surprise because there had been no rings.

"Steven, it's Franc Kovač from Slovenia here. Got a few minutes?"

"Sure. How are things?"

"Complicated, to say the least. Other than that, I'm fine, thanks. And you?"

"Not too bad. Bored of the ever-increasing administration the bureaucrats dream up. So, what's up, Franc?"

"I would be grateful if you could run a few checks on one of your nationals for me. Robert Krane. He's been missing since yesterday morning from the guesthouse where he's been staying in Postojna. We think he was at the Hotel Kras here at the time of the mass killings you've probably heard about."

"Sure, happy to run some checks for you. Yes, heard about the killings, so anything we can do, just let me know. Do you think our boy was involved?"

"Not sure. Nothing is making sense. Everyone was killed except for this Robert Krane and a nine-year old French girl who is presumed abducted as she's disappeared, but her mother, Evelyne Dubois, was amongst the dead. Henri Simmonet is looking into her and has already found a few matters of intrigue, all of which appear to coincide with the young girl, namely additional finances from an unknown source and multiple visits to neighbouring countries, except for Turkey, two visits, and Slovenia, first visit. None of those trips were paid for out of her own or only known bank account."

"Sounds like they were meeting someone, quite possibly a secretive fellow who fathered the girl and for whatever reason does not want to be identified. Whether he was at the hotel and/ or could have been involved with the disappearance is, of course, the question. No one else unaccounted for, I presume?"

"Correct, everything checked. Other guests at the hotel and all of the guesthouses throughout the town. No one is missing, except for your Robert Krane, and no one checked out that morning." Kovač always appreciated his conversations with Steven Gurning. The man was razor sharp, perceptive, and generally helpful.

"Any chance that our boy was with the girl and her mother?"

"No. He was busy chatting-up a waitress.

"Ah. Well, as always, my old friend, I'll run some checks and let you know what I find, or if I can't tell you."

There had been one previous occasion when Gurning had uncovered a conflict of national interests, but even then, instead of lying, he had been up front and informed his counterpart of the position so their political lords and masters could adjudicate on whether the information could be shared. Neither had liked the situation, but Kovač appreciated the other's candour. "What I can say straight-up is that this chap, Krane, is not currently on our radar. Just typed his name into dispatches." The two hung up, and Kovač thought about what to do next.

———◆———

Madam Kos was simultaneously swelling with pride at the thought of being of such great importance to the authorities, especially as all of the neighbours were watching and totally aware of the situation. She had made sure of that herself. However, she was also beside herself. The team of police investigators had clumped in with wet boots and dirtied the carpets throughout the house. She understood as they explained that a criminal would secrete incriminating items all over, not only, if at all, in his or her room. But that did not assuage her mood at the prospect of so much cleaning and tidying up, particularly when she overheard the team boss calling Inspector Kovač to report that nothing of any interest had been found. She acknowledged that the team had been careful and thorough, and it was the thoroughness that troubled her. There was a huge amount of resulting work and what would she say to the nice young man when, or if, he returned?

———◆———

Kovač wasn't thinking about that as he took in the report that had just been relayed to him on the findings from the guesthouse and signalled for Chief Horvat, his assistant, and a few others to join him.

"Nothing's been found at the guesthouse, absolutely nothing," he announced. "I will wait for a response from the British, but in the meanwhile, this Robert Krane should not absorb too much thinking. Do not, I emphasise, do not ignore him, but focus on other leads. For the time being, I would like Chief Horvat and his men to concentrate on locating the missing man. He is, after all, missing and therefore deserves consideration."

———◆———

Rob would have been appreciative, had he known, but he was far too interested in where he was and what he was discovering. Having slithered along a short, narrow tunnel, he found himself gawping as the beam from his torch cut through the pitch-blackness of a cave the size of medium-sized house. There was everything he had read about in the guidebooks, only this particular cave was not in those books. There were jaw-dropping stalagmites and stalactites at the edges whilst the floor of the cave was a pool of water across which ripples of concentric circles flowed, caused by the *plink, plink, plink* of dripping water from high up on the cave roof. He thought of his camera back at the guesthouse and cursed his misfortune and lack of imagination for not having kept it by his side at all times.

After heading back to where he had slept, Rob returned with a white bag to leave a mark so he could find his exit, and then he gingerly set out around the pool to explore deeper into the network he had stumbled across. Venturing into and back out of dead-end galleries and smaller caves, Rob lost track of time thanks to the marvel of nature and his discovery. He had even experienced a unique picnic. *A lakeside lunch with a difference,* he had thought to himself at the time, wishing once more that he had his camera to mark the occasion.

As he turned back upon reaching what he thought was yet another dead end, he stopped in his tracks. Off to his left he could just make out a light in the distance, whether near or far he could not tell. And unless the sun had broken through with a vengeance, which was unlikely, this light was almost certainly manmade and therefore, despite being disorientated from the dark and many twists and turns, he reasoned that the light more than likely emanated from somewhere belonging to the kidnappers. Shining his torch around the walls and ceiling of his passage and running his hand across the rock as he did, Rob assured himself that there were no lights or cables where he was. "No cables, no lights, no frequent, if any usage by those guys," he muttered to himself. He worked his way forward, turning his torch off as he approached the opening.

"Wow." Rob was looking through an opening easily large enough for him to squeeze through but behind an up-stand of rock that hid his opening from sight for anyone in the cave below. Very cautiously and as quietly as possible, Rob eased himself through and lay on the ledge behind the up-stand of rock. Looking down from his vantage point, he could see the backs of three people facing both the man he now knew was Burak Demir and the girl, both of whom were slumped but awake on the floor at the back of the cave. One of the three was talking.

"...is not coming because of the weather. So, Mr King Pin, or should I say KP, our discussion and your health check will have to wait. I have my tools to assist, if required, and have been assured that your daughter will be well looked after in another room until such a time as I'm able to check on her health. Presumably Emilio has already told you of how well I care for my younger patients?"

Burak Demir, addressed as King Pin, nodded once.

"Good. Until tomorrow then, unless I become impatient to start my health check on your daughter, that is." With that, the three turned and left, the speaker audibly chuckling to himself.

There was silence for a few minutes after the sound of retreating footsteps had faded and the echoing clunk of a door being firmly closed and locked. King Pin then uneasily raised his arms, hands still handcuffed, and placed them over the little girl and hugged her. She wriggled further into his body until she was comfortable. Rob watched, partially embarrassed due to his voyeurism during these very personal moments for father and daughter. His mind had blanked in terms of what he should do now. The speaker had sounded very threatening, and the insinuations regarding the health check on the little girl were extremely unsettling.

With a frown of confusion, Rob watched with intrigue as Burak's hands deftly slipped his belt off without even so much as disturbing the drowsiness of his daughter, who was soon fast asleep. He noticed with equal puzzlement that there were tears running down his cheeks. Then, as Burak wrapped one end of the belt around each hand, Rob realised with horror that the man was crying because he intended to murder his own daughter! No doubt it was because he knew what the other man was capable of.

No! This just can't be happening. My intervention is required now or never. I can't let this guy, regardless of who he really is or what he's done, murder his daughter, nor allow that other man to get his hands on her, he thought. Picking up a small stone, Rob lobbed it over to where Burak and girl were slumped. Although he was certain there was no one else in visual proximity, Rob had no idea about sound so did not dare raise his voice.

Time went into slow motion as Rob watched, petrified as Burak (a.k.a., King Pin) raised the belt towards the girl's neck, tears now streaming down his cheeks, and as the stone arced through the air, then landed, tinkled, and skipped over the uneven rock surface towards them. Burak tensed and looked up and around sharply, the jerky movement disturbing and waking his daughter. Burak also rapidly moved the belt away from his daughter's neck and concealed it to one side. As Rob stuck his head above the rocky up-stand, he could see their eyes opening wide in disbelief. Rob held his finger to his lips. The man nodded and promptly whispered something to his terrified daughter.

For a while Rob didn't move but merely exchanged stares with the two from his vantage point and thought, *I must be mad. This is crazy.* Then, with a concerted effort, Rob pushed himself up and looked around the space before dropping down onto the cave floor and hesitantly walked over to the captives.

Looking down at the man, he said, "Burak Demir, I presume?" The man nodded.

"I wouldn't be here if it wasn't for your daughter. Whatever it is that you're involved with has got to be of dubious nature and is therefore your problem. I'm sorry, I don't want any part of it, so I'll help your daughter to get away, but that's it! I'm sure you've made arrangements so she'll be adequately looked after."

Burak Demir shook his head sadly before responding. "That won't do any good. I'm a dead man anyway," he said in a thick accent.

The young girl immediately burst into tears upon hearing this and continued sobbing as Burak Demir added, "My daughter is only here to make me talk. Without her they know I won't talk, and consequently, you *will* be hunted down." He emphasised the word *will* with a strong finality about it. "And no, sadly it has not been possible to make arrangements for my daughter yet, so without me alive for a little while longer, Anja will not be provided for. I've been too clever in the past and have not been able to untangle matters sufficiently yet to consider my personal arrangements."

Rob frowned uncomprehendingly and did not move, so the man had to plough on. "I'm sorry that you have to hear this, sweetheart," he said gently to the girl and then turned back to Rob. "I have tried to keep my personal life a secret, although clearly I have failed. This is because there are certain elements who resent my attempts at creating a distance between myself and those many aspects of my business operations that are of, should we say, a less-legitimate nature.

"One is not meant to settle down when one enters my overall line of business. One is supposed to merely live for the moment and for fun. Upon meeting Evelyne, Anja's mother, I came to realise the lack of fulfilment in my life and sought to change it. That has so far proved impossible. Therefore, young man, whilst hurtful, I can understand your sentiments towards me, but the future security for my daughter is now inextricably tied to my well-being and no one else's."

Anja was still sobbing but more quietly now and did not appear to give any indication of listening much, but even so, Burak fixed Rob with a knowing look and sadly shook his head. This was no place to address her mother's death. Burak then continued with such a finality of tone that Rob was momentarily lost for words. "She needs me to somehow provide for her financially."

"If I help you to escape as well, you will continue to live your privileged life, albeit tragic and threatened. It will be a life of privilege, and I don't think that's fair, nor is it just." Burak remained silent, so Rob blurted out, "Okay, I help you, but you must agree to transfer absolutely everything to me and I will then set up some form of trust fund for your daughter and sufficient for yourself." After a pregnant pause, during which Rob realised how silly what he had just said must have sounded, he continued, "Yes, yes, I know that's a naïve statement, but you just said that you wanted out, so why not? There must be a way."

With that and not waiting for a response, Rob walked purposefully to a table a few metres away, watched by a curious Burak and Anja. Rob picked up a pen and a pad of paper and scribbled

I, Burak Demir, transfer all assets, businesses, possessions, shares, and everything to Robert Krane. I do so totally willingly. Robert Krane accepts such transfer and acknowledges that he will provide for Burak Demir's only daughter.
Signed ....
Dated ....

Rob signed, shaking his head at what he knew was a worthless piece of paper, but he was trying to buy time as he thought. He walked back to Burak and dropped the pen and pad on his knees, noticing for the first time the bar embedded into the rock to which they were attached. He then returned to the desk and continued his search of the drawers. Ignoring the array of knives and other items in the desk, Rob collected keys, another three pairs of handcuffs, a handgun, a semi-automatic machine pistol, and a number of additional loaded magazines for each weapon. *I can be confident up to the point of the cave's exit,* he thought. *Then matters will get interesting.*

Returning to Burak, he sensed that the man was trying to size him up. His appearance should be troubling the man. How could someone have followed the captors, evaded their sentries, and made his way into what must be the depths of their hideaway? Had Burak recognised him from the hotel? He had no idea. Rob picked the signed paper out of Burak's lap and removed the pen from his fingers, allowing the man to glimpse the weapons Rob had left atop his back sack a few metres away to avoid giving the man any temptation.

Burak simply watched every move attentively and nodded when Rob unlocked the bar, enabling Burak to slide Anja's and his cuffs out and stand up. Picking up his belongings, Rob said, "Follow me, preferably without scuffing the walls to show the direction of our exit."

With that, Rob nimbly climbed back up to his earlier vantage point and reached down to help Anja clamber up. Burak was up in no time, showing a surprising agility and signalling that he kept himself in shape. Wasting no time, Rob led them through the hole and turning his torch on once more, through the maze of passages and caves to the originating entrance. Having ignored Burak's protests to remove Anja's handcuffs, Rob periodically reached back to assist her, particularly around the underground lake, as Rob now liked to think of it. He had no idea whether her father had trained her at all, although probably not, and consequently what the young girl may be capable of. *But caution is the best part of valour,* he reminded himself.

At the entrance of his little cave, Rob handed out some food, which was gratefully accepted, as he noted it was still raining. Should they risk the descent and leave now to get as much distance between themselves and this place as soon as possible or wait for safer climbing conditions? It would only be a matter of time before their escape was noticed and their route established, so Rob announced, "I know it's getting late, but we need to get going. You're going to get wet and uncomfortable in the rain without appropriate clothing, but there's nothing I can do to help that, sorry. I'll go first. Anja, you follow. Your dad will help you down the first part and then I will support you from below for the final part of the descent. Burak, I'm having to trust that you won't play any games."

"Young man, or seeing your name on the paper, may I call you Robert?"

"Rob's fine."

"Okay. Rob it is. You have my word. I accept that you will be unwilling to trust me. That is natural. But for Anja, and I have to say, for your foolery for getting involved, I can assure you that I have no intention of playing any games. My life has been all about Anja for a number of years, and I will not intentionally place her in any danger. How you fit into all this will, I am sure, become clear at some point, but you don't appear to be associated with any of my businesses or the authorities. I'm simply relieved to let another lead and to have the opportunity for Anja to escape. By the way, what time is it? My watch was taken."

Looking at Burak, Rob thought he was looking into the eyes of a tired, broken man, but a dangerous one all the same and one who could not be underestimated. He had learnt the hard way not to underestimate his opponents, and on this occasion, the stakes—his own life—were the highest he had ever played for. "Not quite six-thirty, so barely two hours of daylight remaining."

Swinging his legs over the edge, Rob clambered down the cliff, his feet slipping on the rain-slicked rock. Anja followed, Burak holding her by the wrists and leaning down as far as he could before handing responsibility for his daughter's safety over to Rob, who steadied her ankles and continued to guide her down. Burak, again demonstrating a degree of agility that belied his general appearance, easily followed his daughter down.

"Sorry both of you, but please hold your arms out." Rob was holding the handgun he had found earlier. Obediently, both did as he had requested, and Rob used another of the handcuffs to link father and daughter together. "I know this will make the going harder and slower and I am sorry for that, but that's the way it has to be." Burak simply nodded.

The trio set off, staying tucked against the cliff face until well out of sight of the cabin, at which point Rob headed off downhill, picking his way around trees, bushes, and other natural obstacles. Dusk was falling fast as they passed another small cliff with a few potential caves that offered shelter, but Rob pressed on. As they skirted a fourth rocky outcrop, Rob, quite by chance, saw what he was looking for—a small opening in the rock behind some scrub and a small tree growing out of a small fissure. Rob estimated that they had travelled between four and six kilometres.

Signalling to Burak and Anja, he secured Burak to a tree using another pair of handcuffs before climbing up to the opening to check it out. Leaving the food, he returned, released Anja from Burak, and helped her patiently up the rocks. Eventually he returned a second time and accompanied Burak up the rock face and into the cover of the small cave. This one, Rob had discovered when he first looked around, held no similar excitements as his previous cave. Rob handed out some food and then secured his two companions together once more and one of Burak's legs to the small tree before moving further into the cave himself to settle down for yet another uncomfortable night.

Anja was soon fast asleep, cradled warmly in her father's arms. In the darkness, Burak quietly cleared his throat and enquired of Rob, "You awake?"

"Yes," came the cautious reply.

"I do run legitimate businesses, you know. Really quite successfully."

Taken aback by Burak's attempt at conversation and not entirely sure where this could be leading, Rob hesitated a few moments before responding.

"With an undercurrent of illegitimate activity as well, no doubt."

"Ouch and touché. I have been focusing on the legitimate a great deal more in recent years. There are a lot of good people involved who are unaware of the, err, other activities—okay, criminal activities. There you go, I've said it. The first time ever."

Rob was relieved that he had been fiddling with his iPhone and had initiated voice recording when Burak had asked if he were awake. This was an amazing, if not surreal, conversation to be having.

"Evelyne, Anja's mother, without saying anything started an unexpected change in me. Anja's arrival, beautiful innocence, and innate excitement about life have reinforced my desire to change what I can, while I can.

"For years, all I've been is a dead man walking. I had an unknown life span that was most likely to end suddenly. Now, if we are able to respect your crude little piece of paper, I will have no wealth to look forward to. That leaves what I've come to realise is of greatest value for me personally: Anja. I don't know what was going through your mind when you wrote down what you did on your piece of paper, but I was mostly happy to sign. Removing the burden of running legitimate businesses and keeping my not-so-legitimate colleagues away from muscling in on those businesses has weighed heavily on me for a long time. Whilst passing that burden on will be a relief, I am prepared to be on the side-lines and help. Mind you, being totally reliant upon someone else to live will be interesting to say the least and I am therefore concerned how that will transpire, but I guess we need to extricate ourselves from this place first, which presumably is also foremost in your mind."

Rob wasn't quite sure what to say, if anything at all. This level of openness was not at all what he would ever have expected. This King Pin, or Burak, or whatever, was complex and difficult to read. Also, his willingness to relinquish such an enormous wealth defied sense. It had been far too easy. Rob mentally acknowledged that the likelihood for future tricks, if they ever escaped, was both high and to be expected from someone as wealthy and powerful as Burak who had proved himself masterful at covering up his criminal activities. "You're right. All I want to do is get away from this place to safety," was therefore all Rob could think of as a response.

"Unfortunately for you, young man, should your involvement with my escape ever become known, you will never be able to take your safety for granted again, wherever you may be."

With little that could be said in reply to Burak's prediction of Rob's future life, an awkward silence was established in the cave, and both men eventually drifted off into their own unsettled sleep.

◆

Of the seven men in the cabin, five were playing cards at a large, rectangular table of very bashed and stained wood. Another, the one who had been speaking to Burak in the cave, was lounging on one of the set of bunk beds lining a wall, in the middle of which was a single door of heavy wood within a thick frame and two substantial locks. The seventh man, the leader of the group, was sitting apart from the rest at a smaller table studying some maps whilst also speaking quietly on his satellite phone and scribbling a series of instructions on a pad of paper.

There was a pair of small windows at each end of the cabin and another two windows on either side of the front door. At the opposite end from where the leader sat was a small counter on which stood a camping gas stove, a battered metal kettle, and a couple of equally battered pans. A pile of food-encrusted metal plates, goblets, and cutlery were strewn across the rest of the surface. A plastic bowl, presumably for washing up, was propped up against the side. Otherwise, the place was very spartan, with no pictures or other furnishings.

The group leader put the phone down gently and continued scrawling away on his pad whilst referring to the maps. After a while, he turned his head and contemplated the team before saying, "Okay, let's go check on KP and the girl and make sure that lazy so-and-so Kristin is still awake. Doc, Mauricio, you're with me."

Scraping the chair on the wooden floor, he stood up and crossed to the door, unlocked it, and led the way into the passage behind, the first few metres of which had been hewn out of the rock. Then he entered the naturally formed section of the cave and passage network. Walking past a few doors, they came upon Kristin, asleep on his chair, head propped up against the doorframe behind him. The leader merely hooked his foot behind one of the chair legs and up-ended the whole thing, tipping the sleeping man roughly onto the floor.

"Idiot!" he yelled at Kristin, who was clearly shaken. He proceeded to unlock the door, leaving Kristin to scramble to his feet and follow the trio into the brightly lit cave, only to find it devoid of the expected prisoners.

The ensuing ruckus that followed the discovery of the captives' escape was messy. The leader promptly set about Kristin, delivering a series of powerful blows to the man's face and abdomen, forcing him against the rocky wall.

All the while the leader yelled obscenities in his face before storming off and shouting over his shoulder, "Rip this place apart, and rip him apart as well if need be," nodding down to the fallen, groaning Kristin. "Just find them, or we'll all be history. And Doc, feel free to have a practice on him as well just to make sure he was not part of the escape or that there is nothing in his subconscious that he has not told us. This will be the last time he falls asleep on duty!"

He needlessly kicked out at another member of the group as he passed, dialling a number into his satellite phone. Doc and another man dragged the felled man off to a side room whilst the others started a thorough search of the cave as the rest of the men made their way in.

"Oh shit!" said one of the three searching the cave some thirty-five minutes later. He pointed up to the barely visible opening through which Rob, Burak, and Anja had escaped. "Someone's in for the high-jump."

He was standing about as far back as he could and had stretched despondently, figuring the search to be fruitless, when he had looked up and saw the gap in the rock. Moments later one of the others had scrambled up to confirm their worst suspicion. Someone had not surveyed the place fully and missed the escape route.

"Toss you for who tells the boss about this and the guns," the first guy said, digging a coin out of a pocket.

"Tell me about what?" growled their boss, who walked into the room at that precise moment.

"Guns, keys, and handcuffs taken from the table, and looks like the escape was through a previously unseen hole in the cave behind that ledge up there," Mauricio said as he pointed up to the place where Rob had been lying some three hours earlier. "I peered through, but we don't have any torches to explore. Haven't thought of how to get started immediately yet. Don't want to wait until the morning to go get torches from a nearby village."

"Too right we won't wait, nor go buy torches. It'd raise attention. Figure it out with the lighting in here, and check the sheds outside. There may be something there."

They waited until he had left before Gustov said, "Stephane, you go check the sheds. Mauricio and I can start on the electrics. Unless there's a heap of slack, this cable won't get us far."

———

It was nearly four o'clock when Steven Gurning called Kovač again.

A few minutes earlier, Gurning had tapped in his password on his computer for the Alerts Registry System (or ARS for short). He then filled in the requisite fields so any mention or query on Robert Krane's name by any of the UK's authorities would be immediately flagged to him. So far, since the application's surprisingly smooth introduction a few years back, his was the only record for Krane.

Franc Kovač was frustrated to say the least, and that came across in the tone of his voice, despite his attempt to disguise it. He wasn't an actor who could turn on differing personas and vocal output at will. He had read all of the completed reports into the incident, had reviewed the ballistics results and the initial reports of stolen vehicles, and had cross-checked those against the partial tyre treads that had been found at the scene. He had then shouted when forensics called to say that there were no fingerprints on any of the cartridges collected and that it would be a fool's task to try to take prints from any of the fixtures at the hotel that could, on the off chance, have been touched. Steven Gurning's report did little to help his temperament.

"Hello, Franc, Steven here from MI5."

"Steven, hi. I really hope you can tell me something helpful. The investigations at this end are going nowhere, and I'm getting a lot of heat."

After a slight pause, indicating that the MI5 officer was considering his words carefully, Steven Gurning ran through his list of bullet points about Robert Krane, all neatly set out on a single piece of paper placed on his desk. "Not sure if this helps in the way I anticipate you want, as it would move Robert Krane to the low end of my investigations or possibly discount him altogether. Except, of course, from the annoying obligation of having to locate a missing foreigner. Born and still lives in London. Thirty-one years of age. Unexciting family background. Single. Clean record from all authorities, not even a flicker. Even no points on his driving licence. No political associations known. No financial pressures identified. All bills paid on time, often by standing order.

"Made redundant recently, along with many others from some US bank where he was in a back-office support function when his department was shipped off to India and Hungary. Was highly regarded and popular but apparently vocal with his disagreement about the wisdom of the reorganisation, so a prepared offer to relocate him with the work was never presented. Various degrees and some voluntary work for a housing association. Talented amateur photographer who has exhibited, but not seriously or to any great acclaim.

"Now here's the interesting bit: won gold a few weeks back at the European Combined Martial Arts and Unarmed Combat Championships. That tops and complements quite a lot of awards received. Apparently he has been rather successful on that circuit for a couple of years now. Thrives on touring to participate in competitions and nearly always arranges to speak to groups of underprivileged kids at the end of a competition to inspire them into activities, whether work, artistic stuff, or sport. I got one of the girls here to try phoning his mobile a few times, but only got voicemail. So to sum up, essentially one of those good, likeable people who excel at rather a lot."

"You're right. I had been hoping for a lead, but that was too much to hope for bearing in mind how well organised the entire operation appears to have been." Kovač then added with a hint of irony, "No CCTV anywhere, of course, because serious crime doesn't happen in Postojna."

"I know the feeling all too well, I'm afraid. Well, I've tagged Robert's name so that should anything come in, I will be alerted immediately.

72

Also, trying to get a tap on his phone, but that may not be approved. When do we inform his parents? We don't want this getting into the press first."

"Hmm. You're right, of course. Possibly better to inform them sooner rather than later. Can you arrange that?"

"No problem. Will do. Story will be that he is unaccounted for and un-contactable, but that may be expected because of the nature of his planned holiday. Speak to you anon. Bye for now."

"Thank you, Steven. Good-bye."

Steven sighed as he turned to gaze out over the River Thames from his small office in Thames House. He briefly mused the oddity of being on the north side when in actuality, because of the meandering nature of the great river, one could say quite legitimately that Thames House was on the west side. A pleasure cruiser was struggling to make headway against the strong incoming tide, churning the water up in its wake. He glanced at his notepad, knowing full well what he had scribbled as a to-do list earlier whilst sitting in a dull meeting.

Call Franc Kovač

Set up an all-systems flag against Krane's name, priority and alert for himself only. Just in case.
Call 6 (his shorthand for MI6)
Call Krane's family?
Boss?

He drew a firm line through the first two items on the list. Should he or should he not mention this to his boss? He was still not sure. Ordinarily the usual channels within the Foreign Office would manage these matters, and assisting a counterpart in another country was standard practice, particularly when nothing untoward was flagged. So why would he even consider troubling his boss, the DG or director general? Instinct was whispering madly at him. No, he had absolutely nothing, so he rapidly typed up a file note of his conversations with Kovač to circulate to relevant parties. He would let them pick this one up if there was any interest, which from past experience was a rarity. That way he wouldn't have to deal with awkward questions from the family and could avoid getting his peer at MI6 unnecessarily engaged. Whilst Graeme Spreachley was pleasant enough, Steven was not entirely comfortable engaging with the man, let alone sharing information when it was not absolutely necessary.

4

Rob awoke after yet another uncomfortable night and listened yet again to the pattering rain on the leaves of trees and splattering onto the rock. Burak and his daughter appeared to still be asleep. He checked his watch. It was 7:30 a.m. and the light had made its silent way into the depths of their small cave. He shook his head violently as Burak's comments from last night started to filter through his mind, thick and fuzzy because of lack of decent sleep. He did not want to face the truth of those comments, at least not yet. Looking at his companions, he was of two minds about whether to let them continue to sleep or to wake them and get moving. The imperative to keep moving and seek help made the decision for him.

"Come on, folks, time to get going," he said loudly. He watched with keen interest the different ways in which the child woke as opposed to an adult who was always on alert.

Passing out some food, less than previously because their supply was getting distinctly low, he commented, "At least the rain appears to be letting up."

"Won't make a jot of a difference for us," muttered Burak as Anja sneezed and sniffed.

Soon the bedraggled trio were threading their way through the dense trees and undergrowth once more, looking for routes that would leave as little trace of their passage as possible. They paused briefly before crossing a stream to drink and splash their faces from its refreshing waters before crossing and sending clouds of mud spreading through the racing, rippling, crystal-clear water. The cool water temporarily shocked any vestiges of tiredness from their minds and bodies, reenergising them to press ahead. Rob decided to follow an approximate parallel route to the stream, heading constantly downhill in the vain hope that it would lead somewhere worthwhile.

At last, as the rain ceased, that plan paid off as they encountered a small road, which they crossed with caution, even though there was not a sound other than the occasional bird. Taking another drink from the stream, Rob varied his previous approach and directed his companions to follow him, tracking the road some fifty metres into the forest. His heart was racing at the thought of potentially coming across signs of life and what he should do once they did.

After checking on Burak and Anja once more, he was relieved that Burak was quietly talking to the young girl and more importantly, that they were both still handcuffed and also handcuffed together. It made their movements and progress awkward but also meant that Burak was substantially hindered should he ever consider trying to make a break for it or even try taking on Rob. Whilst Rob was confident in his own abilities, he did not want to take Burak on. Not only was he unsure of Burak's capabilities, which he was sure were both great and unpleasant, Rob had an aversion to doing so in front of such a young girl

By late morning, they lost the cover of the trees as they arrived at a steep, rocky cliff, explaining why the road had taken yet another change in direction. "Let's have a rest before we continue on the other side," Rob announced.

Gazing out across a valley below, Rob could look along another valley between the hills in front of them and noticed twinkles of light as an occasional ray of sunlight broke through the cloud and caught on the windows of passing traffic and buildings. His heart both leapt at the thought of possible help but also thumped at the prospect of somehow having to explain what he was doing guiding a handcuffed man and small girl whilst also carrying a pair of weapons.

Michael Stanley! Why hadn't he thought of him before? Michael was something at the Metropolitan Police in London and trained with Rob at a martial arts centre in Wembley. They weren't so much friends as periodic drinking or even cheap dinner partners after a training session. Rob had always enjoyed the odd evening with Michael chatting about anything and everything, except for Michael's work, about which he was always cagey. He would know what to do, although Rob didn't know what to say. Rob had Michael's personal e-mail address and mobile. An e-mail would help structure his thoughts, so seeing that at last he had a signal, he settled down with his iPad and typed out an e-mail, with the words, "As per text message" written in the subject line. He would send Michael a text as soon as he had sent the e-mail.

Michael,

Hi. I'm in a spot of bother here in Slovenia and need advice and a whole heap of help. There was a shooting and kidnapping where I was staying. To escape, I hid in the attackers' vehicle. This was a few days ago. Quite by chance, I was able to free the two kidnapped people and escape with them. Am now sitting at the edge of a forest overlooking a cliff and wondering what to do. Photo of the two attached. The man is Burak Demir, who at his own admission is a criminal. The little girl is his daughter, Anja. Signal has been nonexistent, but I can see a well-used road

*in the distance so presume signal should stay
reasonable from now on.*

   Help!
   Rob

Quickly scanning what he had written before sending, Rob corrected a couple of typos, attached the photo, gulped at the thought of the likely reaction the receipt of his e-mail would create, and then tapped the send button. Checking that it had gone, he sent Michael a simple text. "URGENT! Please check your personal e-mail. I need help. Rob Krane." If that didn't grab Michael's attention, nothing would. With that, he scanned an approximate track down into and across the valley and over and through the smaller valley nearly opposite that led to the barely visible road. "Okay, let's get going," he said and stood up.

Once they had crossed the road, Burak drew close. "Enlisting help?"

"That's right. Sent an e-mail and a text to a friend who will know what to do."

"I hope so and also hope that it won't involve staying in this country. I doubt that would be very safe given how I was traced by my power-hungry cohorts."

Rob didn't reply but merely kept trudging onwards and downwards, watching his step as the terrain became steeper and keeping an ear and eye open for any traffic and a way of proceeding with as much cover from the road as possible.

The *bleep, bleep* of his mobile drew Michael from his reverie whilst he was queuing for a sandwich from one of the counters at Scotland Yard's canteen. He wanted a distraction from the tedious report writing that necessarily followed the conclusion of an operation, even though nothing had come of it. He had to read the text twice for the contents to fully sink in. Rob had never been one for dramatics, so Michael quickly paid for the first sandwich he could lay his hands on and went in search of his boss for clearance to access an external and personal webmail account.

Kevin Barnes was where he nearly always was, in his office. Unless he was called to a meeting by the "lords and masters" of Scotland Yard, everything either happened in his office or in the adjoining meeting room. Michael quickly explained what he wanted and received the requisite curt nod of approval and signature on the inevitable form to be handed to the tech guys down in the basement.

"Let me know what is so urgent, please," said Superintendent Barnes as the form was passed back across the desk. He knew Rob Krane had beaten Michael in the semi-finals of some sort of championships a few weeks earlier, and like Michael, he was curious about what could fluster such an incredibly accomplished man to the extent of using such attention-grabbing words as Rob Krane had in his text.

Twenty minutes later Michael was back at his desk in a large, open-plan area of the famous grey building in St James'. Most of the thirty-odd desks were still empty, their occupants either out for lunch or on an operation.

"Strewth!" Michael said both far more loudly than he had intended and with great emphasis as he read his friend's e-mail.

Controlling his volume, again he muttered to himself, "How the blazes did he get himself wrapped up with someone like Demir?" as he forwarded the mail to his work account and logged off his personal mail account. As soon as the e-mail arrived, he sent it to print, locked his PC, and went to grab the piece of paper off the printer. Walking briskly down the bland, featureless corridor, he found himself once more at his boss's office, but this time, he was in the adjacent meeting room with a meeting in progress.

Ignoring that, he knocked on the door and entered. "Sorry, boss. You need to read the e-mail I mentioned earlier."

With that, Michael walked around the table under the incredulous stares of the six others sitting at the rectangular table for twelve. It was littered with files, pads of paper, and cups of steaming coffee. Two were direct colleagues of Michael's, explaining their vacant desks. Interrupting one of Barnes's meetings was not something one did lightly.

Kevin Barnes scanned the short e-mail very quickly. "Let's go next door. Continue without me," he said to the others as he stood and walked out. "Doris, please get everyone's work roster for me. I may have to rearrange workloads for young Michael here. He's likely to be busy for a while."

That latter statement sounded more ominous than Michael had expected, but at least it meant this could be leading somewhere interesting. Doris, the battle-axe of an assistant who had been with Kevin Barnes throughout his career, gave the appearance of not changing a thing, but in reality she was deftly switching activities to what her boss had just ordered.

Kevin Barnes closed his office door behind them and gave Michael a wry smile. "Well, it appears that your friend has got himself into a pickle." Settling himself behind his large desk, he enquired, "Have you registered this on the systems yet?"

"Not yet sir, no. It appeared to be of sufficient interest to come straight to you."

"Agreed. Right, let's see what we have," the superintendent continued as he opened up ARS and started filling in various fields as he cross-referenced the e-mail. When he had finished a few minutes later, he looked up to address Michael once more.

"So, other than the fighting stuff that you two get up to, what can you tell me about Mr Robert Krane? That way I should be able to figure out who else to contact, if anyone."

"That's not very easy, sir, I'm afraid. Whilst we have shared a drink and/or dinner quite a few times now, in reality, I don't know much about him. And vice versa, as you'd expect."

"I'd sincerely hope so," chipped in the superintendent.

A few minutes into a brief exposé of Michael's friend, the phone rang, interrupting the flow. Kevin Barnes scowled through the glass panel of his office at Doris, who simply shrugged and mouthed, "Sorry, urgent."

Barnes hit the hands-free button of his phone and enunciated a pointedly sharp-sounding, "What?"

"Inspector Steven Gurning of MI5 for you, sir. Said it had to be immediate."

"Okay then," he replied to accept the call whilst rolling his eyes skywards for Michael's benefit. At the sound of the transfer, he announced, "Superintendent Barnes," at the little red light on his phone and winked at Michael, with a sly grin announcing an intended game of brinkmanship with this spook who had dared have the temerity of overriding his request not to be disturbed.

"Ah, Superintendent. About your ARS entry a few minutes ago—we need to speak."

All thoughts of any games went flying out of the window, and their attention was well and truly grabbed.

"Go on," he said warily.

"It sounds as though you're on speaker. I prefer to know who is listening, and considering the potential ramifications of this matter, I would prefer to meet in person."

The superintendent mouthed "*smart-ass*" before replying, "I'm with Michael Stanley, who reported Robert Krane's contact and who also, I have the pleasure to add, whipped one of your boys at the inter-divisional martial-arts contest last year."

There was only the briefest of pauses before Steven Gurning continued. "Yes, I do remember that and will be pleased to work with Michael on this, presuming your agreement, of course, sir. May I ask why you entered Robert Krane's name on ARS? Unfortunately, this has potential international and broad national security consequences, as well as political ramifications."

"Yes, Inspector, I'm coming to appreciate that, and apologies for the initial sarcasm." One of the things Michael really appreciated about his boss was his down-to-earthness and his humour, as well as his readiness to acknowledge when a comment may have been made out of place.

"That's okay, sir. I appreciate that my approach would not have been expected. The thing is, our Slovenian friends are investigating a mass murder in relation to the apparent and inexplicable kidnapping of a young girl in Postojna in Slovenia. Your contact, Robert Krane, is currently unaccounted for and was known to be present at the time of the shooting. Information regarding him is urgently sought to either discount him from the Slovenians' enquiries or tag him for potentially being involved. The introduction of Burak Demir, as you noted on the system, adds a level of intrigue that cannot be ignored at a national level and may override other considerations, such as our general tendency to want to cooperate with the intelligence services of friendly nations. No doubt Demir's name will have started other alerts ringing as well, so I'll need to identify those and coordinate things. We really need to meet." After the briefest of pauses, he added, "Urgently. I will sort a room here at Thames House."

The superintendent simply raised an eyebrow. "As always, we're here to assist our colleagues from the intelligence services." His words were full of a blend of sarcasm and sincerity that Michael had heard before and could only marvel at. "Send Michael an inter-services message on where and when and he will join you. I had already anticipated that I'd have to relieve him of his other duties—at least for the time being."

"Much appreciated. Michael, please be here within the hour. Ask for me at reception. See you then. Not a word to anyone else, please. I'll ask my director to sort out the political niceties and overlapping conflicts between the services. Oh, just one thing—when was the initial contact, and what is the expected follow-up, when, and how?"

"Not quite an hour ago and not stipulated," Michael replied, noting how Gurning neatly ignored the request for an inter-services message.

"Okay, thanks. See you soon."

With that, the line went dead, and Michael regarded his boss carefully. "Well, my lad, your friend appears to have ticked all the boxes for a right royal situation. You'd better hot-foot it over to Thames House, but don't let the allure of the intelligences services draw you away from where the real work gets done!"

Michael knew that a few of his number had left their elite group for MI5 or MI6, but he had never really considered it himself. Nor had he really had contact with those services before, so had not appreciated the possible allure his boss referred to. Therefore, all he could think of to say was, "Fat chance, sir. I'll keep you posted."

With that, he picked-up the e-mail he had printed a while before and returned to his desk to close everything down before heading off to Thames House. He closed the door behind him, certain that his boss would be making some private phone calls.

Superintendent Barnes regarded Michael Stanley's departing back before picking up the phone.

◆

Barely forty-five minutes later, Michael found himself in a large, nondescript meeting room very similar to those he was used to at Scotland Yard. The only splash of colour on the bland magnolia painted walls were some fading prints of traditional British scenery. Steven Gurning commented that he would wait a few more minutes for people to gather. Those who had arrived were grouped in their own little cliques, having secretive, muttered conversations. The body language screamed that interaction with others was not welcome. Michael moved over to the windows and lifted a blind to look out over the river whilst he waited, but he was bitterly disappointed to find no view at all. They were in an internal meeting room overlooking an unexciting, grey light well. He let the blind drop again with a rattle and took a seat as Steven called the meeting to order. *No allure here then,* he thought to himself as he took a seat, thinking back to his boss's earlier comment.

"Okay all, thanks for coming at such short notice. I've a very simple agenda this afternoon. First, to brief everyone here about the situation as we know it and take a note of vested interests and queries. Second, as an even smaller group, to establish contact with Robert Krane and agree on next steps with him. Needless to say, everything discussed here today is to be treated with the highest confidentiality and sensitivity, so before you leave you will be required to sign another of those beastly Acknowledgement of Restricted and Confidential Information Forms, so no onward dissemination of information. Your bosses will be brought into the picture as soon as they sign the form as well. Right, let me introduce Detective Michael Stanley from Scotland Yard, who received the initial contact and can brief us on all he knows. I'll then provide an overview of my conversations with the Slovenians. Michael."

It took Michael less than ten minutes to finish his briefing and answer what questions he could, acknowledging that it was not much. It was then Steven's turn.

"Okay, myself and Laura Harding here are both MI5," he started and waved a hand at a youngish woman sitting opposite Michael. "We became involved when Inspector Kovač of the Slovenian Intelligence and Security Agency called me. Their current supposition is that the shootings were so well executed and unusually well-equipped that some form of terrorism must lie behind the inexplicable kidnapping. Robert Krane's unaccounted-for status potentially linked him to those thought-to-be terrorists, possibly as a spotter. MI5 will continue to have a close involvement with this case because we believe that Demir's activities and extensive networks have links to and/or fund and/or are associated with organisations that intend to harm British interests both at home and abroad. The latter, of course, being the reason why MI6 is here, represented by Graeme Spreachley." Steven gave a nod in the direction of another man, neatly turned out in a light grey suit.

"The thing is, we also have reason to believe that Demir may be merrily oblivious to his links to terrorism. As far as we can tell, he started as a petty, small-time criminal somewhere in Turkey. However, such was his aptitude for his chosen direction in life that he was soon hitting the big-time in Istanbul. Whilst there, he also discovered that he was equally successful with legitimate business and at times was able to merge or blend the two. Inevitably, success there and the confluence for Europe and Asia soon tempted the increasingly powerful young man to spread his wings further afield. His operations spread rapidly, both in scale and type of activity. This assessment has been corroborated with the National Intelligence Organisation in Turkey.

"Demir's purely criminal activities are known to operate across the UK, although direct links to Demir himself are hard to come by, as you'd expect. Hence the failure of the French prosecution a few years back and for inviting our colleagues from SOCA, the National Criminal Intelligence Service, and Scotland Yard. To round matters off, to help tread the paths of the government's political relationships with Slovenia, we have our friends from the Foreign Office.

"We will keep everyone here briefed via e-mail reports. For those who know me, I don't appreciate unnecessary meetings cluttering up my diary. The key thing I want to establish today is that we do not engage with any of our Slovenian counterparts for the time being." Holding up his hand to wave off objections and attempts to interject, Steven ploughed on. "Yes, yes, I realise that is awkward for all of us with relationships to preserve, not least political. However, there is a lone British national overseeing a man who evaded questioning when he walked free from that French court, and we are desperate to get Demir to the UK and hold him for questioning. We don't want red tape, whether Slovenian or international, getting in our way. Okay, I can see a few of you are bursting to jump in, so ask away."

Fifteen minutes later, following much debate, Steven brought the meeting to a close and invited all but four to depart. "Right, before replenishing our cups or breaking for nature, while I was talking I had the terrible realisation that Robert may well be using his mobile whilst we sit here cogitating. We need to put a stop to that first and foremost. Michael, the honours please—by text. We don't want the Slovenians catching onto him. Advise him that we will contact him again by e-mail."

The other three, Steven, Laura, and Graeme, politely waited in silence while Michael sent Rob a quick text.

At the bleeping sound of a successful text transmission, Gurning continued. "At least the Foreign Office chaps eventually saw sense and agreed that we don't involve the Slovenians until we have our chap and his companions safely on home soil. I thought it touch and go for a while there. What a hassle. Okay, as I see it, the questions we need to resolve for are: One, how do we sensibly communicate with Robert without calling his mobile and giving the Slovenians an opportunity to trace his location? Two, where is he? Three, how do we extract them in short order? Time is not on their, nor our side. Four, where do we keep them once in the UK? Five, how safe will Robert be if he returns to an unprotected life as normal? Comments."

"I can help with point three. We have a very able young lady based in Ljubljana. The one good thing about that country is that it is quite small, so a pick-up and delivery to a safe house should be possible with relative ease. My only concern is how to keep hold of Demir. By all accounts, he is a tricky and slippery character. I'd be so bold as to say that point two is easily answered provided we can overcome your first point, Steven."

"Agreed to that."

"May I make a suggestion to cover point one?" Michael asked.

"By all means, my man," responded Gurning encouragingly. "At this stage, anything is a good start."

"Well, Rob is the sort of guy who likes his techie toys. He sent an e-mail whilst clearly on the move, and the photo he sent was not of standard scale, meaning he had cropped it."

"Yes, so go on," said Gurning, following a momentary silence. "I'm a bit of a dinosaur when it comes to technology and don't have any children to keep me current, so you'll need to explain."

Michael caught a glimpse of Laura's slight affirming nod and wry smile at her boss's frank admission. Michael placed Gurning in his mid-fifties with his grey, silvery, and receding hair. His face was, however, virtually ageless, no doubt helped by a healthy and physical lifestyle evidenced by his trim physique and easy movements.

"Of course. Depending upon what Rob has with him, we could either exchange instant messages or even hook up through Skype or similar Internet video and/or audio conferencing application."

"You're kidding me," Gurning exclaimed. "Laura, please fire up the computer over there," he added, pointing to the credenza along the far wall. "We could certainly give that a go. You sure it can't be traced?"

"Actually, sir, it can, but only if you are specifically monitoring for that Internet traffic, and it most likely takes somewhat longer because of the wireless nature of the technology. I'll text Rob that that's what we intend to do, assuming that you either already have the applications on your own systems or are permitted to download it. If you're anything like Scotland Yard, however, that's unlikely and authorisation will be required."

"Oh grief, more techie protection. I accept they're necessary but so tedious to deal with. Laura, you've always said that you know someone. I will approve the request."

As Laura navigated through MI5's various systems, Michael sent another text to Rob saying what was planned and asking what application he had, adding that he would send another text when they were ready to start communication. The response was almost barely two minutes in the coming, and Michael slid his phone across the table for Laura to review the screen and complete the electronic form on the screen in front of them before pressing "submit" and giving the phone a gentle shove back across to Michael. It was then Steven's turn to log into his own system, asking for everyone to turn around as he did so before validating the request.

Laura then went through the rigmarole of logging back onto her own system from the meeting room's PC, downloaded the same video- and audio-conferencing application that Rob used, and established the settings. Eventually, she was able to search the contacts for the abbreviated name "*fitnessman*" that Rob had included in his final text.

At the back of the meeting room, Graeme had been speaking quietly on his own mobile phone whilst the others were sorting out the technology. Now, as Laura was tapping her fingers waiting for the excruciating egg-timer to disappear from the screen, he said, "I've put our Slovenian agent on standby to support whatever action we deem appropriate. She will await further instructions."

———◆———

A muffled bleep and buzz emanated from Rob's back sack, alerting him to a text. It was a reassuring sound, making him think that just maybe life could soon return to normal. But checking the message would have to wait. He was in the process of part treading, part scrabbling, and part sliding down a patch of bare earth littered with loose stones and muddy from the earlier incessant rain. He hoped beyond hope that it was Michael. It had been well over three hours since he had sent his text, and while he knew a meaningful response would take time to sort, simply knowing that people were acting would provide an immense boost to his ragged spirits.

The journey downhill had been strenuous, and whilst not particularly of great distance, at least for him, it had been steep. Anja had struggled so much, in large part because of her inappropriate footwear, that Rob agreed to separate her from Burak and permitted Burak to lift her onto his shoulders and carry her. Rob's greatest concern had been the distinct lack of cover. The topography was not conducive for pedestrians, and not surprisingly, there was no pavement, not even a track or worn earth or grass to indicate that people walked around the area. Those facts, coupled with their dishevelled appearance, was more than adequate to make a passing motorist suspicious.

Burak had been equally wary. "I agree that we don't have any choice, but we should think about our actions and response should a car come along and we are spotted," he had advised.

Rob had agreed but immediately quashed Burak's first suggestion that they try to wave the vehicle down, explain that their car had broken down and that Anja was unwell and they were taking her to the hospital. Then they would kidnap the person and take the car to make a break for it. As far as Rob was aware, he had not done anything illegal thus far and did not want to start. That way, if they were found or caught, he should have nothing to fear from the authorities. He was sure he could explain the weapons if he had to. He also did not want to release Burak from his handcuffs.

They had eventually agreed on progressing sufficiently far from the road that their appearance would hopefully not attract attention and that Rob would give a cheery wave. With Anja on Burak's shoulders, there would be no reason for either of them to wave and show their handcuffs. Burak was not particularly thrilled but accepted the proposal, mostly because he had little choice. He could also appreciate the wisdom of the decision from Rob's perspective, and his admiration for the young man increased further as he nodded a few times whilst sucking his lips in silent thought.

Now they were approaching the valley floor, and Rob charted for a last time their route across to the opposite side, through another smaller valley and on towards the cluster of buildings beyond. He wasn't quite sure yet what he would do at that point, possibly flag down a passing motorist to seek help. That was if Michael did not get back to him by that point with a better solution.

"Rob, I will need a rest when we get to the bottom," Burak called from behind him.

"Okay, no problem. That makes sense for all of us, particularly as we'll have a hill to climb once on the other side," he replied, half-relieved that he could agree with Burak on something. "Let's keep going until we reach the cover of the tress over there," he added pointing across the valley. "At least the ground will be more or less level so the going should be far easier."

"Agreed."

Anja was on foot again, improving their progress somewhat, but once again handcuffed to her father as a precaution against anything that Burak could possibly contemplate. As a result, Rob still had to contain his impatience at wanting to know who had sent him a text and matched his walking speed to theirs. It was therefore late afternoon when they again reached cover and could sag down onto a damp, fallen tree trunk. They were all hungry but had no food left.

Rob moved away from the other two to check his text, and he decided to use his technology to pinpoint their location with the GPS tracking associated with Google Maps. Wiping his hands on his jacket to clean away the grime before using his gadgets, he then opened up his bag.

The sudden rush of blood as he read the text, coupled with his hunger, made him feel weak and dizzy. Why hadn't he thought about it himself? At least someone was on his behalf, and he was grateful to Michael for the warning not to use the mobile phone because of the potential for him to be tracked by both the good and the bad guys. Hopefully the calls he had made to his parents' answer-phone and his voicemail had not jeopardised them. He had left quite a lengthy message for his parents, and there had been quite a few voice messages for him. Could either or both calls have been long enough to be traced? He had no idea.

After sending his text in reply, Rob did as directed and turned the signal for his iPhone off. That left his iPad, through which his friend could contact him by e-mail and/or by web-conferencing. He shook his head in amazement that Michael had recalled their conversation some months before that he had the iPhone and iPad working off different connections. That probably had something to do with why he was some sort of detective, although he had never been explicit about his job.

Swapping devices, Rob flipped open the cover for the iPad and felt some of his tension ease at seeing a very recent e-mail from a Laura Harding with a "from Michael Stanley" in the header. It was a very simple one-liner asking for a response when ready to connect and requesting confirmation of his web audio and video conference application link. Before sending the reply, Rob rummaged around in the bag to dig out his earpiece with built-in microphone. This was one conversation he did not want Burak to hear.

Relieved that he was thinking rationally again, Rob adeptly tapped through the menus on the screen, and with the benefit of Google Maps, he pinpointed their location. The collection of buildings they had seen and decided to head for was Podgraje, a small village in the neighbouring valley just off what appeared to be a reasonably main road heading north-south before turning west towards a distinctly main road that crossed over into Croatia, which as the crow flies was less than five kilometres directly south. After a deep breath, he replied to Laura's e-mail that he was ready, switched to his conferencing application, and waited with great trepidation, nerves tingling and butterflies in his stomach. How were things going to turn out? Who was Laura Harding, and who was he going to be speaking to?

5

The soft *duh-buh, duh-buh, duh-buh* gongs of the conferencing application soon flashed on the screen of Rob's iPad. Burak had been watching Rob curiously ever since Rob had inserted the earpieces. Rob stood and pretended to stretch as a forefinger tapped the accept button to acknowledge and start the incoming video conference. He then ambled a bit further away, leant back against a tree facing Burak and Anja, and said, "Hello" in as nonchalant a manner as he could.

Four faces stared up at him from the screen. Thankfully, one was Michael's, who waved. "Hello, Rob. It appears that you've got more of an adventure from this holiday than you'd bargained for! First up and before any introductions, you obviously got my text?"

"Yes, I did, but unfortunately, not before I'd left a message for my parents on their answer-phone and listened to my voicemails." Anticipating the obvious next question, he continued, "The first, for my parents, was probably no more than ninety seconds or so. The second was probably also a couple of minutes as there were quite a few messages, including from the landlady at the guesthouse where I've been staying and two from different policemen whose names I couldn't hear properly. The numbers they gave were different, although I didn't have any paper or a pen to write them down with."

"Okay, thanks for that. We'll have to keep this brief and quick in that case. It's doubtful that the first call could have been traced, but it was probably long enough to register and flag that you are now active again. It's a given that the Slovenian authorities will have tagged your phone by now. The second call, on the other hand, was almost certainly of sufficient length to get at least a partial fix, if not reasonably accurate, depending upon where you are, of course. The more rural, the fewer masts and therefore the harder to secure a really good fix. I don't suppose you know where you are, do you?"

"As it happens, I do. Checked before replying. We're in the neighbouring and by all appearances uninhabited valley to the east of a place called Podgraje, just north of the Croatian border. I'll spell it: P-o-d-g-r-a-j-e. Appears to be a small village."

"Great. Laura here will just call it up on another screen for us whilst we talk. Now, with me there are Steven Gurning and Laura Harding, both from MI5, and also Graeme Spreachley from MI6."

Rob blanched at hearing those organisations' names. What had he got himself involved in?

"Rob, are you okay?"

He nodded once and muttered, "Yes."

"I guess hearing that MI5 and MI6 are involved is somewhat disconcerting. It's because of Burak Demir, who you mentioned is with you. Is that still the case?"

"Yes. He's with his daughter. I can see them both now, and they're out of earshot. He's not looking this way, except for the very occasional glance. He's mostly focused on his daughter, so I'm confident that there's no lip-reading going on, although I suspect he's guessed that I have contacted the British authorities. He knows that I know who he is."

"Ah." The four people on the screen all looked at each other, clearly concerned about the potential implications for Rob's safety.

"I've handcuffed them, both individually and then together."

The undisguised look of startled surprise was evident from the four.

"Good man," Michael responded with feeling. "I think it's safe to say that we're all impressed. How that came to be and the story of your escape will have to wait. The key thing is to arrange a pick up and get you back to Blighty. Laura has already sent your location details to a MI6 operative in Slovenia. She left Ljubljana an hour ago, already anticipating that you were very possibly somewhere in the region that you are. Crucially, we really don't want the Slovenian authorities involved, and therefore you must continue to stay as inconspicuous as possible. As far as you can tell, could you have been seen by anyone?"

"Not that I'm aware of, no."

"Good. That's something. I don't suppose that with that clever piece of technology of yours you can show us precisely where you think you are."

"Should be possible," Rob replied, and he tapped the screen a few times to file share and brought-up Google Maps on the screen, losing the visual link with the four people at the other end. A blue dot glowed in the centre of the screen, showing his location as Rob said, "Here" at the same time.

"Got you." From the female voice, it was presumably Laura speaking now. "That's great. I suggest that the pick-up be at the first junction up the hill as you travel towards that Podgraje place. We'll send you an e-mail with details of type of vehicle and who, possibly also a photograph," she said with a sideways glance at one of the other men, who simply nodded. "The reasonably good news is that being in such a rural area and near mountains, it is very possible that if anyone was tracing your calls, they would not have been able to place you accurately, thereby necessitating a time-consuming and labour-intensive search. Be aware of airborne surveillance as well please, so do stay under the cover of trees as much as possible."

"Not a problem. We are under trees at the moment, and there'll be tree cover all the way to the meeting point. We can get there and take a rest. After an uphill walk on top of everything we've already done today, we'll need a rest anyway. We'd possibly have to also start looking for shelter by then. It'll be getting dark in a few hours."

"Damn good point, Rob," chimed in Michael. "We'd better let you go now. We don't want to attract attention, even though this will be far, far harder to trace. Oh, I don't suppose your technology can also show us your captives without giving the game away can it?"

Without saying anything, Rob deftly tapped away once more on the screen, and barely moving, he provided his audience with a zoomed-in shot of Burak and Anja.

"That's Burak all right," said one of the other men. "Had no idea that he had a daughter though."

"Okay, thanks, Rob. We'll drop now and hopefully see you in a day or so. Good luck." It had been Michael again. With that, the connection closed, and strangely, Rob felt incredibly lonely all of a sudden. Paradoxically, at the same time, he was relieved to know that people were mobilising to come and help.

Looking at his watch, they had only been at the rest stop for thirty minutes. "Let's take another thirty minutes before making tracks," he said to Burak as he sauntered back to the fallen tree trunk and sat down with a sigh.

"No news, then?" Burak enquired casually, looking up from Anja and sideways towards Rob.

"Nothing noteworthy yet, no."

"You make a lousy liar, Rob. You'll have to work on that. A good poker face for commercial negotiations, I suspect, but a lousy liar. There are subtle differences, but I'm sure you can learn."

Somewhat taken aback, Rob merely humphed, to which Burak commented, "Such responses only serve to give you away further. Let's hope that we won't have to rely on verbal reasoning to get us out of this place and that whoever you were just conversing with can really help."

Rob stifled a yawn, leant back against another tree, and stared out from the trees, looking at the way they had come. Still no vehicles. With a slight shake of the head, he thought about how isolated this region must be and the consequent challenges to receiving help.

Some two and a half hours later, it had become really quite dark beneath the trees, exacerbated by the east-facing nature of the hill up which they were walking. A few rays of the evening sun were catching the higher hills on the opposite side of the valley. They had to cross the road at one point where it brushed up against a small cliff face. Rob, becoming a little blasé about their remoteness, was about to leave the cover of the trees and cross when he caught the sound of a car. Quickly signalling to the other two, they lay on the ground as a car raced past unseen. If they could not see it, the theory went that they in turn could not be seen, so long as they weren't hiding ostrich-style with their heads in the sand!

Now, closing in on the road junction at which he was to meet their pick-up, Rob was concerned to see another set of headlights twinkling between the trees coming down the road along which they had descended earlier that day. Two cars in the space of an hour or so. Was that possible in this remote area? Of course it was, but…

He let the thought hang as he watched Burak, who was carrying Anja on his shoulders once more. Somehow, he had swung her up without a word or a request to take the set of handcuffs off them that held Anja and himself together. Could Burak really be genuine in his desire to hand everything over and focus on his daughter? It appeared highly illogical, but if actions were to be believed, maybe. He really could not figure this man out.

The distant revving of a vehicle's engine echoed dimly and hung in the air. Was that the one he had just seen or another car? There was no way to tell, but as they drew closer to the pick-up point, Rob became decidedly more nervous. Surely the cars were simply coincidence and to be expected.

It was, after all, evening, and it was to be expected that people would want to head home.

Fifty metres or so ahead, Rob could see the fork in the road where the pick-up was to be. Quite sure that Burak could not see the junction from where he was five or six metres behind, Rob announced, "Okay, let's have a break here before looking for somewhere to spend the night."

Anja required no further motivation, simply flopping off her father's shoulders and falling into a heap on the ground, promptly falling asleep. Burak looked down upon his daughter with a fond, loving smile and muttered, "Probably for the best." Looking up from his crouched position next to Anja and changing his tone, he queried, "So what next?"

"Let me find out" was the easy reply as Rob also dropped to the ground. "That position looks mightily uncomfortable," Rob commented, noticing Burak's forced crouched position because he and Anja were still handcuffed together. Standing up, he walked over to Burak and undid the handcuffs linking father to daughter before returning to the spot he had found for himself.

The forest was virtually silent. A few birds were still warbling away, but that was it. He shrugged off his sack. It was time to check for e-mails again. The simple task was completed in less than a minute, and in doing so Rob's stomach muscles tightened. Another e-mail from Laura gave him the news he had longed for.

Yasmin Gorski will meet you at the junction discussed at 6:45 p.m. She will be driving a medium-sized blue van with a logo of three trees on each side. See the attached photo for your familiarisation. She is of medium height and build. Don't worry about language. In addition to her mother tongue, she speaks fluent English and Italian. At the junction, she will slow down, pull over, get out, and open the rear doors. She will then sit in the rear under a light eating a couple of sandwiches for a maximum of ten minutes before leaving. Please confirm receipt of this e-mail so we can let Yasmin know to proceed as planned.

Great, he thought as he looked at the mug shot. *That could be a million and one women except for the fact that she'll be here in the middle of nowhere.* The photograph was of a woman with short, straight brown hair and stern features.

The confirming mail flashed through the ether moments later, and he sat back to wait. They had ten minutes to wait, which was not too bad, except for the fact that his nerves were stretched to their limits. At least he could justify a wait of that length without difficulty, particularly on the basis that Anja was fast asleep. Burak had repositioned himself so that he could manoeuvre Anja's head onto his lap, making her more comfortable. Rob marvelled at the unlikely relationship and the caring that Burak, a man with no doubt a horrendous history of violence, was displaying. He was more impressed by Anja's stoicism. The young girl had not caused a fuss nor been any trouble throughout the ordeal of their escape. *Hopefully there will be no long-term consequences for her mentally,* he thought.

As Rob's thoughts wandered, the minutes ticked by rapidly, and soon the sound of a vehicle shifting down a gear to address the road's gradient could be heard. Both men looked about warily and at each other.

"This may be our ride," Rob announced. "We stay here in the shadows until I can verify it."

Burak simply nodded his acknowledgement.

Less than two minutes later, a dark-coloured van pulled up on the other side of the road. The three-tree logo was clear to see, although it was impossible to tell the colour. However, as per the e-mailed directions, the driver got out and sat in the rear with a light shining down upon her as she ate a sandwich. Rob glanced between the woman and the photo numerous times to make sure. There was no doubt in his mind, and he turned to say as much to Burak, but he was gone!

Anja was still there. What had happened? Rob was at a complete loss and had not heard a thing. "Sod it!" he whispered to himself vehemently. Looking at Anja, he knew he had to take her with him but was thoroughly shocked that Burak would desert her after the loving attention he had poured out upon the young girl. *Maybe a leopard can't change its spots after all,* he thought miserably.

Picking the girl up as gently as he could, Rob walked over to the rear of the van. "Yasmin?"

The woman looked up. "Yes. And who are you?"

"I'm Rob, and this is Anja."

The woman stood and scrutinised the area with a sweep of her eyes. "I was told to expect three of you. Where's the other man?"

"I think he did a runner whilst I was checking you out. I'm sorry. I didn't expect him to leave his daughter, and I have no idea what he can be thinking. He's still wearing handcuffs."

"We can't wait or look for him. Apparently he's resourceful, so he'll have to look after himself. Everyone is surprised that he hasn't tried to kill you, handcuffs or no. Get the girl into the back and strap her in securely please. Then follow suit. I'll close the doors behind you once you're all done."

Anja hardly stirred as Rob followed the first part of the instructions, thoroughly deflated that he had come so far and failed. After he had finished, he turned to the woman and got back out from the van. "Please, may I have a moment to look for him?"

"No! The girl is still attractive for the kidnappers to use against Demir. We need to get going. Please get back in."

"Oh come on. A couple of minutes won't hurt."

"No!" came the very firm response.

"Okay," replied Rob in a deflated manner. He turned and climbed into the rear of the van.

"Go, go, go! We've got company!" It was Burak, yelling loudly at them as he crashed out through bushes and low branches and onto the opposite side of the road.

Rob leapt out of the van as the woman spun round to meet the oncoming man and drew a handgun from her jacket. Burak skidded to a halt at the rear of the van, breathing heavily. "Standard procedure. Tail reports ahead and then drops back so not to be seen nor heard. Attackers, usually the police for me, move into position silently, often with electric or hybrid car. I went ahead to scout it out." With that he jumped into the rear of the van just as the further crashing of bushes and branches announced the arrival of four armed men some fifty metres away and closing.

Without hesitation, Yasmin opened fire at the same time as the men, everyone's shots wild and missing their intended targets. Rob, whilst he was aware of the weapons tucked into his trousers, relied instead upon his instinct and training. He rolled across the road, narrowly being missed by a burst of bullets as they spat pieces of the tarmac into his face, and he leapt up for a close-quarters fight, which was far and away his personal preference. By doing so, he successfully unsettled his opposing combatants, who tried to keep their distance and use their guns.

The initial volleys of shots ceased because Rob's actions took him too close. As he mingled between the four, varying his kicks and punches, it became too dangerous for any of them to use their weapons. Either the attackers risked hitting one of their own or Yasmin risked hitting Rob. Instead, she moved to one side to give a clear line of sight. By doing so, she exposed herself, and as Rob turned his attention to one of the others, the assailant closest to Yasmin twisted around and squeezed off a number of rounds. Two bullets ripped into her, one slicing through the upper leg, the other just catching her in the side sending her spiralling against the van and onto the tarmac.

Rob kept himself in the middle of the four who were now circling him, trying to either get a shot in or attack with their more basic fighting skills, but they were superbly outclassed. Rob smiled to himself as an image for these men sprung to mind. He thought of them as a group of gangly adolescent boys prancing around a dance floor trying to impress some unfortunate girl who had attracted their attention.

Rob comfortably ducked a swinging right-handed punch from one. A glancing blow immediately followed to his right shoulder from another's gun barrel. However, Rob used the momentum of that to spin around and deliver a forceful, straight-armed punch into the chest of one of the men. In the ring, he knew that would fell most of his competitors. To his amazement, however, the man simply stepped back, apparently unfazed and only slightly off-balance.

The man was tough.

Half-crouching now, Rob realised his predicament and that this fight would be no pushover. He needed another ploy. These guys might not be able to fight well, but so far they were completely undeterred by what he had thrown at them. He kept moving, parrying their lunges and immediately counterattacking, trying to disable at least one of them to even up the numbers.

This standoff lasted quite a while until Rob spun, dropping to his hands and lashing both feet into the nearest man, one foot to the solar plexus the other into the nose, which scrunched with a gush of blood and a high-pitched shriek. The handgun scuttled across the road out of harm's way and disappeared under some bushes and piles of leaves.

Rob followed through, landing on his feet and lunged forward, catching a second man totally by surprise. They spun briefly, struggling to maintain balance. The man got an arm around Rob's throat. Rob feigned a collapse, forcing the man to adjust his position and grasp and in doing so, lessening the pressure slightly. Rob then spun around to bring the man down onto his back with Rob on top. He rapidly sprang up and stood over the man before pummelling him in the chest and face, feeling both a great satisfaction and a stupendous revulsion at his intent to hurt or even kill. The man became still after a couple of twitches.

The remaining two circled Rob, Yasmin groaning in the distance as she tried to stem the flow of blood. Rob kept himself between them to avert the use of firearms. After a while of noncontact circling, Rob suddenly and swiftly struck out at the man nearest him with a sharp, flat-handed stab to the throat as he dropped into a crouch. The man dropped like a sack of potatoes with a grunt while Rob rolled behind him as a couple of his comrade's bullets tore into the man's body, killing him instantly. Rob pulled one of his own weapons from his waistband and squeezed off three shots in rapid succession. One found its mark, spinning the man. That gave both Rob and Yasmin the time they required to line up their respective shots, and they hammered the man multiple times, sending him staggering backwards into some of the roadside bushes and ending up on top of them.

In great pain, Yasmin called, "Quickly, into the van. There will be others, and the authorities will be alerted by the disruption."

"Are you okay to drive?"

"Yes, I'll have to be. I'm known as the driver of this van. Get in!"

Yasmin steadied herself on the front of the van with one hand before stumbling around the front of the van, dragging her hand along the bonnet for support before clambering in through the driver's door. As Yasmin was moving to the driver's side, Rob ran to the rear, checked Burak and Anja were securely strapped in and okay, slammed the doors closed, and ran round to the front passenger side, slamming his door closed behind him. As he clambered in, Yasmin was in the process of strapping her belt around the top of her leg to stem the flow of blood. The engine roared into life, and the van lurched forward, Yasmin groaning with pain.

"I'm changing the plans," she said simply.

Rob leant to one side to look back in the wing mirror. The one man who had not been killed was lying on the road speaking on a radio. "Blast! The injured one is reporting in. We'll need to be ready."

Within moments and as Yasmin continued to accelerate, they passed a deserted car pulled into the verge that must have belonged to their attackers. From the tone of the engine and the ease with which it accelerated, Rob deduced that this had been customised, no doubt for situations such as this. A short while later, a single shot echoed through the valley, clearly distant, so it was not aimed at them.

They looked at each other, and Yasmin commented grimly, "It appears they don't look after their injured." Rob's shocked expression said enough. "You're clearly new to this, despite your abilities."

"Yes."

"We need to hole up and patch me up. I won't be able to drive for long. We also need to switch vehicles. This one will stand out a mile. I know of a place nearby. We use it when receiving or preparing for crossings into or from Croatia."

Driving hard, flinging the van around corners, they careered between the trees on either side of the road along the valley. Fewer than five minutes later, lights could be seen ahead at the village of Podgraje. Yasmin slowed, picking her way through the streets of the village, avoiding the centre where most people would be. As it was, they passed one middle-aged coupled, who stopped and watched their progress.

"Is it to be expected that people stop and watch around here, or do we stand out?" Rob asked.

"Generally, yes, they will watch. This van is known, so unless they saw the bullet holes, we should be okay, provided no one asks specifically for this van, in which case we're stuffed!"

Yasmin's delivery was very matter-of-fact, and Rob gained the impression this was her standard mode of speaking and had nothing to do with the pain she was in. He glanced sideways at her. Her brown hair was now somewhat dishevelled. The thin brown leather jacket soaked in blood was over a light blue shirt and worn jeans. As they headed out of the village, they passed a number of parked cars and one driving in the opposite direction. They charted its progress into the village in the wing mirrors and were relieved to see that it appeared to continue without even a tap on the brakes.

As another car approached, Yasmin pointed the van towards the main north-south road along the valley, making out to join that carriageway, but as the other vehicle briefly disappeared, she swung the wheel round and took once more to the country lanes, skirting the village of Zabiče without encountering anybody else. They could now hear sirens in the distance. "They won't be coming down this road, so we're OK."

As they passed an apparently disused and ramshackle house, Yasmin switched off all the lights and continued in the half-light provided by the moon through the layers of cloud. Upon entering the forest again, Yasmin reduced their speed to a crawl to navigate the narrow lanes and sharp corners.

"It's not about speed now but about not being seen so our adversaries have to spread themselves far more thinly to cover a wider territory in search of us," she said in acknowledgment of a sideways glance from Rob. "You were pretty useful back there. I wasn't expecting anyone to be able to assist in a scrap. If you hadn't, I doubt we would have made it, so thanks."

"No problem." Rob tried to sound unconcerned by what had just happened, but the truth was that he was very troubled at having played a part in killing a number of people, even if they had threatened his own life.

Some twenty minutes later of silent driving, Rob gasped and held on, expecting a violent, bone-wrenching crash as Yasmin turned off the lane and drove straight at a group of trees. They drove five metres like this with branches scraping the sides of the van, the twigs screeching on the metal before they emerged on a narrow track winding between trees and closely-knit shrubs. After no more than one minute, they arrived outside a couple of small huts nestled between trees.

"Please, open the doors to the one on the left," Yasmin asked Rob, who bounded out, grateful to be outside and fill his lungs with fresh air. Yasmin had opened her window so the cold air flowing over her face would help keep her awake, but even so, the smell of drying blood was all-pervasive.

The doors swung open easily, revealing that the small hut was actually narrow and long, with another rugged-looking country-type vehicle at the far end. Barely giving Rob sufficient time to jump out of the way, giving rise to a startled exclamation from Rob, Yasmin drove in and parked.

"Let our passengers out, and then come and help me over to the other hut," she called, and Rob started to do as requested.

The hut's interior was, as expected, sparse but pleasantly and surprisingly warm. Burak and Anja had already settled themselves in a far corner on a mattress and looked up as the others hobbled in. Anja was wide-eyed, clearly terrified and silent, staying close to her father. Rob guided Yasmin to a chair, where she sat down, shaking slightly from the shock. "You'll find medicines in the cabinet over there," she said, pointing to the far wall and

117

a row of cupboards. "Please bring all that you find. I'll need your help."

As he walked over and rummaged through the cabinet, Rob asked, "I don't suppose that there's any food here as well? We haven't eaten for quite a while."

"Yes there is; in the cabinets over on the side wall. You can help yourselves."

"Burak, please take a look and see what you can put together for us while I help out here." As Burak laboured to his feet, Yasmin dropped her handgun onto the table within easy reach and with a loud thump. Burak regarded her momentarily and nodded an acknowledgment to her unspoken warning not to try anything. Injured she might be, but she was still very alert.

Rob set about tending to Yasmin, cutting her trouser-leg off and cleansing her injured leg. The puncture hole had a few strands of the material in the wound but was otherwise clean, as was the exit wound. He cleansed the wound and then wrapped some gauze, padding, and bandages around the injury before starting on Yasmin's side.

"Please, some morphine first," she asked.

Rob found a couple of pre-prepared syringes, jabbed one into her arm, and then continued with her side, gently removing her jacket and easing her shirt off to get to the wound.

Burak and Rob finished their respective exertions at the same time, Burak having been hampered by the handcuffs. As Anja and Rob joined him sitting at the rickety table in the centre of the room. Rob then looked over at Yasmin, trying desperately to keep his eyes only on her face and not her shirtless chest. "Want any?"

He was taken aback that Burak had not prepared any of the dried meat, bread, and fruit for her. However, Burak replied, "Not a good idea. Food on top of the shock that her body is going through will exacerbate the situation, quite possibly making her vomit, which would weaken her further. Drink is all that she needs." Rob didn't argue, sure that Burak knew a lot more about such matters than himself. He took her a cup of water instead.

As they ate, Yasmin typed and sent a text on her mobile phone, the confirmatory bleeps of a successful transmission disturbing the otherwise silent evening.

Franc Kovač was not happy as he dropped the phone into its cradle. He was sitting in his office back in Ljubljana. Having realised that there was little more he and his team could do in Postojna, they had returned to base, leaving only a few men on the ground to wrap up the remaining lines of enquiry. All forensics and other evidence had been bagged, tagged, and sent away for assessment. All the statements they were able to obtain were similar. Didn't see anything, only heard the racket and stayed put so as not to take any risks. No one had even come forward to admit having seen the departing vehicles. He was frustrated and under pressure from all sides: his boss, the local police, politicians, and the media. And now, the reason for him being so late in the office, reports of more gunfire not that far from Postojna and in the middle of absolutely nowhere, so it would take time even for the local emergency services to arrive at the scene, let alone his teams. In this case, the word *local* was clearly an inappropriate euphemism.

"Nina," he barked at his assistant, "get two of whoever's in the team room and tell them to contact the locals with respect to the latest shootings. Drop everything else. And Nina, I don't want anything disturbed until our guys have assessed the situation on the ground themselves. Nothing!"

This latest set of shootings was bound to heap further pressure on his stretched team, particularly if they were not linked. Kovač was, however, absolutely certain that they were linked, so he had to ensure that the evidence was preserved. The locals, being too keen, could disturb aspects of the evidence without realising it. The coincidence that the shootings were not related would be too hard to swallow, and those facts would also not be lost on the locals. With his limited resources, it had been essential to share the intel that Robert Krane's mobile phone had been used twice, and it coincided with the region in which these latest shootings had occurred. That way, all possible authorities would have people if not directly looking for Krane at least being alert to spot and identify him if he appeared in public, or indeed, to report possible hideouts.

The great frustration was that it was already dark so the location would have to be effectively sealed off until either the morning, which was most likely, or mobile lighting arrived. What could have happened to prompt further shootings though? The little girl had already been kidnapped, so unless there had been a falling out or a rescue bid, Kovač could not understand why there would be further shootings. Krane must be involved, but how? The Brits were adamant that there was no reason why he would pose a threat. Something just did not stack up. Why was this young girl so important? There had to be a key piece, or pieces, of information missing.

He didn't have to wait long until the first phone call came through from the local police at the scene, and they sounded nervous. Kovač could hear the talk in the background as well as the comments from the caller. There appeared to have been both armed and hand-to-hand combat, leaving four men dead, all of whom were wearing similar dress. None fitted Krane's description. One appeared to have been executed with a single shot to the head. Dark tyre tracks suggested that someone had left in a hurry.

In the densely forested area, the local police, who were unused to gun fights, were concerned that others could be lurking and so were telling each other to keep their eyes open and stay in the shadows themselves. Kovač tried to assure them that the perpetrators would be long gone but to no avail. At least they would not be disturbing the scene of crime, but he really hoped they would not leave and give the perpetrators the opportunity to come back and clear up.

The execution of one worried him, however. That didn't happen when someone was in a hurry to leave, which was suggested by the tyre tracks. So what had really happened there? Something did not make sense, unless, of course, someone had already followed up to ensure no one could talk. If that were the case, this matter had taken an even more macabre turn after similarly executing all those in Postojna.

6

As day four dawned, there was a hive of activity around the fight site. Police, the Slovenian Intelligence and Security Agency, crime-scene specialists, and of course the media, who were being kept at a distance, were all there. Detailed notes and measurements were being taken together with hundreds of photographs. Particular attention was given to, first, the blood on the ground around where it was presumed a vehicle had been parked. Second, the apparently executed man was also receiving close attention.

The initial impressions from the person heading the crime-scene unit that day were relayed back to Kovač as he drove to work in Ljubjana. It was as he feared, if not worse.

"We've found four bodies, as you know sir," the senior on-site investigator was saying. "Three died from multiple bullet wounds, one from differing directions and one from an execution-style shot to the head. However, I suspect that he had been incapacitated for quite some time before that following two kicks, one to the face, obliterating the man's nose, and the other to the solar plexus region, judging by the muddy footprint on his clothes. The execution shot was from an entirely different weapon than any of the others used. Not only was the calibre clearly different, but there was also no cartridge whereas there are dozens of cartridges lying around from other weapons. The bullet is buried in the relatively soft tarmac and is being carefully retrieved. Whether we can get any useful forensics will depend upon how damaged the bullet is once we've retrieved it. The fourth man died from blunt force trauma, and judging by the marks, it was hand combat.

Possibly Krane, thought Kovač, immediately acknowledging how ridiculous a conclusion that was considering the number of people suitably skilled in such combat. But all the same, it was a bit too much of a coincidence.

The man paused for breath before continuing. He was gabbling to get the information out, knowing how keyed up the Inspector was. "Timing of the execution shot was such that the deaths were too close together to make an immediate distinction, but appearances here are such that a clean-up squad may have come after the fact to ensure that no one who could talk was left alive.

It is possible that the executed man had used his radio at some point. The body is in the centre of the road facing the direction in which the fleeing vehicle went. The size of the tyre tracks indicated it was either a large car or a light van. Probably the latter judging by the muddy footprints that simply disappear to the rear of the vehicle's apparent position. I expect that the vehicle is of dark blue colour based on the flakes of paint found on the tarmac, suggesting that it was hit by multiple bullets. Even though it was evening and dark, I would be surprised if it could have gone far without being noticed, so either there was a local switch or they've had to hole up somewhere.

"As you also know, we found additional blood on the road surface, indicating that at least one of the group that drove away has been hit. We conclude this because, like the muddy footprints, there is a trail from initial strike point to a place close to where I put the front of the vehicle as being. Curiously, it appears to be on the driver's side, unless it's a British vehicle. The wound does not appear to be superficial from the extent of blood loss, so I would expect that medical assistance will be required." Then, anticipating the obvious, he said, "All doctors and hospitals have been alerted, as well as the Croatian border guards, as they are less than ten kilometres away. We've also alerted the Croatian authorities in case the suspects already made it across the border. Border CCTV footage is also being reviewed."

Kovač listened patiently. There was no need to interrupt, as all the information he wanted was forthcoming. He knew the guys on the ground were working hard and making progress, but he was impatient for results. Everyone could sense the urgency and importance of this investigation, but even so it was generally going nowhere. They were in a constant game of catch-up and guesswork, which was highly unsatisfactory, particularly because so far there was absolutely no reason or rationale behind any of this.

Kovač was therefore relieved to receive another call ten or twelve minutes later with a further update. Even as the update was being relayed, he could hear further excitement in the background. The same investigator was saying, "There are clear tracks leading through the woods directly from the unclaimed and unregistered car found a few hundred metres further up the road to the attack site. An initial search revealed nothing, but the vehicle has been seized for a forensic search back at the lab. What is more surprising is that the attackers were not able to ambush the targets because one of the target group had walked forward in their direction, seen them, and come running back through the bushes.

"There are slightly broken branches at the side of the road, and these guided a sharp-eyed colleague to have a closer look. She found small threads of material that do not match any of the deceased on the rough edges of the snapped wood. Following the tracks back, it was clear that he, from the foot prints, saw the car and/or the attackers early and then ran to the road."

This was an intriguing find, but it did nothing to help solve who everyone was. Why would one of the target group have walked forward? There was no sign of urination or other bodily activity, so could that individual have been trained in some way?

There then followed a series of whispered messages relayed from an out-of-breath colleague. "We have found where three people were apparently waiting for a period of time, quite probably for the pick-up. The prints in the earth and mud indicate three people, and none of the prints match any of the deceased. One set is sufficiently small, with only light indents in the mud such that they could belong to a child. A team is following the tracks back to see where they came from. However, those tracks do not head toward the vehicle, the fight, or anywhere. They simply vanish. We've started a thorough search of the area in case the child is in hiding, although it is possible he or she was carried to the vehicle."

A child! Yes! Kovač felt vindicated. His instinct that the girl was somehow involved was correct. "But why? Why are so many people dying for a young girl?" he asked himself quietly.

Three days had passed, and there had been no reports of a ransom demand. Ordinarily one would expect a ransom demand within the first twenty-four hours—that is, of course, if the purpose of the kidnapping was for ransom. "If this isn't for a ransom, what could all this be for?" Kovač shook his head. *The poor child is caught in the middle of goodness knows what,* he thought.

What's more, if the girl was there with someone skilled in unarmed combat, it has to mean Krane was also there. He has to be involved; he was at the hotel at the time of the kidnapping and is also unaccounted for. It's all too coincidental. Could the British be covering for something? It's unlike Gurning, unless it is something very big. Although his own investigations on Krane drew a similar conclusion to that of Gurning's, that Krane was an innocent, his instinct said otherwise. But what didn't make sense was why Krane would now be with the girl when he had apparently been a part of the kidnapping. Kovač's head began to spin with all of the unanswered questions, which made him all the more certain that there was a lot more to the case than he realised.

"Thank you," he said as the briefing ended and he put the phone down.

"Nina," he called, "please ensure that the photographs of both the girl and Krane are circulated once again. They may or may not be together, and please drum it into all border controls, especially along the Croatian border, to be on alert." Kovač sat back in his chair to think.

In peculiar contrast to Franc Kovač, life at the MI6 hut in the middle of the dense forest was remarkably relaxed. Rob awoke first, his mattress across the front and only door. Yasmin was between himself and the other two, at her insistence. Burak and Anja also remained fast asleep, a cord tied around their handcuffs to an electronic buzzer should they move more than expected so it could alert Yasmin. Rob was not sure how they could be a danger as both had been securely tied to the hut's corner post. But anyway, it was the only way to get Yasmin to settle and sleep, which she was in desperate need of.

He watched the gentle heave of her chest beneath the light blanket that covered her as she breathed and was relieved that there was someone on his side and with him, even though she was injured. What was it that made someone place herself at risk for the sake of another, particularly when they were strangers and what's more, place herself at risk for the interests an entirely different nation? Rob did not know, but as he lay there watching her, he was extremely grateful, not only to her but to all of the security forces. There was no way he would take them for granted again.

Yasmin's phone vibrated, and she answered groggily, presumably in Slovenian, but Rob was unsure. Upon hanging up, she announced, "We have a visitor. A good visitor." Moments later the there was a buzzing of alarms in the hut, immediately followed by the screeching sound of branches on metal. Another vehicle was arriving.

The sound of an opening and closing door was the prelude to a knock on the hut door, giving Rob the precious seconds he needed to both leap up and pull the mattress out of the way. A young, skinny-looking youth came striding in and slumped down on a chair, completely at ease with the place and the circumstances and totally unfazed by Yasmin having a gun trained on the door, just in case. He dropped a parcel on the table.

"Rob, please could you look through the parcel and hand me the set of clothes most suited for me? I hope they are obvious. The other clothes are for you three once we arrive at the safe house and you've had a chance to clean up. There are also some toiletries in there for you all. Ignore my glum colleague; he doesn't like getting up early."

Rob did as requested and then politely turned his back on Yasmin as she changed, somewhat taken aback that the new arrival did not. Once Yasmin was ready, signalled by a heavy breath of relief after a series of painful groans, she said, "Right, all of you get yourselves into the transport. It won't be comfortable as you're going to be hidden beneath the floor and the load we're transporting, whatever it is that we've been given on this occasion."

The nameless, skinny youth, Rob, Anja, and Burak trooped out, closing the door behind them, and started the laborious process of unpacking the van to slip beneath the false floor. The youth was then left with the task of heaving the stacks of boxes and furniture back into the van. A while later, the van started and moved gingerly off.

＊

Steven, Laura, and Graeme were huddled at one end of another internal meeting room on the fourth floor of Thames House, beakers of steaming coffee in front of them on the table. They had barely said anything since their arrival some forty minutes earlier, and it had just turned to eight in the morning; all were still bleary eyed from a restless night wondering what could have gone so wrong that the pick-up had been compromised and ambushed. At least they had escaped, even though Yasmin had been injured. Elsewhere in the meeting room, alongside a map of Slovenia and its neighbouring countries, there were pictures of Rob, Burak, and Anja all pinned on the wall. At the opposite end of the room was a white board stretching the full width of the room with a timeline drawn across the top, annotated at various points, and a large grid beneath with only a few of the boxes filled in, all done in Laura's neat handwriting.

The silence was broken by the Polycom audio conference equipment sitting on the table between them *bing-bonging* noisily, its lights flashing. As Steven leant over to answer the incoming call, Laura fiddled with the mouse that had been next to her, and a large, wall-mounted screen flickered into life. Yasmin's voice filled the room in strong, strident tones that belied the reality of how she felt.

"Gregory has arrived and taken our friends outside to settle them into their transport," she was saying, her language cautious despite the fact that they were using a secured satellite link.

By launching right in, she signalled that she did not want to discuss her own well-being and wanted to control the agenda. Steven, Laura, and Graeme shared quick glances and went with the flow. Those in the operational field had to dictate the pace as they were the ones putting themselves at risk. "The journey to the guesthouse should not be too long nor too strenuous. They will be well looked after when we arrive and be able to relax and be available for conversations late in the day if you wish. You should be able to stream the footage from the van's cameras now."

Laura clicked on the pre-established icon for secure sharing of files or other material. The three watched intently as Yasmin described the events of the previous evening and consequently the need to change plans. When the film clip had finished, Yasmin said quickly, "I should go now. I heard the transport doors close, so my passengers are waiting for me." With that, she simply dropped all connections.

"Wow," Gurning said. "Your girl doesn't waste words, does she, Graeme?"

"Apparently not," he replied dryly. "I guess she simply wants to get to the safe house in Piran, where we've already arranged for her to receive medical attention. Some folks are heading over there from Italy." Holding up a hand to defend any comment, he added, "They're using a very different route to cross over so as not to increase traffic through the port. Laura, are you sure you still want to participate in the extraction?"

"Absolutely," she replied, possibly a little too eagerly, as she eyed the pictures of Rob on the wall and thought of the fighting skills he had exhibited on the film they had just watched. If her eagerness was noticed, neither of the men commented.

"Okay, no problem. In which case, as planned, you fly out this afternoon. We'll keep you updated on events. A cover team has already arrived, and they have the safe house and general area under observation. They have already reported an increase of police activity and tightening of border controls, so the operation will be a challenge. You'll meet Stefano Cassini, typically Italian as far as I'm concerned and a really great guy. Extremely capable and will love taking you for the journey on his boat. At the moment, we still intend that you will meet Yasmin for a briefing at the Skocjan Caves, but clearly, depending upon her condition, that plan may have to change."

"Agreed. Before that, I suggest we review the footage again and try to get identifications for the four attackers. Then, and only then, we can start to establish their connection to Burak Demir and why they are targeting him. Whilst I am sure he has many enemies, this is the first time on record that he has been threatened, so what has changed? If there is a power-shift in his network, we need to know and try to understand any new forces at play."

"I agree with you, Laura. The potential ramifications for serious criminal activity in Britain and possibly national security cannot be ignored if Burak is being removed. And Graeme, I suspect that you need to touch base with our Slovenian friends to show an interest in the recent events and if they have anything to connect Robert Krane to all this. It would be great to keep him out of this as far as possible until we really know the extent of his involvement. Then, if feasible, he could disappear back into the daily world of anonymity."

"Yes, I'll do that and see what I can learn."

"One final point before we review the footage again. It is imperative that we establish how the pick-up was compromised to ensure that none of the next stages go the same way."

Laura stepped in, saying, "I've been mulling that over and have had a few ideas. First, and most worryingly, it could be at our end, whether MI5, MI6, or through Robert's friend and associates at Scotland Yard. Second, it could have happened at the Slovenians' end if they were able to trace Robert's call and were sloppy with their interdepartmental communication. It does appear that their Intelligence and Security Services are stretched and have involved the local police forces and border controls. That would provide a very wide net for any of the bad guys to link into and zero in on our guys. Third, it could purely be a combination of bad luck, instinct on behalf of the bad guys, chance, and/or a combination of any of the preceding matters. We know that the roads around there are infrequently used, hence being prepared to arrange the pick-up there and for MI6 to have a safe house. The van could have stood out and been followed by putting two and two together to make four, coupling the knowledge that our guys would have to be in that region because that was where they were held and/or noise picked up from police channels, etc."

"I can accept any and all of that, Laura. It was a good assessment, but it does not lessen the need to at the very least discount a leak from our end. Before you leave, please brief one of your colleagues. Bring him or her over the wall in respect of the confidentiality so he or she can start working out if we have a leak. Who do you recommend?"

"Jim Aitcheson," she responded with no hesitation at all. "He has a great nose for leads and is very discreet."

"Yes, I agree, Jim is a good choice. Okay, let's review that footage again and see who, if anyone, we can identify."

The creaking of the van's doors opening alerted the three dozy occupants of the under-floor compartment that they had stopped and something was happening. It was hard to distinguish from the muffled voices whether they were at their final destination or if this was something more sinister. Burak whispered urgently and quietly to Anja not to move and to remain silent. They were all now wide awake, senses straining to hear what was happening, heartbeats sounding like bass drums in their ears. The muffled voices continued, all male. Then the sound of the wooden furniture grinding and sliding against the wood floor was heard as some of the furniture was hauled out. Could this be a good or a bad sign? The muffled voices continued. The tapping along both sides of the van was the first sign that this was not what was intended.

The van had arrived at a checkpoint, and police were separating cars from all other vehicles and pulling all of the latter type over for questioning and possibly inspection. That Yasmin was asleep and her companion, Gregory, had refused to wake her had roused irritation with the police, who did, however, respect those wishes. Instead they decided to give Gregory a hard time and give the van a thorough going over. Gregory tried to balance being reasonable with being suitably challenging of their approach, giving rise to occasional animated and loud disagreements.

When a couple of policemen started tapping the sides of the van with small rubber mallets,

Gregory's protestations increased to being incensed. He made out that the little marks created would create a whole heap of trouble for him with his boss, making the police laugh and find other cosmetic aspects to wind Gregory up, distracting all but one from the purpose of the checkpoint. The one was shining his torch into the rear, tapped the floor of the van, and tried to shift some of the furniture to get a better look. Gregory came back round to the rear and pushed the man aside, rummaged around, and emerged with a can of polish and rag cloth. He then started vigorously polishing a couple of marks at the rear, partially disrupting the one diligent policeman, who had to cease his exertions to address the belligerent driver, the ninth of the still-young day.

Their exchange, now some twenty-five minutes since the van was first stopped and five since the search started, was interrupted by a ruckus near the end of the queue coming in the opposite direction, temporarily distracting the attention of the four policemen surrounding Gregory and his van. Seven of the eight police working the other side were headed down towards the disturbance, watched by their colleagues on the other side of the road, while the eighth was trying to prevent vehicles from moving off prior to clearance. However, the seven soon proved insufficient as impatience and anger flared amongst numerous drivers and passengers up-and-down the queue. Soon, therefore, all police from both sides had to leave their stations to quell the multiple outbreaks of disturbances before matters escalated too far. This left other drivers, including Gregory, to simply drive off without their checks being completed.

Yasmin, of course, had not been asleep and immediately sat up once they were underway. "Okay, guys, keep it up for a few minutes longer. We're moving and almost clear," she uttered into a collar microphone. As they moved well beyond the police checkpoint and any potential for the police to easily wave them down once more, she said, "Right, we are clear. You can let matters ease, and many thanks. A great diversion."

"That was close," she said to Gregory. "I'm glad that I called in for the support early. Otherwise it may have turned out very differently." Gregory merely nodded, kept his eyes facing front and drove on, wiping the sweat off his brow with his forearm. "I just hope they do not get into too much trouble and that whilst necessary, it does not occur to either the authorities or the other side that the outbreak of discontent was what it was—a diversion to get us through."

After a nerve-tingling ten minutes, they took an exit off route 111 heading into Portorož, joined the coast road Obala and passed the smart hotels in the centre. A few minutes later they pulled over into a small dockside complex of long, nondescript sheds. Gregory leapt out to open the roller-shutter doors, drove into the space beyond, and then closed the doors behind them. Five minutes of strenuous effort later, Rob, Burak, and Anja staggered to their feet on wobbly legs into the semidarkness of the warehouse, partially full of old, cheap furniture stacked and labelled as though it was an official storage unit of some sort or another. Two mid-range and inconspicuous Slovenian registered cars were parked to one side of the van.

As the three wandered around the unit, stretching and getting life back into their cramped and stiff limbs, Gregory helped Yasmin out of the van. He helped her move about a little and then settle into the driver's seat of the lead car. Leaving the door open, Yasmin called out, "Rob, Mr Demir. Please take the wash bags from Gregory here and freshen up a little, as well as shave please. Mr Demir, you will need to help your daughter as well. The objective is to be sufficiently normal and presentable to be everyday passengers in a car so as not to draw unwanted attention. The next stop will have an adequate bathroom to fully wash and change into the spare clothes that we have for you. Gregory will show you the way. Please be reasonably quick. Rob, you will have to remove their handcuffs for this part. Gregory will guard the outside of their door and there is no window, so no need to worry."

When they emerged, Burak preceded Gregory who had a handgun strategically placed in the small of Burak's back. Their clothes were still looking slightly dishevelled, but they felt far brighter having been able to wash properly for the first time.

Gregory handed a pair of sunglasses to Rob and Burak as Yasmin said, "Mr Demir, you are with Gregory riding in the front passenger seat. He will not talk to you but has the potential to be extremely violent if attacked. Rob, please do the honours and handcuff him again. Mr Demir, you will kindly hold your jacket over the handcuffs, as casually as possible. I should add that the doors have been modified so you won't be able to open any of them without me being in close proximity. Rob and the young girl will travel with me, Rob in the front as though we are a family. We will take different routes but end at the same location. It's not far, although we shall take circuitous routes. I'm trusting that there won't be any, but are there any questions?"

After the required silence, Yasmin simply said, "Okay, everyone to their respective positions." Burak gave Anja a hug and whispered something to her before walking over to the second car. Once Rob and Anja were settled in the lead car, Yasmin continued, "Ordinarily I'd be happy to talk whilst driving, but not today. Silence please."

Gregory opened the roller-shutter door once more, and they drove out. Yasmin dawdled sufficiently to watch as Gregory got out of his car, closed the roller-shutter door to the warehouse, and drove off in the opposite direction. Anja could not help but turn and watch her father disappear.

She was watched in turn by Yasmin in the driver's mirror. "Don't worry, little girl, you will be back together again soon." With that, Anja sat back, facing the front, and Yasmin drove off.

The two cars drove through the narrow streets of Portorož and eventually the short distance to the eastern outskirts of Piran. Leaving the built-up areas behind, they drove sedately through the predominantly wooded areas on the north, less-populated side of the peninsular and pulled into the driveway of a medium-sized house. Yasmin, Rob, and Anja arrived first to find a man and two women waiting for them inside. Immediately, the two women took Yasmin off to the rear of the house, one carrying a medical bag. As they went, Yasmin threw her handbag to the man, saying, "The proximity device to open Gregory's car doors is inside. They should be here soon."

Watched with an irritating intensity by the man, Rob collapsed into a comfortable sofa to wait. Anja, on the other hand, trotted over to the window overlooking the driveway and positioned herself to wait and watch for her father's arrival. She didn't have to wait long, but as she instinctively moved to the front door to go and greet him, she was stopped by the man, who simply pointed to a chair.

"Wait inside please."

Rob spoke for the first time in a long time and found his jaw was stiff. "It will be okay, Anja. Your dad will be inside very soon. All this is for everyone's safety, as I'm sure your dad has already said."

The little girl nodded whilst keeping her eyes glued to the open front door. An audible *thunk* of the locks preceded the opening and closing of doors, with Burak entering the house moments later, still carrying the jacket over the handcuffs. Anja ran over to give him a hug as he draped his arms over her head.

Gregory and the other man spoke in lowered tones for a few moments before Gregory went back outside, leaving the parcel of clothes and toiletries behind.

"Hi, I'm also Gregory for the purposes of our acquaintanceship," the man said.

His appearance, like that of the other Gregory, as well as his accent, clearly suggested that the assumed name also did not match the nationality. "This house is fully secured, as is the perimeter. You will find fresh clothes in this parcel, along with toiletries. The bathroom is down that corridor there on the left. Robert, you first please. There is no rush, so you can take your time. Once you're ready, there are some people who would like to speak with you briefly while those two are getting ready and before we all have something to eat."

With a little shove of his foot, the parcel slid across the wood floor to where Rob sat. He stooped to pick up some of the items inside and made his way in the direction indicated.

Upon emerging, Rob exchanged places with Burak and Anja. Gregory II, as Rob had decided to refer to him, nodded towards one of the women sitting on the sofa.

"This is a nurse who will check you over to make sure that you haven't suffered unduly from your ordeal; she's already given a generally clean bill of health to the other two, the girl's cold aside. Layla, over there, is my partner for looking after you whilst you remain here. We've taken over from Yasmin and Gregory, who have left."

After the quick medical exam, the nurse left, and Gregory II motioned to Rob to follow him. Opening a door beneath the stairs to the first floor, they descended into a well-lit basement corridor and entered a room of about three metres by three metres. The small table in the centre had a bottle of water and a couple of glasses on it with two chairs facing a video conferencing screen. Gregory II motioned for him to take a seat. "I'll leave you now. The conference will start automatically. I'll know when it's finished and come to collect you." Turning to go, Gregory II paused and added, "Yasmin says good luck and thank you for your intervention with the attackers. You saved her life, which deserves the thanks of us all." With that, he left, locking the door behind him.

Moments later, the screen burst into life, with Steven Gurning and Graeme Spreachley filling the picture.

"Afternoon, Rob. Although no doubt still somewhat exhausted, we hope you feel slightly brighter now you've had the chance to freshen up. Laura Harding, who was with us before, is on audio. She's travelling at the moment so is unable to join us in person."

Laura was actually at home and grateful that none of them could see her as she sorted through her drawers and cupboards to pack for the next few days.

"Hello, Rob," she said, announcing her presence.

She was excited by the prospect of foreign travel again, a rarity in her role, but she knew she would miss her modern yet spacious two-bedroom flat on the tenth floor of the St. George Wharf complex overlooking the Thames at Vauxhall, a fifteen-minute stroll from the office. Laura stopped her packing and looked out over the Thames, enjoying the view as she concentrated on the conference call. She loved the light, minimalist, ultra-modern effect she had accomplished. She had been able to buy the flat with the legacy left by her grandparents some years earlier and was delighted that she had done so, benefitting from the sharp price rise for flats in the development should she ever want to sell.

"What about Michael? Where's he?" Rob asked.

"Michael's back on his normal duties. I appreciate that he's your friend and that is why you contacted him in the first place, and we all agree that was a decision of inestimable wisdom. Considering the current circumstances, we decided that friendship could affect decision-making and/or response times and did not want to take the risk, even though with Michael that would be extremely unlikely. I hope that you understand." Rob merely nodded. He had welcomed the sight of a friend and the reassurance that had come with it.

"Good. I just mentioned bringing you back to Blighty. Well that's what we're going to do just as soon as possible. Follow the directions when given by your hosts. You're in good hands. For now, though, we'd like to ask a few questions. We can cover the full detail once you're back. More importantly, we need to understand what, if anything, Burak Demir has said during the few days you've been together. Please think carefully. Even a passing comment that to you may appear inconsequential may hold a greater meaning for us with a wider network of intelligence gathering. We're also interested in why he appears to have been so willing to come with you. Okay, you had him handcuffed, but has he tried to escape? Was he ever out of your sight?"

Rob took the sudden silence as an indication that he was expected to talk. He took a deep breath and heaved a sighed. "Personally, I think he was not expecting any of this. At one point he commented that he'd tried to keep the relationship with the lady who was shot and his daughter a secret, and he clearly regrets them becoming involved. He said that upon meeting Anja's mother and then particularly once Anja was born, he realised how much more there is to life and started trying to distance himself as much as possible from his criminal activities and focus on his legitimate businesses. Apparently those have grown substantially over the years. However, this created issues with his criminal associates, who noticed that he was spending less time with them and more time on other matters, although they do not know the extent of his legitimate interests, or at least Burak has not told them."

"He openly admitted to being a criminal?" Laura jumped in, querying Rob's phraseology with an amazed expression in her voice.

"Yes, he did. I remember it well because I was fiddling with my iPhone at the time and started recording our conversation."

"So you have recorded him admitting to being a criminal?" Gurning asked incredulously.

"Yes, that's exactly what I've just said," Rob responded, slightly frustrated.

"Just checking that we understood you, Robert. Please, I'm sorry if at times we come across as infuriating, but in our business we have to be absolutely precise. Presumably, you don't have your iPhone with you at the moment?"

"No, I don't. Sorry."

"Oh well, next time please bring it with you, and we may need the actual machine when you get

146

here. If that's the case, we will, of course, replace it with a new one for you."

"Sure," Rob said in a non-committal manner.

"Did he ever comment on why he thinks his associates were trying to kidnap him or worse?" Laura prompted again to re-gain the focus that had suddenly lapsed.

"Oh, he's sure they were going to kill him, without a doubt, but they needed to know the details of his networks. At one point he commented that he intentionally maintained many separations in his activities but did not elaborate. He also said that he'd take that information to the grave instead of letting some chap called Emilio pull the strings, and Emilio knows that. That's why they kidnapped his daughter along with him to use as leverage to get him talking."

"Hold on," Spreachley interrupted. "Sorry, but you mentioned Emilio. Who's he?"

"No idea. Nothing was said about him. Burak simply mentioned his name a few times."

"Okay. So you were saying why he was kidnapped and why these people want to kill him."

"As I've already said, Burak wants to spend more time focused on his legitimate businesses and grow those and encourage the people in those businesses. That rankled his associates. They were concerned that his apparent changing of allegiances to other matters that placed them and their operations at risk, that he was going soft. Not that Burak sees it like that, but he acknowledges that's how his associates will view it. Time with Anja and her mother started to change his values, away from only himself, away from the hard loyalties of the network and making money in any way he could.

"However, he is sure that his associates would not, could not understand this and remained focused only on increasing their own wealth and power, and to a certain extent, they enjoy the process. Burak said in the past, he also looked on similar changes in people as them going soft, placing the network at risk through split loyalties. He acknowledges that, which is why he kept his relationship a secret, or at least thought he had. Whilst he still spent time managing the criminal activities, his heart is focused on the legitimate side and the new challenges that came with it. Ideally, he would completely split the two, legitimate from criminal, and has done so in a couple of instances.

"However, making the separation is not at all simple because in many cases he built the legitimate businesses on top of the criminal activities to help hide the criminal aspects, often without many of those involved knowing there was criminality involved. To simply cease the criminal aspect would hurt many innocents, which he did not want. Hence his focus was to try and build up the legitimate so there would not be the reliance should a separation ever become possible. That's what he's been struggling with for a number of years, and he has become worn out with trying and with the tension between the two sides. It's also why he said he is willing to hand everything over to me."

"He what!" launched in Gurning, almost shouting in an incredulous tone. Spreachley simply slumped dramatically, shaking his head in disbelief.

"I've no idea what prompted me, but whilst he was still trapped there in the cave and I had to decide whether to leave him and/or Anja, I thought I wanted something for the risk. I'd read how wealthy he is, so scribbled on a piece of paper that he had to pass everything over to me and asked him to sign. I expected some degree of negotiation, but instead he simply signed. Only later did we discuss why he had done so, and that is when he admitted that he is tired of his current way of life. All he wanted was an assurance that Anja would be looked after, but he did not elaborate on what he considers as being looked after."

"I can't believe this," Spreachley said, shaking his head again. "It's the height of naivety. There's no way that a man like Demir would agree to such a thing. He must be scheming, and therefore, the fact that he's still with you suggests that this is all part of his intended plan. What on earth possessed you, man?"

"As I've said," Rob commented in a tired manner, "I've no idea what possessed me, and yes, after the fact I also considered my actions to be naïve and that the likelihood of Burak living up to his side of the agreement as being zero. Only time will tell." He finished with a shrug.

A faint fuzzy buzz sound from the conferencing equipment filled the silence that ensued, each mulling over the exchanges that had occurred. Laura broke the silence between them.

"Actually, this has potential."

"You must be joking," Spreachley said sharply. "I always gave you more credit than this, Laura."

"Graeme," Gurning said quickly, knowing how Laura would leap at the chance of a sparring match with Spreachley, which was something he really did not want in front of an outsider. "I suggest we listen to Laura's reasoning before leaping to a conclusion. I asked her to join this case precisely to be insightful and consider the possibilities and angles in ways you and I rarely do."

"Humph," was all that Spreachley could manage as a response.

"Well, clearly Demir could well have been playing Rob all along, but first, he wasn't to know that Rob would come riding to the rescue and second, it would be an incredibly cynical thing to achieve at such an emotionally charged time with his daughter's welfare and life in the balance. So—"

"Ah, that reminds me," Rob interrupted. "I didn't say that Burak was about to murder his daughter when I intervened."

"What!" the three exclaimed.

"This is simply unreal," muttered Spreachley.

"Another man was in the cave when I arrived. Along with others, he was there to speak with Burak, and the innuendo was dreadful for what he planned for Anja. It was clear that Burak knew what that could be, so he was about to murder her to avoid her being put through whatever this other man had planned. I could see tears streaming down his face as he prepared himself to kill her."

"Oh my word," Laura gasped in response to Rob's revelation. Gurning and Spreachley were struck silent.

"That leads to my supposition," said Laura after a moment to compose herself following Rob's startling revelation. "Maybe, just maybe, Demir *is*"—Laura stressed the word *is*, paused, and repeated the word—"is looking for a way out and found a way in the face of his death. Whether truly through Rob or using his agreement with Rob as the signal of his intent, we can only find out, but we should, I suggest, give him the chance to prove it."

"Why not put his hands up as part of the French justice system then a few years back?" Gurning countered before Spreachley had the chance to and no doubt dig a larger hole for himself as a consequence.

"Fair point, but my instinct is that Demir doesn't want his conversion, so to speak, to be public but wants to do it his way. He is a man used to being in control, so he tried to do it his way. Now that opportunity has gone. For us to get him out of Slovenia, it has to be covert, and who else would Rob enlist to help other than the British authorities? Bear in mind that we are still one of the most respected security authorities the world over for our treatment of people. Demir would know that for sure. Once he is sure he is out of reach of the Slovenian authorities and fully in our hands and before we have the chance to go public with his capture, he will have the opportunity to declare his intentions."

"Why not public?" Spreachley asked.

"First, in order to protect his daughter and possibly himself. Second, if he goes public, his associates will have the chance to counterattack. There must be plenty of inmates in many countries who would finish him off if given the nod. Also, if he went public, his associates would have the opportunity to reorganise their operations so that whatever Demir is able to structure to disrupt their operations and protect the legitimate businesses would fail. To achieve his ultimate goal, he needs help and a lot of it. Quite by chance, this could provide the route to his dream. Okay, okay, it sounds far-fetched, I know, but what if, just what if?" By now Laura was pacing around her flat, waving her arms around animatedly.

"I buy that," said Rob. "In my view, he's a broken man. I saw it. He fell hard—I mean so hard and so quickly. He watched as the woman he loved was shot in front of him, and then the mere threat of harming Anja as well must have nailed it for him. So when I materialised, why not? He just went for it. He had absolutely nothing to lose and absolutely everything to gain."

Another silence played out whilst all four thought about this. On screen, Rob could see Gurning and Spreachley fidgeting as they tried to get their minds around the possibility and if even partially true, the potential ramifications, of which he could not even hope to imagine.

"Fine," announced Gurning. "Let's play this out. Flush him out. Give him every opportunity. Robert, please, we need to trust and rely on you not to breathe a word of this to anyone, not even other members of our teams helping to extricate you, and especially not to Demir. Only the three of us please."

"No problem. And by the way, drop Robert please and call me Rob. Everyone else does."

"Good. That will limit the credibility damage to each of us if this is wrong. It will also limit the potential that this has if the story goes down avenues we cannot control and lets the cat out of the bag. Everyone so far involved needs to be muzzled as tight as can be, and we will limit even more so who and how many people we involve with this extraction. Everyone agreed?"

"Agreed," the others said in unison.

"Good. Well, let's get to it. And Rob?"

"Yes."

"Great stuff. I'm looking forward to meeting you."

7

Later that evening, Laura's plane touched down at Marco Polo Airport outside Venice. Stefano Cassini watched as the passengers disembarked, noticing and nodding approvingly as a young, slim but not skinny woman with short, fair hair tied back in a ponytail walked down the steps with athletic ease, her cream blouse and tan linen trousers flattering her female curves. He knew from photographs that she had hazelnut brown eyes. Stefano walked away from the viewing platform, elegant in his flannel trousers and lightweight, pale blue shirt accentuating his own brown eyes and olive tan, to wait for Laura in the arrivals area.

"Miss Grahams," he called, using the cover name under which she travelled as she came through the sliding doors. Stefano gave a polite bow and held out his hand. "Welcome to Venice," he said. "May I help you with your luggage?"

"Thank you. Stefano, I presume?" she replied, scrutinising his facial features to compare to the photograph she had been given.

"At your service. I'm delighted to be able to welcome you to Venice. Come, you must be hungry. There's a pleasant restaurant not far from the harbour that I know. A table is booked with a view you'll adore—the sea, the boats. The only thing missing is the sunset, but we'll have that tomorrow in Piran."

Laura smiled warmly at his charm. She had been warned of Stefano's flattery and was prepared and also able to appreciate his eloquent, smooth talking in the knowledge that apparently it was all show, for his commitment to his wife and family was legendary.

An hour later, once Laura had dropped her bags at the safe house, they were seated, as described, overlooking the Mediterranean and tucking into a fine Italian seafood dish accompanied by a crisp, dry white Sicilian wine.

"So tomorrow we will sail to Piran," Stefano said in perfect English. "It should take a relaxed five hours or so to cover the approximately eighty kilometres, so there will be no need to rush the morning. If we rise early, we can swing around Venice and enjoy the sights from an angle not usually experienced and see the route to our friends' house should they be available the following evening."

Laura was only too well aware that this was business and Stefano was talking about their plan B should they decide that upon their return it would not be safe to return to the same port as their departure.

"Then I propose a lunch bobbing around in the middle of the Med. You never know, I may even be lucky and catch a fish or two for us to share. Otherwise it'll be mixed charcuterie, breads, and salad that I will prepare. We'll be in Piran to watch the sun come down whilst we have our aperitifs and dinner at a lovely restaurant I know. It's a wonderful town. I'm sure you'll love it. The following day I recommend the Skocjan Caves. They're magnificent, I never tire of them. Then we can take an evening cruise into the sunset and back home. How does that sound, my darling?"

Laura marvelled at the way he was briefing her on their planned schedule in public by turning it into some sort of romantic foray. She joined in by asking pertinent questions about their friends' house in Venice, such as would they be able to tie their boat up close to the house, and she also asked questions about Piran and the Skocjan Caves. As she did, she relaxed into the evening, and their conversation soon moved on to their pastimes and hobbies, holidays, and dreams, just like any courting couple. It was, therefore, a wrench to share a last grappa with the restaurant owners, who appeared to know Stefano well, and head back home, as Stefano referred to the safe house in

Porto di Piave Vecchia. It was not far from the small harbour where the boat was apparently moored. They could have spent the night on board the motor yacht, but Laura knew the next day would provide ample time to familiarise herself with that environment, and she also wanted to get to know the safe house and its layout and facilities, should they return to it.

━━━

The fifth day since the kidnapping was calm and relaxing for Rob, Burak, and Anja and mostly so for their protectors. Gregory II and Layla were vigilant at all times and regularly talked on their mobile phones.

They woke late and spent the morning relaxing, reading a newspaper, and in the case of Anja, watching children's television. Sometimes the adults joined her to take their minds off matters. Despite the pleasant, sunny weather, they were not permitted to go outside, although Gregory II and Layla did so they could do some gardening or other chores, providing the pretence of normality should any neighbours be taking note. It was unlikely thanks to the position and privacy, but no risks were to be taken.

It was not until lunch, whilst Layla was serving dessert, that Gregory II provided an update. "I know it's frustrating, but please stay indoors and away from the windows at the front. Continue to rest and regain your strength. Our intention is that tomorrow we will smuggle you all out of Slovenia and to a protective environment in England. I won't answer any questions, but I do want you to be aware that the trip, at least the first part, may not be as easy going as we'd hoped. We won't leave until the afternoon—unless, that is, plans have to change for whatever reason. Unfortunately, that is very possible, so please ensure that you are ready to go at a moment's notice following this meal. Our scouts are telling us that the Slovenian authorities are working on the assumption that our diversionary tactics to get us through the road block yesterday were exactly that.

"Consequently, the entire area is crawling with police and other agents, whether to the borders with Italy and Croatia or the harbours. Unfortunately, it also appears that there's been an influx of others as well, presumably linked to the kidnappers. They're tripping over each other, and the authorities are suspicious. However, having nothing to pin on these guys, they have to leave them be. As a result, tensions are apparently running pretty high on the streets as the search continues for you.

"The one thing that benefits us is the presumption that you are operating alone and either waylaid a passing van or enrolled a friend to help. They don't appear to think you're well organised. We're not expecting house-to-house enquiries, but we need to be ready. You'll all

159

remain indoors and ready to decamp down into the basement if the alarm is raised. Now, enjoy the apple pie. As you'll have already realised, Layla is an excellent cook."

Rob wanted to but refrained from asking *If we are operating alone and are not organised, then how could I arrange a diversion? It doesn't make sense!* But after one look at Burak he let the matter drop.

—

Stefano and Laura, meanwhile, were enjoying the sun whilst speeding across the wide-open sea of the Med. It had been difficult to concentrate during the trip around some of the sights of Venice to learn the way to the plan B safe house. This was her first time, and she marvelled at the place. Stefano had quickly realised that and kept testing her every time they turned left or right to make sure she knew the landmarks. That way she could recognise the route should she need to without his assistance. His thoroughness and casual acceptance that harm could befall him impressed her.

Now, however, she was sitting back replete after a wonderful lunch. The mere sight of the delectable food, coupled with their surroundings, gave no hesitation, and any thought of her diet was cast to the wind. As the afternoon sun started to wane, drink in hand and soaking up the sun, she watched Stefano as he stood at the helm on the flying bridge, the wind ruffling his hair, and she couldn't believe she was doing this courtesy of her work. *No small wonder he loves his job,* she thought. *I could get used to this as well.* She had walked around the 17.5-metre motor cruiser a couple of times already, just to absorb the experience. Stefano kept it immaculate, so the age did not show other than for the few aspects of styling he had not been able to change. It was pure white, sleek, low-lying, and oozed opulence. The thought that James Bond would be impressed sprung easily to mind.

Stefano had explained as they set off on their voyage that the boat had been confiscated following a huge drug haul six years earlier by a British naval vessel just inside international waters. Then, whilst waiting for London bureaucrats to decide what to do with it, he had taken it out at a moment's notice following a tipoff and had been able to prevent the kidnapping of an influential British businessman at sea. Shortly after that and another tipoff, he helped the Italian authorities bring down a jewellery-smuggling ring by posing as a potential smuggler. With those two results in the bag, Stefano had successfully persuaded London to let him keep the craft, and many subsequent success stories could also be recounted—plus, he added with an elaborate shrug, a few not-so-successful episodes!

No alcohol had passed their lips, however, because they knew they would need their wits about them. They had heard that security and searches had increased immeasurably. It was presumed to be the Slovenian authorities' working assumption that Rob, Burak, and Anja were in the vicinity.

Throttling back on their speed, Stefano called over his shoulder, "We're approaching Piran. It's worth a look. I love the approach into this small harbour."

Laura joined Stefano as they cruised into the harbour. Stefano's approach was intentionally slow for Laura to take in the Venetian Gothic architecture surrounding the harbour, dominated by the bell tower of the Church of St. George. She loved the market town–type busyness of the place and the colourful, small fishing boats.

"It's wonderful, amazing. Will there be time to just wander about, nose in the shops, and explore some of the streets?" she asked.

"Absolutely," he replied. "Don't forget that we're on a romantic trip and I'm out to woo you." He glanced over at her, winked, and grinned mischievously. "All part of the cover."

She couldn't help but return the smile, saying, "Great for the first part, although I'm going to be very difficult to get for the second part!" They both roared with laughter.

It didn't take long after they had moored for security to arrive to check their papers, accompanied by the harbour master, who wasted no time in saying, "Ah, Mr Cassini, it's a delight to welcome you back and to welcome your friend. Please bear with us today as there are some additional formalities. My apologies for any inconvenience."

"That's not a problem," Stefano replied, shaking hands with everyone. "Anything we can do to help? I'm sorry you felt you needed to come down and meet us. As you know, I always come to your office as soon as I arrive." Laura recognised that Stefano was clearly fishing for information, but none was forthcoming.

"I know, I know, Mr Cassini," the harbour master mumbled. "It is a sad indictment of life that trust is a scarce commodity these days."

After a perfunctory search and check of their papers, they were left in peace. Stefano went below decks and extracted what looked like a mobile phone. Laura immediately recognised it as a portable electronic bug detector. The screen flashed green. Stefano grinned and said softly, "We can't be too careful on this trip, but it does help being a frequent visitor."

For the next hour or so, they meandered through the streets, soaking up the atmosphere and blending in as the tourists that effectively they were for the evening, whilst being very aware of the increased police and other authorities' presence. Dinner at Tri Vdove was everything and more than Stefano had promised. They sat on the terrace as the sun set with glorious food and ambiance and the sound of gentle waves on the rocks just a stone's throw away.

◆

The next morning Laura emerged from her cabin amid the tolling of the church bells and to the aroma of fresh bread. She was wearing a pair of lightweight walking trousers and a short-sleeved shirt.

Stefano was busy in the galley. "We'll be busy today, so we will require all our strength. Anyhow, breakfast is the best meal of the day. You'll need a warmer outer layer for when we get to the caves. Do you have anything because otherwise I will lend you something?"

"I agree, and the bread smells divine. And yes, I do have an outer layer with some robust lightweight walking boots. Thank you for the thought and the offer."

Forty-five minutes later they hailed a taxi as it was about to move off, having disgorged the previous occupants, who were clearly tourists. "Probably from a nearby hotel coming to look around the old town," whispered Stefano in Laura's ear, pretending to be romantic.

"The Skocjan Caves please," Stefano called through the window.

The journey was uneventful and mostly quiet, both looking out of the window. From time to time they would point something out to each other, using expressions such as, "Oh look, darling," to give credibility to their cover story of a romantic weekend away just in case the police questioned the driver at some future point.

Much to Laura's amusement, Stefano was playing the gallant gentleman brilliantly as he bought the entrance tickets for the caves and insisted upon carrying all the extra items in his back sack. They opted for a short tour and joined the queue. Another couple joined the queue immediately behind them. The man was equally making suitable caring noises and actions towards the woman, justifying that pleasantries and lighthearted conversation would naturally be exchanged between couples. Thus, introductions already made, by the end of the tour, the four tourists agreed to have a drink together and sat apart from everyone else in the sun.

Layla introduced one of the scouts who had been watching over the safe house, monitoring activities in Piran, and more importantly, seeking an appropriate spot to make the exchange to pass Rob, Burak, and Anja into Stefano's and Laura's care. She apologised for Yasmin explaining that her injuries were such that she could not meet them as initially planned.

As he said, "It'll be far too risky within the town limits," the others responded with lots of nodding and laughter, as though he had just cracked an excellent joke. "I recommend a water-borne exchange close to the northern coast line of the peninsula. There is a good stretch of wooded coastline west of the Bioenergy Resort Salinera. Pick-up could occur without attracting attention two hundred metres west of the pier there. We can hire small boats, canoes, etc., at the resort, float along the coast, pick up our friends, and relay them out to you upon your arrival. There'll be plenty of cover and nothing unusual to have people from the resort exploring the coastline. We'll just make sure that no one else has the same idea," He added with a grin and a wink. "So far, we've seen very little boating activity from either the authorities or the other side. We'll have folks stationed at the approach roads and around the cove just in case we are needed."

More laughter by all ensued before Laura asked, "And how are our friends?"

"They're all fine," Layla replied. "The girl, Anja, has a bit of a cold but is otherwise okay. Nothing to be concerned about or to change the nature of the pick-up."

"Good," said Stefano. "And what time should we be making our sweep? I'm tempted to leave earlier, swing past the Italian border, and then come back for the pick-up. That way we'll be able to review if we're being shadowed."

"Fair point," the other man said. "I prefer that approach as well. Presumably we'll all have our mobiles to keep in touch?"

Following more laughter and nods all around, he continued, "So I suggest we swap our false identities and contact details as though we intend to stay in touch and call it a day."

So with polite handshakes and hugs, they exchanged scribbled bits of paper and parted. Stefano and Laura headed back to the harbour and found a café for a late lunch before cruising off under the watchful eye of the authorities, but they were not followed.

———

Upon her return, Layla changed her appearance with a wig, makeup, and some padding in various strategic places. She then turned her focused on Anja, who loved the attention and dressing up, particularly the new hair styling. The two chatted away about their ideas for the new look, and Anja giggled at the additional padding given to her, increasing the appearance of her age by a few years. Rob and Burak were mere spectators and left to wonder about themselves.

After a light lunch, they were led through an internal door to the garage where a large, family-type car was parked. Layla opened the trunk and motioned for both Rob and Burak to get in and lie down. It was a tight fit for the two men, but they made it. Layla draped a lightweight sheet over them, dumped a few groceries on top for good measure, and partially pulled the roll-top cover over before closing it once more. With the slamming of car doors, the engine kicked into life, and they moved off. The journey was short and uneventful. They bumped off the coast road and into the trees, where Layla dropped her passengers off, left them with Gregory II, and drove off. They threaded their way through the trees in a manner reminiscent of their earlier escape and made their way down to the rocky coastline, staying just inside of the trees and out of sight.

After what seemed an age, two sailing dinghies scrunched into the rocky and stony shore, and two men got out. As they did, Gregory II's radio sounded. It was Layla. "I've got a tail. Can't make out who. Picked me up as I passed the resort. Won't return to the safe house, and neither should you. Good luck."

Gregory II immediately hustled his three charges towards the new arrivals, everyone scanning the trees for unwanted visitors. They didn't see anyone, but they heard the whine of bullets flying through the air. Gregory II and Burak felt the full impact thudding into their sides, sending them sprawling onto the rocks, and Anja screamed as she saw her father fall. Rob placed one arm around Anja's waist to both place her in front of him and shield her from the danger, as well as to keep her moving. Then, as he reached the place where Burak had fallen moments before, Rob reached down and grabbed Burak by the scruff of the neck and hauled him to his feet. Gregory II rolled over once before he found his feet and a footing to stand and continue his running.

There hadn't been any other sounds, so they had to assume their attackers were using suppressors in the same way they had silencers on their weapons. If shooting was involved, they did not want too much sound alerting the local police or security forces and getting tangled up in an unintentional shootout with them and the consequent political ramifications of that.

The two new men strafed the trees in the general direction of the received fire with their own machine pistols as Gregory II, struggling with pain, bundled them all into the dinghies as another salvo of bullets smashed into the surrounding rocks, sending pieces flying in all directions, stinging exposed skin and shredding the lightweight fabric of their shirtsleeves. The two men shoved the boats off the rocks and jumped in behind them as a further salvo of bullets struck the fibreglass hulls. The two men were returning fire as Rob and Gregory II, in different dinghies, took charge and started to sail out to sea and towards a white motor cruiser that was approaching at speed.

With Laura at the helm, Stefano shouldered a rifle and also provided covering fire. As soon as she could, Laura positioned the cruiser between the shore and the dinghies with reverse engine on hard, the water frothing up as though a saucepan boiling over, to slow it down and not overrun its intended covering position. The motor yacht was taking fire now but at a slower rate. Laura scampered down to throw ropes and a ladder over the side for Rob, Burak, and Anja to climb up once the dinghies bumped against the boat.

Stefano kept his eye to the sights of his rifle, trying to spot and eliminate their attackers. Although it felt like an eternity, the exchange continued for a further twenty or thirty seconds before coming to a sudden and silent halt. Laura helped haul Anja onto the boat as Rob manhandled Burak over the side. The man's face screwed up in pain from having taken the earlier hits.

Once everyone was on board, Laura yelled, "All clear, let's go," and Stefano rammed the throttle to full speed and steered directly out to sea, leaving the two dinghies to make their way back to the resort, taking on water and with some awkward explaining to do. The intention was to stay out for as long as possible so as not to attract attention, but that wasn't going to happen. They were sinking, which in the circumstances was probably for the best. They would simply swim to shore and confess stupidity, leading to a collision between them!

The motor cruiser was riddled with holes but fortunately nothing to impede their passage. Laura went to check on Burak, who merely groaned and through gritted teeth, muttered that he would be fine and was glad for the bullet-proof vest Gregory II had insisted he wear. Stefano yelled down, "I need someone up here to spot. Should be Laura. All others to keep out of sight."

When she arrived by his side on the flying bridge, she could tell that he had been hit by some fibreglass splinters and was bleeding slightly. She was as well but for the more silly reason of having caught her arm as she raced down to help the boarders.

"We're going to have to adopt plan B," Stefano yelled into the rushing air. "The bullet holes will attract far too much attention in Porto di Piave Vecchia, and we certainly don't want the Slovenians getting an easy view. We need to get to the Italian side as quickly as possible."

A few moments later he added, "Clean my face, please, and look as though you're enjoying yourself!" He winked mischievously. "If the authorities decide to take a closer look because of our speed, we need to be looking our best, but I don't want to slow down in case the other side have a speed boat and decide to give chase. As it is, we won't be hard to track."

The headland was not far away, but the minutes seemed to drag before they were able to change course and pass the promontory. As they rounded the headland and could look back towards Piran harbour, there were only a few yachts milling around and mostly heading back for the evening.

"Nothing out of the ordinary," Stefano yelled over the rushing wind and crashing waves against the bow. "Please keep watching, but as though you're enjoying the scene. See any motor boats travelling fast and I want to know. You'll need to keep a watch for the entire trip with greater vigilance for anything remotely suspicious once we approach Venice, as those waterways are busy."

"Understood," Laura replied, her heart beating fast from both the adrenalin of the fire fight and the nervous expectation of a potential chase. "I'll go down and check on our passengers. Then I'll keep watch with the binoculars from the windows, as they should give me cover should the Slovenians be watching us."

"Good idea for now, but I'll want you up here as we approach Venice. There'll be far too many boats, and you'll need the 360-degree view afforded by being up here instead of constantly moving between windows."

"Okay, see you in a few hours, unless you'd like a drink and something to eat?"

"Just a large glass of water, please."

With that provided, each settled in for their high-speed and thankfully uneventful journey. Laura reappeared at Stefano's side as he throttled back to cruise past Porto di Piave Vecchia and towards Venice. The sun was setting directly in their eyes, making them both squint even though they were wearing sunglasses. Stefano carefully navigated around the islands and various channels, occasionally doubling back until they arrived at the boat yard to be used as plan B. A colleague waved as he swung a pair of timber gates open, leading to a shed built over a short inlet, all designed for boat maintenance. The sound of the gates rattling shut brought a wave of relief to all on board but afforded no rest. Stefano immediately leapt into action, calling out instructions.

"Guido, get the work boat to take us to the airport transportation. Laura, give these passports to our passengers. Rob is your husband, Anja your daughter, and Mr Demir your father. You take after your absent mother," he added, noticing her sceptical look. "Please make sure that they all understand their respective roles. As soon as Guido is back with the work boat, we will leave. A people carrier is waiting to take us to the airport, where our London colleagues have arranged for a private flight to take you all home. I'm sure the boat will have been tracked, so I don't want anyone hanging around."

The exhausted group sat in utter silence at the stern of the workboat as they were ferried across to the mainland, where they piled into a people carrier for the short drive to the airport. Even at their sedate pace and using normal urban roads, the journey took less than fifteen minutes, mainly thanks to the light traffic. At the private terminal, Rob and Laura shared a couple of nervous glances over Anja's head as their driver exchanged more than a minute's worth of quick-fire repartee with the guard. Eventually and with an exuberant display of grudging reluctance, the guard waved them through, glowering through the windows. Their driver muttered to himself in rapid, expressive Italian as they drove past but only once the windows were firmly closed.

A few minutes later and after a perfunctory passport check at passport control, they were headed for an isolated private jet near some outlying hangars. Once they were out of the vehicle and as Rob approached the plane as nonchalantly as possible, he commented, "I only hope that there won't be any of the dramatics as frequently seen on the films." Laura simply smiled in acknowledgment, noting as she did that Burak had also heard and was constantly sweeping the area with his eyes.

"My thoughts entirely," Burak said, regarding the heavy-set men on either side of the steps with unease. "So this must be what they call rendition," he quipped as he passed them by. Laura found it hard to suppress a smile as the two heavies bristled but held their position. They all had strict instructions to bring this man back to Britain safely and without arousing attention, linking their services to the operation. That Burak still had the presence of mind to crack such comments was impressive, at least as far as she was concerned and from Rob's smirk, his as well!

Shortly afterwards, they were airborne and settling back for a light dinner, after which they all dozed for the remainder of the nearly four-hour flight. It was approaching 1:30 in the morning when they were all gently shaken awake by one of the heavies. "Ten minutes to landing," he said in a monotone voice. "Strap in."

Bleary-eyed, Rob asked Laura, who was sitting adjacent to him, "Where are we landing?"

"Northolt in west London," she replied.

"How come we're able to land at this hour? I thought that there were restrictions on aircraft over London at this hour."

"There are," she replied. "A restriction is what it implies—simply restricting such landings or take-offs. That provides suitable flexibility to occasionally—well, ignore them, I suppose."

"Oh well, whatever. It's just good to be back," he said, looking out of the window at the lights below. "I would like to get my belongings back from the guesthouse somehow and say thank you to Mrs Kos, who was a great hostess, despite being more than a tad overwhelming with the meals that she served." Rob paused, before adding with a sigh, "But I guess I am now persona non-grata in Slovenia, and there were still quite a few places I wanted to see."

"Don't worry," Laura replied. "We've already thought of that and intend to set about the task of retrieving your belongings once everyone's safely on British soil. As regards you returning to Slovenia again, I'd agree, that is possibly a little more questionable, but we'll just have to see. It will depend upon how the Slovenian authorities respond to the news that Mr Demir got out of their country and has ended up in Britain under our care and attention." Laura had nodded her head towards Burak as she was talking.

8

The chilly morning air of the westerly breeze hit them fully in their faces as they more stumbled than walked down the steps that had been pushed up against the side of the plane. If they hadn't been fully awake, they certainly had no choice now as their bodies instinctively started shivering, their thin summer clothes, which were more suitable for the weather they had left behind, providing little protection against the typical British climate.

Laura stepped forward to greet their welcoming committee, speaking to them in hushed tones. Behind them, engines still purring, were two nondescript cars, one silver, one a pale blue, and a small minibus with blacked-out windows. Laura waved them to the minibus. Anja stayed close to Burak, who was holding her hand. They headed for the back seats and made themselves comfortable.

Anja, struggling with tiredness, snuggled up against her father, who merely looked about him.

Rob hesitated at the front of the minibus, wondering where to sit. He also wanted to be at the back and put distance between himself and the two heavies from the airplane, but Rob also did not want to be seen as aligning himself too much with Burak. He therefore opted for a seat two-thirds of the way back, leaving a couple of rows of seats between himself and Burak, and he also sat on the opposite side from that taken by Burak.

Several minutes later, they joined the westbound carriageway of the A40. Rob couldn't see the two cars anymore, but knew that they had been with them as they left the airbase, one ahead and one behind. At first Rob stared blankly out from the windows marking off the various landmarks that he knew well from his own use of the A40 travelling out of London, but gradually drifted off into a light sleep.

When he woke up, Rob realised they were stationary and dawn was breaking. The engine was still running so the heater could continue to blast warm air into the cabin. The driver had disappeared, but the two heavies from the plane were still seated at the front on either side of the aisle. Rob glanced over his shoulder and noted that Burak and Anja were still fast asleep. One of the heavies ambled over to him and whispered, "If you go into the house, you'll find the facilities on your right under the stairs or the kitchen straight ahead. I know it's still early, but there's a good breakfast and strong coffee ready. Alternatively, head up the stairs and find a room with your name stuck to the door. You could lie down again if you feel like it."

Whilst the man's tone was pleasant, it was clear that he was expected to leave the minibus and head inside, so Rob obliged. Stepping down off the minibus, Rob looked about him, blinking in the cool air. It was a good few degrees cooler than at Northolt, and the only sounds belonged to the birds and the engine of the minibus. Whether the latter drowned out other man-made sounds or whether they were totally isolated Rob could not work out. He walked towards the house and the front door that stood ajar, ready for him.

Nice, he thought to himself. *Must be the Cotswolds judging by the architecture. Must cost a fortune.* The two cars from Northolt were also in the driveway, as were another two, one black, one silver. *More people*, Rob thought, sighing inwardly.

"Rob, we're in here," Laura called as he pushed the front door open. The smells of a typical home-cooked English breakfast were hanging in the air and very appealing. He wavered momentarily between taking the stairs and finding a bed for some more sleep or responding to Laura's hail and heading to the kitchen. With a sigh he relented, knowing what was expected of him. As he entered, Rob recognised Steven Gurning and Graeme Spreachley from his video call a few days earlier. He shook hands with the two men, who were dressed casually, unlike the suits he had last seen them in, as Laura placed a plate laden with food and a steaming mug of coffee on the table, ready for him to sit down.

"It's good to have you back in the UK," Gurning said to Rob. "You've been an immense credit to the country, and we will work with you to help return your life to a semblance of normality, as well as getting your belongings back."

"Thank you," Rob mumbled, mouth stuffed with oozing, juicy food.

"I expect it will be a good couple of days before you can consider going back home. During that time, we will want to meet with you a few times and go over as much as possible with you. We will also be talking matters through with Mr Demir."

"What will happen to him and to Anja?"

"That hasn't been decided yet. We would like Mr Demir's input into that, although I suspect we will try to have Anja fostered to give her a life apart from her father's criminal activities and the consequences thereof. Almost certainly we will need to give her a new identity, which for one so young should not pose too many difficulties. We'll also make sure she gets whatever counselling she needs."

Rob nodded before looking up to say, "I'd like to say good-bye to them both before we head in our separate directions."

"Of course, we'd expect that, and there will be plenty of time for that as well. We'll keep you all together until you go home. After your exertions, we expect that a level of connection has developed between the three of you."

Gurning held his hand up as Rob jerked his head up with a look of alarm. "That is perfectly normal, and I am not insinuating anything at all, Rob. You were simply in the wrong place at the wrong time and got caught up in this terrible mess, but you acted brilliantly by saving people's lives. More than once, I might add. As a consequence, we hope to get information from Mr Demir that will both break various criminal networks and also terrorist activities, which is why we are involved instead of the police. No, Mr Demir is not a terrorist," Gurning countered quickly on seeing Rob's troubled expression. "However, whether he realises or not, there do appear to be linkages. We have reason to believe that it's more than a series of coincidences that when we've thwarted some terrorist activity in Britain, there has been too much evidence connecting the supporting activities to some of Mr Demir's associates."

The radio lying on the table sprang to life. "Our other two guests will be with you shortly."

"Okay, thanks, Jim. Once they are indoors, please secure the front door, and then you'll be free to head home. Thanks for all your help," Gurning replied, having picked up the handheld device.

A few moments later, a buzzer sounded quietly in the kitchen, followed by the closing of the front door and footsteps in the hallway. Laura stood and went to greet Burak and Anja. As they entered the kitchen, Laura said, "I'm sorry we didn't really get the chance to be properly introduced until now. I'm Lisa Grahams."

She gave Rob a kindly but pointed look as she said it, hoping he would understand she had to use a cover name in front of Burak. At the same time, she was cursing herself for not having mentioned this to Rob at an earlier stage. "Rob you know, of course, and these are my colleagues, David and Adrian," she continued, motioning to Gurning and Spreachley.

As she had done for Rob, as Burak shook hands and introduced his daughter, Laura laid the table for them, but instead of providing laden platefuls, she placed a selection of food and drink in front of them for them to take what they wanted. "I hope this will be okay for now. We can discuss likes and dislikes later in the day before I go shopping," she said.

"This is fine. Thank you," Burak replied politely.

"Now it's just us," started Gurning. "I'll fill you in with our more immediate intentions and how the next few days will pan out. First, after breakfast we will leave this place and head to somewhere different. Whilst we have total confidence in the security both here and with the operation that brought you all here, there are a lot of people who know about it, even though they don't know who you are. Given your status, Mr Demir, we prefer to be ultra-cautious, and move everyone immediately to another safe house that is known only to our director general. The address was unknown to us prior to yesterday.

"The guardians live there on a permanent basis. They are known in the nearby village for their hospitality, and in preparation for this visit, the man of the house unfortunately did not have his work contract extended. That should provide a suitable reason for his remaining at home. Friends and neighbours won't be overly concerned for them because his cover was being employed as a highly successful specialist IT contractor in the city, and whilst they live modestly, the clear impression has been created that the couple are extremely wealthy. He's taken many breaks from work before as needs required, enabling them to either work on their house or take extended breaks. Their house is nicely secluded, with a walled garden within the larger grounds enabling guests to spend time outside without risk of being observed. This is, of course, for your personal security as well as for our benefit of being able to converse with you undisturbed in relaxed and congenial surroundings.

"We don't know for how long you will be their guests, and we will be regular visitors, sometimes staying over as well. The objectives, very simply, will be to debrief and discuss future cooperation before deciding upon the future. For young Rob here, clearly we anticipate him returning home and being provided with support to return to a normal life, if ever there is such a thing."

"I'm not sure of how possible that will be," interjected Burak. "I've promised and signed away my entire wealth to him, so unless he wishes to relinquish all or the greater proportion of that, Rob is tied in. I intend to honour that promise, so it's entirely his choice, and I suggest that he and I have a separate conversation on that subject once we are settled at the new safe house. Whether he accepts your participation in or attendance during that discussion will again be his choice. I'm relaxed either way."

It was clear from everyone's expressions that this was totally unexpected, even though Rob had briefed them previously on this agreement. "Surely, Rob, you didn't think I'd reneged on that?"

"I don't really know what I expected," admitted Rob, "although I had informed our friends here. What about my other friend who I first contacted?" Rob asked, careful not to name names to protect his friend, Michael Stanley, who had been his initial contact to seek help.

"He's essentially out of this now and understands that upon your return, assuming your return, his brief will be to revert to your previous level of friendship. We have every confidence of his ability to do that, which we also believe will help you in that regard as well."

"Okay, I understand," Rob said unconvincingly. He was not entirely sure that he either understood or knew how he should proceed. He had hoped for Michael's involvement, even though they were not close friends, because whenever they had spoken before, Michael had struck Rob as being a remarkably sensible and wise person, one for whom he had a great deal of respect. Rob also noticed Burak's knowing look that indicated that he, at least, recognised Rob's disappointment.

"Okay, let's finish up here," said Gurning, "and get ready to head out in fifteen minutes. Mr Demir, your daughter and you can continue to eat. That's not a problem, and I don't want to hurry you. It appears as though you're nearly done, but if not, no problem. Lisa, leave everything. The cleaners will come along later. The new house is not far, so your lengthy journey is close to an end. Adrian and I will be driving, and as we leave, I'd ask that people keep their heads below window level. That way even our spotters won't know you've gone until much later. We'll be swapping cars as well after a short distance."

An hour and a half later, they were comfortably ensconced in the living room of the new safe house. Anja was upstairs fast asleep, and their new hosts, William and Jessica, had provided more coffee as they explained they were protective hosts with ready means to ensure their safety, after which they excused themselves. Gurning and Spreachley had left, and Laura had stayed.

Burak broke the silence. "Rob, do you mind if Lisa listens in?"

Glancing cautiously at Laura, Rob said, "No, not at all. It may be helpful in the long run."

"Good point. Look, I'm serious that you are welcome to my wealth. When I signed your piece of paper, I was prepared to renege on the deal as I simply wanted to save Anja. I am confident in my ability to judge character, and having spent time with you, I am confident you will manage any wealth that you gain wisely. Having thought it through over the past few days, I do think it best that I withdraw from what I was doing.

"If you want or are prepared to accept everything, I have to advise you that there is quite a lot of unpleasant baggage that comes with it. I am sure Lisa and her colleagues can help, or should I say will insist on helping with that baggage. Otherwise, I am equally sure they will be willing to assist clearing the way for you to receive my completely clean wealth. That's still a reasonable amount, but you wouldn't be able to retire immediately. Much of the clean wealth is unfortunately reliant upon the criminal. It's entirely up to you. Whether you opt for everything or not, I can assure you that I am prepared to help your authorities unravel everything in exchange for a good standard of living, education, and care for Anja, as well as periodic access.

"As I said during our travels, I want out and have been trying to distance myself for her sake. She means so much, and I loathe myself that she has lost her mother and been drawn into this all because of who I am. She's all that matters now. My life is effectively over. How Emilio thought he could take over I have no idea. I always kept the many strands of my network separate. No other person has an overview of my network, although a number were clearly aware that my reach went well beyond their own particular areas, simply because of the way I could assist their operations when they required. One thing I want to make clear from the outset is that it will take time, possibly a number of years, to unravel my operations in a way that prevents them from scattering and re-emerging later simply to restart on their own accord, stronger and wiser for the experience. That is what I want— them to be closed down for good."

From Laura's expression and the phraseology of that last remark, Rob was certain it was meant for her ears. It also came across as genuine, which he now believed, even though it could easily be interpreted as being a way in which Burak kept the upper hand. Rob was sure that was the case as well. He was equally sure such an approach would lead to some serious confrontations with Gurning and Spreachley but that Burak probably could not have cared less.

Burak was still talking, so Rob quickly re-focused. "I don't want to put you under undue pressure, Rob, but we do need to agree on how to proceed really quite quickly. If the leaders across my network don't hear from me soon, they may assume I'm out of the equation and scatter anyway.

I am sure Lisa's colleagues are aware that it will be important that I retain a semblance of control and strength to provide them with the time to close in and take operations out.

"Lisa, which part or parts of the British security services do you represent?"

After a slight pause to think the question over, she replied, "Both David and I are MI5. Adrian is MI6."

Burak scowled in surprise and thought. "Why are you involved? I was expecting you to say one of the agencies interested in serious organised crime. Now I am confused and more than a little concerned."

"I take it from that remark that you are unaware of how some of your network either source, transport, or pay for their merchandise and how some have expanded their activities and relationships."

"Generally, correct. Sometimes I get involved when it is beneficial for other parts of my network, whether legitimate business or not. I don't like the idea that my network is supporting terrorism, which is the underlying assumption from your involvement. Okay, people still suffer because of many parts of my business activities, but terrorism operates at an entirely different level. I don't like what I am hearing at all."

"You know what, Mr Demir?"

"Burak, please."

"Burak, I actually believe you on that, as do my colleagues. But the reality is that potential terrorist and espionage activities have benefited from your network, as you call it, and we can provide evidence of that. The problem is that we cannot fully trace the linkages, or we do not have adequate intelligence or evidence to act. We have had limited success within Britain, and thus far nothing has transpired elsewhere when we review British interests or in the United States. Otherwise your extradition would be a certainty once our American counterparts hear that you are in our care. Other countries will almost certainly also apply for your extradition because successful terrorist activities have occurred and are linked to your network. In those cases, we are confident that if we provide adequate information, we will be able to deflect those extradition requests.

"That's why we're involved, why you're here, and why we have made extreme efforts to get you here. For what it's worth, your conspicuous, increasing, and successful involvement in legitimate business has been noticed, albeit with intrigue. We suspected you weren't aware, but we weren't certain. We are, however, absolutely certain that through you we can disrupt terrorist and espionage plots both here and abroad, as well as nailing a substantial amount of seriously nasty criminal activity."

"Damn it, that casts a very different complexion on the situation. Of course I will help."

Again, Burak came across as being genuine, but only time would tell. From their exchanged glances, both Laura and Rob were clearly thinking the same thing. Rob was also intrigued. In part, he wanted to know more and be involved. On the other hand, it all sounded quite scary. What should he do?

9

After two days of intense planning, Kovač and his team were ready.

Gurning had invited one of Kovač's men to Britain to interview Rob as soon as possible after the initial debriefings, and they had pored over maps for a few days, together with aerial photographs taken by reconnaissance helicopters.

It had been part of Gurning's plan to reconcile himself with his opposite number. Understandably, Kovač was furious when he was informed that the British had undertaken an operation on his patch and prevented him from the potential glory of capturing Burak Demir.

Only time would tell if it would work, and for that to happen, Kovač would require a breakthrough of some kind to show for all his efforts. Gurning really hoped that would occur.

Otherwise Kovač had been very clear that he would have to inform his political masters of what had transpired, and both agreed that was far from ideal. If that happened, some details would inevitably get to the world's press that Britain had worked against Slovenian interests, and that would be a tough one to calm down without mentioning why. Gurning appreciated Kovač's position and the competing tensions of their profession and their ruling politicians.

Despite their best efforts previously to search the area around where Yasmin had made the pick-up, the team had come away empty handed. All the forensics from the three crime scenes—in Postojna, at the pick-up, and also outside Piran—had not provided any leads. All that had been established was that each incident was linked. Kovač had read and re-read the reports a million times and each time found only the same information. The manufacture of many of the brass bullet casings was the same and from one of the former Soviet republics, but which one was not apparent. All interviews had equally drawn a blank, and trying to follow the tracks back had failed, no doubt because of the incessant rain.

Finally, and surreptitiously, a couple from Kovač's team had set out on a "camping and photography holiday" around the area identified by Rob following the visit by Kovač's men. It had taken three days of apparent fruitless meandering between rocky outcrops before they came across the scattered leftovers of human food clearly eaten by a wolf and a rocky outcrop visible in the distance through the trees. Staying well back, the couple surveyed the scene, easily identifying the place against Rob's description.

This time they were prepared to face the gauntlet of calling in. This time, they would turn the tables on their many colleagues who jibed them for being a couple in love and on holiday together. This time they had results.

Kovač and the raiding team approached from the valley to the east of the hideout, the opposite direction from the path leading down to the road. Separate teams were in place to block the roads and all identified forest paths. Kovač quietly urged his team forward. Timing could not have been better. The couple, as they had become known, had informed him that a quad bike with a trailer had arrived during the night. Although they had not seen anyone during the day, the quad bike was still there, and Kovač was therefore eager to proceed and not let whoever was there slip through his fingers.

As they approached, the team split into three groups. Two sections approached the main cabin from opposite ends of the rocky outcrop. Kovač sent the third group to identify and guard all cave entrances. He did not want anyone escaping from him in the same way that Rob had slipped Demir away from under his captors' noses. Teams of specialist search-and-rescue folks would come in

193

behind them to search the entire complex of caves and tunnels that evidently existed from Rob's briefing. They were uncomfortable with the task, but at least they would have an armed escort. Kovač really hoped it would not be necessary, other than as a precautionary check.

They held position as one man from each section approached the two outbuildings, each staying out of the line of sight of the main cabin's windows. Each man extracted a flexible cable camera from his back sack and slipped it into the hut through one of the many holes or cracks that were evident.

"Clear," came the first whispered report over the radio. "As described and expected, a food store but little remaining."

"Clear," came the second report. "There's another quad bike but partially dismantled. Appears to be under repair. Otherwise, bits and pieces, various tools, etc., as you'd expect to be reasonably self-sufficient out in the mountains."

"Understood. Proceed to disable the quad without it being obvious, just in case an escape is attempted. Everyone, prepare to move in."

The second man shuffled along on his stomach through the grass to the quad in front of the cabin whilst the first man returned to his position with the rest of the team. Arriving at the quad bike, the man set about tinkering with the engine. It was a quick task, and once he had identified the location of the fuel pump, he simply switched it off. He also drained the tank into a small plastic can he had produced from his back sack. They had strict instructions not to damage or destroy anything of value that could be sold to generate revenue for the service. With that, he too returned to his team, ready for Kovač to give the word and storm the cabin.

The day's warmth was reaching its height as it approached midday, not that it was particularly warm or sunny.

"At least it isn't raining," Kovač said to himself as he cast his eyes around, appreciating the quiet beauty of the space, the fresh smell of the trees, as well as the isolation. "This would be the perfect spot for my dreamed-of get-away-from-everything cabin."

Dragging himself reluctantly back to the moment, he considered the time. With luck whoever was inside would either be preparing lunch or already eating. It would be a perfect distraction as long as he, she, or they did not look out of a window. So far none of his spotters had indicated any sign of a person at a window, and his final check confirmed the same. The blinds remained down and had not moved.

Kovač gave the signal to move in.

Cognisant of Rob's warning that there could be alarms, they approached with caution. One man buzzed his radio briefly, the signal that an alarm had been found, and they all froze for precious seconds whilst the individual marked the area with aerosol paint as he worked his way around the danger area. Then, following another buzz, the approach started once more. As soon as the teams reached the sides of the cabin, they were able to move along the walls to the doorway. Moments after the lead man had inspected the door for strength, he comfortably smashed it in with a handheld steel battering ram. The door splintered and came off its hinges, falling into the space beyond with a thud as it hit the floor. Even before the door hit the floor, the lead man and two colleagues threw some flash-bang stun grenades in at differing angles to cover the entire space. They waited for the near-immediate blasts and then stormed inside, masks on, weapons at the ready.

Kovač watched from a distance, tensed up and waiting for the sounds of gunfire, but none came. His radio clicked. "Clear," the leader called. Kovač would now have further anxious minutes of waiting as the team worked their way systematically through the place and whatever tunnels and caves lay beyond. The element of surprise was now surely lost.

"Sir," started the team leader, "the cabin is clear. There are obvious signs of current life—an overnight bag and food ready to be eaten. There is also a substantial supply of cleaning materials and solvents. Whoever is here must be further back, inside the caves that the British reported."

"Understood, proceed," replied Kovač.

Having thoroughly checked the cabin for trap doors or other concealed areas, the men took up positions on either side of the apparent back door, only the back of the cabin was built against the rock face. This door presented an entirely greater challenge. The two locks, a third of the way from the top and bottom, were firmly fastened, and the door opened towards them into the cabin, making battering it down far more difficult. Placing a strong piece of thick wire into each lock in turn, they determined that the key was in place on the other side in the top lock.

Surely, Kovač thought, *this must be a good sign. Someone has to be on the other side—unless, of course, there is an exit we have yet to discover.*

Methodically and swiftly, Kovač's men rummaged through their sacks and in seconds extracted three flat squares of flexible explosive. They fixed one above each lock and the door handle, set the fuses, stood back, lined up against the rear wall, and pressed the miniature detonator. The blast blew the windows out and rumbled through the forest, sending birds squawking into the air, flapping their wings noisily in agitation at the sudden disruption to their usually tranquil environment.

The door remained where it was momentarily before swinging forward on its hinges. The residue of smoke billowed out across the room before dissipating in the breeze that emanated from the door and now-open windows. Kovač cursed. "Why didn't they open the windows?"

Mercifully, the lights were on in the corridor-cum-tunnel beyond. It was long and straight, with at least ten metres to the nearest doors, one on either side. There was at least another five metres beyond that before the tunnel ended in darkness. Their infrared scopes on their assault rifles revealed nothing. This was not the sort of tunnel you wanted to be caught in partway along.

One man, back as flat against the wall as he could get it, inched along the tunnel whilst covered by three colleagues, two kneeling and one standing in the doorway. The face of the tunnel, whilst not rough, was also not smooth. The surface of bare rock almost rippled, casting shadows all over from the bare bulbs overhead. As the first man reached the doorway on his side, a second man slipped along to join him. They wanted to be quiet simply to hear any other noises and also to give as little indication as possible to whoever was there how far along they were.

Now, one man on either side of the door, the second man tried the handle. It turned, and the heavy door swung open silently on well-oiled hinges. The men gagged at the sudden stench that flowed out and the sight that met their eyes. They barely gave themselves adequate time to scan the room before they closed the door once more. No sane living person could remain in there for long. The door provided a good seal, and they noted a step down into the room.

They gave the signal that the room was clear of life and that they were about to change sides. Reluctantly, they swung the opposite door open, identical to the first. Gagging once more, even though they were prepared, they rapidly made their way back for some fresh air. The room was the same.

Nothing had to be said. All those at the entrance to the tunnel shared all too clearly the smell of death as the cooler tunnel air was sucked out into the relative warmth of the cabin.

"Okay," the team leader started, keeping his voice low as he spoke through the radios incorporated into their helmets, "time to find this sucker. As before, three cover from one side of the passage. The rest will hug the opposite wall. I'll lead. Once close enough, we'll deliver a couple of flash bangs into the area. Then we take the space at speed. Ready?"

All affirmed their readiness with a sharp, "Sir!" before taking up positions.

"And we take him alive. The boss has made it clear anything less is unacceptable. Got it?"

Another sharp chorus of, "Sir!" echoed through the radios.

The leader then led the way, covering his advance with his assault rifle constantly at the ready and one eye firmly against the infrared sight. They progressed without incident to the point where the leader chose to throw the flash bangs. Through his sights, he could only make out some relatively cold chairs, a table, and packing crates. There was nothing to signify life of any form.

"Cover!" he ordered and then lowered his rifle and prepared the first flash bang, at which point he grunted loudly as two bullets slammed into him, one in the chest and the other in his throwing arm. The report of the firing weapon followed the shots, echoing around the cavernous room and tunnels.

The team leader was thrown back into the next man in line, making both men stumble. He also dropped the flash bang, which promptly went off at their feet, flipping the two men up with the blast and onto their backs. The flash bang also had its intended consequences of disorienting the others who were close to it, both through sight and sound. More bullets followed, thumping into the body armour of the next two men, knocking them off their feet and winding them terribly. More bullets ricocheted off the tunnel walls, bouncing around off the rock with terrifying twangs and sending splinters of rock flying into the men's faces, stinging them in the process.

The three men at the far end started to open fire, having identified where the bullets were emanating from, only to be ordered to halt by the shouting of their colleagues, some of whom were desperately trying to move their fallen comrades back to safety and did not want to be hit by friendly fire. It was mayhem. The others, aware that to retreat would be disastrous, stormed forward through the chaos, oblivious to their personal danger, opening fire as soon as they were clear of their colleagues, at which point they also lobbed more flash bangs into the area beyond to try to disorient and disable their opponent. As they entered the dark space beyond the tunnel, they spread out, seeking whatever cover they could.

Another man fell, taking a couple of well-placed bullets in the chest, leaving him to curl up into a protective position to minimise the unprotected areas of his body, hoping desperately that the body armour would continue to protect him. The remaining two lobbed more flash-bang stun grenades in the direction of the shooter, wishing they were the real thing. They rolled aside once more as the flash and boom caused glass from the darkened overhead light bulbs to come sprinkling down upon them like a short, heavy rain shower.

Cautiously, with rifles raised, they rounded either side of the pile of packing crates. Midway between them was a young, plump, fair-haired man with at least two days stubble. He was sitting up, back against the wall, watching them through night goggles. His guns lay at his feet, poking through the crates. In his left hand he held a detonator, but the men could not see any explosives in the dark. He smiled sadly.

One said, "Put it down slowly. You've caused enough harm. No more is needed, and you can live."

His reply, loud enough to be heard by all the others over their radios, sent a chill through their spines. "I suppose you've seen inside the other rooms? That'll happen to me if I leave this place without my job done."

These men had not seen inside those rooms, and they started to feel glad that that was the case; only their colleagues had, and they had left for air without reporting any detail. Nevertheless, they did not want to die in an explosion with this man. "No it won't," one said confidently.

"There's no way that you can keep me safe. They can get to anyone, anywhere."

Knowing the best ploy was to keep him talking, they did just that. "Who are they? Tell us and we will be able to help you."

"No you won't. Not forever you won't, and Emilio says that W has long tentacles and a longer memory. It was W that ordered us to do those others in for letting KP escape. Doc enjoys that sort of stuff."

"So there you go, people do escape from these guys. With our help, so can you. We can get you out, as though one of us. Then we create the explosion and report that an unknown person was left inside. We can then remove a fake body, just to preserve appearances."

The man was clearly mulling this over, so the officer pressed his point home. "I can call in for an extra suit now if you like. How about it?"

So far it had been the same person speaking, keeping the young man's attention. The other was merely keeping careful watch from the other side.

Kovač was pacing around outside, listening to the conversation, extremely concerned at the turn of events, the injuries sustained, and the tone of the conversation. As a precaution, he had ordered as many men back as he feasibly could. He wanted to call those on point back as well; he loved these men, but he knew he could not. They all knew and accepted the risks.

Instead, he listened to the team chatter with one ear as they planned how to save those inside from almost certain death. With the other ear, he listened to the dialogue between his man and the unknown defender.

Now as their plan approached its execution phase, Kovač prayed silently to any god that would listen and paced back and forth under the trees, scrunching the dried leaves and twigs, not bothering anymore with their previously intended silence. The lives of his men were threatened and at stake!

◆

The silence of the dark cavern was suddenly shattered with a single, deafening shot. Another team member had silently positioned himself a few metres behind his colleague who was not speaking and had taken the shot.

The young man screamed and howled as his left wrist disintegrated in an explosion of blood, skin, and bone. A large-bore, hollow-point bullet had been used; the shot was accurate and virtually took the young man's hand off at the wrist. The detonator skidded across the floor, and the nearest of Kovač's men scooped it up carefully. They all then waited. They waited for the fizz and then the rumbling and subsequent explosion of noise that would announce their death and send them to meet at their maker. But other than the constant howls of pain from the young man, no sound came.

Permitting themselves just a few seconds of space to appreciate their success and immense relief, they informed Kovač of a successful disarm. The three men then set about giving the young man medical assistance whilst waiting for their colleagues to arrive with a stretcher. A couple of helicopters had already arrived and were waiting to deliver doctors and medical supplies, as well as to take the injured to hospital.

Kovač met the team upon their exit, receiving them warmly and heaping on his congratulations.

As one team left, having done their job of storming and securing the area, another two teams arrived, one to guard the place and the other to forensically search it. As the yet-to-be identified young man was whisked away by the medics, Kovač emphasised that he expected to interrogate him as soon as possible, no excuses. In his opinion, no one involved with atrocities in his country could expect any sympathy, merely the basics of what human rights afforded them. He was prepared to sail as close to the wind on this one as he could to get results. His country had been thrown into turmoil and fright because of all these atrocities, and he wanted to get someone and make him pay!

Kovač waited for the forensics team to make an initial assessment before donning his own paper overalls and shoes to venture inside and have a first-hand experience of the place. He wanted to see for himself before returning to head office and reporting to both his superiors and the British. Taking on board the recommendation of his team, he left the "slaughter rooms," as they had been called, to the end.

The cabin was nothing exceptional. Fairly basic, in fact. No comforts at all. The single tunnel had been carved out of the rock well, almost professionally but without regard for the finish. *How could this have been done without anyone knowing,* he wondered, *and where did they dispose of the waste?*

At the end was a large open space behind a heavy wooden door, reinforced with steel bands. This was where the young man had holed up and met his comeuppance behind the packing crates. Also, judging from the steel hoops inserted into the rock face and various chains along the floor, this must have been where Demir and his daughter had been held. Looking up, he saw the opening through which Krane had spirited the pair from under their captors' eyes. *What an exceptionally lucky break for all concerned,* he thought. Kovač was keenly aware that had Krane not intervened, then

Demir and his daughter would very possibly have disappeared for good.

Kovač had seen enough, and it was time to go, but first, to see these so-called slaughter rooms. He opened the first door, feeling confident that his men had been teasing him; they were all hardened, after all. He had been surprised that those who had looked in had been so affected by the stench. Again, and sadly, they were hardened to that, or as far as he was concerned should have been. *Maybe their training needs to get toughened-up*, he thought as his hand fell onto the door handle.

He swung the door open, half-nonchalantly, and immediately knew why his men had reacted as they had. He froze. He wanted to gag, to retch, but was too shocked. It wasn't the stench, although that was bad enough. He understood why they had used the expression "slaughter rooms." Three men were hanging on poles facing each other, severely beaten and mutilated, most likely tortured. A pile of extremities lay at the base of each pole, fingers, toes, feet, hands, ears, nose, kneecaps. There were pools of dried blood at the foot of each pole, aligned with the ends of the remaining limbs, bones protruding from the ragged, dried skin. Kovač could not imagine the warped, demented mind of those responsible or the horror faced by those subjected to the brutality or the torment for those witnessing the brutality, knowing they would be next. He could imagine that the perpetrators inflicted their sadism on one man at a time, leaving the others to watch what awaited them.

There was no need to go inside. Kovač closed the door with his gloved hand and looked briefly into the opposite room, anticipating what he would see. There were three poles but two men, so five dead in total. At the base of the unoccupied pole, he could see from the age of the floor that these had not been installed recently. The poles had been there for quite some time, so there was no telling how many people had been subjected to such horrors, right here in his own country, the security for which he was partially responsible.

Whoever these Emilio, W, and Doc were, he wanted them badly, desperately even. There was now no doubt in his mind. He would help the British, despite the embarrassment they had caused by sneaking Demir out from under his nose. He acknowledged that Demir was of far greater importance to the British than to his own organisation. He now also accepted, reluctantly, what he had known since Gurning's call informing him of their operation to extract Demir and Rob. He would have done precisely the same thing in Gurning's position.

Kovač closed the door and headed off, back to the office. As he walked briskly downhill to the waiting car, he took deep breaths of fresh, mountain air and tried to focus on the scent of the pine trees. He gazed around at the beauty of the countryside, searching for wild animals, for flowers, for anything to counter the horrific images that kept working their way back into his mind. He recognised that he would be haunted by this day for years to come, until the culprits were caught and in time, also killed.

In the car he called Gurning to brief him, particularly in relation to W and Doc.

"I've no idea who they could be," Gurning said, "but will certainly ask Demir if he knows their identities. I do seem to recall either Rob or Demir mentioning a Doc, as you express it, so it may be the same chap. Let me know how you get on with the cleaner."

"I will do. Good-bye, Steven, and thank you. This should satisfy my lords and masters and the media."

Kovač sat back and pondered what sort of person the young man in their custody really was. There could be no doubt he was a cleaner—someone coming in behind the perpetrators to clean up their mess and leave no evidence behind. Hopefully he had not been able to clean very much so Kovač's own forensics team could come up with something.

10

Several days later, a plan was emerging. At times the discussions had been fractious, at times genteel. There had been many harsh words, threatening at times, but the underlying message throughout was loud and clear. Burak was not going to spill all of the beans in one go. He intended to keep a strong grip on how and when his network would be dismantled. That it would be dismantled was beyond dispute. That Burak was prepared to participate and support its dismantling was also not in question. Gurning and Spreachley were clearly frustrated at being thwarted and not being in ultimate control. Burak was convinced that he knew best in this instance and handing control over to the authorities would be a huge mistake because they would not proceed appropriately.

The number of overnight stays at the safe house were also more numerous than they had ever expected. Initially they had been extremely reluctant for Burak to contact anyone associated with his network, but after two days, they had relented, recognising the logic in Burak's argument. Listening in with Rob and Laura, they had marvelled at how Burak handled the explanation of his temporary absence to his network leaders, instilling confidence and loyalty once more. The only person within his network Burak did not contact was Emilio, for obvious reasons.

They were all terribly uncomfortable as Burak discussed future criminal activities and helped formulate the plans, but they acknowledged that unless he did so, the game would be over. They became even more uncomfortable as they reluctantly accepted that they would have to let many of the activities occur, whether in Britain or not, because by intervening, the game would also be over, and they just did not have the resources available to jump in and disrupt everything. The scale of his network was far beyond anything they had expected. Despite his criminality, a high degree of respect for Burak's intellect and acumen had developed.

Burak was clearly in his element. Enjoying and treasuring his time with Anja, he relished his regular engagements with Gurning and Spreachley and seeing how they came to accept that their initial expectations of simply milking him for all his information and to come crashing down on his network to close it down had been utterly misguided. Lengthy briefings back at MI5 and MI6 were taking their toll, and the two men were visibly exhausted. The pressure for results was immense, and so the euphemistically titled debriefing sessions became more intense.

Thus it was so that one mid-afternoon a week later, Gurning and Spreachley met with Laura and Rob to discuss what they had gleaned and what their options really were. They sat outside at one end of the walled garden bathed in sun, sipping their chilled drinks and watching Burak play with Anja at the far end of the walled garden, enjoying the little girl's regular bursts of laughter. It was, Rob mused, really rather surreal considering the topics of discussion just completed and about to be embarked upon.

"Okay, so who wants to summarise where we stand, if we are standing, that is?" asked Gurning sardonically.

Without hesitation Laura launched in, riffling through notes in her writing pad whilst Spreachley watched, his eyes fixed intently on the young woman, hands clasped with his two forefingers stretched upright and pressed against his pursed lips in concentration. Rob and Gurning, on the other hand, were relaxed in their chairs but no less focused with their listening.

"We've had our showdown with Demir, and I'd say we came off a poor second. He appears to still hold all of the cards but is willing to play them for our benefit to take his network down, but in his own way and time. That he is best placed to make those calls he is adamant beyond belief, leaving us with very little scope to dictate otherwise. The only bargaining chip we have is Anja, and quite honestly, there's not much bargaining we can do on that side either. Demir knows full well that whatever happens to him, we will ensure that she is looked after. Yes, he wants to spend time with her, and I'm sure he accepts that at some point she will be taken from him, possibly for good. Thereafter, in his own words, he has little to live for other than to dismantle the criminal aspects of his network and support Rob in boosting the legitimate side.

"We have a criminal network that is far broader than we had ever conceived. It ranges from money laundering, drugs, the smuggling of people, antiquities, gems, and other valuable commodities to bribery, protection rackets, dubious construction and public works contracts, gambling, prostitution, and local and regional gangs involved with petty and/organised crime and intimidation to order and for the sake of it. You name it, it's there and frequently coupled intimately with apparent legitimate businesses that are more often than not run by completely innocent people who at worst could be accused of naivety and being overly trusting of their business owner.

"Demir clearly has a handle on the entire network and from this week's discussions and the contacts made he is a master at running the show. However, he leaves much of the operational side to those he has put in charge, relying upon both their reports and an intricate network of loyal henchmen who somehow or another also validate what his appointed lead men are telling him. He controls those people, to a greater or lesser extent, with these henchmen, who also act as his own personal protection and enforcement squad, as well as middlemen when required. Unfortunately, in the case of this Emilio chap and possibly others, that level of control appears to be slipping. He had to leave his henchmen behind when he visited his lover and Anja, thereby exposing himself to kidnap.

"His henchmen are a tough bunch and a fiercely loyal fighting team, and by all accounts, Demir is equally loyal and generous to them. The curious aspect is that he appears to have at least two of these teams, neither of which is aware of the other or others. These groups act, when required, as go-betweens to link the criminal elements and his legitimate businesses so the two do not have to communicate directly or have an inkling that Demir controls all sides.

"Demir is adamant that as we proceed, we must cut a deal for these guys. He accepts that they, like him, must face judgement, but he says we must cut them some slack because otherwise they could fragment and go to pieces without their support network that operates more akin to a family.

The result of any fragmentation of these squads would potentially be very unpleasant, to say the least. If these individuals go off the rails, they will resort to new crime of varying sorts to quell their frustration, and their desire for incurring pain and death will probably turn on the innocent instead of for controlling other criminals. All in all, a very unpleasant crowd. That he has more than one such group says a lot about his lack of trust of others, a desire to keep the components parts of the network independent and importantly, fragmented so no one other person or group of people can determine the structure. It also clearly provides a great degree of separation for him personally.

"There are hundreds, if not thousands of innocent people employed directly or indirectly by his legitimate businesses, only some of which are viable in their own right. Others are on the verge of being marginally viable, but many are totally unviable. Those businesses are supported, in the main by Burak pushing criminal activities through their hands to generate revenue. As a result, he effectively launders the proceeds of criminal activities through his own network of businesses. All very clever as it keeps the money in the same family, so to speak.

"His operations are geographically dispersed, although primarily in the wider definition of Europe and the immediately neighbouring countries. There is some involvement in the

Middle East and southern or central Americas and limited involvement in Asian countries and the United States.

"Demir has an almost encyclopaedic memory, committing everything to memory instead of to paper or computer, or so he says, and not surprisingly he hasn't trusted anyone with the information. What I can't work out is whether during any of his calls to his henchmen he has communicated in code, tipping anyone off that he is in trouble. It doesn't come across that way, but we can't be sure.

"He appears willing to help us but wants to go at his own pace and is insistent upon trying to help the legitimate businesses, viable or not, to become meaningful entities in their own right without the throughput of the criminal operations.

"As I've said, we really don't appear to have much to bargain with. He appears to accept that his life is all but over, whether he ends up in prison or dead with a bullet in his head or worse. He wants Anja looked after and supported but is relaxed at knowing that being in Britain, even if there is no deal done with us, we will still ensure she is taken care of, albeit not to the standard to which he aspires for her. This is where Rob fits in.

"Assuming that Rob does inherit everything, Demir expects Rob to ensure that Anja is well looked after, as well as investing in his various businesses. Curiously, he also wants Rob to cover a good proportion of the cost of our operations to accomplish the dismantling of his network. I'm not sure how feasible that is, but I do like the idea. Then the rest is essentially for Rob as he sees fit. Demir is really pretty confident that he either has more than adequate funds to accomplish all this or that the funds can be generated, which from the way he talks is probably accurate.

"Demir is also adamant that we should strike first at this chap Emilio and strike soon. Emilio, whose surname is Arroz, is the man who initiated Demir's kidnapping and the murder of his lover, Evelyne Dubois. His opinion of Emilio's character and nature is that if Emilio is hit and hit hard, but in planned and apparently unconnected phases, Emilio will be too busy reacting and protecting himself to think about restructuring his activities to disappear out of Demir's and by inference our reach. If anything, that could play into our hands because Emilio could realise the extent of his reliance on Demir's brilliance and seek atonement to come back into the fold. But that is highly unlikely.

"Finally, Demir claims to be appalled at the links to terrorism."

"You have a smart young lady here, Gurning," started Spreachley. "I'd say, Laura, that you've neatly summarised everything. I'd certainly agree that whilst we appear to have a willing tool to make an impact on terrorism and espionage, as well as a huge dent in organised crime, we're a far cry from having any control, and that makes me nervous.

I don't think that he's playing with us, however. I honestly think he considers himself superior to us and that he knows best.

"And you know what? He may just be right on that score! It hurts to admit it, but it's possibly right. Think about it: we've only had a few successes against his network and have nothing but limited circumstantial evidence against the man. So why should we know best? A black-and-white list of names, addresses, and activities will hardly tell us what activities we need to stop permanently. What we need to know is how everything operates effectively. I'd say that we have to go with him. On the timing front, what's to say we have to do things at his pace if either we're not ready or some other matter crops up? All he's saying is that he should be responsible for determining the order of any op against his network so the ripple effect does not tip off other parts unwittingly. Seems to make sense. What do you say?"

"I'd agree," confirmed Gurning, amazed by Spreachley's conversion. "The one matter we haven't fully covered is you, Rob. Demir appears to have taken a shine to you and not only because you saved his and Anja's lives. He also appears to respect you as a person, something on which I totally concur.

"So the question is, young man, are you prepared to join this venture with us or try to return to your previous life? Before you answer, please be aware that if you do join us, there will be

217

risks, and above all, you won't be able to disclose a thing, let alone discuss matters outside of a pre-cleared group of people. We'll have to determine what your cover story would be because it's not normal for one so young to come into such large sums of money. But that's by the by. You'll find us supportive whichever way you choose. Life on our side is unusual, to say the least, and many can't adapt to it, so we won't think any less of you if you say no. Are you in?"

There was a silent pause as the enormity of Rob's decision weighed heavily on each of the four. "I presume that I can't use the 'call a friend' option," Rob eventually remarked, referring to a television quiz show.

Whilst his comment had broken the tension in the air by providing a little joviality, the decision would not go away, and he was acutely aware of that. After a few more moments to build the tension once more, he said with a wide smile, "It's a no brainer; of course I'm in. I wouldn't miss it for the world. I abhor much of Burak's life and activities, but I totally respect what he wants to achieve for his legitimate businesses, and it'd be a great honour if I can be the man to deliver that."

The subsequent and immediate chorus of, "Wonderful!" from the others was genuine and heartfelt.

"This does mean, of course," continued Rob, "that I have to be involved with all matters pertaining to the network, whether the legitimate businesses or closing down the criminal elements. I want—no, I *require* an *absolute assurance* on that.

"What's more, my involvement will be as an outsider running the businesses. I will not be a member of one of your services. That's got nothing to do with what you do but more a case of wanting to work for the benefit of the legitimate network and not be subject to whatever conflicting policies and procedures your respective organisations may have in place!"

That the three others were stunned was an understatement, and it was left to Gurning to break the silence. "Well, well. It would appear that you've given this a lot of advance thought and have clearly enjoyed the moment to boot!" he said with a smile. "I have to say that whilst your proposal will make life more than a little awkward internally, I see the sense in your approach from your perspective and potentially from an all-around point of view as well. It will also certainly keep us on our toes, which is no bad thing either."

"The only thing is that it could preclude your total involvement in the planning of our operations because of our internal requirements for confidentiality," chipped in Spreachley, somewhat aghast at the prospect of someone not wanting to join the service.

"Oh, I doubt that," said Rob confidently. "I'm sure there are many times when you need to involve external people in your operations so they don't unintentionally upset matters by, for example, turning up at the wrong time!"

Gurning's and Laura's pinched smiles could not hide either their admiration for his punchiness and pluckiness or the fact that he was spot on and had blown Spreachley's argument to pieces.

"I'm sure that settles the principles then," said Gurning to cover Spreachley's embarrassment. "There will, of course, be plenty of form filling and technicalities to complete for the details, but we're essentially there, and I, for one, am delighted to have you on board, Rob."

"I echo that," chimed in Laura.

"May I join you?"

They all looked up to see Burak approaching. "Of course," replied Rob. "Our conversation had petered out, so good timing."

"Well, from the laughter, it certainly sounded a jovial end to a conversation, so I trust that is a positive sign?" Burak paused only fleetingly since he received no reaction. "As you can see," he continued, gesturing towards Anja with a smile, "my daughter has found a new interest." Anja was evidently enjoying herself skipping on the terrace and singing in time with the rhythm of her skipping.

"So it would appear," agreed Gurning. "I've heard friends say that young children have a short attention span."

"Absolutely," Burak agreed with feeling. "No children of your own, then, if you don't mind me asking?"

"Oh, that's not a problem. No, no children. My wife and I weren't able, and we have very happily filled our lives accordingly. It's always struck us, however, how rewarding family life can be even though children are a severe drain on their parents' time, not to mention resources! The positive thing is that none of our friends regret not being the free agents that we are. And whilst we often wonder about family life, we know we had established a lifestyle totally unsuited to family life long before we even discussed having a family, only to then find out that we weren't able!"

Rob could see a strange expression on Laura's face, one he couldn't quite place. Following Gurning's startling revelation and the then awkward silence that ensued, the group all stood and dispersed. Rob and Laura wandered over to where Anja was still skipping and joined in her play.

———◆———

Later, when Rob and Laura were sitting alone on the terrace, he asked her, "Remember this afternoon and Gurning's comments about family life?"

"Yes" she replied guardedly.

"Well, you had an expression that I couldn't place, and I'm just curious, I guess. Normally, it is impossible to read your near-expressionless face, unless in more relaxed moments when you are not in work mode."

Laura smiled appreciatively. "It is rare indeed to get a glimpse into Steven's personal life, so I was surprised. I guess it was one of those moments when circumstances conspired to put him at ease." At Rob's questioning, furrowed forehead, she explained, "Well, we were all delighted by your agreeing to stay with us, we had shared some laughs, the sun was shining, we were relaxed, and young Anja was merrily skipping and singing. You could almost say that the atmosphere was akin to a being round at a friend's house of a weekend, so the conversation slipped easily and comfortably along. It's a positive reflection on all of us in my mind, and I'm sure Steven both appreciates that and won't forget it. I have the distinct impression that he likes you."

"That's good to hear. And he also appears to both like and respect you."

"Yes, I've been very lucky and have worked with him almost from day one. Whilst I've had to move around various departments for experience, I've always come back to his team. I enjoy it. And he's a great boss, looking out for his people. He still picks up a few operations, despite his seniority. The service wants the benefit of his experience and wisdom across the board, but he insists that he still run some ops to stay fresh."

"Good for him. Why did he get this one?"

"Oh, that's simple! First, his Slovenian counterpart contacted him enquiring about you. Then once you made contact and mentioned

Demir, well, it was a slam-dunk. Demir is such a high-profile catch, and the implications for the UK alone are immense. Add the international layer and the need to work between services, as well as with other countries' services, then there was only one choice—Steven."

"Hmmm, I'm with you. I can understand why you want to work with him, and he's one of the contributory factors to my decision to stay with this."

"That doesn't surprise me. We're both looking forward to working with you, and I think you've been very shrewd in wanting to stay outside of the services and retain an element of independence. Just don't let anyone know I said that!" she said with a broad smile and a glinting twinkle in her eye.

"Understood." They fell into a period of relaxed silence at that point, although they sat there grinning at each other, knowing they had shared a secret or two of their own.

━━◆━━

Later that evening, after seeing Anja to bed, over dinner Burak announced that he would like to bring everyone together in the morning.

"I've had a few ideas of how to start closing down Emilio's UK network and disrupt the international one," he said whilst munching on some food. "We should meet in the morning to test my thinking and discuss the implications, particularly how to keep the legitimate side of the businesses running after any operation. I suspect that from your perspective there would be value by keeping them running because an initial swoop may not intercept everyone you'd want to bring to justice and the on-going, unconnected businesses could provide useful information. I've also got some thoughts on how to stage the handover of the network to young Rob here," he said, bobbing his head in Rob's direction.

"That sounds positive," mumbled Gurning, also chewing on his food, "but best to wait until the morning when we'll be fresh. I don't want any misunderstandings occurring as a consequence of tired discussions. So, does anyone know when and where the next Formula 1 race is due?" he asked, neatly changing the subject and signalling that no further business was to be raised that evening.

The next morning, whilst their hosts entertained Anja, they gathered in the dining room, a digital voice recorder in the centre of the table as usual and pads of paper and a glass of water beside each chair. Coffee, milk, sugar, and bottled water had been placed on a side cabinet, together with a plentiful supply of biscuits and fruit.

"I trust everyone slept well," started Gurning. "Following Burak's welcome remarks last night,

I'd suggest that we get right down to business and allow Burak to expand on his ideas. Let's try to keep this cordial because it appears we are going to be working together for a lot longer than we had initially anticipated. We have agreed both between ourselves and with our superiors that it is best that from now on we adopt our real names. In doing so, Burak, I hope that you realise you will be effectively muzzled for the rest of your life, so before reintroducing ourselves, I just want to check that you fully understand."

"Yes, yes, I do. It comes as no surprise that you've been using cover names, and once you reveal your true identities, it comes as no surprise that I will never be left alone in public."

"Very well. In which case, I am Steven, this is Laura, and that's Graeme," Steven said, indicating to each in turn. "Rob, of course, you know, and his name has not changed! And now, to business.

"First, I would like to remind you, Burak, that whilst Rob is an integral part of this group and we value his involvement, it is Graeme and myself who will agree on the direction and the acts to be taken going forward, as well as to the timing. We respect that you have insightful perspectives on how to proceed. However, with all due respect, please remember that your skills are the polar opposite of ours. Of course, we fervently hope that you can convince us of your ability to flip your thinking to dismember your network that up until now has really been quite resilient to our investigations and probes. By sharing your skills at evading our best efforts and staying one step ahead of us, we acknowledge that you have a deserved, albeit unique, somewhat distinct and uneasy place at the table. How that will work once due process of the law is complete, I honestly have no idea. When such due process will take place is another matter that is beyond my authority. Enough of me—over to you to share your ideas."

"Yes, well, a neat combination of encouragement and I have to accept, unpleasant reality to start the day.

"I appreciate that, for the security services and the police, the instinctive preference is for me to simply tell all I know and leave you to remove me from the equation and close the network down as best you can. Regardless of that, the reality is that it is not practical to do so and would not achieve your objectives, namely to put as many people behind bars as possible and stop and prevent criminal activities in the long term. All that would happen is you would partially succeed, fragment the rest, and be chasing your tails forevermore. In particular, you would not break the relationships with terrorism and espionage that you so desperately want to tackle. I believe from our more recent discussions that you now appreciate that?" Burak looked around the table and received the affirming nods and mumbled acceptances that he was hoping for.

"So, the dismantling and handover needs to be gradual. By handover, I refer to Rob picking up the pieces afterwards to take businesses forward in a legitimate manner. That also will need to be planned to provide a semblance of continuity and assurance to those unwillingly but necessarily impacted by your operations. Otherwise their lives will potentially be substantially and detrimentally impacted. Moreover, there would be many of them. So far, so clear?"

Again Burak got a round of nods, each person listening intently.

"Good, no questions so far. At present, you will not have sufficient evidence against any of the leaders of the various strands of my network, and it will probably take a while before you could conceivably place any of them behind bars. After a break, if we can have a flip board I will sketch the network out for you. That way I can explain how my network grew. It was so piecemeal that even as I contemplate it now I am amazed and I have to say pleasantly surprised that it all hangs together. Therefore, I propose that each strand be impacted bit by bit until such a time as you have both sufficient evidence to nail them and—may I emphasise *and*—adequate information to come crashing down on the rest of that particular strand. There really is far too much to attempt in a short space of time."

Spreachley jumped in, eager to draw first blood. "We should be judge of that! I can see the face value of your logic, but it permits criminal activities to continue unabated and the criminals to enjoy the good life. We should go in hard and fast, involving our counterparts in all other services and countries. That's what the Americans would do, and we'll have a dashed hard time preventing them from going off half-cocked anyhow, let alone taking this in phases! There may be no or little direct activity in the US that you know of, but internationally, their interests are sure to be impacted."

"If I may say, Graeme," interjected Burak, "whilst the Americans do have the reputation of charging in with all guns blazing with no care of the consequences, they are not all like that, and I am sure the soothing British attitudes will be able to ease any impatient American temperament to secure their patience. The thing is, if that approach is taken, the network will fragment, and yes, crime will reduce, but only for a time. People will resurface undetected and crime will increase once again, along with the established links to terrorism we've all discussed."

"Yeah, I get that, but you won't have to answer to the politicians and all those people affected by crime whilst waiting on your plan to conclude! That's what I struggle with."

"Which is a very fair point," added Gurning. "But Graeme, that is what we are paid to determine. What are the risks for long-term security of ploughing ahead versus a steady-as-you-go approach and the associated benefits of each approach? Whichever way we decide, our briefings higher up will be tough. That's one reason I'm here. Once out, the profile of this will be huge, even if we manage to retain the required confidentiality of it all. As a FYI, together with Laura, I am on this full time."

"Why should it be tough?" asked Burak innocently.

"Because, you great ass, you're a criminal and our bosses and politicians are highly unlikely to believe you!" exclaimed Spreachley in a highly exacerbated tone.

"Really, Graeme, that was a little harsh. Now let's just all calm down a tad and consider this rationally," soothed Gurning. "For the sake of all of us, we have to get to an agreed approach on the way forward."

"Look, okay, I don't appreciate what hoops you guys are going to have to jump through or the politics of it all, but I do recognise the politics of life and relationships, and I do appreciate their frustrating necessity," acknowledged Burak as calmly as possible. "Surely, please, between us, we can agree on the approach and accept that however arrogant I may sound, I do know how best to dismantle what I have created?"

"Yes we can," Gurning replied before anyone else could speak, "and I am pleased that you acknowledge that getting whatever approved will be more than challenging. Key will be a rational set of reasons to not only support but crucially, to justify the incongruity of permitting criminality to continue to close down more in the long run and prevent the re-emergence of further criminality after an unspecified period of time.

"Laura, please work with Mr Demir and sort these arguments, or should I say briefings, out for us. You may want to use Rob as a sounding board to give him some exposure to what lies ahead. We cannot let this fail; the potential is far too great. I suggest that we can draw this little meeting to a close. Laura, please let me know as soon as you've pulled everything together. Are we done?"

"I'm not sure," Rob said. "I've also been thinking, and whilst I am looking forward to being involved, as Burak says, we need to plan for the aftermath of any operation and when necessary, my taking over the ownership and running of things. To structure how best to run those businesses, I will need to have an overall picture of what is coming my way and an inkling of when. Presumably you'll be fine if Burak and I have some conversations along those lines? Additionally, part of that may link into whatever Laura needs to provide for you. I'm sure the politicians and others will want to know how long the dismantling will take to manage any other stakeholders. They will also want to know that we are also concerned with the protection of employment and business."

"Spoken like a true businessman," commented Spreachley. "And yes, they would want an idea of the possible timeframe. However, I sincerely hope there won't be other stakeholders, as you say. These discussions and whatever comes out from them as briefings will by their nature be kept to a very few who need to know."

"Got you, thanks."

"But Laura should be present at all such discussions. I'm sure both she and Steven would agree." The two nodded as Spreachley looked around the table.

"Right," announced Gurning, "I think we all know what the three of you have to do over the next few days so we can wrap this up. Burak, I'd like a separate conversation with you once the others have left about both your and Anja's futures."

Taking the hint, Spreachley, Laura, and Rob left the room, Spreachley pulling his cars keys from his pocket whilst mumbling something about having to get back to the office. Laura and Rob headed outside to sit on the terrace with a couple of cold Cokes taken from the fridge.

"You haven't mentioned a girl or other special friend to contact to provide some assurance to whilst you've been here," commented Laura casually as they settled on some chairs out on the terrace.

"Oh man, thank goodness I split from Jemima before I went to Slovenia. She'd be impossible at the moment, driving my parents crazy. I guess this lifestyle must play havoc with your personal life as well?"

"It does, yes, hence no man in my life at present. My mother keeps badgering me to settle down and have kids. Thankfully, Dad keeps her in check as much as possible and tells her to leave me alone, so I only get the hassle when he's out. Dad is great. He's really cool about things, and I am sure he's guessed what I do, whilst Mum just doesn't have a clue."

"What do you say to them?" asked Rob curiously. "I guess I'm going to have to come up with some cock and bull story as to what I'm doing."

Laura laughed. "Oh, I'm a travelling representative supporting cohesive communities for the government. Mum thinks that's absolutely great. Dad thinks it's funny. I'm sure he saw through the story immediately but decided to play along. How about your parents?"

Rob partly snorted through his nose. "They're wonderful and loving. I'm very fortunate. They are very concerned that I don't have a job but cool with me taking time out. Yeah, yeah, there's a bit of a contradiction there, but that's them. They know that I saved enough to be comfortable for nearly a year, even allowing for holidays. They've even said that I could rent out my apartment in Vauxhall and move back in with them if money becomes an issue."

"Vauxhall," exclaimed Laura, "that's where I am!"

"Wow! I'm in a converted vinegar factory, of all places, just off Fentiman Road."

"Oh, I know, that's on Rita Road, isn't it? That's a lovely development. I'm at St George's Wharf."

"Yes, it is a great development, and yes, you're spot on about Rita Road. Do you ever go to the

Fentiman Arms, or do you frequent the many other places somewhat closer to home?"

"I've heard of the Fentiman Arms but never been there."

"Oh, you should, it's a great gastro pub. I often eat there when I'm feeling lazy, which is also quite often!"

Laughing, Laura went on, saying, "Well, when we eventually get way from this place, you can introduce me."

At that moment Anja appeared and rushed up to Rob to give him one of her regular hugs and burst into rapid chatter, telling him all she had been up to that morning.

A few minutes later an alarming and persistently irritating buzzing was heard throughout the house and areas of the garden into which they were permitted to venture.

"Security breach!" exclaimed Laura, eyes wide with surprise as she leapt up gun in hand surveying the area.

Rob picked Anja up in his arms. She had started to cry again and struggled to rush off and find her father. They rushed into the house as Laura followed behind covering their retreat. Rob could sense Anja's fear as she clutched on to him. She had become limp in his arms having given up the earlier struggling. *Poor girl. She's been through too much torment already and now this* thought Rob as he headed for the basement and secure bolt room. They were the first there, but Burak and Gurning materialised shortly afterwards, as did their hosts. Anja immediately ran into Burak's arms and buried her face in his side.

William Lees, the man of the house quickly briefed them. "Our far perimeter alarms have been tripped, which is not that infrequent. However, the cameras have tracked and identified a man moving very cautiously towards the house carrying a gun and making use of all the cover he can. He has now tripped the middle perimeter alarms, hence the need to congregate here. You are all required to remain in here while Jessica and I investigate. There are ample provisions, so you need not worry. London is aware and reinforcements are on the way."

With that he closed the door and the terrified group huddled inside the cramped room as they heard the rumbling of the false wall sliding into place in front of the door completely concealing their whereabouts. Burak picked up a couple of large cushions and dropped them onto the floor in a corner before he and Anja slumped down onto them.

◆

"Good luck darling." remarked William as he and Jessica dashed back up the basement steps towards the gardens and the known position of the intruder. Jessica merely followed and did not respond. They both had their iPhones that showed clearly where the intruder currently was, and he was still headed their way!

Just before they separated to go their own ways to approach the man in a pincer movement Jessica commented "This isn't right. Something's doesn't fit. For such a high profile target I would expect more than one assassin."

"Agreed, unless he's really good!"

"So why has he tripped our detection systems then?"

"Don't know. Hopefully because we're better than him! Good luck, I love you." William quickly kissed his wife and then moved off in the opposite direction to her.

They quickly skirted the formal gardens that comprised the near perimeter before heading into the wooded areas beyond. Guided by their iPhones, that were strapped to their wrists, they closed in on the last registered position of the intruder. They knew the land inside out and had prepared for such an eventuality many times.

Grateful for the dreadful English weather they were able to move silently over the damp ground, always crouching low to remain concealed behind the numerous bushes and shrubs. A gentle vibration on William's arm alerted him to the fact that the intruder had tripped another hidden alarm point. He knew that the same alert would simultaneously be transmitted to his wife. On he crept towards the interloper, adjusting direction slightly to allow for the latest alert.

Meanwhile Burak and Rob exchanged silent, knowing looks of concern. *Was this place really as safe as Gurning had originally intimated?* They were not convinced. But how could anyone have found Burak so quickly?

Laura and Gurning had taken up position on either side of the doorway, weapons drawn and ready for confrontation.

"I suspect we will have quite a while to wait." commented Gurning as he shuffled himself into a comfortable position. "Hopefully it will turn out to be a false alarm."

"That's what you hope because otherwise you have a leak in your organisation" commented Burak sourly.

Gurning ignored the dig. Although he was confident in the background checks on team members this thought concerned him. Pushing the prospect from his mind he thought *That's a matter for afterwards. We need to get through this first.*

The man came into view as William continued his way forward carefully. He was moving slowly and deliberately and was definitely carrying a long-barrelled weapon of some sort, but William was still too far away to see what it was.

"Target sighted." he announced quietly into his collar microphone that was connected not only to Jessica but also to some speakers in the bolt room where Rob and company were hiding. "He's still headed towards the house and appears to know the lay of the land."

"I'm to his right and in front of him." said Jessica.

"I'm to his left and behind him."

"Good. Then I will emerge and confront him and if he moves you can take him out!"

"Jess. No. You can't!"

"Yes, William, this is what we've trained for remember. I have confidence in you and I love you whatever happens."

The intimate discussion played out over the loudspeakers in the small and protected room made embarrassing and awkward listening for Rob, Burak, Laura and Gurning. Anja was far too scared to listen.

"William, I'm going now."

Jessica stepped out from behind a broad trunked tree in front of the intruder, her handgun concealed in a pocket of her lightweight garden cloak. "Oh, hello." she said casually.

The tension in the basement room was unbearable. Everyone's heart was racing as they held their breath and braced for the unwanted sound of gunshots and accompanying groans of dying people. The few seconds of silence weighed heavily on each person. Eyes darted from one to another in expectation of calamity.

"Err, hi." came the reply in a failed attempt at casualness. "Nice day, for a change. Out for a stroll?" the man was eyeing Jessica up and down recognising that she was alone.

"Yes, a lovely stroll in the woods." said William as he emerged behind the man. "And I have a gun directed at the base of your neck, so drop the weapon!" he continued in a threatening and hostile voice. "We are armed police!"

Jessica raised her handgun at the same time along with her identity badge.

"Oh shit!" exclaimed the man as he allowed his double barrelled shotgun to drop to the leaf covered ground and raised his hands. "Honest guv, I have a licence." The man trembled in a barely audible voice.

"What are you doing here?" barked William.

"Err, oh, umm, looking for some food." the man stammered.

"You what?! You get food from the supermarket! What are you, a poacher after out of season wild fowl?!"

After a lengthy pause the man admitted "Yes, I guess that sums me up. What's going to happen now?" Then, after a few more seconds of silence he questioned "So why you are armed police here?"

Laura and Gurning gasped in the basement hideaway. *Surely the safe house could not be uncovered in such a mundane manner?* they thought.

"Because there have been reports of someone with a weapon in the area." responded Jessica calmly. "You have many of the locals concerned judging by the number of calls the police have received."

William had in the meanwhile walked silently up to the man and suddenly kicked his legs from under him, grabbed his wrists and slapped a pair of handcuffs on to him. Reading the man his rights, William hauled him to his feet and led him to a nearby road to await a police car and the uniformed police to take it from there. The man would not see daylight for a good couple of weeks, if he was lucky!

Thirty-five minutes later everyone emerged from the basement hideout room. The relief that the safe house had not been compromised was immense. They flopped into the comfortable sofas in the living room ready for dinner and copious quantities of wine. Burak, meanwhile, took Anja up to bed and stayed with her for most of the night to comfort her in case of nightmares.

"We should consider a change of location." commented Laura to no one in particular. No one bothered to reply, they were all too exhausted.

11

"Okay, everyone, listen up. First, please can anyone who has not signed the register or the additional confidentiality forms please say so now."

Gurning looked around the crowded meeting room in Thames House at the expectant faces. Sunlight periodically broke through the clouds sending sparkling rays through the windows making people blink and squint. It was an unusually civilised hour for such a briefing, and Laura had overheard various mutterings that the pleasant time must either come with a catch, or something really big was going down, making her smile inwardly. *These folks are in for a pleasant surprise, hopefully,* she thought.

At the lack of response, Gurning smiled and continued. "Good. Welcome to our colleagues from the various organisations that will also be participating in this matter. Laura will pass round the detailed briefing as I speak. Each document is named and has to be signed for, both for standard procedure and also because each has a separate section at the back detailing your own particular involvement in this series of ops. Yes, I say 'series' for good reason. I am pleased to announce that a major crime lord is currently in our custody and has been for a couple of weeks. He is cooperating almost beyond expectations, and today we start to dismantle his criminal empire. Unfortunately, I cannot divulge his name for security reasons. In any case, for the purposes of these operations his name is unimportant because somehow or another he has successfully kept himself anonymous as far as those operating from each location are concerned."

The murmurs around the room were of both satisfaction that a crime lord had been caught and also of mild irritation that the name was not going to be divulged. Gurning waited patiently for the hubbub to die down.

"Nothing can be mentioned of these operations beyond those in this room because it is possible that others may be able to put two and two together and make four. That would jeopardise other, future operations by potentially alerting other connected locations within the same arm of this individual's network. Before anyone asks, no, it is not possible to take the whole thing down in one go. We have looked at that in detail. However, the breadth of operations is far more extensive than anticipated and can only be taken down over time. When appropriate, we will involve our counterparts in other countries because this does have an international flavour.

"That communication will not be handled by any of you, regardless of how good your contacts are. The level of interdependencies and other sensitivities far outweigh everything else. This afternoon we will start the surveillance on part of just one strand of this network. In this instance we will be looking to close down some money-laundering and drug operations. However, we must keep our eyes peeled because it is very probable that all or any of the locations listed are occasionally used for other purposes as well, potentially including terrorism, hence the involvement of both five and of six," said Gurning, colloquially referring to MI5 and MI6.

"There are four locations attracting our attention for this series of ops, two in London and one each in Bradford and Leicester, hence our colleagues from those cities joining us today. For the drugs element, we expect raids on various houses will follow as dealers' home bases are also identified. Please remember that in large part the target locations are legitimate businesses that have simply been hijacked for other purposes. We are informed that there is a concealed room within the roof area of the primary Leicester building that is used for the splitting, dilution, and packing of drugs received ready for onward distribution.

"You are required to study your briefing document carefully immediately after this meeting and then attend the separate briefings as outlined in your packs at the times stipulated. Forthwith, your other work will be reassigned. You will be allocated additional teams at the follow-on briefings. Those teams will not be dedicated, in recognition of our respective scarce resources, so I ask you to keep me informed should there be any conflicts, but I do expect each of you to do your best to manage without having to involve me. Questions should wait until you've read your personalised briefing and the follow-on briefings that are already arranged.

"Okay, that's a wrap. Good luck, and enjoy your role in bringing many to justice, dismantling a substantial criminal network, and cutting the tentacles that feed the terrorism that threatens our nation!

"Please could the core team remain, as I have some news."

Gurning waited for everyone to leave the room with the exception of Laura, Spreachley, and Rob. "I thought you'd all be interested that I have some news from my Slovenian counterpart from whom we spirited Demir away."

Rob glanced at Laura once again. His previous glances throughout the briefing had been more respectful of her as a woman, and he had been pleased to receive a warm and friendly reciprocating smile on more than a few occasions. This time was different, however. This time he was concerned, and from Laura's expression, she was equally in the dark.

"Thanks to Rob, again, our Slovenian colleagues have located the hideout where Demir was being held. Yesterday, they stormed the place. It may not make the media here, so thought I'd let you know. Some of Inspector Kovač's team were injured in the process, but the operation was a success. They captured the cleaner, who was also injured, and they hope to interrogate him soon. They found five bodies in the process, all badly beaten and all of whom were blamed for letting Demir slip from his captor's fingers. So, in other words, Rob, most of the guys you would have seen participating in the kidnap.

"What they did get from the cleaner, who is yet to be identified, is that someone called W required their deaths at the hands of the Doc and very possibly Emilio, although as yet we don't know whether he played an active role in the brutalisation of his own people. Demir says it is very possible that Emilio would have played a part.

"As you know, it is part of his network we are targeting now. How this W person connects with Emilio we don't know, nor where he fits in since Demir swears that he doesn't know him and that Emilio worked for him—Demir, that is. Whilst Demir doesn't know the Doc's true identity, he does know his reputation as one of Emilio's principal sidekicks and as a really nasty character by all accounts. Kovač wants this guy—well, all of them, in fact—so he's joining the queue. What Kovač said was that the two rooms in which the five were found were clearly set up as torture-cum-interrogation rooms and gave the impression that they were far from new. He's hoping that the cleaner will be able to provide some detail around how long the place has been in use.

"Well, that's it and good luck. Let's all keep in touch and watch how you go."

As they left the room, Laura whispered to Rob, "Lunch at the Tate Britain. It's a great place." He simply nodded imperceptibly and walked on.

Rob wandered off to Tate Britain, a ten- to fifteen-minute walk from Thames House, as Laura had suggested, to fill his time whilst she continued her work. He walked along the banks of the Thames, breathing in the air, freshened by some heavy overnight rain showers, and watching the diverse river craft making slow progress along the meanders through London. They had agreed to meet there for a late lunch, the restaurant providing both pleasant fare as well as adequate space for them to speak discreetly.

Laura re-read the briefing pack she had prepared for the surveillance team prior to meeting them. Then she left her desk in the open plan fourth-floor office and walked along the anonymous corridors and down a couple of flights of stairs to the assigned meeting room that would double as a dedicated and secured "war room" where their regular reviews on progress would be held and the information gathered analysed.

Her heart was pounding as she approached the meeting room and the adrenalin kicked in. The excitement of playing a leading role in the crackdown on one of the world's largest criminal networks ever was palpable. Trying desperately to keep her nerves in check, she took a deep breath as her hand took hold of the door handle and she opened the door.

"Morning all," she said brightly as she surveyed the room of familiar faces. "Good to see you all again."

———◆———

Shortly after two in the afternoon, Rob's phone beeped, signalling the arrival of a text. His usual placid face wrinkled in puzzlement as he read Laura's text.

"Sorry, can't make lunch. Something's up. Speak later."

Rob's response belied his apprehension. "How about dinner at the Fentiman Arms? I can wait. Let me know when convenient." Rob snacked at a cafe in the Tate and idled his afternoon perusing the various exhibits, not really focused on anything as he wondered what had arisen.

Eventually returning home, he paced his apartment, frustrated at the lack of news and being in the dark. There was nothing much on the BBC news as he watched, just the typical political infighting and gossip-mongering of government. Some company he had never heard of had called in the administrators, a man in his fifties had been shot in north London, and England had lost the second test against Australia at the Oval by twenty runs.

Since he knew he couldn't call anyone, he went for a workout at the gym, followed by a swim and a run. Marginally refreshed, but still highly strung, he nearly leapt through the ceiling when, at nearly eight that evening, his phone beeped again with another text message: "See you there in 20. :-)"

He smiled. At least she was betraying a semblance of friendliness, but he dearly wanted to know what the afternoon had held.

Twenty-five minutes later Laura walked into the pub, and Rob waved to her from a corner table he had found and stood as she approached. "Hi, sorry I'm a little late," she announced with joviality, kissing him briefly on the cheek before seating herself.

"Evening, good to see you," he replied, rather surprised at her friendly welcome. "Fancy a drink?" he asked, heading to the bar.

"Oh, a rum and coke please."

Rob returned a few minutes later with one rum and coke and a gin and tonic, as well as a couple of menus. "So, is there anything you can recommend? Also, how was the Tate?" Laura asked whilst studying the menu.

"Great, it's been a while since I've been so it was interesting to see the new exhibits. I didn't leave until nearly three o'clock. Oh, I can recommend the salmon. I had it two nights ago, so I think it'll be the chicken for me tonight. How about a basket of bread and some olives whilst we're waiting?"

"Sounds a good idea, and yes, the salmon does sound good. This is a great place. I can understand why you come here."

"I was very pleasantly surprised to find so many cool places around here within walking distance. There's also a great tapas restaurant a little way along South Lambeth Road that I like."

"Evening, Rob. It's good to see you here again. We were beginning to think you'd either moved away or given up on us," commented the landlady cheerily as she came to take their order.

"Not at all. I've just been away for a while, although I was here a couple of days ago." He paused for a moment before continuing with the order. "A basket of bread and some olives as starters, please, followed by one salmon for my friend and the chicken for myself, with a bottle of your Minuty rosé wine please."

"Certainly, with a selection of sides, as usual?"

"Oh, yes please," Rob said spontaneously, only looking to Laura as he finished talking to see that she was smiling and nodding in agreement with his order.

Once the olives and bread had arrived and the landlady had wandered away, Rob asked, "So, how did the briefings go?"

Laura laughed gently, sipped her rum and coke, and teasingly said, "You mean why couldn't I make lunch?"

Rob feigned shock. "Not at all. Just interested. Presumably something occurred. I understand that as it was my life at the bank, dreadful place that it was. Well, in fairness, that was towards the end. It started off well. The outsourcing process was a shambles from the start. Quite a few of us were convinced it was rigged in favour of one particular company. Needless to say the least favoured by those affected."

"I will look forward to hearing about that one day. Chapter and verse. In the meantime, I think our presence has caused some considerable interest," Laura commented, surreptitiously nodding towards the bar.

"Let me guess—there's been a steady stream of people materialising behind the bar, looking over at us, and then disappearing again."

"Spot on. How did you guess?"

"Well, I'm reasonably well known here as a regular and usually by myself so have got chatting to everyone over time. As a consequence, my love life, and continued general lack thereof, combined with my various wins at the Martial Arts and Unarmed Combat Championships has attracted people's attention. They have even had me autograph some of the photos of me on a podium on the other side of the pub where they have the display. That's why I sit over here. It's rather nice really, flattering, but odd all the same. They are almost paternalistic. Anyway, you can't get away that easily from telling me about your afternoon, however hard you try to deflect my train of thought."

They both smiled at each other as the landlord this time brought the olives and wine over, bowing politely to Laura as he poured the wine.

"Hmm, nice," Laura said appreciatively as she tried the lightly chilled wine. "Good choice. The briefings were fine, all standard stuff. I've some good surveillance teams working with me. Surveillance will start tomorrow with others separately trying to identify apartments overlooking the subject addresses where we can install some folks around the clock. The good news is that the briefings we put together for the powers that be were accepted and will be submitted. Steven was really quite complimentary, and having got to recognise my style, he quickly identified those sections you had written. I'm sure he'll tell you himself, but he did say you've the makings of a good agent!"

"Yeah, right, as if compliments are enough to entice me. No chance!" Rob said with a wink and grin.

"Anyway, I was about to leave to join you for lunch when Demir called Steven with something entirely more newsworthy."

"By the way, why do you always use his last name? What's wrong with his first name?"

"Who's trying to deflect who now?" Laura countered with a smile. "Habit, I suppose. It's just the way we refer to people in the Service. Anyway, you may remember that Demir hadn't been able to contact the lawyer he had put in place to oversee and support Emilio. Well, his tortured body has been found floating in one of the back canals on the outskirts of Amsterdam, not far from his home."

Rob looked shocked. "Why on earth torture a lawyer?"

"We presume Emilio is searching for Demir and also wants to get hold of whatever paperwork exists for elements of the network, particularly his own. Fortunately for us, this guy knew nothing of Demir's whereabouts and never has. He was merely a communications conduit to maintain a suitable distance between Demir and his network. The next lawyer in the line of communication is based in Lichtenstein. Preliminary checks confirm that he is okay, and a protective surveillance unit is being arranged without his knowledge. We suspect that he will be targeted. Demir assures us that even he does not have connections to the one lawyer who is based in Vienna and knows Demir. This is the lawyer who manages his affairs in conjunction with a few private banks in various tax havens. He also holds the majority of Demir's legal documentation, either directly or through other firms of lawyers in appropriate countries."

The conversation paused as their meals arrived and they tucked in.

"Delicious. I can see why you come here."

"Pleased you like it. As the menu doesn't vary that often, I'll have to introduce you to some of the other places around here, like the tapas place I mentioned, and you can introduce me to those places you know and like. That should keep us occupied for a while!"

Laura laughed again, relaxed after a long, tiring day. "Sounds like an excellent plan. The firm's legal team are working on ways for the Viennese lawyer to transfer all matters firstly into the firm's hands, through some circuitous routes and ultimately to someone representing you. Demir's not entirely happy at the speed of this approach, but he does agree to its necessity. You need to think how you will manage everything. It's going to be complex."

"Agreed. And I have been thinking it through. I rather fancy a private equity type approach." Rob paused, despite Laura's querying raised eyebrow, whilst the plates were removed. "That's to say, simplistically, to have a few really good people taking an overseeing governance and guidance type role, leaving the daily functioning to those at the coal face and who are already running the various businesses, unless, of course, it's determined that they aren't able. The issue is who and how to set it up. There are a few models around the world where extremely wealthy families have teams of people on board to manage their holdings. I'm thinking of emulating them." He added, after a thoughtful pause, "You know, it's truly bizarre to be talking like this. I know I need to be thinking this way, but to have such wealth thrust upon me is, quite simply, weird!"

An hour later, Rob held up his hand for the bill. "Let me walk you home. I suspect we've a busy day tomorrow."

Rob hardly saw Laura the next day, their paths rarely crossing and even then only as Rob passed through the corridors and offices around Gurning's office. First thing that morning he discussed with Gurning his thoughts on how to run the disparate group of business he was about to inherit, receiving a warm reception to the idea.

"You know, Rob," Gurning said, "your plan makes eminent sense, and the contacts we have here at the firm will be sure to help identify some suitable candidates to support you if you'd like us to assist finding people, that is. And the legal team are close to finalising how to transfer all of the holdings through some complex structures that keeps your name clean and doesn't leave a trail for anyone to follow. Best to go and see Jed Milligan on both matters as Jed will be able to coordinate contact with potential recruits for your enterprise, as well as undertake the various background and security checks on each."

"Sounds good," Rob responded. Then, after a brief pause, he said, "To all aspects, that is. Thank you. Has Burak provided the full list of holdings and assets yet?"

"It's still in the making, as I understand it, but certainly growing. The intensity to complete it has increased. Presumably you have heard about yesterday's news of the lawyer found dead in Amsterdam?"

"Yes I have. A shocking thing to have happened."

"Good. I want you involved and kept up to date. I agree that it is shocking, but sadly, it is the nature of the beast that we deal with, and it also demonstrates why we are so pleased that you managed to bring Demir in. It sounds corny, but the world really will be a better place once his network has been closed down. Well, I'll leave you to get on and find Jed. Thanks for popping in, and please continue to do so."

With that, Gurning turned his attention to his computer, and Rob took the hint to leave. Jed wouldn't be available until after lunch, so he went for yet another walk. When the time came, Gurning's assistant, Jill, guided Rob through the labyrinth of Thames House to Jed Milligan's office, strategically placed in the corner of an otherwise L-shaped open plan space with meeting rooms at each end. Rob could feel eyes boring into his back as heads rose at the rare presence of a stranger, clearly an external.

On their way, Jill chatted away, merrily informing Rob that Jed had left one of the big law firms some years back, where he had been a highly successful litigator covering fraud, intellectual property rights, complex corporate restructuring projects, and complex cross-border commercial contracts, which was how he had come to the service's attention. It hadn't taken much to persuade him to cross over. He had relished the opportunity and had been providing invaluable contributions of hard-hitting, pragmatic thinking, as well as great lateral thinking across the Service, ever since, becoming one of Gurning's few fully trusted inner circle.

Jed rose from behind his desk as Rob entered the enormous office with a large meeting table and mountains of files on a small coffee table adjacent to the nearly clear desk. *I guess that's one way to get round a clear desk policy*, Rob thought wryly. Rob had instantly recognised the tall man with strong features from the briefing the day before as having been standing at the back of the room. That he exercised hard to keep fit was obvious.

"You must be Rob. Great to meet you," Jed said, warmly shaking hands before they settled round the unexciting, institutional meeting table in adjacent chairs. Jed had pulled a bottle of branded mineral water from under his desk before coming over to join Rob. "I keep my own supply," he said with a sly grin. "Nothing stronger, I'm afraid, but far better than the governmental tap water that rattles around ancient pipes! Just joking. Fancy a glass?"

"Please, thank you," replied Rob.

"Well, what a spider's web Mr Demir has spun, and may I add my thanks to you for bringing him in?" Rob took to Jed immediately and his confident yet easy-going manner. "Now Steven has both got me working on the transfer of Mr Demir's assets and has also told me about your inspired plans for managing the businesses heading your way. Here's a list of potential names and associated bios of folks that could be of interest to join your enterprise," Jed continued as he pushed a few sheets of paper over to Rob. "You should start on these as soon as possible, if I may be so bold; time is not really on your side now that the surveillance is starting. I'm more than happy to help during the interviews and also discuss any names you may have.

"I have two further lists for you. The first," Jed said, ploughing on rapidly in the style that only litigators have and passing another fistful of papers over, "is a list of the businesses and their addresses, financial positions, and employees that are under the current spotlight. Once we've discussed those in detail and what needs to happen next, I'll send you away with the list of the initial holdings, bank accounts, and assets Mr Demir intends to transfer over to you.

"Amazingly, this long list is not exhaustive. It makes for interesting reading, although, as you know, Demir has asked that the amount of cash you receive will be limited to pay for a reasonable proportion of these operations, ensuring that the taxpayer does not have to fund your wealth creation. Ordinarily, everything would come to Her Majesty's Government and be auctioned off, but an exception has been made in your case so legitimate businesses are allowed to continue without becoming tarnished by association and employment maintained, all of which I trust you accept as fair?"

Rob merely nodded. He was simply too keen to get started with his new life to discuss the point. This was all very surreal, and whilst there was a tinge of disappointment that he was not getting everything, he did acknowledge that it was entirely fair. In fact, it was amazing that he was getting anything at all, and he was both excited by the prospect as well as determined not to become some obnoxious rich kid. An hour and a half later, Rob left one of the most intense meetings of his life and departed from Thames House, head pounding, for a nearby café. Jed had been tough but uncompromisingly fair, and Rob thoroughly respected the man, as he did Gurning. Rob also found himself liking Jed. His personality, humour, and apparent values struck a pleasant chord.

Sipping an iced coffee, Rob pored over the papers in a quiet corner. That he was—at least initially—a puppet for the government and its agencies was neither here nor there. He recognised and accepted this fact comfortably; it was the longer-term that attracted. At some point, he would have control of his own business empire; he had been assured of that in writing. Jed had presented him with a long letter, signed by the director general, that they had read through line by line. How long he would remain indebted to the government depended entirely upon the cost of the operations to close down Burak's criminal network and the cash in Burak's accounts, as well as the success of his businesses. The cost of closing down the network would be immense. He was going to have to cover part of that cost and that share was to be treated as a form of debt, a large millstone around his neck.

He was pleased with some of the compromises he had secured, but now came the hard part—preparing to receive and secure the cooperation of unsuspecting business owners. He wanted those people to continue to run those businesses but knew that would be very challenging when to date they had been at best partially funded and/or at worst predominantly funded by criminal activity! Many were well integrated and important within their local communities, and such a revelation could be extremely damaging to both the business and the morale and motivation of the people.

As he sat there, he decided that some of the more liquid assets could be sold upfront, whilst those properties not already leased out should be used to generate much-needed revenue to support his businesses as well as start repaying the debts. Why they weren't already leased out he decided to ignore. He was sure that he wouldn't like the answer. Those that were not already part of one of Burak's property companies would be transferred as soon as possible. Let the professionals handle them, although he would have to make sure the people involved were professionals.

Those properties not deemed eminently lettable would also be sold. He would need to determine how much money he needed to employ his small band of private equity folks and how much needed to be injected into the businesses. He would fight to keep those funds before handing anything over to the government. Having at least some of those being recommended by Jed should hopefully help that cause, so he turned to that list. Of the many names on the pages before him, three stood out, a couple of which were recognisable from reading the papers. Steven Gurning and Jed Milligan would be non-executives on any board of the overarching holding company that would be set up.

Sir William Shields
Fifty-four years old. Former CEO of two medium-sized international companies (one in real estate, one in logistics) brought in as a turnaround specialist and proved very successful leaving both companies in capable hands upon his departure,

with both still thriving ten and three years on respectively. He worked up to those positions as a group strategist at a major conglomerate before becoming the head of two sizeable divisions at that same organisation with an initial background in a highly reputable consultancy. Currently not employed.

Timothy Havering
Forty-nine years old. Lifetime career in international banking, having shone at all disciplines encountered. He has lived in Hong Kong, Tokyo, Frankfurt, Geneva, and Mexico City during his career, although he is now based in London. Multilingual and currently working at Rothschild. Known to Jed through many business deals conducted together and now subsequently known to Gurning, having undertaken numerous highly successful financial advisory roles for the Service as a part of various operations in the past. He was intrigued by what he saw from the outside and frequently expressed an interest in becoming more involved should the opportunity ever arise.

Karen Ayles
Forty-seven years old. The CFO of a government quango currently in the process of being wound down after five years, having achieved and exceeded the objectives set. She is highly regarded throughout Whitehall as a consequence. Came

from a variety of finance roles across multiple sectors, including CFO and finance director positions. She is frequently hailed as a role model for women in industry and for demonstrating women's equality with men.

Rob also thought of people he knew and trusted, connections made over the years through both university and work. He wanted and needed a balance of people to ensure he would not be too much of a Service puppet. Whilst he didn't know suitable senior people immediately, or nearly immediately, who were available to step in and provide invaluable advice and guidance, he did know suitably qualified people he could trust to be part of such an enterprise. Rob wanted a good cultural mix to reflect the many communities and countries in which Burak conducted business. The initial contact would have a substantial impact upon the on-going relationship with the various business managers, and Rob dearly wanted those people on his side. There were many business entities coming his way and soon. Rob made notes on those he would like to join him on the back of the papers Jed had handed to him.

Huw Thomas
Thirty-eight years old. A very sharp corporate lawyer at the bank I just left. Rose to number two for EMEA, but like me, Huw is disillusioned with senior management, has no real prospects,

and is seeking the right exit route, having turned down a large handful of offers, all of which he considered unsuitable.

Julian Smith
Thirty-one years old. A trusted friend from university days and now the chief operations officer at a medium-sized professional services and consultancy firm with offices throughout Europe. Since he works at a smallish organisation, Julian has proven his worth as the central project manager for a number of corporate acquisitions as the firm expanded its reach, driving the subsequent synergies and integration successfully in each case. I am sure that many of the skills required for successful M&A work and integration will be required for the challenges that lay ahead for me.

Khalid Shalabi
Forty-six years old. A Qatari national from a wealthy family Khalid is now based between London and Geneva working for a Qatari bank. Met me through a number of merger and acquisition transactions over the years, both on opposing and the same sides for different transactions. He is sufficiently mature, in terms of age, mannerisms, and appearance, to relate to the older generations, whilst having an apparently inexhaustible supply of energy to keep up with those half his age. Although not religious, he was brought up to adhere to his

parents' beliefs and remains utterly respectful of the cultural and religious aspects of his heritage. Whilst Khalid's background was one of privilege, I'm sure his friendly, easy demeanour will comfortably establish the essential trust with some of the businessmen and communities that could otherwise perhaps be resistant to working hand in glove with the Services, as that connection will inevitably have to be declared.

Yves Aussourd
Thirty-three years old. Swiss national from Geneva living in London. The son of a diplomat, Yves was brought up and schooled in the US before travelling extensively, first with his family because his father held numerous foreign assignments before returning to New York for a posting at the United Nations. Consequently, he is multilingual, with excellent global networks thanks to his natural ability to relate to people. Now working for a niche private wealth firm focused on the ultra-high net worth sector. Yves has regularly commented to me that after four years in the role, whilst fun and interesting, it did not provide adequate stretch, and consequently he is seeking a new opportunity.

Rob reviewed the list again and shook his head. Why on earth would he need so much help? Instinctively he knew he did, if not more. The list of businesses was extensive, and they would need all the help possible to become viable in their own right without the unwitting reliance on the criminal revenue Burak had pushed their way. It was also highly likely that Sir William would play only an advisory role to get them started, with Timothy Havering subsequently taking the lead role, but that was supposition on his part.

They would need a base as an office, ideally not too far from Thames House. Rob instinctively knew he would be spending a lot of time shuttling between Thames House and wherever his office was based until the network had been fully unravelled, and he had no idea how long that would take—possibly years. No doubt, he thought grimly, Sir William, Timothy, and Karen would likewise be regular visitors to Thames House as well! He would go in search of a small office shortly, but he wanted company whilst doing so. Both Laura and Julian would be good.

Rob quickly typed up some notes to capture his thinking on an e-mail, creating persuasive bios for his friends, and sent it through to Gurning and to Jed. He didn't expect a rapid response; it was a certainty that they would run a lot of background checks on his friends to determine suitability. Hopefully he would not be confronted with any awkward findings that could affect his relationship with these trusted friends and contacts.

He needed a drink, something stronger than his iced coffee. Looking at his watch, he saw it was nearly six o'clock. May be Michael would be able to join him.

Two days later, Rob and his parents were having afternoon tea in the garden. The conversation had finally moved from Rob to their nattering about their plans for reshaping the lawn to make room for more plants when Rob's iPhone bleeped to announce the receipt of a text. It was his first in many days and gave both Rob and his parents a surprise. Before his holiday, he had averaged just under one hundred texts or messages a day from his friends, but that had since dropped off. He had not been inclined to announce his reappearance just yet.

When Michael had reluctantly declined a drink a couple of days earlier because he was on duty that evening, Rob realised that all he really wanted was the comfort of his parents' home and the pampering that would come with it. With a great feeling of guilt, he called them, realising he had not been in touch properly since his return, other than to say he was in Britain and was safe to provide a level of reassurance for them.

Too much had happened in a short period of time, and Rob now wanted, and needed, some space, so there was no place like home. As expected, his parents were delighted to have him back. They were also exceptionally concerned when he had to say there was not much he could tell them, at the request of the police, other than he had been an innocent bystander caught up in some unpleasantness that required absolute confidentiality. He successfully assured them that he was not in trouble but actually was in the police's good books. After a while, they grudgingly accepted this state of affairs and settled into making a fuss of him, which ordinarily would have made him flee back to his flat, but just now the comfort of their proximity far outweighed anything else.

"Now that's one thing we haven't missed," his mother commented, smiling. "That said, we have both been surprised."

"Probably something to do with not having told everyone I'm back," he replied, looking and feeling a little guilty as he did. "I've been so wrapped up with sorting matters out and helping the police with stuff that I haven't really had the time," he continued thumbing the security code on his phone and glancing at the text. "Ah."

"Well?" queried his father after a good twenty seconds, during which Rob had neither said nor done anything other than to look exceedingly puzzled.

"It's Laura. She's asking if I want to join her for a couple of days checking out some places up north. We would leave tomorrow morning."

"Well, darling, I'm sure that would be lovely, and a break with a friend would do you good. Are you going to introduce us at some point?" his mother asked as innocently as she could.

"Well yes, but she also said she's in the neighbourhood and will be here in a few minutes to give me a lift home so I can pack the necessary stuff and get…" Rob broke off midsentence, realising the obvious direction of his mother's thinking. "Aw, Mu-um, it's not like that. Laura is—well, police," he stammered, realising how it must have come across and feeling a little embarrassment and blush creeping into his face.

"Why would a policewoman want you to take a trip with her?" his mother countered, probing.

"Look, you have to take this at face value. There is nothing, absolutely nothing, going on between us. It's just that I am continuing to help with their enquiries," he added, suddenly realising as he spoke that the denial probably made matters sound even worse, but whether from the police side or the insinuated romanticism he wasn't quite sure.

"Rob, come on—you need to tell us something," his father jumped in. "We are simply concerned for you. If you have a new lady friend, that's fantastic, whether she's police or not. If this is simply a police matter, please help us to understand. They held you for goodness knows how long since your return, and now you expect us to believe that you are willingly considering going on some trip around Britain to help their enquiries when you've been an unsuspecting bystander caught up in nothing to do with you in another country! I'm sorry, it doesn't make sense!" His dad's voice had risen, not to the angry stage but to the clearly exacerbated.

The doorbell saved him, and his dad got up, fixing Rob with a hard stare. Moments later his father re-emerged. "Rob, it's for you." Then, after a pause for effect, he continued, "It's Laura."

Rob squirmed in his chair, completely lost for words and totally unsure of what his suddenly spinning mind and churning stomach meant. Was it confusion or excitement, and if so, was it for an imminent adventure or for Laura being at his parents' house? All Rob did know was that his intended inward groan had sounded so loud to him that the entire village must have heard it! Anyhow, how had she known his whereabouts, and why did she come here? Whatever, he now felt an increasing level of irritation. Not forgetting his manners, however, he stood to welcome the smiling Laura, recognising his parents sizing her up, a matter that was clearly not lost on Laura either.

"Mr and Mrs Krane, I do apologise for barging in unannounced like this. I'm with Her Majesty's Government and assigned to the case Rob has brilliantly helped us with. A few things have cropped up for which we'd welcome Rob's further assistance, and knowing that he came out to visit by train, I thought I would come to meet him to make the return journey simpler."

"Not at all," his father said smoothly. "Whilst he's not told us anything, much to our frustration, we're delighted that he can be of help. Although," he continued with the slightest of hesitation, "Rob intimated that you are with the police?"

Laura smiled again. "Yes, I suppose I am. That's the best description. You could say we are a branch of the police dealing with specific types of crime. Consequently, and in so doing, we usually disassociate ourselves with the word *police* because of how people usually relate to it. Snobbishness I suppose. Apologies if that's caused any confusion."

Rob felt relieved. Laura had been so smooth, so immediate, so compelling that he hoped his parents accepted her at her word. From their countenance, his mother clearly had, but he wasn't so sure about his dad.

As soon as they turned out from his parents' driveway, Rob virtually leapt down Laura's throat. "How on earth did you know where I was, and how dare you intrude like that!"

"Rob, I'm really sorry. Steven has assigned a protective squad for you so they followed you. I did tell him that you should have been informed, but—"

"Too damn right I should have been told!" Rob interrupted angrily. "And why do I need protecting?"

"A fair question and one we have no answer for. It's precautionary. Anyhow, that's how we knew where you were, and I came to meet you so we could chat whilst I drive. I need to bring you up to speed on the last couple of days. Personally, I'm pleased you've had the opportunity to relax, even though only for a couple of days. It would have been best to let us know that you intended to leave London, though."

"What!" Rob exclaimed. "I thought I'm a free man?"

"Of course you are. Please, we really appreciate all you've done and have promised to do. You have been and still are brilliant. Consequently, we don't want anything untoward to happen, and until matters are completely nailed down, we don't want to take any risks, which leads into why the pick-up and our intended trip, assuming you still want to actively participate?"

"You bet I do," he replied, his tone softening from aggressive to interested.

For the rest of the journey, Laura briefed Rob on the surveillance of the four locations and the break-in of the lawyer's offices in Lichtenstein. Whilst the lawyer remained under protective surveillance and untouched, there was the concern that papers that should not have existed, but did, may have led to Burak's principal lawyer in Vienna. He was now under protective surveillance. Also, because of Rob's known nationality, it could be reasonably presumed that Rob and Burak would have headed back to Britain. Laura assured Rob that his parents would also be provided with protection, again without them having to know so it would not raise concerns.

Eventually, and lightening the tone, Laura enlightened Rob, informing him that his belongings had been returned from Postojna. Following a bit of prodding, Laura admitted that soothing the offended feelings of the Slovenian authorities had turned out to be the challenge they had expected. The Slovenian authorities had required to know as much detail as possible and were subsequently enlisted to root out leads on Emilio's operations in their country. Responding to Rob's unconcealed surprise, she went on to explain that Kovač's investigations could provide a useful distraction for Emilio, keeping his focus away from MI5's own investigations. Laura admitted this was a longshot, but any distraction, however little, could be helpful, to which Rob felt compelled to agree. As they approached London, Rob recognised that his earlier frustrations had subsided and his intrigue towards the future and his excitement for the imminent trip had taken a firm grip.

◆

Later that evening, comfortably settled back on his soft leather sofa, Rob called his parents to apologise for both the intrusion and having to rush off so unexpectedly. As always, his mother, who had picked up the phone, did most of the talking, and as was often the case, he partially tuned out for much of it. However, he was suddenly listening intently again as her tone shifted perceptibly.

"Well, it was lovely to see you again, looking so fit and healthy, as always. And Laura seems to be such a pleasant young lady, attractive too."

Mental alarm bells started ringing in his head as his mother paused, clearly expecting him to respond. "Mum, I've already said, there's nothing going on between us. We simply met because of the Slovenian mess."

"Well, give it time, darling. Even if it's inconvenient at the moment, as you say, things will settle down and the interaction that is necessary now will not be required. Both your father and I noticed how the two of you looked at each. We do know you."

"Oh, Mum," Rob said, sighing, for that was all he could think of to say.

"And darling, we are both concerned that all this Slovenian business is distracting you from finding another job. The authorities have to understand that and give you time to look and network. I know money's not tight yet, but don't underestimate how long it will take."

"You're right, Mum, but don't worry. I am reasonably confident that an opportunity I'm working on will come to fruition. I don't want to say anything about it at the moment because I'm not sure how it will turn out, but I will let you know."

"Oh, that's wonderful, darling. You father will be pleased."

"Anyway, Mum, it's getting late, and I have an early start tomorrow."

"Of course. Well, love from us both. Goodnight."

"Yes, goodnight, Mum. Love you both lots."

12

The buzzer was shrill in the early morning quiet of the flat, announcing Laura's arrival at the gates to the private development to pick Rob up, and yes, Laura would appreciate a coffee before they set off. Rob quickly scanned the apartment, closed the doors to rooms into which Laura would have no need to venture or see, and rapidly tidied up his breakfast things and the pile of post he was still working through. That was the one thing he hated about going away for any period of time. The post would mount up and demand attention upon his return when all he wanted to do was catch up with his friends. Personal paperwork was not his thing; it was bad enough having had loads to do at work, where everyone thought of him as organised. With a final satisfied glance around, he was pleased with its reasonably tidy, lived-in appearance, as opposed to the museum-like neatness of his parents' house. Moments later he buzzed Laura through the door to the block and opened his own front door, where she kissed him briefly on the cheek.

Over coffee Laura ran through the planned itinerary. Leicester that day and the next, followed by Bradford for a day and finally down to cover the two London locations. Gurning was keen for matters to be moved along but not rushed and jeopardised. Whilst they did not have sufficient resources to mount a larger operation without involving others, and he did not wish to, he equally wanted Burak to divulge more, and an early conclusion to this first op would place Burak under pressure to do so. Rob smiled, noting Laura's use of Burak instead of Demir, which hitherto had been her preference.

The surveillance teams had secured accommodation overlooking both locations in Leicester and Bradford. Although the latter did not have a direct line of sight, most comings and goings could be observed, and thus far all had been of no discernible interest, hence only a fleeting visit.

Shortly afterwards they set off, Laura having insisted upon washing up despite the presence of dishwasher. She gave her opinion by saying dirty cups should not be left for such a long time, leaving Rob feeling suitably chastised, and he wondered if Laura had been speaking to his mother! *Women,* he thought to himself as they walked downstairs to the car.

Laura guided her car across Vauxhall Bridge, along Park Lane, and out to the A40 before joining the North Circular round to the M1 motorway heading north. They were taking the long way around, she explained, avoiding any risk of the central London congestion charge and the inevitable traffic jams.

Rob slept during the journey up the motorway, lulled to sleep by the monotony of the tyres thrumming on the roadway. He woke as Laura turned off the motorway and navigated through the centre of Leicester towards their objective on the west side of Belgrave Road. The going was slower than anticipated as they had hit the morning's rush hour traffic.

Turning right into a side street, Laura pointed out their dual objective and commented on why Leicester had proven more interesting than expected. Both premises were on the west side of Belgrave Road, opposite each other across a side road. One was a money exchange, complete with a recently freshened-up facia board, and the other was a carwash opposite.

"Abdul will explain once we are in the flat," she commented.

"Welcome, welcome," a young man announced, opening the door to a small flat overlooking both objectives almost directly opposite. He showed them into the living room, where another man was perched on the edge of rickety chair taking photographs through a gap in the old, yellowed net curtains. "Hey, Stu, our visitors have arrived. Stop pretending you're busy. I'm Abdul, by the way," he announced, shaking hands with each in turn. "Coffee?" he called over his shoulder as he disappeared in the direction of the kitchen.

Rob surveyed the apartment, recognising the musty smell and poorly looked after condition of the decorations as being very studentesque, which was logical considering the large student population in Leicester.

Half an hour later, as they took turns viewing the scene through the camera, Stu explained the set up. Abdul had rented the flat and set up a temporary home, with the rest of the team paying regular visits to support the surveillance and Abdul's training. Abdul was the newest and youngest member of the team and had a part-time job locally that helped his integration with the local community.

They had not been able to determine if the two operations opposite were connected. The carwash appeared to be hive of activity, and Stu thought they had identified who the three targets were, whilst the rest, including the owner, were merely innocent bystanders, unintentionally caught up in something they had no knowledge of.

It appeared that the targets would receive a phone call to inform them of which car to engage with for either a pickup or a drop-off. The car would arrive, and the targets would emerge and converse with the driver. Then the driver, as with many customers, would enter the unkempt building to the rear of the forecourt to wait whilst the valets completed their job. On one occasion, a member of Stu's team had managed to time his car's valet with a suspect arrival, and whilst waiting inside, he had watched the target driver enter the washroom carrying a heavy bag, followed by one of the targets. They presumed the switch happened then but had no evidence to support such presumption, other than the driver did not labour quite so much with the weight of his bag as he left. They also could not be certain but were reasonably sure that the targets were up to something inside of the cars. Otherwise, why else would they take personal charge of the in-car valet?

On occasion cars were taken inside for the more expensive, full-blown inside-and-out valet, known as "the Extensive." Another of Stu's team took his car through that service and was amazed by the sparkling result. The problem with that, however, was that the vehicle was out of sight, so any exchange, regardless of size, was invisible to the watchers.

What had become obvious was that rarely did the trio, as they had become known, do any work other than after having received a phone call. Therefore, when the trio performed the Extensive, they again presumed this was because an exchange occurred and was most likely one that could not simply be disguised in a bag or two.

Coincidently, when the trio were involved with the Extensive, there had either just been an intensive period of standard car-washing activity or one followed immediately afterwards. They could only surmise the reason for such activity as having to be a large consignment of drugs or bulky smuggled items that were subsequently redistributed. No one could conceive that cash only would warrant the same level of consideration.

Later, if there had been a presumed money drop, one or more members of the trio paid a visit over the road to the money exchange-cum-launderer. It all depended, presumably, on how much money was collected. It was also presumed, as a consequence of a subsequent increase in the number of cars a few days later, that any drugs received by the trio had been split and were ready for collection and distribution.

"But guys," Rob queried, "the money laundering doesn't make sense. There's all this cash. Surely the money exchange chap has to account for it?"

"Fair question," said Laura. "We don't know in this instance, but very probably the money launder will be a hawala dealer. Before you ask, hawala is widely used by various communities, often Middle Eastern or from the subcontinent, to transfer money around the world. Hawaladars are a network of trusted hawala dealers, often with family connections, or long-standing regional connections. Rarely does the physical money pass between the hawala dealers, thus confounding our concepts of the financial system, particularly because they rarely require anything to be written down in ways our investigators are able to understand.

"In this way, money can easily pass throughout a country and across borders, with the hawala taking a nice cut at each turn. Often we suspect that dirty money will pass through the hands of many hawalas before ending up, thoroughly clean, in the hands of the intended recipient, whether here or in some other country and whether as cash or as an investment in some construction or other project. The thing is, these guys—and they are guys—can operate wherever with little more than a notepad in which they scribble their own personal code. Here it may be as part of the money exchange, but more often than not it is in the back room of another enterprise in a very informal, as far as we are concerned, manner. Some countries have made the practice illegal or have tried to regulate it, although as far as we can tell, to little effect. We haven't come to grips with it in the UK yet, and if truth be told, I doubt we ever will.

"One could be excused for wondering why, with so much cash at stake, no hawala has been recorded as doing a runner. Well, it always comes back to trust, relationships, and of course, the fact that they become wealthy and respected pillars of their communities. The latter, very possibly, is of equal or even greater importance than the extent of wealth thanks to the prestige that is conferred on the hawala. We are forever frustrated that a substantial amount of illegal money slips through our hands by these means. Steven hopes for a positive consequence from this operation and that this hawala stays in business but is brought into the fold, so to speak; that he learns to distinguish between the outright criminal and the occasional bit of dubious dealing for a poor family trying to help relations back home. That would be a major result for us."

"Wow," responded Rob. "And I suppose you are referring to the guy over there running a business that is or will become mine and that somehow or another either myself or someone who will work for me needs to persuade him?"

"Spot on," Laura replied, smiling broadly.

"Great, no pressure then!" he said, smiling and then returning his gaze to the activities across the road.

The next day and a half passed in an expected and uneventful manner. They witnessed a couple of possible exchanges, nothing certain, but everything was caught on camera, and car registration numbers were recorded for subsequent checks and investigation. Numerous vehicles without adequate insurance or other documentation were also identified, thanks to the established computerised links they had, and the details were passed on to the local police an hour or so later so as not to provide any connection back to the carwash and jeopardise the on-going op.

"The thing with this type of operation, Rob," commented Stu at one point, "is that our colleagues in other parts of law enforcement never know whether to thank us or not. We can end up giving them so much good information it keeps them busy for ages to come!"

"That, of course, is the point of joined-up working," chipped in Laura, "but they are never quite expecting or ready for such an influx of work."

Rob was buzzing as they climbed into Laura's car late afternoon on the second day to head off to Bradford. He was on a serious adrenalin high, and if it weren't for the seatbelt, he would have been bouncing around the car like a helium balloon at a children's birthday party. They arrived at yet another anonymous, cheap hotel in time for dinner. Laura had scowled at Rob when, in Leicester the night before, he had suggested that he cover the cost for higher quality lodgings. At that point, Laura had patiently explained that they wanted to blend into everyday life and not draw attention to themselves, unlike James Bond, leaving Rob more than a little deflated.

—

The next day Laura drove out to Leeds Road Hospital and parked in the visitors' car park. They then walked back, twisting through a variety of residential side streets towards Leeds Road. As they meandered between other pedestrians, Laura initiated a mundane conversation typical of young couples working through the teething problems of starting out life together. She was relieved that Rob easily caught on so no one paid any particular attention to them. On reaching the memorised address, Laura linked her arm through his to guide Rob to the correct doorway and rang the doorbell for a flat above a parade of shops and diagonally opposite the subject travel agent Laura had mentioned a few days earlier as they drove away from Rob's parents' home.

Ranjeev answered the intercom, inviting them up to a small but comfortable flat. The setup was very similar to that in Leicester, except only Ranjeev was present in the flat, looking very tired. Recognising Laura's quizzical expression, he sighed and admitted that his partner was unwell and the local branch had not been able to find a replacement to join him. Rob had not seen Laura so angry before as she pulled her phone from a pocket and called in the digression from standard protocol. After giving Ranjeev a dressing down for not having escalated his situation when the local office could not respond, she invited him to brief them.

As expected, his report was uninspiring. There had been a slow but steady stream of people in and out of the travel agency. The frontage was faded but well maintained. As with Leicester, Ranjeev handed over a series of USB memory sticks and flash cards taken from the camera as he shared his knowledge in a flat, matter-of-fact manner. Laura then stuffed them into a zipped pocket in her jacket. Ranjeev was certain there had to be a rear exit to the building because a few people, one in particular, had entered through the front door and had not reappeared by closing time. However, despite one sortie and umpteen searches on Google Maps, he had been unable to identify where that exit could be.

Laura scowled at him once again. He really should not be undertaking such enterprises by himself and certainly should not be holed up without maintaining a semblance of normal life, however one defined normal. Ranjeev merely gave an acknowledging "what should I do?"-type shrug as he pointed out the arrival of his prime suspect for delivering money to the hawala somewhere in the rear of the shop.

By mid-afternoon, with nothing else having happened, Laura suggested that it was time to leave and head back to London. As they left, Laura assured Ranjeev of how grateful they all were for his dedication and that she would kick up a stink to get him some support just as soon as possible. He was clearly grateful and shook their hands warmly before opening the door for them to slip out and head back to the hospital and the car.

Halfway there Laura changed the casual, chatty conversation, saying, "Don't look back, but we have company and have had since we left the flat. And they're getting closer after each corner. We won't go to the car but will find the hospital restaurant and take stock of the situation. I trust you remember the emergency number should we need it?"

"Of course, but I am sure we won't need it."

Two corners later, they came face-to-face with two young Asians and another two immediately behind them. "What you doing back there at that flat?" the shorter, but stockier of the facing two spat as he squared up to them.

Rob felt his heart pounding and a trickle of sweat dribble down his back as he relaxed his arms and legs in the same way he did prior to any championship fight.

"Visiting a friend in his new home," Rob replied, taking the lead from Laura, as that would be expected.

"Don't believe you," the man shot back, pulling a knife out from behind his back, a signal that the others should as well. "Want to change your mind before white skin turns red?"

Rob didn't hesitate; he spun so fast, sending his right foot slamming into the speaker's nose, that the man had no chance to react. Rob's follow-through was like a whirlwind of action, focused on the accomplice, pummelling him with both fists, first to the face and then to the abdomen. Both men were floored instantaneously and left writhing in agony.

Rob cautiously approached them, reaching out to remove the knives from further use. As he reached for the second knife, the man lashed out, catching Rob with the tip, drawing blood across the palm. Rob lurched back, fell onto his behind and kicked out hard, sending his right, hard leather heel into the man's jaw. The man's head snapped back. Rob felt the crunching as his foot passed across the man's face. The man part gurgled from the blood in his mouth and part screamed in excruciating agony before passing out from the shock. Rob barely looked at the youth in his desire to help Laura, but he noticed that both his jaw and his nose were clearly badly broken.

Laura, meanwhile, had swung round to face the other two men, who were stunned by Rob's sudden, unexpected, and highly effective counterattack.

One of the men lashed out at Laura with his knife. She ducked and took evasive action, letting out a muffled cry that brought Rob quickly around to her help. As Laura tackled her attacker, Rob approached the other, who immediately turned to flee. However, Rob gave chase and soon grabbed him from behind. He didn't know the protocol in situations such as this, but he instinctively knew he didn't want this guy escaping and tipping any others off that the intended victims had gotten away. The man twisted and slashed out with his knife, deftly fended off by Rob, who blocked the thrust with a parry to the forearm. The two circled each other briefly as Rob caught glimpses of faces in windows and heard the reassuring sound of sirens in the distance. Laura was likewise facing her assailant.

"Don't let him get away!" Rob called as his man attacked with a series of wild, vicious swipes and stabs that Rob had no difficultly evading.

He soon established the man's rhythm and waited for the opportune moment before catching the man's wrist, twisting sharply and bringing his other hand down hard on the back of the man's elbow. The screech of pain muffled the crack of bone as the arm folded back on itself. Rob then proceeded to kick the man's knee from under him, flooring him to leave him writhing in agony on the pavement. That distraction was sufficient for Laura to take her man down with a couple of stinging blows to the head.

"You okay?" Rob gasped as he tried to catch his breath and control his adrenalin whilst looking around to make sure none of their assailants could slip away.

"Yes. We should wait for the police. I'll call Ranjeev, and you let Steven know."

As Laura was on the phone listening to seemingly endless ringing, she patted down their assailants, relieving them of wallets and various forms of identification, as well as a couple of knuckle-dusters, and scribbled down names and descriptions in her notebook.

Seconds later, three squad cars came tearing down the street from opposite directions. Laura jogged up to the first, even before it came to a halt, ID card held out in front of her, yelling out Ranjeev's address and that they must immediately go there because an agent was not answering.

As those police tore off again, Laura summoned the other policemen, handed over the items taken from the four attackers, and said, "The four men on the ground must be detained under the Terrorism Act and not be permitted to see or speak to anyone until MI5 gives the signal. Get statements from anyone who was watching from the windows and is willing to speak." Because she took the initiative, none of the police asked about Rob, despite their frequent glances in his direction.

Laura hailed Rob with a wave, calling, "We've got to get back to the office," and she headed off toward the hospital and her car at a brisk walk.

Once they were out of earshot, Rob suggested, "What about Leicester?" Shouldn't they be warned?"

"Yes, good thinking," replied Laura, pulling her mobile from a pocket once more. "Abdul, hi. Is everything okay? Has there been anything out of the ordinary?" Then, after a moment's pause to listen to his response, Laura said, "Good. There's been a problem here in Bradford. Rob and I were just attacked, and Ranjeev is not answering his phone. Can I speak to Stu, please?

"Stu, hi. Bradford has been blown. We don't know how. Please watch out for any unusual activity and beef up the security and arrangements at your flat. Will keep you informed. Yes, that's right. Of course I will let you know about Ranjeev. Okay, bye for now."

It had been a long time since Rob had actively listened to another's telephone conversation, and the staccato nature of it struck him. Had he not known the circumstances, he would have had no clue what was really being said.

Looking at Rob as they continued their march, she said, "This is not exactly what Steven had in mind when he wanted progress. I really hope Ranjeev is okay and that the Leicester guys have not been blown. It will be interesting to see if the money laundering there increases. If so, that should be an answer. I'm confident we weren't tailed before we arrived, so there must have been some sort of counter-surveillance on Ranjeev's flat."

She then looked down at Rob's hand, having noticed that he had clenched his fist around a bundle of tissues. "You're hurt!" she exclaimed.

"Not too badly."

"Well, let me take a look at it once we're back at the car and then decide whether you have to go to the hospital. At least we won't have far to go if you do!"

Rob merely smiled weakly as the pulsing throb in his hand and the warmth of the blood distracted his thinking from the witty reply he wanted to respond with.

As they continued to walk, Laura said, "Once we've cleaned the area, you'll need to swing into action with your team, if you have one yet, to provide some reassurance to the remaining business here and determine if this one can be salvaged. You may want Burak's guidance first because I suspect you haven't had the chance to get your team assembled yet, and it may fall to you, unless you can piece something together in a couple of days. Steven's preference is that you don't become directly involved with the people, at least initially anyhow.

"And after the contretemps just now and the appearance of the police, I suspect that we need to get some sort of identification for you as well. It could become a little awkward otherwise." Then, holding her hand out to ward off the obvious riposte, she continued, "Yes, I know, you don't want to become part of the Service, and I acknowledge that. But some sort of compromise position has to be found. Otherwise you may just find yourself arrested unnecessarily."

They had reached Laura's car, and she sat him down on the passenger seat as she took out a medical box and opened his hand to inspect the wound. Rob sucked in his breath sharply as Laura dabbed on some antiseptic and started to clean the wound. "You're fortunate; it's long but superficial. It'll be uncomfortable for a while because of where it is, but it shouldn't take too long to heal."

As she finished up, Rob said, "Thanks. You'd make a great nurse."

"I'll take that as a compliment, but the profession holds no appeal. Whilst I have to know how to do it, I could not face cleaning up wounds day in, day out. I have the greatest respect for both doctors and nurses; they are unsung heroes."

As Laura was about to get in her car, the phone rang. "Yes? Oh, hello, officer, what's the status? Okay, many thanks, and yes, please place a guard on the door. We will require the space to be sealed off, ready for the forensics."

Rob waited patiently in the car, knowing Laura would fill him in when she was done. Having hung up, Laura climbed into the car and sat for a few moments in silence, staring straight ahead. After a deep sigh, she started the engine and set off at pace back to London, calling Gurning on the hands free to brief him, enabling Rob to listen in and get up to speed.

Ranjeev had been found dead, beaten and viciously stabbed. The flat had been ransacked, and by all appearances, it had been a hasty job. The police had to break into the flat, indicating that Ranjeev had opened the door to his attacker or most likely, attackers. It was assumed that the assailants had left the same way because there was no sign of an open alternative exit.

The tone of the conversation was very flat at the loss of a colleague in such circumstances. Gurning also expressed extreme anger that Ranjeev had been by himself and consequently did not have a second pair of eyes and thinking to consider the validity and necessity of actions taken or not taken, such as Ranjeev's walk about to look for the rear exit to the travel agency. Someone would pay for this.

After a brief pause for reflection, Gurning changed the subject to Leicester. At long last the members of the trio had been identified and warrants received to monitor their phone calls. Surprisingly, they did not appear to be discarding their phones on a regular basis, like many in the drug business. Since they didn't, it would make it much easier to eavesdrop.

They had also received warrants to enter both premises to conceal cameras and bugs so they could monitor what went on inside. That way, the camera in the flat could be removed, just in case someone had spotted that in Bradford to give the game away. Everything was pointing to the trio using the carwash as a hub for collections and distribution, presumably of both drugs and money. They wanted the cameras in place to find out if there was anything else as well. At the end, just to emphasise the seriousness the turn of events had taken, Gurning confirmed that the DG had been briefed and had asked to be kept informed of all developments, adding to their pressure. Ranjeev's death was not, however, the sort of development Gurning had expected to brief him on.

With the conversation over, Laura disengaged from Steven and drove for a while in silence. Eventually, Laura sighed deeply. "We've got to catch whoever killed Ranjeev. And thank you. I doubt I'd have coped with those four by myself.

Well, I know I wouldn't have been able to. I know you've seen the good side to Burak, and I'm pleased that there is one. The problem is the bad, legacy side now has way too much momentum, and sadly, I suspect that more people will lose their lives before this is over. How are you doing?"

"I'm not sure. At least the hand is not too bad. This is still all very surreal. I don't really know what to make if it all. The closeted, rarefied world at the bank did not expose me to such dreadful realities of life. Yes, it was dull, but it was safe. Being so close to so much death and being threatened myself— well, I don't know."

Rob paused, shaking his head, unable to complete the sentence. "I'm relieved I was there to help you. The thing that will keep me going is to try and keep those unwittingly caught up in Burak's enterprises safe and on the right side of the law. What sort of a man is he? Really, deep down I mean. To knowingly and actively encourage activities that will result in other people's death and/or injury is something I just can't conceive."

"Well yes, I can fully empathise. It took quite a time for me to adjust to this game and even longer when a colleague was first killed during an op— someone I had known reasonably well. I suggest a good dinner and some stiff drinks when we get back to London. My place, that way we can talk openly."

"I'd appreciate that. Hearing of your past and experiences would be interesting and possibly

helpful. And after all, you've seen my place!"
With both of them laughing at that last comment,
the rest of the journey and evening took on a far
lighter mood, although the memory of Ranjeev's
exuberant face was to remain for a long time to
come.

13

The next ten days were a whirlwind of interviews and meetings for Rob to get his business put together. Laura joined him early on for the viewings of potential offices, and they quickly settled for one in Millbank Tower overlooking the River Thames. Not only was it reasonably close to home and very close to Thames House, but the view was also good, and it provided great accommodation. The previous occupier had been a firm of lobbyists funded by some large corporates with deep pockets. As a consequence of quite a few upcoming statues and changes to the law, considered detrimental to their clients, the firm had grown rapidly, relocating to larger premises after only sixteen months. They left the fit out, including much of the furniture, that Rob considered eminently suitable for his purposes and thereby accelerating the speed with which his new firm, Zouches, could start occupying the space and coming to grips with the challenges that lay ahead.

Security was good, thanks to the presence of numerous politically affiliated organisations and at differing times, having formerly housed offices for both the Conservative and Labour parties thanks to its proximity to the Houses of Parliament.

Rob was delighted that everyone he approached to join his enterprise wanted to participate, and he was relieved that he immediately clicked with those put forward by Steven and Jed. He also secured the services of two assistants and other administrative and operations people to manage the team of people, the office, and the necessary financial, reporting and other administrative-type matters that come with any and every business. Both of the assistants were pleasant, chatty young women seconded from MI5 as they were looking for a new challenge and came highly recommended.

It was, however, with great trepidation that Rob signed the lease and the employment contracts, staggered that he was in a position to be employing people. If it hadn't been for the HR team at Thames House, he was sure he would not have succeeded. Now he would have to wait for people to work out their notice periods and for the office to be fitted out, for which again the folks from Thames House were also equally supportive and involved. Thankfully, they were able to create a nongovernmental style of workspace, so the end result would be tastefully modern and young and very spacious.

As a typical grey, damp, and drizzly morning dawned, Rob set off for his early-morning run, a habit he had started years ago to keep fit, fully wake up, and think about his objectives for the forthcoming day. He was already deep in thought by the time he entered Vauxhall Park and came out on South Lambeth Road heading towards his usual route along the river and its pathway all along the South Bank away from the traffic.

As he exited the maze of tunnels under Vauxhall Cross, his split-second instinctive reflexes enabled him to leap one of two other runners who collided just in front of him, sending one sprawling onto the dirty, damp ground directly in Rob's path. His leap saved him from ending up on the cold pavement alongside the man. The other runner, apparently off balance, made a grab for Rob, as though as to regain balance, but Rob's pace carried him forward, beyond the man's reach. In doing so, whatever was in his hand just caught Rob's sleeve, pulling the threads of his shirt. "Watch out!" Rob yelled at them, annoyed. He glanced over his shoulder, and seeing both men back on their feet talking and apparently okay, he continued out of the tunnels, past a van parked illegally by the roadside and down onto the river path, passing two attractive young women who were also out for a jog.

Such a pleasant frontal vision had to be checked out further, so he turned around to run backwards for the rear view. Hopefully he would see them again. All those thoughts rapidly vanished as he glimpsed the two men with whom he had collided standing watching him before they ducked back behind a wall. Somewhat perturbed by this and seeing St Georges' Wharf rising high above their heads on the other side of the road, Rob, in his usual decisive manner, decided to run a loop around the MI6 building where he currently was and then circled back to pay Laura a visit, keeping a wary eye open for the two men.

Five minutes later, he was feeling fuzzy-headed as Laura buzzed him up to her apartment. By the time he walked through her door, he was wobbling and dazed, as though he were drunk, and was barely able to describe what had happened. Immediately Laura had him lie down and phoned for an ambulance explaining, all Rob had managed to stutter out and her presumption of a failed full scrape of contact poison. Then she made a required call to Thames House both to alert the powers that be and also, more importantly, to place the medical services on notice to support, if necessary, the doctors who would attend to Rob at the hospital.

Laura was frantic by the time the paramedic arrived, daubing the now-unconscious Rob with cold water. An ambulance arrived a few minutes later to find the paramedic working hard to keep

Rob's vital signs functioning. Rapid exchanges between the paramedic, the ambulance crew, and the Thames House medics on the phone were had as Rob's heartbeat and temperature rose. His eyes were dilated, and his tongue had dried quickly as sweat poured off his body.

"I've never seen or learnt about anything like this," the paramedic uttered to the crew, looking bewildered and hoping for some inspiration from the ambulance crew.

"Can we move him? If we do, there will be periods when we can't have him hooked up to your monitoring equipment, and from where I'm standing, I'd want to keep a close eye on all organs and respiratory activity," said one.

"Agreed, but he needs to be in hospital to stand any chance of cleansing his system of whatever has got in, assuming that's possible. There's nothing for it but to move him. How about keeping my stuff and I'll follow you on my bike?"

"We wouldn't be able to secure your equipment in the ambulance. Ours is designed for that purpose—idiotic, I know. A universal kit will be issued shortly to get over situations just such as this, but that doesn't help this chap."

"Don't be daft; he needs it, so just drive more slowly and smoothly." Then turning to Rob, the paramedic leaned close to his left ear and spoke clearly. "Rob, I'm the paramedic. We spoke earlier. An ambulance has arrived, and we are going to lift you onto a stretcher to take you to hospital; we'll be a gentle as we can. Hang in there. We'll have you right as rain in no time."

Then, to everyone else, he said, "I'm sure both this guy's fitness and the fact that this appears to have been such a slight graze has saved him from the worst effects of whatever this is. Right, let's get him onto the stretcher. Everyone ready? On the count of three."

Following a series of nods, he continued, "One, two, three," and with that, they lifted Rob from the floor and onto the stretcher as Laura watched on, very concerned. Just as they were about to leave, she stopped them. "Hold up, let me call for a police escort. Damn, why didn't I think of that earlier? We'll need his shirt for forensic examination. Can we remove it now and cover him with something else? That way it will get to analysis more quickly, and the faster we know what we're dealing with, the better."

"How about simply cutting the sleeve off?"

"That'll do fine. Just don't disturb where the material was cut by the attacker."

Five minutes later, the ambulance was escorted to St Thomas' Hospital, and Rob was rushed into surgery.

While Rob was in surgery, Gurning and Laura waited impatiently for news in a side waiting room. Gurning called the DG to let him know what had happened and agreed that Laura should be moved to a safe house; there was no way of knowing if Rob had been followed or why Rob had been targeted. This had been a professional hit, so it had to have something to do with the Service.

With that resolved, Laura arranged for one of her female colleagues to go to her apartment, with a couple of male guards, to pack her necessities. She felt awkward standing there in front of Gurning giving directions to someone as to what personal items she would require and where to find them, but needs must. The question on everyone's mind was who had attacked Rob and why?

———

By the end of the day, Rob was conscious again and starting to show signs of a strong recovery. He was in bed in a single room at St Thomas' Hospital with two policemen standing guard outside. Meanwhile, the forensics teams were running numerous tests on some blood samples and on the material of Rob's shirt.

The next day, at the earliest opportunity, Gurning and Laura paid Rob a visit after many hours of anxious waiting. After the inevitable pleasantries, Gurning took on a serious tone. "I'm pleased to hear that the doctors have given you a clean bill of health, Rob. We suspect that this was an attempted kidnapping and therefore need to keep you under close protection until we get to the bottom of this. You were lucky—very lucky. Once again, your training, instincts, and reactions saved you. If you'd hesitated or even paused to check on the two men, for that matter, the story could have been very different. We're reviewing all CCTV footage and have circulated the images of the two men. I'm sure we will identify them soon."

"Could it be related to Burak and this Emilio chap?" Rob enquired.

"Quite frankly, we don't know at this stage. Clearly that is a very real possibility. Another possibility that has to be considered is partially related to the blown stakeout in Bradford and a cold case Laura worked on a year or so ago." At Rob's puzzled expression glancing between the two of them, Gurning continued.

"The one saving grace of your visit to Bradford was that Ranjeev passed Laura all of his material collected during his surveillance. We are fairly sure he did not retain copies on site for the attackers to find. What was found, discarded a few streets away by an alert dog walker yesterday, was Ranjeev's photographic collection of cars, also kept on camera flash disks. Ranjeev was an absolute car nut—not just sports cars but of all models, both glamorous and run-of-the-mill mass production types, which could explain a camera looking down onto Leeds Road. We are hopeful that, as a consequence, the attackers have been comforted that the stakeout was not a stakeout at all but was totally innocuous from their perspective.

"This is important because, aside from those tagged by Ranjeev as being of potential interest, when the guys were trawling through the photos yesterday and earlier today, there was one other face that stood out during a review of everyone coming and going from the travel agency: Sharif Al Rashid. He's a trusted number two for Mustafa Khartoum, who narrowly evaded capture eighteen months ago as we thwarted an attempted terror attack in London. Other parts of the Service are currently working on intel that Khartoum is planning another attack, so the Bradford connection is of extreme interest. As soon as we found Al Rashid's photograph, we arranged a re-lamp of all the streetlights along Leeds Road and the surrounding side streets, during which an operative fixed a number of wireless cameras onto the lights overlooking both the front and the back of the travel agency. The good news is that Al Rashid has returned twice, giving credence to our supposition that Ranjeev's cover was not blown. That also suggests that Laura was not recognised by those who sent the thugs to attack you both."

"As an aside," commented Laura, "those thugs are still locked up and so far, we've managed to cook up enough to keep them under lock and key until trial, which we've asked to be delayed for as long as possible."

Gurning then continued once more. "We think Khartoum somehow identified that Laura worked on the op that disrupted his last attempted terrorist attack. We also think he has had folks watching out for her but not for that long. It is possible that they may have seen you with her, which is very troubling indeed. Every member of the team has had to up their own personal security as a result. Taking out an agent does not overly hinder an op focused on terrorist matters. Khartoum knows that. If it wasn't for the Demir project, code named Network Break, by the way, it would be logical that Laura would work with the same team on the latest op against Khartoum.

"So if simply removing an agent won't get Khartoum anywhere, what about kidnapping a perceived boyfriend and attempting extortion for inside information? If they've been following you, they'd have noticed that you haven't been to Thames House, at least not since returning from Bradford, when we suspect they started watching you. And may I say, everything about you clearly suggests that you do not work for Her Majesty's Government. On that basis, we assume they pegged you as Laura's boyfriend or at least someone close."

Gurning paused to give Rob the opportunity to take everything in. Whilst the bewilderment in his face was evident, the tension inside and the cold sweat running down his back were not. He also wondered whether Gurning had seen Rob taking the odd furtive glance towards Laura. She was attractive, but then many men took second looks when she passed, so why would Gurning think differently of him. *Grief, am I really up to all this?*

he thought to himself for the thousandth time. Both Steven and Laura were looking at him with a mixture of concern and possibly something else.

"We can come back later if you'd like," said Laura. "I'm sure you're still tired and this is a lot to take in."

"No. No, I'm fine. Thanks for asking, anyhow. Please, do continue and brief me on as much as you think I need to know. But I am curious—if they'd been following me, as you suggest, where was this surveillance team that you've got watching my back?"

"There's not actually much more to say, and that is an excellent question I have asked myself. There are some folks who are feeling my wrath at the moment for having been way too lax," Gurning went on. "Anyway, just to be on the safe side, I've decided that you both are to be relocated to a safe house in west London, Ealing, as a matter of fact. That will provide accessibility both for those at Thames House who will need to visit as well as for you to get out and about to meet Demir when required and Rob, for you to meet your new employees. I bet that sounds strange, 'your employees,'" Gurning repeated with a grin.

Smiling in return, Rob said, "You bet it does. But what about our respective families?"

"That has all been considered, and protective surveillance has been installed for Laura's family. The team covering your family has not gone anywhere, although have been told in no uncertain terms to make sure there are no lapses. Everyone concerned have learnt not to let their guard down."

"Thanks," Rob replied. He tried desperately to suppress a growing smirk, but failed and so Rob felt compelled to explain to his evidently puzzled companions. "My parents are going to just love this. First Laura pays a visit, then we go for a three-day trip around England together, and now I'm moving in with her! Mum will make my life a nightmare."

All three burst out laughing, and after another ten minutes or so of chitchat, Gurning and Laura left and Rob drifted off to sleep.

14

Laura had explained that they were in a long-term safe house, hence the furnishings and general fixtures and fittings being of reasonable standard. Meetings with his own future team were arranged at pre-cleared restaurants with private function rooms to discuss strategy and the best approach to the task ahead and importantly, to get to know each other. The future office in Millbank Tower was still a construction site and would be off-limits for a while to come, so even if folks weren't working out their notice periods, they wouldn't have been able to start work for Zouches, the name Rob had given his new enterprise.

Laura meanwhile was able to work remotely from the safe house. On the second day, as they were working alongside each other in the room set aside for them to do so, cups of coffee close at hand, Laura gasped, "Who would do that!"

"What's that?"

"It's those two men we heard about on the news—you know, the ones found floating in the Thames earlier this morning. I'm just reading an internal report seeking assistance with their identification. They were both beaten severely, brutally even. Take a look at these mug shots, would you? I'll spare you the photos of their bodies. Fortunately, their faces were spared, to a degree. Steven sent it across because they were both wearing running clothes. It's a hunch, but well, take a look."

"You mean you think they could be the guys who attacked me?" Rob said, strolling over from his desk. There was no hesitation when he said, "Absolutely, that's them. Why kill them? Surely that depletes his own organisation."

"Khartoum's way. We know little about him, but he does have a brutal track record and does not tolerate failure, so this will be meant as a message to the others on his team: succeed or else. As far as depleting his team, unlikely. These guys, like the thugs in Bradford, would not be part of his core team chosen for the serious work. They'd have been pulled from the sadly growing ranks of marginalised and disillusioned people of any race or creed who fit Khartoum's profile for gradually becoming radicalised. The prolonged tough economic climate has not been helping, and he often sets challenges such as Bradford and here with you to test whether the recruit has what it takes. Once the recruits are in and once criminality has been committed, there is unlikely to be any turning back."

"Makes it all the more important to provide continuity, something firm and tangible, and to build a successful business out of whatever remains once the criminal activities being syphoned through a business have been removed," Rob remarked.

"Very astute, and I wholeheartedly agree with you. Steven and Graeme will be impressed. You're definitely becoming an honouree member of the Services!"

"Gee, thanks! Anyway, what's the news from the four stakeouts?"

"Good question. Pull up a chair. I've the reports open and am due on a series of conference calls shortly. You can listen in if you want."

Two and a half hours later, they sat back and looked at each other. "Conference calls like that are far harder than meeting in person," Laura commented. "That was exhausting!"

Laughing, Rob said, "That's life in the private sector, especially when covering multiple geographies."

"Well, I don't know about you, but I fancy lunch. There's a Carluccios just off the Broadway, so not far. How does that sound? The protective chaps will be there as well, and I'm sure they'd appreciate a treat."

The reports and conference calls had provided an encouraging update. Matters were moving rapidly, and Laura and Rob would soon have to be springing into action for their respective roles. Rob would head up to Leicester to follow the raids on both the money exchange and the carwash, providing assurance to those who were present legitimately. Laura, on the other hand, would be in Bradford trying to piece together the money trail and understand what Al Rashid intended. So far, there had been no sign of Khartoum. He had dropped off the radar entirely after the last and thwarted attack, and Laura hoped Al Rashid would lead them to him.

Over the following days, it was decided that they would go their separate ways the following Sunday evening, leaving them just a few days to fully familiarise themselves with the layouts of the respective buildings and all the intelligence thus far collected on each location and both the people based at those premises and their visitors. Everything pointed to an imminent attack, but still there was no clue as to what, let alone where, and nothing untoward had been detected at the London locations. Stress was running high.

The London surveillance had been relatively unexciting compared to Bradford and Leicester but no less revealing. The organised crime teams from Scotland Yard were delighted to have additional help and a regular flow of information as more and more was uncovered through the days of generally tedious surveillance work.

Rob was shocked as he read through the near-daily briefings provided from both locations whilst holed up in Ealing with Laura and their assigned protection team.

"Sadly, this reflects the daily life for far too many people in our home city," she said. "I couldn't cope with it, which is rich coming from someone who specialises in counter-terrorism and the associated atrocities that go with that!"

Despite the wealth of valuable information coming from both surveillance teams, nothing had attracted MI5's attention from the potential terrorism perspective. Steven, on the other hand, was keen to make sure Rob kept on top of the businesses because he would be picking up the pieces once the criminal contributions were taken down.

The Pimlico All Hours General Store and Money Exchange on Wilton Road at the Victoria end had a booming trade, thankfully, mostly legitimate and therefore of little concern to Rob as a future viable going concern. However, some of the successful tails of the drugs couriers from Leicester had provided follow-on identifications of the local dealers throughout Westminster, Kensington, and Chelsea. A large narcotics team from Scotland Yard was brought in as support to tail the identified suppliers without being briefed on the wider operation. Whilst it was clear to those teams that something else was brewing, they were kept more than sufficiently busy and were delighted with the results that were in effect being handed to them.

The circle was closed as the dealers passed part of the money collected to an intermediary, who then turned up at the Pimlico All Hours store to avail themselves of the hawala in the rear, who also operated the money exchange, which was aimed predominantly at the tourist trade. Thanks to the bugged telephones, it became clear that much of the intermediaries' money returned to Leicester. The frustrating aspect was that they had still not identified the source of the drugs working back from Leicester.

Likewise, the Fonthill Clothes store had not shown any sign of interesting activity to the teams supporting Steven and Laura. No links to Leicester been established either, but the surveillance and research teams had uncovered some very unpleasant criminal activity. Fonthill Clothes occupied three ground-floor units turned into one at the lower end of Fonthill Road in Finsbury Park, close to the junction with Seven Sisters Road. A popular and busy store in the area, trade was reasonably brisk. The business manager had an informal arrangement with a hawala who operated out of a rear office, and both appeared to support the other in bringing business in. Land Registry records indicated that the manager had sub-leased the first floor out to two separate organisations. The name on the documentation—Roberto Borzi—was the same, however. Relations between the sub-landlord and sub-tenant appeared fraught at best, each trying their best to avoid the other.

Laura's favourite researcher, David Spalding, had proved his tenacity once again, delighting Laura and amazing Rob with his news in the briefings and when he paid a visit to the Ealing safe house.

"It's great getting out of the office occasionally," he said as they settled around a table with cups of coffee. "I know I say that I like the relative safety of Thames House and the routine of my work, but the odd excursion is great."

"Glad you could come, David," Laura replied. "Coffee?"

"Oh, yes please," he said with feeling.

"So what have you got for us?" Laura asked, pouring the coffee.

"Nothing much of interest for the Service, so far as I can tell, but plenty that'll be of interest to the Yard. To think that I've been part of getting one up on them!" he said excitedly.

"This Borzi chap runs both a modelling agency and a temp agency, specialising in Eastern European women, and I use the expression Eastern European in its widest sense. Essentially it appears to be a front for people smuggling, prostitution, pornography, and extortion. I can't believe there is any other organisation in Britain with a higher turnover rate of staff. Young, mostly attractive women arrive, apparently legitimately and with valid work visas, and then disappear, only to be replaced. Borzi reports the disappearances as the women having simply not turned up for work and their whereabouts as unknown, having left the given contact address. Consequently, he has kept himself on the good books with the Borders Agency.

"The women—I could probably say girls because some are so young it's unreal—sometimes work for both of Borzi's companies, depending upon the woman's skills and beauty. His clients are not particularly reputable either." He handed Laura and Rob a list of those he had identified, and a large minority had an asterisk next to them as an identifier of either a criminal record or being under suspicion.

"I've passed details on to the vice team, and they have tracked a few of the girls already to various types of establishment throughout the country. As of yesterday, it appears that a wanted people trafficker has been identified, so the team are tailing him and are hopeful of tracing other locations and women."

Changing tack somewhat and taking a deep breath from having talked so much, David continued. "I'm not sure Fonthill Clothes would be able to cover the rent for the entire premises without the income received from Borzi.

Otherwise I have no doubt the manager would kick him out at a moment's notice, assuming he was entitled to. To explain, I could not understand why Fonthill Clothes leased the entire building in the first place given that the sub-leases were signed on the same day as Fonthill Clothes signed its lease on the building, so I did some digging. The freehold is owned by Templar Real Estate Services, which is, as you know, one of your friend Demir's organisations. Interestingly, Templar Real Estate Services also owns the Wilton Road premises occupied by Pimlico All Hours as well as the parade in Bradford, of which the travel agency is just one tenant, as well as the carwash in Leicester and the parade along Belgrave Street in which the money exchange is a tenant."

"You're joking!" exclaimed Laura. "Burak really does live up to his word that he set out to control as much of his operations as possible."

"What better way to launder the money you're earning in other dubious ways than to own the buildings that you rent to yourself and keep the money in the family, so to speak?" David added.

Rob sat there shaking his head. "How soon are we able to close those operations down? I know a little about leases, and they generally all have 'no immoral, etcetera, uses' as a requirement. Any lawyer putting a new lease in place would be highly suspicious if he was asked not to include those words."

"Steady on, Rob," Laura said. "From what David has said, it does sound as though we have sufficient grounds to raid Borzi's premises. The necessary information will be passed on so the appropriate actions can be taken. However, don't forget, we have a terrorist threat to deal with, and at least some of Burak's network is being used as a cover. The raids can occur after we've nailed Khartoum and Al Rashid. As yet, we have no idea of how extensive an act Khartoum is planning, and that has to take priority, however unpalatable the consequences are of permitting the status quo of other activities to continue for a while.

"A raid on Pimlico All Hours is possibly harder to justify but would at least provide an appropriate opportunity to introduce you as the new owner."

"Got you," Rob said simply, albeit with a great deal of personal difficulty in accepting such an approach.

◆

As they were talking, the London team, led by Brian Jeffries, were debating the previous evening's football and some of the more questionable decisions by the referee. As always, the views were diametrically opposed, dependent upon team and supporter.

"There was no way that was a penalty," Keith protested. "Terry, your chap dived. Clear as day!"

"Utter crap!" responded Andy. "You don't limp around as he did for five minutes if you dive. That was fair and square a penalty. Terry's game was badly weakened after that. It was!"

"Oh shut up, you two," cut in Brian, "and come look at these guys paying a visit to Borzi. Seems intros are being made."

"How about a lottery draw again to decide which we follow?" asked Keith. "And when are we going to get adequate resource? This is the fourth time we can't tail all those we want."

"Keep your knickers on," Brian scolded in a friendly way, indicating he was equally frustrated. "You know the score and the money constraints.

"No, this time we take the guy on the left. I've a hunch. He appears to be calling most of the shots, even at times over Borzi, which is a first. Make sure we get good photos of these guys."

"So far we've only got partials and their backs at that."

"What!" exclaimed Brian in annoyance. "What about when they entered the place?"

"It wasn't through the front, that's for sure, and somehow or another they evaded the CCTV focused on the rear."

"Right, we get folks stationed to follow these guys, particularly the more senior, the moment they leave. And get photos!"

"Got you. Okay, I'll start and coordinate with the others. Will let you know how we get on. See you later, guv."

An hour later, a dejected team were in the surveillance room, having let the two unknowns slip through their net without so much as a photograph, let alone a chase, leaving Brian to pick up the pieces and try to re-motivate them. They always responded to energy and action, so he knew what to do.

"Right lads, the priority is to get inside that building and understand how those guys gave us the slip. Keith, Andy, how do you fancy a bit of environmental protection work?" he said with a smirk.

They both knew he was up to something but could not fathom what, so they played along.

"Urrrg!" they both grimaced. "Sounds dreadful."

"Well my view is that you get your overalls on and get some duplicate IDs sharpish, then with the help of a cover letter I will compose, you go in there to check all sinks, toilets, drains, etcetera, for risk of backing up because of reported problems by Thames Water further up the system. That will require the mandatory inspection of basement areas, the whole lot. Otherwise the force of law will come down on them. Got that?"

"Always the glamorous jobs," complained Andy with a grin of enthusiasm. "But aren't we sailing a bit close to the wind on this?"

"Very possibly, but so what! The system has let us down, and we need to know the layout of that place. I don't want any more folks giving us the slip again. You in or do we bottle?"

"We're in!" chorused everyone together.

15

Meanwhile, Al Rashid had been traced to an unassuming terraced house in Morley, just outside of Leeds, close to the station and the many junctions serving the north-south, the east-west, and the Leeds ring-road motorway networks. The surveillance teams were rotated regularly and constantly frustrated by Al Rashid's total lack of routine, preventing the easy placement of tails to take over one from another. Alerted by his vigilance in Bradford, the team remained away from the terraced house, and when Laura arrived, she based herself in the anonymous Bradford office, listening to the numerous communications as the teams kept their vigil for Al Rashid's next move.

Two days earlier Al Rashid had visited the travel agency and by all appearances had been frustrated with something. Somehow, at last timing worked in their favour, and an agent was able to walk past the frontage just as Al Rashid left, yelling, "In two days," and crashing the door closed behind him, leaving a concerned-looking assistant behind him.

Now, at 10:25 a.m., from the corner at the end of his street an agent reported that Al Rashid was on the move, getting into his car accompanied by an as-yet-unknown white male. As he turned out of his street, an old Peugeot 205 also turned on the same road from another side street with a young couple inside, call sign Unit 1.

"Target Alpha in sight, two cars ahead, proceeding along Queen Street. Hold on that, Alpha pulling up. Having to pass. Alpha picking up another male, white, unknown. Alpha re-joining traffic behind us, turning left, left, left. No further visual." Shots from the on-board camera mounted in all of the surveillance vehicles were largely blocked by other cars, but everyone craned their necks to try for a glimpse of the new passenger, as though they were there and doing so would provide them with a different angle of the scene and an improved view.

"Unit 1, take next left. Roads will connect. Try to intercept. All foot units take position on street corners to look out," called the controller. "All others hold position." Laura felt quite giddy watching the streamed footage as Unit 1 raced through the side streets, trying to re-connect.

"Foot 3, Alpha has circled round and is passing along home street once more. Turning left, left, left on Queen Street again. Out of visual."

"Unit 4 nearly in position, will pick up." Then, following a few tense seconds of silence, not knowing if Al Rashid had slipped their net, they heard, "Unit 4, have contact approaching turning with Corporation Street. Left on Corporation Street."

Everyone in the control room expelled a collective sigh as the controller explained to Laura that this was one of Alpha's standard routes for starting his journey to Bradford.

"Unit 4, right on Fountain Street." The controller nodded to Laura again. There would be a few minutes as Alpha headed down Fountain Street to Bruntcliffe Road and the motorway.

"Unit 4, Alpha takes left, left, left on Baker Street going at speed. Unable to pursue without blowing cover."

"What the!" exclaimed the controller, studying the map and calmly relaying orders to all units directing cover for the possible exits Al Rashid had. Long, silent seconds ticked by as they waited for news.

"Unit 2, have Alpha emerging into Chartists Way. Will pick up."

Everyone watched the streamed video of Unit 2's progress as they followed Al Rashid, listening to the commentary for added flavour.

"This is not going well," muttered the controller to Laura. "This is the first time we're getting the run-around. Either we're blown or he's taking additional precautions because something's up. Do we stick with him?"

"Yes," replied Laura emphatically. "We must follow, if at all possible without making it overtly obvious, and hope he is simply taking precautionary measures because today is special. If it is, we really must not lose him."

"Unit 2, taking left into the High Street and the one-way system. Will follow."

"Unit 2, Alpha has circled the one-way system. Across roundabout, continuing on the High Street. Right, right, right into Harlington Road at speed. Unable to pursue."

"Damn, damn, damn," cursed the controller. "Potential exits again are limited, which is good for us, but I don't like this one bit. Units, take up positions on Fountain Street, Chartists Way, and motorway junctions. Unit 2, remain where you are and monitor Harlington Road. Report when in position."

To Laura, studying the map in front of her, Al Rashid had simply been going around in awkward circles, getting their units out of position and giving him maximum opportunity to either slip or spot a net if there was one. Why would he assume such tactics unless he either knew of the surveillance or wanted absolute certainty of not being followed?

A silent five minutes ticked to ten and then to thirty, and then eventually the controller turned to Laura. "We've lost him. He either slipped out of the net or has gone to ground within this area." He circled the Fountain Street, Chartists Way, High Street, and Britannia Road quadrant. "What do you want us to do?"

"Stand down for now, keeping roving teams around the area on the off chance. Alert the teams around the travel agency, although I suspect he will be a no-show," was her dejected reply. "Good effort, though, folks, thank you. He gave us a real run-around and hopefully still doesn't know we've been tracking him." With that, Laura stood and walked off to a quiet meeting room, grabbing a coffee on her way. She had to think.

Should she order a raid on Al Rashid's house? She could see who else was there, if anyone and find whatever information might be available to point them in the right direction. The thought was very tempting. There was, however, one potentially massive flaw that nagged at her instinct. If, as she suspected, Al Rashid's evasive actions indicated Khartoum was on the verge of a terror attack, then the house had no further purposes and had been abandoned. As an experienced operative, he would not leave anything incriminating behind. Therefore, nothing of use would turn up following a raid, and Al Rashid would potentially be tipped off and would take additional precautions, which they really did not want. The opposite would be preferable. No raid, then—at least not for now.

A few hours later, a technician monitoring the surveillance cameras popped his head round the door. "Thought you may like these," he said, placing a range of unappetising-looking sandwiches on her desk. "You'll need the sustenance. Also, Khalif hasn't returned from lunch. He usually takes just thirty minutes, but it's been ninety. What would you like us to do?"

Laura did not bother to smother her groan. She leaned back in her chair and rubbed both sides of her head with her hands. After a few moments of contemplation, she responded, "Have someone call in and ask for him to talk about some genuine-sounding travel plan that has supposedly been discussed with Khalif previously. I'd like to speak to whoever makes that call as soon as he or she has finished."

Laura sighed as she watched the retreating back of the young man who had come to break the news. The tension throughout the small office was palpable, and this latest twist did nothing to alleviate it.

Less than ten minutes later, the same young man knocked politely on her door and waited to be invited in. "Come on in and take a seat. What's up?"

"Well, I made the call you asked for. Thought it best that I did since we'd had the conversation." Laura smiled. She was warming to this unknown member of the team.

"I like your initiative. I'm sorry, I don't know your name."

"Talal Fara, and thank you. Not encouraging news, however. Mr Singh sounded a little frustrated, although he was trying to hide it. All he'd say was that Khalif has taken some holiday and will be back after Thursday, whatever that means."

"Oh great. Our leads are disappearing like flies in front of a waving hand, and we're nowhere nearer knowing what they're up to. Well, it appears that we have three days, and my hunch is either Wednesday or Thursday, most likely the Thursday, leaving today, tomorrow, and Wednesday for gathering and preparations. I'll speak to London. Thank you, and please let the team know how much I appreciate all your efforts."

Laura called Gurning and patched in Stu and Rob at the Leicester base to update them all on the morning's happenings. "In conclusion, Steven, my hunch is that whatever is intended will take place on Thursday unless we can stop it."

"I agree. Stu, any update from your side? I'll have Jill dig around to find out what, if anything, official may be happening over the coming few days. Stu?"

"Well, our trio appear to have been a little busier than usual, but nothing that would raise any alarms. The only matter of real interest has been that they've been visited by the same Range Rover five times now over the past week and a half. Other than that, there have been a couple of guys bringing different cars in on separate occasions. All went for the top-of-the-range valet, so they drove out of sight into the building and the one area where we weren't able to gain access ourselves to place a concealed camera. If you remember, we mentioned that area of the building is very well secured, and we didn't want to risk leaving any evidence of an encroachment and tip them off should they look for tell-tale signs."

"Yes, I remember," said Gurning, "and I still agree that your decision was the right one, even though I'd love to know what goes on inside that area. Anything else?"

"Yes, a couple of things. First, as we review footage of the cars going in for the 'the Extensive,' they generally leave either a lot lighter or are a lot heavier laden. That's not drugs or cash. And before you ask, getting a tail on them has failed. We tried, but they disappeared down circuitous side streets far too rapidly.

"Second, we have more evidence of the trio making exchanges in the toilets and visits to the hawala over the road. When they don't visit him, our presumption remains drugs, and we've been able to follow a couple of the couriers to drop-offs with known dealers throughout the Midlands. Unfortunately, we have not been able to follow those bringing the primary supply in, and that's a frustration. Hold on a tick, Abdul's waving."

A few moments later, Stu was back on line. "Two of the trio are on the phone. We can expect to be busy in the next few hours. Whether this is linked to the other matter we have running is impossible to say."

"Well we can certainly discount the drugs," said Laura.

"Unless they provide the funding," commented Gurning.

"True. More interesting would be to know what goes on behind those closed doors. It could, of course, merely be far larger consignments of drugs ready for splitting and the trio provide that service, but on the basis of the comments on car loadings, I suspect not. Steven, I think we are at the stage of having to act and find out. We need to either discount aspects from a possible terrorist link or disrupt it, potentially forcing Khartoum's hand so he may make a mistake and/or we will gain a useful lead."

"Agreed. Stu, make the arrangements for when a vehicle goes inside the building. If we learn nothing by close of the day, go in anyway before close, making sure you take the trio. Clear?"

"Crystal. Not a problem."

"Good. Ah, here comes Jill with what appears to be news." Everyone waited patiently whilst Steven scanned whatever she had brought in. "As always, there's a raft of high-level engagements and activities going on, not that their target has to be a particular activity. Jill has already sent a copy to you all by email. They could be focused on any number of power stations or other facility public, private, or even military, come to that. Laura, please establish what facilities could be a target within say a hundred-mile and a fifty-mile radius of Leeds, where Al Rashid appears to have made his base. I'll get the team down here to assess what could be going on in or around London in case they're using the Midlands simply for grouping purposes."

"Steven, if I may?"

"Of course, Rob. You're part of the team."

"Well I've scanned the list that Jill sent through on Stu's machine."

"Yeah, and oh boy does Rob go fast. I had to give up trying to keep pace with him!" interjected Stu.

"It's just that towards the bottom of the list for Thursday, there's a pharmaceutical conference in the Peak District with both a flag and a tentative against it. What does that mean?" Rob asked.

"Hmm. Interesting. I'll get Jill to pull up the details on computer."

Everyone could visualise Gurning waving a hand to Jill, as was his way, pointing the entry on the list out to her and waiting patiently as she tapped away on his computer for some more detail and then scurrying off on this latest errand to find out as much as she could.

"I agree with you, Rob. This is potentially interesting," Gurning commented, reading off the screen. "The tentative indicates that there is currently nothing requiring our specific attention, so it is of note only should we hear anything necessitating action. The flag appears to contradict the tentative notation because—and this is where we should have been informed and what could well be of interest now—our Minister for Business and Enterprise, along with many of her European counterparts, could be attending the conference. This is crazy. Two days to go and it's not confirmed what senior members of various governments are or are not doing! Jill! I want this prioritised!" Gurning called, ignoring or forgetting those on the phone and consequently nearly deafening them in the process.

"It appears that the CEOs and their COOs and heads of distribution from Europe's top pharmaceutical companies are meeting to discuss the increasing disruptions to the supplies of critical medicines across Europe. Incidences of serious illnesses and deaths have increased over the past month due to the apparent sabotage of the distribution channels for these medicines, and rightly, this is being taken very seriously. No wonder the various ministers may want to be present.

"Jill, I want to know why this conference was not explicitly flagged. It certainly meets all criteria!" he called again.

Everyone on the phone could clearly picture the scene as Steven became more engaged. "And I want to speak to the Minister immediately after this call ends. We require her intention to attend or not. She needs to be aware of the security implications of the Service not having been kept informed, for her sake and that of her counterparts. This is a travesty! Then I want the DG to speak to Sir Gus MacDonald as head of the Civil Service. He must make sure this never happens again.

"Right, Laura, pending the Minister's response, I still want you to focus on other possible targets, as discussed. Stu, you are to raid both the Leicester premises regardless. God help us if we are to secure a conference venue in just a couple of days!"

"Can it be postponed?" enquired Rob.

"Probably not, considering the topic. Blasted politicians—you'd have thought they'd learn or at least have someone appointed to babysit them properly! Ah, this is the Minister on the other line now. Chop to it, folks, and good luck. We'll speak later." With that, the line dropped.

Abdul and Rob returned to their surveillance, while Stu made arrangements for the raid upon minimal notice. He hated having to put people on standby without an explicit time to work to. The team could be waiting for hours, which could take the edge off their reactions. However, there was nothing for it sometimes.

Laura set to trying to identify other potential targets. By the time Gurning had everyone on the phone again a little over thirty minutes later, Laura had identified two, e-mailing Gurning accordingly. The first was a military research establishment in the Peak District and the other a research and development centre north of Birmingham and west of Nottingham supporting

GCHQ in Cheltenham. Both facilities should be totally anonymous and highly secure, as well as presenting attractive targets for terrorists.

"Interesting research on possible targets, Laura," Steven started. "Either could be a target. You'll need to assess both. As we speak, Jill is arranging for you to be expected at both. You'll have to figure how you will manage everything. Sorry, it's going to be a pressurised few days. Unfortunately, to add to the burden, we have a very sheepish Minister. Both she and her European counterparts will be at the pharmaceutical conference. She has no idea why it was presented as being tentative because her attendance has been scheduled as confirmed for weeks. To me this is either unacceptable incompetence or something more sinister—something deliberate. Whichever, it will have to wait until we have thwarted Khartoum again.

"I'm arranging for a team to secure the hotel as a matter of urgency and contact all attendees. The details are being sent to you all as well. You'll all have to find as well as follow the leads necessary to narrow the field to a single target."

"Steven, I appreciate that a witch hunt within the Ministry would distract and take time, but if it was deliberate that we didn't hear about the conference, wouldn't that be a strong indicator of where our attention should be focused?"

"A fair comment, Stu, but there is deliberate and deliberate. There's deliberate to avoid fuss and aggravation on top of a heavy workload, which sadly does happen all too frequently. Then there's deliberate to place a person or persons at risk, which would suggest a mole and a wider conspiracy to hit at the heart of Europe's governments and in this case, if true, to also adversely affect the European health system. Otherwise why target this conference, unless it was simply identified as a soft target, which as of now it is?! No, I don't want to discount options too early in case this is just another instance of lazy deliberate. And if it is a sinister deliberate, then any investigation would take far more time than we've got. Anyway, how are things looking at your end?"

"All quiet at present. The team is on standby to raid at a moment's notice. Quite frankly, the sooner the better for the chaps. They're getting restless. You know how it is. But I do want to wait to see if either of the calls received by the trio requires the enhanced valet service, the Extensive, before pressing the button."

"Okay. That seems sensible. I'll leave you guys to it. Laura, if you leave now, you should be able to assess the military establishment today. Rob, welcome to the deep end of our work. Exciting, but the ramifications are immense. They also cannot be discussed with anyone other than those already in the know, not even trusted friends who are on our side, such as Michael. We're all reminded of this regularly, so don't worry, the reminder is not a reflection on you. Keep in touch one and all. Good luck, and safe endeavours."

Despite Steven's assurances, Rob did wonder if he could read minds. Had Michael mentioned that Rob suggested they get together for a drink a couple of weeks back? Oh man, what a life! But time to contemplate that life was cut very short; Stu was tapping him on the shoulder.

When Rob looked out across the street, he saw that the trio were looking agitated and no wonder. A standard delivery or pickup car had just arrived and was parked outside for a more basic wash. Meanwhile, a Ford people carrier had pulled in and positioned itself in front of the roller-shutter door reserved for the enhanced valet, and Stu was barking orders into his radio to mobilise everyone and initiate the raid. Rob would accompany Stu, who did not want anyone to be left alone.

16

Upon Stu's orders, two matte black armoured vans with POLICE emblazoned across the sides and front travelled rapidly and silently up Belgrave Road from their holding position and came to a halt, one each at the entrance and exit to the carwash. Police cars both followed and came from all other directions to cordon off the vicinity, blocking the side roads and running tape across pavements to keep innocent bystanders away from the activities at the carwash and money exchange. More police officers from accompanying standard police vans entered the shops in the cordoned-off area, requesting people to remain inside and apologising for the inconvenience.

The rear doors of the armoured vans swung open as soon as the vans were stationary, and armed police, in their dark-blue padded uniforms, flak jackets, and helmets, stormed out. Four approached the money exchange. The two at the front door waited for the signal that the other two were ready at the back door. The others focused upon the carwash forecourt and building, with a team charging around both sides to cover the rear.

A small group of the armed officers quickly entered the waiting area inside the building and following a confirmatory check of each person there, guided them outside to a waiting van in the side street. A further group of officers stormed the toilet area to apprehend the one member of the trio who had entered the area behind the suspected drugs or money courier. As they burst in, the courier, with head bowed, was in the process of checking the contents of the plastic shopping bags handed to him for stuffing into his own large brown holdall. Immediately the trio member shoved the courier hard in his chest, sending him sprawling into the oncoming police officers, a flurry of bank notes flying into the air as a result.

The trio member raced in the opposite direction, flinging yet another bag at the officers, covering them in a white powder that would later test positive for heroin, making the officers grateful for their masks, which protected them from inhaling the stuff. Having lost ground, all but one of the officers set off in pursuit, seeking the exit taken by their quarry. One remained behind to apprehend the courier.

Meanwhile, Stu, Abdul, and Rob had entered the waiting room and looked around the spacious area. Whilst not designed for comfort, it was certainly pleasant enough, with a reasonable-sized confectionary and car parts and accessories shop off to one side. Two televisions, one with the BBC News Channel and the other with a cartoon network, were placed high on the wall in opposite corners. As they looked about themselves, a burst of gunfire sent them scurrying into the shop area for cover.

The rest of the armed officers had tackled the enclosed valet area. Two stood guard outside the vehicular entrance, having earlier decided that access that way would be futile because it would take too long and permit the targets to escape via some other route. Instead, they forced a way through the heavy, well-secured internal side door they had been unwilling to force to install some concealed cameras. The inevitable noise alerted those inside, giving the other two members of the trio sufficient time to arm themselves and dive behind various crates at the rear of the oversized garage.

The driver of the Ford people carrier, on the other hand, decided to jump into the driver's seat and start the engine. The boot was still wide open and the rear seats were down, with a couple of long cases still sticking out of the rear. Moments later, he rammed the car into the closed doors and reversed once more, slamming into mobile equipment racks near the rear of the garage, sending them spinning in all directions and spilling their contents over the floor. Accelerating forwards once more, the car managed to crash through the doors, debris from the frame and surrounding brickwork flying in the wake of his attempted escape.

A few well-placed shots into the tyres from the two police officers outside, coupled with the blocked access routes by the police vans, put paid to the driver's escape. Moments later, staring up the barrel of a sub-machine gun, the driver was hauled roughly from the car and virtually hurled onto the ground before being cuffed and led away.

The gun battle inside the garage had settled down to periodic exchange of fire as the officers repeatedly called out the standard warnings of, "Armed police, you are surrounded. Lay down your weapons, come out with your hands above your heads, and lie down on the floor."

In response, the two members of the trio squeezed off a few more rounds from behind the steel crates where they had based themselves. Following a radio exchange with Stu laying out the scene and situation, the officers were advised to secure the area and position themselves safely to establish a siege to minimise gunfire and avoid unwanted injury. The objective was to take these two alive. They were too important and could hopefully provide useful information to understand what Khartoum was planning, when, and where.

The team following the other member of the trio pursued him through a doorway, along a narrow corridor, and up some open-sided timber stairs that were not shown on the building's floor plans, leading up to a mezzanine floor. The man had produced a handgun from his clothing and sent a couple of wild shots slamming into the concrete block walls. The police followed cautiously, crouching low as they emerged on the mezzanine floor, just in time to see the man, now accompanied by two others and all gripping larger firearms taken from the lockers lined up along one side of the otherwise open but cluttered space, exiting through a hatch in a side wall and firing wildly over their shoulders. The other few occupants, some screaming in alarm at the gunshots and apparently workers of some sort, went scrambling for cover behind benches and chairs.

As the officers shouted at these folks to stay down, they made their way across the floor to the hatch. Suddenly three shots rang out. Two of the four officers fell to the floor, one unmoving. The other, groaning loudly in pain, rolled away from his position, seeking any sort of cover. The remaining officers flung themselves aside, rolling to end up in a crouched position from where they both fired well-placed rounds to the head and chest of the new gunman, killing him outright.

Whilst covering the other people to avoid further ambush and keeping a wary eye on the hatch through which the others had escaped, one of the two officers radioed Stu.

"Urgent assistance required on the mezzanine! Two officers down, one in need of medical attention. Guarding five unknowns with a further assailant dead. Trio target plus two others at large, escaped towards rear of building in the roof area."

As he spoke, the other unwounded officer shuffled in a crouched position over to his fallen colleagues, keeping his gun levelled and pointed towards the remaining men. After confirming that the first colleague was dead by checking for signs of a pulse at the neck, he continued his shuffle over to the other to rest a hand on his arm.

"Hang in there, mate. Help's on the way. We downed the bugger that got you."

"Heard," responded Stu. Then to the others in the garage he said, "Need the team split. Half maintain position and secure the siege status to keep the trio two in place. Expect them to test resolve as they see forces leave. All others are to assist downed officers upstairs. Go!"

A group of four broke away from the garage and headed cautiously to the mezzanine. Stu and Abdul readied their own weapons and hailed the two officers from outside to support them now that the Ford driver was firmly in custody.

Minutes ticked by as near silence fell across the building and the group of four edged their way to support their colleagues, checking that the end of the corridor was secure before climbing the stairs.

Across the road at the money exchange, the four officers entered the building, two from the rear and two from the front. As expected, the business manager and hawala were both present, chatting to each other from across the room. Their eyes opened wide at the sight of the armed police. A rapid glance around the shop, which also acted as a card store and stationers to attract a greater flow of business, confirmed the pre-raid reports that no one else was present, at least at ground level. Giving no resistance, the two elderly men accompanied one of the officers outside for a quick search before joining the others who had been safely evacuated from the carwash.

The remaining three officers rapidly went from room to room, first covering the remainder of the ground floor and then slowly mounting the stairs. They eased the first of the closed doors off the landing open, senses on high alert following the initial burst of gunfire they heard moments earlier from across the street. Gradually, thoroughly, they worked through the upstairs flat, not letting their guard down one iota as regular reminders of the unexpected dangers of raids were heard from across the way as sporadic gunfire continued to rattle out. Finally, they eased the hatch open that led to the roof space, wary from the signs of regular use. Using a ladder propped up against the wall, the first of the officers mounted the

343

steps. The flashlight atop his weapon illuminated the space, beams of light slicing through the darkness, seeking out any potential threat. His relief was evident from the tone of his voice as he announced, "All clear. The space is empty, but there's an opening between buildings that leads all the way along the terrace."

A few minutes later, he and his colleagues emerged at the far end back at street level, having followed and cleared all of the roof spaces and the presumed route taken by those who had not been observed re-emerging from the shop. Having cleared that space, the four officers jogged briskly back towards the carwash to support their under-fire colleagues, who were facing far greater challenges.

———◄———

The team of four reinforcements emerged on the mezzanine to take over from their colleagues. Three stayed behind whilst one accompanied his colleagues back out of the building, covering them as they carried the wounded officer away from the building and to a waiting ambulance.

As they finished up there, they combined forces with the four coming back up the street. The team leader agreed with them that they would enter the hatch to try and flush out the missing member of the trio and his two unidentified companions. Those officers laying siege to the two trio members holed up in the garage appeared to be secure, as were the three guarding the scared car valets up on the mezzanine.

Re-opening the hatch, they went in, surprised by the amount of light pouring in through the roof lights. In pairs they worked their way along the series of narrow metal walkways covering the remainder of the roof void. Try as they might, they couldn't stop the loose metal sheets from clanking with every step, preventing any chance of stealth. As they peered around the corner of the wall to the mezzanine floor locker and break room, a single shot twanged off a steel roof truss beside one officer's head. The other officers all dived onto their stomachs, craning their necks to try and spy their quarry and identify where the threat came from.

Suddenly there was a deafening boom from an explosion, the noise reverberating throughout the building. Clouds of billowing grey-white smoke rapidly filled the space as dust and other debris from the roof filled the air, disorienting the officers. The lingering ringing in the officers' ears partially disguised the cracking and crunching sound of smashed masonry, wood, and plasterboard. The rapid-fire radio conversation that ensued confirmed that no one could determine the direction from which the sound came. With such poor visibility, it was going to be slow work worming their way back along the narrow walkways on which they found themselves.

Stu, Abdul, Rob, and the two armed officers with them looked around in horror at what sounded like an explosion above their heads, instinctively ducking as ceiling tiles and debris poured down upon them. They were startled to find that amongst the debris, the one trio member and his two new colleagues had dropped through the ceiling, landing nimbly on their feet, spraying bullets all around. Abdul and the two armed officers fell, wounded, taking a number of bullets in their arms and legs.

Rob and Stu rolled for cover, Stu opening fire. One of the injured armed officers, who had been chatting to Rob, shoved his weapon over to Rob, grunting in pain with the effort.

—◆—

A second explosion, coming from the garage, rocked the building as the three men dropped in from the ceiling. This second blast had blown a hole through the outer wall of the building. The previously trapped two of the trio sent a hail of bullets throughout the garage as they fled the space and ran down the side street away from Belgrave Road. As they raced past the rear of the building, the second man was hit firmly in the belly with the butt of a police officer's firearm who had been guarding the rear for just such an eventuality. He doubled over in agony, breathless and unable to move. The leading runner swung around, spraying bullets as he did so, but another officer, who had also been covering the rear, dropped him with two well-placed bullets to the chest. The writhing trio member on the ground was rapidly disarmed, searched, and cuffed by the officers, who had followed their targets out through the mangled side of the building.

◄►

Stu and Rob found themselves separated at opposite ends of the car accessories shop, heads down, peering around themselves. Stu waved to Rob that the three hostiles were in front of them and two aisles away. A spanner clattered across the floor as Stu and the remaining trio member exchanged fire.

Rob ran crouching to the next aisle and came face to face with the other two hostiles, who had closed the distance unknown to Stu and Rob. In surprise, they swung their weapons up to fire at Rob, who first flung the firearm he was holding at their faces and then dropped backwards onto his hands and kicked up at their faces.

Startled by this unexpected tactic, the two men staggered backwards to avoid being hit. One dropped his gun as he stumbled on some screwdrivers and other tools spread across the floor. The other tried to squeeze off some shots at Rob but was left frustrated as his weapon jammed. Both grabbed at some stainless steel exhaust tubing from a nearby rack as new weapons more suited for close-up combat. Flipping himself upright as though a gymnast, Rob soon found himself between them, ducking to avoid the first few manic onslaughts of swinging pipe, which clanged loudly on the metal shelving as each missed Rob's head.

A further exchange of fire rang out as Rob heard messages in his earpiece that informed everyone that of the trio members from the garage one was dead and the other apprehended. At the same time, Stu was calling for assistance.

There were tense moments as the two on either side of Rob squared up for the next assault, waving their respective pipes in the air to look menacing. Reading the moves correctly, as drummed into his reflexes during his training, Rob ducked, grabbed a piece of cloth from a shelf and used it to dampen the incoming swing from one of the pipes. Wrapping the cloth around the pipe, Rob twisted sharply, sending the pipe flying from the attacker's hand and clattering onto the concrete floor a few metres away, out of harm's way. Totally surprised, the man stumbled forwards and off-balance from Rob's move. He immediately received a well-placed kick to the solar plexus, sending him crashing into some shelving before slumping to the floor with loose items from the shelves raining down on top of him.

Yet another exchange of gunfire followed, and Stu's voice rang out loud above the heavy breathing of the two close-quarters combatants. "Assailant down!"

Whilst not used to fighting people with steel piping, Rob was in his element, so not to be left out, he in turn yelled, "One down, one soon to follow!"

He grinned and took up his standard fighting position before launching a series of wicked and rapid kicks at his opponent, who quickly saw sense, dropped the pipe, and held his hands up in submission whilst kneeling on the floor, just as Stu came around the corner, gun up and levelled, ready for action.

He quickly took the situation in, cuffed the kneeling man, and then followed up with cuffing the other, who was still curled up in agony from Rob's kick.

As he pulled them up, ready to be led from the building, Stu added with a broad grin, "Laura said you were useful in a scrap. I wish I had seen the action for real. I've watched a few of your championship bouts on *YouTube* over the last couple of days and they were impressive, but I suspect the real thing is something to behold. Well done!" he said, clapping Rob on the back. "I think we're done."

Then, picking up his radio, Stu called for urgent assistance for Abdul and the two officers, one of whom, despite the pain, commented to Stu, "I did see the action, and boy, it gave me some real pleasure!"

As they walked out into the sunlight, Stu turned to Rob. "Great work, Rob. A real pleasure. This was a tough one. I want to follow Abdul and the chaps to hospital to check up on them. However, you still have some work to do. Let me introduce you to the local Community Police Officers as they'll take you to the holding area for all those who've been working here and as far as we can tell are legitimate. These people know the CPOs, whereas we need to retain anonymity. They will introduce you so you can explain whatever it is you need to about what's been going on, the transfer of ownership, and their allegiance. Good luck."

"Thanks, Stu. I've learnt lots." With that, Stu made the introductions and left.

◆

An hour and a half later, Rob felt exhausted. The adrenalin from the operation had worn off, and for the past sixty minutes, he had been chatting with the impacted people from both businesses in a rapidly commandeered hall nearby, where he had to depend upon his wits, his best influencing skills, and blending a carefully balanced combination of charm, reasonableness, and firmness.

Initially he had addressed everyone, saying that the previous owner of the buildings was also part owner of their businesses. This, he explained, had been achieved through a network of offshore companies so that it was not clear the same person was involved. That person was now in police custody for criminality, and all assets, including the buildings and the part ownership of their businesses, had been transferred to Rob's new company, Zouches. This was because that same individual was a much-wanted international criminal who had abused his position to funnel criminal activities through their businesses.

This represented a new approach by the government, introduced by Rob, to support those impacted by crime through no fault of their own. The objective was to keep businesses running and people employed. It would be Rob's job, together with his team, to support their businesses going forward, to help re-build where necessary, and to assist developing new business to replace any that was lost as a result of closing down the criminal elements.

He emphasised that he was totally independent of the government, and therefore, so were they. That was why there were no government representatives at these meetings and why the Community Police Officers had left after making the introductions. Their presence at the start was simply to provide an assurance that Rob was legitimate. This arrangement had only become possible because of his involvement in bringing the mastermind behind the initial criminal enterprise to justice.

Following that, he had met with the two business owners and the hawala to reiterate his support for legitimate enterprise and that they were not currently under suspicion. He explained that there would have to be the inevitable checks to confirm this presumption and he hoped they would understand. Only then could the police, other agencies, plus Rob and his team support them and vouch for their integrity, helping to rebuild reputations that very possibly would have been tarnished purely by association with criminal activity. After that, they would not see any interference from the police or the government. These institutions respected that communities throughout the country did not want interference. His firm, likewise, would not interfere. They would merely take an active interest in how their business was progressing and assist when appropriate. They, the people in front of him now, were responsible for running their businesses.

During that second part of the discussions, as confidence in Rob grew, all three mentioned their unease at the involvement of the trio and the other three men who had been previously unidentified by the surveillance. Their attitudes had been threatening, but the owner's representative had introduced these men and required their employment within the carwash business. He had also insisted upon cooperation by the money exchange and hawala as part of the deal to provide the initial start-up investment and accommodate their respective businesses. This representative, they explained, held a lot of influence over them because he had a Power of Attorney to sign documents, collect a share of the profits, and provide additional investment or not, as well as introduce new business or not.

Rob referred to the arrangements each had with respect to the profit sharing and cooperation drawn up as part of that initial investment. As far as Rob was concerned, the type of cooperation that had been required previously was history. The only cooperation he expected was in terms of sharing relevant information on the health and progress of the businesses and agreeing on a business plan for them to work towards into the future. Update meetings or board meetings could be held either at the premises or at a hotel in central Leicester. The choice was theirs.

All he wanted from them at this stage was two things. First, he wanted them to agree when they would meet again and discuss taking the businesses forward. Second, he wanted a copy of the Power of Attorney they had mentioned. Both were promised.

Later that evening and at last in the comfort of a decent hotel after a healthy dinner and a glass of wine, Rob updated Gurning and Laura. As he finished, he assured Gurning that as soon as he had copies of the Power of Attorney, he would send them through for further investigation.

17

As the raid on the Leicester premises had unfolded, Laura was in her car heading south to the first of her destinations: the military research establishment in the Peak District. She had listened anxiously to the escalating events in Leicester, desperately wanting to be where the action was, providing whatever support she could to those engaged in the operation. She felt partially responsible, so not being there was odd. She was also acutely aware that she was too far away, had a vital task to perform, and quite possibly would simply get in the way.

Likewise, she also knew she should not try to make contact with any of her direct colleagues—Stu and Abdul or even Rob—to check on their safety, however desperately she wanted to. They would be far too busy to take a call, particularly if the reports of gunfire were correct.

Late in the afternoon, having at last relaxed sufficiently to enjoy the drive through some beautiful parts of the Peak District, Laura slowed down as she meandered along a narrow, twisty, one-way lane. The directions, which she had been required to commit to memory, had provided that after the seventh corner there would be a very narrow, obscure turn to the right. The appearance was one of a passing point, which for a one-way lane was not required. She was to pull in at that point and then reverse a car length to the next hedge, at which point a further opening would become obvious. She was to then drive slowly along that new lane, ready to stop at any time when challenged. She should expect up to five checkpoints before reaching the security gate and fence. At the gatehouse she was to ask for General Marshall-Jones, who was expecting her but did not know the reason for the visit.

Following the directions explicitly, she found the way—just. She marvelled at the cunning simplicity of the disguised lane as she drove along slowly and was challenged just once, although she did see the other checkpoints because they made their presence known. If it hadn't been for that, there was no way she would have spotted them. She was clearly expected.

Whatever it is that goes on here, not only is it well guarded, but by association, it must be an attractive target, assuming it has been identified in the first place, she thought as she arrived at the gatehouse. But for her trained eye, it appeared to be an averagely maintained cottage in the middle of nowhere; however, she identified some serious firepower at various concealed places in the walls. Ten minutes later, she arrived at the main house, accompanied by an armed escort wearing civilian clothes, driving a Range Rover. The mansion was breathtaking, a perfect hideaway for the wealthy with its immaculately manicured lawns.

Another armed escort, again in casual clothes, materialised at the front door as the Range Rover returned from whence it came. "Ma'am, please follow me. The general is expecting you."

As Laura obediently followed, she tried not to gawk at the magnificence of the place, feeling completely underdressed for such stunning surroundings, with a grand staircase leading from a large, stone-floored entrance hall with portraits of various people hanging throughout. As she looked about her, she did spot some CCTV and movement sensors and was sure there were more she had not seen. Laura was shown into a library and waved to a set of chairs and sofas. "Please take a seat. The general will be with you shortly. Would you like a tea or coffee?"

"Just some water, thank you."

The escort produced some bottled water from a sideboard with a small fridge inside, placed the tray in front of Laura, and left.

"Miss Grahams, I presume?" came a commanding voice from behind her. She turned to find that a powerfully built man in his late fifties had materialised silently through the wall. *Presumably there is a secret door somewhere in the wood panelling,* Laura thought to herself.

"And no doubt a cover name for a lady in your line of work," he said, smiling. "I'm General Marshall-Jones. Pleased to meet you, on the basis that I have to. Please, do sit. I can't say I'm at all happy to meet you. I'm surprised your organisation even knows about the place."

The general was smartly dressed, with a dark blue roll-neck shirt, trousers, and blazer. His comportment and presence were such that one's attention was immediately grabbed. Laura had met many powerful and commanding people in her time, but this was different. The general was the real thing.

"We didn't, not even the DG. It required some digging," Laura said, refocusing herself so as not to be overawed.

"Ah, then you'd better explain just why you were digging, my dear, and how your digging identified this facility," the general said in a kind yet demanding manner. "As you may imagine, I am not best pleased that outsiders are able to find out about our existence, let alone our location."

"Well we're extremely confident there's going to be some sort of terrorist incident within the next few days, quite possibly Thursday, somewhere in this region. However, we have no pointers yet on what or where the target may be. One of the key suspects was able to give us the slip earlier today, and we have raided a facility in Leicester this afternoon. You'll hear about it on the news, if not already, because there was gunfire and some explosions."

"Hmm, yes. It has been flashing across all the newswires imaginable. Caused quite a stir by all accounts."

"No surprise there, then. Well, to answer your question, at least in part, our systems are designed to perform deep searches under specific circumstances. However confidential the matter, it will be registered in the system but only accessible under certain circumstances and provided that appropriate authorities are obtained. Your facility was located following one such search and was identified as one of the possible three targets. My purpose today is simply to meet with you and assess first your security and second the likelihood of your facility being the target. May I ask what happens here? That was not recorded on our system."

"Delighted to hear that no one can simply dial us up, and sorry, no, I'm hardly going to enlighten you with any detail, merely a smidgen to whet the appetite, so to speak, as I'm sure you'll get the same from other sources. What we do here is not done in the house; my ancestors would turn in their graves. Yes, this is my ancestral home. Nor would our business be visible from the sky. From that I'm sure you can figure something out, what!" The general guffawed at his little witticism.

"For all intents and purposes, I'm some oddball former military buffoon living out my years in my ancestral home, previously left to decay somewhat, but I came into the money and did it up. There is the formal driveway that I use, but I have left it unmaintained to actively discourage curious visitors. Clearly, to maintain some sense of life, I do have the odd visitor and even have opened the house and gardens for the village fête. I also do take the occasional trip into the village at the end of the drive to show myself and spend a little money, but that's about it.

"When I had to take on a desk job, I pressed for one of my specialties to be taken more seriously. Got nowhere initially, what! But by gum, it wasn't for the sake of trying! However, after some of our more recent international engagements kicked off, the armed forces asked me to research my ideas. As it became clear that I had indeed hit upon something, we needed somewhere secret to develop the idea. I suggested this place. The rest is history, as the saying goes. There are no relatives for me to leave the place to, so I'll form some sort of trust to maintain the balance of stay away, you're not welcome unless invited, with being semi-amenable to the locals, whilst ensuring the highest level of security to continue with the on-site activities.

"If you'll allow me," the general said, standing up suddenly. Laura got that sinking feeling that she was about to be dismissed and would have to kick up a stink. "If you follow me, I'll show you my security audit room. I developed it for military audit purposes, so the arrangements can be checked without giving anything away about the place. We don't want some bureaucratic auditor spilling the beans now, do we? That should hopefully give you a sense of comfort."

I already have it, thought Laura.

"That said, I will raise the alert status until the weekend. It'll be a good exercise for the chaps, what! But I would appreciate a call when the threat has passed."

"Not a problem. Of course I will."

"Oh, and Miss Grahams, I presume you will require somewhere to spend the night. You're very welcome to use one of the guest rooms and save the Services some money. You'll bump into all sorts of others here, even over dinner and breakfast, but please respect the code of this place. Conversations are actively discouraged."

"A room would be wonderful, thank you. I haven't even had the chance to think about sleep, let alone food. Presumably I can make calls from my room?"

"Absolutely. You'll find it far better equipped than most hotels. All recorded, of course, so make sure you don't say anything you don't want overheard"

An hour later, following a very engaging explanation and question-and-answer session on the facility's security, Laura found herself in a luxurious suite with fabulous views over the grounds. She put in a quick call to Gurning to update him, giving him her instinctive assessment.

"In conclusion, Steven, this facility would be an excellent target, disrupting our research into our next-generation attack and defence capabilities, all of which are of a technological nature that many parties, including terrorists, would love to get their hands on, if they knew about it, which is doubtful.

"Apparently, in the hands of any other organisation, Britain would be at great risk. That aside, a successful attack on this place would also be a tremendous coup, as well as providing a huge propaganda opportunity. However, unless there has been a leak and serious breach of security, it is unlikely to have been identified. Also, if it is the target, they'll be more than able to look after themselves. Therefore, my recommendation is to consider this a target but focus our efforts elsewhere until such a time, if it comes to it, that all other options are discounted.

"I also somehow suspect that the general would not be at all enthused by the idea of having an additional layer of security foisted upon him for three simple reasons. First, the security here is the best I've ever come across, and second, the number of people becoming familiar with the place would in itself be a weakening of security in his eyes. Third, a greater presence would undoubtedly draw more attention to the place, detracting from the anonymity that is currently enjoyed."

"For now I'm happy to go along with your logic and recommendation, but I will want to reconsider the position after your assessment of the next possible target tomorrow," Gurning replied with a sigh. "Have a good night's rest; you'll need all your energy for the next few days."

18

First thing the next day, Rob joined Stu at the carwash with some more members of Stu's team.

"Okay, folks, listen up," Stu called over the chitchat, seeking silence and attention. "Clearly we are going to focus on the garage after the guns that were found in the Ford people carrier and the explosives those guys used to blow their way out through the wall. However," he emphasised, "I'll repeat, however, we need to go through the whole place with a fine-tooth comb. Remember, weapons were taken from the lockers upstairs, and there could well be other locations used to store or even split up their merchandise. We must not lose sight of the initial brief indicating that there is a concealed room in the roof for the drugs. Any questions?"

After a moment of silence, Stu finished up with, "You've got your pre-assigned teams, so let's do it."

The teams of men dispersed for their assignments, leaving Stu and Rob to wander around separately checking on progress. The long packages from the Ford had been taken away the evening before for security reasons after they had revealed two sniper rifles, complete with a substantial amount of munitions, not only for the two rifles. That find had created an air of expectation for the teams.

Rob watched on from the side-lines as two teams in the garage started unpacking many more boxes of munitions of various sizes and types and then started carrying the contents to armoured vans, ready to whisk the items away for further examination. Seeing Rob's interest, Stu walked over to explain.

"We will take the finds to a secure facility ready for tests prior to subsequent disposal. We really hope something will indicate the source of this stuff. Often the manufacturing process will leave little hints for us to follow, provide a trace to an initially legitimate-sounding purchase that ultimately was a cover. Alternatively, we may find that it was siphoned off from a larger consignment. Knowing this detail could help trace the financiers, the locations, and even those involved."

"Stu, over here," a man called, waving. "We've got explosives here, with components for timers and some grenades."

Rob wandered off, not entirely comfortable with his proximity to so much destructive power. Walking across the otherwise-deserted mezzanine floor, he received an enormous fright, jumping back in surprise and shock as the scattered, overturned chairs and small tables also bounced on the slightly bouncy vinyl-covered wooden floor. As he had been walking past the row of lockers, one section just in front of him toppled over with a huge crash, sending a cloud of dust up into the air. A couple of heads materialised from a concealed opening where the lockers had stood. Half-laughing at Rob's expression and half looking rather sheepish, two officers emerged to apologise at the shock created.

"Sorry about that, although your expression was priceless, well worth the racket! Well at least we now know where they split and diluted the drug consignments. A veritable factory in there," he continued whilst signalling behind him with his thumb. "This was a massive operation."

Moments later Stu was at Rob's shoulder, breathing deeply from his sprint to find out what the noise had been all about. "No more of that please!" he barked. "We're not sure yet that all of the explosives downstairs are stable!"

"Come on, guv," one of the men replied, "the whole place would have gone up ages ago if anything was unstable."

"Yeah, yeah, okay," Stu conceded. "Just be careful, okay. So what's up?"

"Come have a look. If we find any CCTV, I want a copy of Rob's expression and reaction. Guv, you should 'ave seen him."

"Okay, okay, now budge over and let's have a look."

They all squeezed through the narrow opening into what appeared to be a dead-end corridor the length of the mezzanine floor room. It was fitted out with a full-length smooth vinyl worktop, a number of chairs, scales, and other drug paraphernalia. Everything was rudimentary but perfectly functional. There was a stockpile of various drugs at one end, and at the halfway point, there were various powders all neatly labelled and ready to mix with and dilute the stocks of drugs of far higher purity that the trio had accumulated. Incongruously and wholly unexpected, at the far end were a number of piles of gold in a variety of forms. There were rings, ear studs, and a surprisingly large pile of shavings. Next to the gold were some more scales and various items for melting the gold, ready to pour into the moulds all neatly lined up against the wall.

Stu whistled a few expletives before ordering, "Right lads, let's have loads of photos, and then bag and label all this up. Then keep on searching. Oh, and guys, good job."

By lunchtime the search was over, so the forensics folks could have the place to themselves. Rob surveyed the haul of weapons, explosives, drugs, gold and an odd assortment of other items found in the packing crates at the rear of the garage, amongst which were garden forks and spades, golf balls, and colourful back sacks. The team milled around, joking about the assortment of items as Stu checked the inventory before clearing everything to be removed.

At the same time as the Leicester team were busy with their searches, the London team were drinking coffee and drawing lots on which regular Borzi customers would turn up that day and who they should follow. After the first few tails, to break the monotony of an otherwise straightforward surveillance op, the team soon realised that many of the regular visitors had something to hide and were building quite an extensive dossier for further examination by other agencies. However, they could not follow everyone at the same time.

"Ah, the young, smart, nervous chap is back," said Keith, not taking his eye from the camera. "Take a look. He appears more apprehensive than usual today."

"Agreed," came Alan's reply not long afterwards. "As the saying goes, 'First come, first served.' Let's follow him. Not quite 08:00 hours. It'd be interesting to see where he works and if any of Borzi's ladies are there, or at least find out the connection. This chap's been here, what, six times now?"

"Five," Keith corrected, looking at his list. "Surely this guy is too young for anything significant, and whilst presentable, the cloth is certainly not of the quality worn by many of the others and neither does this chap have the same swagger. Why not wait for another?"

"That's what makes him interesting. I've a hunch. Contact reference will be Delta." And that was that; they had their target for the day.

Ten minutes later the young man re-emerged and walked directly to Finsbury Park underground station, with Wes easily keeping up with his long-legged, casual strides. Taking the first southbound Victoria line train towards central London, along with many hundreds of other commuters, Wes had to join Delta in the same compartment just to keep him in sight. *Far from ideal*, Wes thought to himself as Delta looked around at his fellow travellers, eventually letting his attention settle on an attractive young woman sitting not far from him. He got out at Green Park. Delta then headed north into Belgrave Square and up the west side of the square. Shortly afterwards Wes called in for support.

"Control, I need support with this tail. Delta has walked right around Belgrave Square and is now heading back south out of the square. This is not going to be easy. He eyeballed everyone in his carriage, so he could well spot me."

"Onto it," responded the team's controller.

"Thanks. Now cutting through an alleyway beside the Holiday Inn towards Dover Street. I'm exposed, too few other people around." A few minutes later, Wes called again. "Back on Piccadilly heading west. Went east on Stafford Street and south on Old Bond Street. Now heading into Green Park."

"Okay, Wes, stand down, but hold position to monitor progress from a distance, just to make sure Delta does not cut back again. Others can pick him up at the other exits to the park."

"Control, I've got a visual. He's approaching the Mall," came an announcement a few minutes later.

"Okay, Marjorie, Delta is yours."

"Thanks. Delta has sat down on a bench and is making a poor show of reading a paper whilst looking around at all the people. Good job Wes held back. I'll need to pass on to Paul. This guy is clearly agitated and concerned about possible tails or is looking out for a meet."

Five minutes later, Paul reported in. "Delta is on the move, heading into St James Park."

"I'm on Birdcage Walk and will pick-up."

"Thanks, Marjorie," responded the controller.

"Have visual again. Delta looking around. Heading east and has cut through to Old Queen Street heading towards Storey's Gate. Damn it, he's turned into Matthew Parker Street. I'll be blown soon."

"Okay, drop back or go into a building. Paul, pick him up on Tothill Street please."

A few tense minutes of not knowing ticked past before Paul's radio burst into life once more. "I have a visual on Delta, heading towards Victoria Street. He's slowed down. Blast it, he's legging it and has crossed Victoria Street on amber. Lots of horn blowing—the idiot could have got run over!"

"Suggests he made you, though," commented the controller unhelpfully. "I'll flood the surrounding streets with cars to try and locate him before he goes to ground."

"He's heading down Great Smith Street, crossing as though towards the DTI or the Department for Business or whatever blasted name the politicians have given it nowadays, and has gone round to the rear but can't see if he's entering or passing it by."

"Okay, keep walking the streets. You may come up lucky. Stranger things have been known."

◆

The London controller called Laura, informing her that they had lost a target, code named Delta, in the Westminster and Victoria area and that they would keep people in the vicinity throughout the day and evening rush hour, as well as staking out all surrounding underground stations.

"Do you have any idea what Borzi and this guy were talking about?" she asked.

"None at all at this stage," came the reply. "The warrants have not come through yet to bug the place."

"Blast! Get a message to Steven and ask for his help to expedite matters. Sounds as if we really need to know. People don't do a runner unless something is up." Then, with a sigh, she said, "okay, well keep me informed how it goes today, but sadly I suspect you won't get very far. Speak to you later." With that, Laura disconnected and refocused on the road ahead.

19

Laura had reluctantly left the grand surroundings of General Marshall-Jones's home. Her room had been exquisite. The bed had enveloped her in silken, soft luxury, giving her the best night's sleep for ages. She had ambled about the room in the extra-long T-shirt that she wore at night, feeling that her attire was totally out of place for her unexpected surroundings while trying to soak up every aspect of the place. For once, she had not rushed to check e-mails, whether personal or work, and neither did she check for any text messages on her phone.

Instead, she spent quite a few relaxing minutes sitting at the dressing table preparing for the day and looked out across the open countryside through the windows. The day that dawned was a perfect British autumnal one, although it was still only late summer. She enjoyed the clear blue skies, the early dew from the snap cold spell twinkling on the lawn in front of the house, and the last of the morning mist rising through the trees and dissipating over the fields as the temperature gradually rose.

There was no sign of the general when she left, merely the note that was handed to her at breakfast thanking her for the visit and asking to be kept informed. The note also reminded her of the checkpoints that she might encounter as she drove down the lane and that he really did not want many people to hear of his home.

With that, Laura climbed into her car and set off on the journey south towards the GCHQ research and development facility. The tranquillity she felt remained as she drove through the Peak District but soon evaporated as she passed through the more urban environments of Sheffield's suburbs. By the time the London controller's call came through, she felt as though all of the benefit gained at the general's house had well and truly gone, but she would still be able to picture the place in her mind's eye and dream.

The facility was not hard to find. It was a little to the south of the Peak District north of Birmingham and almost directly off one of the many main roads that cluttered the otherwise beautiful countryside. It was conveniently sign posted as "The Peaks Business Park," and as she approached the handful of low-rise buildings, she could have been anywhere in the country. The establishment gave the impression of a typical small business park that had sprung up between the late 1980s and early 2000s. The main distinguishing feature was the security, which impressed her for how discreet it was.

Laura pulled up at the gatehouse and the lowered barrier. An elderly uniformed guard emerged as she wound down the window.

"Good morning, young lady. How may I help you?"

"I'm here to meet Simon Jones. He's expecting me. My name is Lisa Grahams."

"Certainly. I'll let him know that you are here. I'll be right back."

Laura followed his progress with her eyes. His expression had not given anything away at all, which was good. She could also see a number of other shadows in the gatehouse, and instinct suggested they would not lack the agility that the guard who had greeted her clearly was deficient of.

"That is all okay, Ms Grahams. Presumably you have a form of identification?"

Laura presented the ID card for her alias and gave him time to inspect it. "Thank you. Please proceed straight ahead; Mr Jones is in the second building on the right. He will meet you in reception. You'll find a visitor's parking space at the front of the building."

"Thank you," replied Laura brightly, and then as the barrier was lifted, she drove forward slowly to give her time to scan and review the complex. As she did, she noted a slight change of sound as the tyres ran over a marginally different texture of roadway. Laura glanced down from her window and saw a couple of rectangular outlines in the road surface that she presumed were concealed tank traps. "Neat," she said to herself.

As she continued her slow drive, she kept her eyes open for other forms of security but saw no clear evidence of anything very much. Although that did not mean additional measures were not present, it was not encouraging. All she did see were a couple of CCTV cameras on the corner of some of the buildings but not all of the buildings by any means. Those she did see appeared new. *Interesting*, she thought. *I'll have to ask about that.* There were none overlooking the fence—well, at least, not as far as she could tell.

Simon Jones came out to meet her as Laura pulled into a parking space and stepped out of the car. "Ms Grahams, pleased to meet you. Simon Jones."

Laura gave him an appraising look. He was reasonably good looking, slim, fit, approaching middle age, and had what had surely been a happy, pleasant face, but the dark bags around the eyes and early greying hair told a story of their own. His pale blue, open-necked shirt complemented his eyes, and dark blue trousers with a black belt completed the picture of a man generally comfortable and confident in himself. It was just the recently tired eyes and streaks of grey hair that suggested otherwise.

"Please, Lisa," said Laura, shaking hands. "It's good to meet you and kind of you to do so at short notice and minimal explanation."

"My curiosity has certainly been piqued, although I suspect that I have a good idea. I've been expecting a visit from someone," he replied, turning towards the building. "Anyway, please come in. Coffee is brewing, and it will be more comfortable to discuss whatever you wish in my office."

Laura frowned a little, evidencing her puzzlement at his comment.

"You chose a fine day for an outing. I trust that you had a pleasant journey?"

"Very pleasant indeed, yes. I spent the night in the Peak District since I was coming down from a job further north, and it was just delightful. It's just a shame not to be able to spend more time in surroundings like that."

"Oh, I agree entirely. It's one of the benefits of living around here. In weather like this that region is stupendous. If the weekend has similar weather, I'll be over there for some wonderful walking. Anyway, this is the admin block and restaurant," he said as he held the door open for Laura to pass through into the large, light lobby running the full width of the building that was glazed floor-to-ceiling along three sides. Two lifts were facing them, with stairs off to one side, the steel handrail gleaming under the lights. To the other side of the lifts was a set of wide glass double doors through which Laura could see a lot of chairs and a variety of small café-type and long bench tables. *That's the restaurant then*, she thought as the lift doors opened.

As they settled down at a small meeting table in Simon's office with a cup of coffee each, Laura decided to take the initiative. "So, why don't you tell me why you've been expecting a visit?"

"Ah, now that would be telling, wouldn't it, particularly if I'm wrong. So it's probably better that you start. I hope you don't mind. I don't want to be rude."

Okay, thought Laura. *Polite, genteel, and comes across as unassuming, but sharp and cautious with it. That's fair enough.*

"No offence taken as that's a perfectly reasonable stance to take." Laura was keen not to antagonise the man so early on because, hopefully, he would become more forthcoming with a gentle approach. "I'm here to discuss your security arrangements because we have reason to believe you're being targeted."

Simon sighed. "As I suspected."

"Really? Why's that?"

"We've had a few security breaches recently. Strangely, they've only been into the perimeter and not the buildings. As far as we can tell, nothing has been taken. All very curious, but alarming all the same."

Laura sat up, even more alert than initially. "I'm sure. How do you know there's been a breach in that case? And when was this?"

"It's been periodic over the past few weeks. The perimeter patrol has found the fence damaged on four occasions now. Of course, I've taken a good look because, as the site manager, I'm responsible for getting the damage fixed. And therein lies the curiosity; only once did it appear that someone could have got through. Of course, it's always possible that whoever it was was disturbed, but our patrols have never reported seeing anyone. We're certain that it's not an animal, however. I've seen animal incursions many times during previous jobs, and the damage to the fence is most definitely man made. I've asked for additional security, even though it's not my responsibility, so we have some troops stationed here now in the gatehouse until arrangements are finalised. I hope they will become permanent. There are also plans to install a lot more CCTV with twenty-four-hour on-site monitoring, even though that will start to destroy the low-key nature of the place."

"Strange indeed, I agree. Why would anyone want to break in? I know you're the research and development section for GCHQ, but from the external appearance, you may as well be a standard office park."

"That's precisely the intention. Create our security through anonymity by being boringly normal in appearance and by being in everyone's face. You know, no one pays attention to what's in front of their noses. But therein also possibly lies the problem." At Laura's raised eyebrow and quizzical look, he continued. "Simple really. Standard offices in these parts rarely have good security and therefore offer easy, rich pickings for the opportunistic thieves: computers, other pieces of technology and stationary, lots of stuff that we workers take for granted, and even grounds maintenance equipment. All has a ready resale value and is easy to pass on."

"Yes, I can see that. Are you sure it's as simple as that?"

"What, you think it could be more serious?"

"Not necessarily. Your explanation is perfectly plausible, but surely, simply because of what this place is, there should be consideration of more serious intentions? And that is precisely why I'm here."

Upon saying that, Simon looked increasingly alarmed. *Simon wouldn't be a good poker player,* Laura thought. *At least that helps my cause because I'll know if he tries to hide something.*

"I have been troubled by these breaches for the reasons I've given," he continued. "Local police, who have no idea what we do here, have warned all office parks and commercial users in the area about a spate of office burglaries. I haven't wanted someone discovering our endeavours as a result of petty crime, particularly because there are a few important initiatives in testing phase and close to formal release. That's why I escalated my concerns back to GCHQ. Don't ask me what these folks are doing. I'm not cleared to know what the clever souls here do; all I do know is that the work is vital for our nation. Now you've got me really worried."

Laura proceeded to give the worried man the same information as she had shared with General Marshall-Jones, bringing a distinctly grey, ashen expression to his face as his shoulders slumped further and further. "Oh gawd," was all he could say as she finished. "Presumably the powers that be in Cheltenham know?"

"Absolutely, they do know now. That's why I'm here. Another quick question, if I may. It's one that I expect you cannot answer, but you may have heard something."

"I will try, fire away."

"Have there been any leaks about the work undertaken here, or has someone been acting strangely or as though under extreme pressure, or even, has anyone disappeared totally?"

"If there have been any leaks, I've not heard. In terms of people's behaviour, well yes, many people are under pressure, and it is showing. All I know is that each of the different work streams are highly sensitive and are to be delivered as soon as possible. From what I pick up, they are on schedule but only just. The entire contingency was eaten away a long time back. No one has disappeared as far as I am aware."

"Okay, thanks, that's helpful. I was hoping you'd be able to show me around and give me the details of the security arrangements here in order to assess the potential risk profile and likelihood that this facility is the target. I would have cut to the chase far earlier had you not said what you did at the outset. I wanted to give you the opportunity to expand in your own way, which you did and that was helpful, so thank you. Maybe you'd be so good as to show me around, if that's possible?"

"Certainly, that's not a problem. A walk will do me the world of good, particularly in such fine weather. We won't have access into any of the other buildings whilst people are working there. Those are the rules. If something breaks and requires attention during the day, a blocked toilet or replacement light bulb, for example, then everyone has to clear their work away before the swipe access is downgraded to a level for me or members of my team to go in. It's a right old palaver.

"We can certainly walk around the perimeter, and I will show you where the damage occurred. It will cost a fortune to place tremblers and covert cameras to cover the entire complex. I suspect that the chiefs of Cheltenham, as I call them, know it is necessary but are trying to delay the spend until the next financial year. As I understand it, they've already over-committed their capital for this year."

"Well that's their problem, not ours," replied Laura comfortingly and smiling at his reference to the chiefs of Cheltenham. "The long and short of it is that they need to, and after today, they are likely to also get hit with the cost of additional guarding and very possibly a severe kicking from my boss!"

With that they stood and had a pleasant stroll around the perimeter, chatting amicably as they went. Simon pointed out places of interest and concern and where the fence had been damaged. Following that, Simon suggested that they have lunch before she left, an idea that she readily accepted. She was hungry and ready for something far more substantial than she would buy for herself on the road. Simon was also an easy man to talk with, and as they ate, he happily chatted away about his wife and family, why he had applied for this job, and how enjoyable it had been until these security breaches had occurred. As Laura prepared to leave, Simon handed her a number of sheets of paper.

"Forgive me—these are copies of all the e-mails I sent about the paucity of the security, even before the breaches. As you'll see, I recommended changes. I've also included my e-mails and reports covering those incidents. Yes, I suppose it's been a bit of an arse-covering exercise, but the primary purpose is because I believe you will be able to make something happen and ideally before anything more serious occurs."

"Thank you, Simon, this is most helpful. Well, very good to meet you, and I am sure you'll be hearing from folks shortly. I hope it doesn't become too much of a headache for you."

They shook hands, and Laura departed, eager to find a deserted lay-by or other place to pull over and read Simon's materials and then to call Gurning.

—◆—

Laura found herself talking with Gurning from the car park of a roadside café, where she had parked as far from any other vehicle as possible.

"I can't believe how amateurish and idealistic the place is, Steven. I've read the e-mails that Simon Jones has given me, and they go back a good few years with him warning people that security could be a lot tighter. Whilst I fully acknowledge the plausibility of Simon's comments that these recent breaches could well be the typical criminality that targets office buildings, because of the many attempts, I would not discount this as a possible target. That said, professionals should have been able to gain access the first time."

"Unless the lack of apparent security perversely put the infiltrators on edge, thinking there might be something a lot more sophisticated. They could have been testing the security. Anyhow, I agree that this facility has to be on the list as a potential target. I have spoken to the head of station at GCHQ, who told me what they're doing there. Essentially, it's a breakthrough that will place us years ahead of everyone else in electronic eavesdropping, both voice and electronic communications. They have also had a breakthrough for encryption and decryption techniques. We are known as a powerhouse nation of technical expertise in this arena, so it would not surprise me if others, whether at the national or terrorist level, would seek to snaffle our ideas and capabilities."

"And to think that such advancements have such poor security. It's inexcusable!"

"Exactly."

"But Steven, we don't know for sure that the breach was only of the perimeter. Nor is there evidence that a subsequent search was undertaken to ensure that no listening or other recording devices were installed. Regardless of being the target or not, the entire facility requires a huge amount of attention."

"Agreed. You need to come back to London and work on both coordinating efforts against Khartoum and also on this. Sorting Demir's wider mess will have to wait a few days. We're going to be stretched horribly thinly, even leaving your general to protect his own."

"My general, indeed," she replied, cheering up slightly at Gurning's leg pulling. "See you in a few hours, but you know I can't help but think we're missing something."

"I agree. That's why last night I asked David Spalding to work on this with you as well. I know the two of you work well together."

"Great, thanks."

20

As Laura disconnected speaking with Gurning, her smartphone started beeping like a thing possessed. As she glanced down at the display, a flood of emails and texts came through. One of the texts indicated she had a number of voice messages. *Great,* she thought to herself. *There's either been a network outage or no signal or the blasted contraption is playing up because it's so old.*

There were two notes from the London team. The first informed her that Delta had not been seen again. The second reported that the two men seen with Borzi two days earlier had given them the slip through a basement tunnel connected to a rear garage hitherto unknown as being connected with the premises and therefore had not been watched. Some photos of the backs of the men's heads were attached, but the small size of the display prevented Laura from getting a reasonable perspective of them. She was pleased to note that David Spalding had been copied on both emails.

David Spalding had also sent a text message, as well as a crisp voice message. "Call me as soon as you can." So, with a sigh, she called him back.

"Gracious, Laura, where have you been? I've tried calling you dozens of times!"

"No dratted signal."

"You sure Rob's not with you?" David teased.

"Humph! So what's got you so excited, David? Certainly not ill-informed and idle gossip!" Laura was smiling widely by now and was sure David would be as well. The two of them enjoyed such sparring and had consequently engendered an excellent, trusting work relationship.

"Not at all. It's the notes from the London surveillance teams. I want your approval to circulate Delta's photograph across the HR departments for all Ministries, particularly the Ministry for Business, since Delta was close at the time of his disappearance. It's just a hunch. The London team are not aware of the European Ministerial Critical Medicines Conference tomorrow so would not have put two and two together. It could be coincidence, but—"

Laura cut across him, having heard more than enough. "Do it. I will e-mail my approval now. I don't believe in such close coincidences. I always like working with you. You catch things the rest of us don't."

"And just to let you know, I'm working on trying to get identifications of those guys in the photographs with Borzi. The one they said was domineering is a complete unknown, but the other—well, it wouldn't stand up in court and the described behavioural traits don't fit, but the posture and ears are very like your old adversary, Khartoum, just with a very different hairstyle."

"Work on Delta until I get back. I want to see the comparatives you are referring to before setting any hares running. It sounds intriguing. I'll be a few hours, that's all. See you then."

As Laura walked through the security turnstiles at Thames House reception, she could sense that tension filled the air. She was also staggered to find that Gurning was sitting with David Spalding in her office. She gave one her famous raised quizzical eyebrow glances at Gurning as she hung her jacket on the stand, left her overnight bag at its base as well, and dropped her handbag behind her desk.

"What's up?" she asked as she continued to unpack her work items, including locking her handgun in the secured desk drawer.

"Delta is up," replied Gurning. "It required some pushing to get the Ministry for Business HR department to engage with us, including an irate Minister, frustrated at the no show of one of her admin team who has been making the arrangements for the conference. With that knowledge and a bit of prompting, it did not take long to get their attention and to get them to look at a photograph, which was immediately recognised as one Nazim Omar, the no-show admin.

"We now focus on the conference. I've alerted the team up there, and sorry, you're on your way out again. I've asked Brian to release one of his lads to join you and for him to do the driving. You've done enough today. Study these photos on your way, and give me your opinion. It's a good enough resemblance for me if you're onside as well. I will have to pull a few favours to get authorisation to raid the Finsbury premises, but with the growing links between Leicester, Bradford, and now this place, I will push for it."

Laura was aghast at how rapidly matters had moved in a few short hours. She was also mightily relieved that she would have a chauffeur for the journey back up north. She started to pack her things again whilst saying with a grin, "You intentionally waited for me to finish unpacking, didn't you?"

"Absolutely! Unfortunately, we have to assume that Khartoum and company are aware by now that we are onto them, or at least sniffing around and also that they realise they are neither as substantially manned nor equipped as planned. From his past record, I can't see him aborting whatever he has planned, so I want you there to take charge.

"Just think—we would have been completely blindsided by this thing if it hadn't been for looking into Demir's operations. I'm heading off to confront him with this now during the proverbial quiet before the storm of what will be tomorrow. Hopefully, with this clear link to terrorism, he will become more amenable to sharing his information more openly and quickly. I'm probably flying a kite, but it's worth a try. By the way, the conference starts at ten o'clock tomorrow morning.

"The news from the venue is that the entire place has been searched and there's nothing to report. With the local police we are flooding the place and the surrounding area, but as we know, the countryside can be like a sieve for anyone sufficiently determined.

"Well, there you have it. Let's jump to it."

"Right you are," replied Laura enthusiastically, caught up in the moment of high tension and imminent action. "However, I still think the GCHQ facility deserves immediate attention as well. I accept that everything now points towards the conference, but that doesn't mean that, like the conference, we haven't stumbled upon something there."

Gurning hesitated at the door, thinking the logic of Laura's comments through and the implications on resource. "I'll speak to the DG," he said eventually, in a thoughtful, cautious manner, showing his hesitancy, despite his apparent agreement. "As always, your logic is faultless." With that he opened the door and left, closing it behind him.

A few minutes later, as Laura finished collecting her things once again, there was a knock at the door, and Rob popped his head in. "Hi! Oh, hello David. How're things?" Then Rob hesitated, seeing Laura with her gun in hand. "I trust you are not intending to use that thing!" he joked. "I saw you walking through reception, so thought I'd come and find out how things are going, but I can come back again later if you want."

"No, it's all right, Rob. Come on in. I'm just packing again. Steven was here with David, and they've just briefed me. I'll fill you in whilst I pack. I also want to hear from you about Leicester."

"I can also update you on the office. It looks fabulous and is nearly ready for occupation. The teams here and their contractors have really pulled all the stops out. When you're back, you'll have to come round."

"We'd love to," Laura replied for them both. Then she went on to summarise the current situation, leaving out the details relating to the two secret facilities, merely commenting that the conference was their focus because there were too many coincidences.

◆

Laura arrived at the conference hotel late that night and ate a tuna sandwich and salad with the ever-present stack of fries on the side as Nat Williams briefed her on the hotel, the grounds, the surrounding land, and the couple of hills overlooking the hotel. He outlined the steps taken to secure the area as far as possible, including regular patrols of the hills, and he covered, in detail, the agenda for the following day.

Nat looked tired, as well he might, not having slept for forty-eight hours. His eyes gleamed, however, and his energy level was so remarkable that Laura was tempted to ask how he did it, but she was not entirely convinced that she would like the answer.

Nat was apparently in his mid-thirties but looked a lot younger. His reputation was legend. Muscles rippled beneath his white, open-necked shirt, with the rolled-up sleeves exposing a string of tattoos on his forearms, all gained during his years in the special forces. Whether a long-term member of his team or a new recruit, everyone said the same thing: they didn't want to work for anyone else. Now that Laura had met the man, she could understand why.

"How are the transfers being covered?" Laura asked.

"A separate team, thankfully," replied Nat. "As each minister arrives at Manchester airport, we'll be informed. A security detail has been allocated to meet and greet and then accompany the minister here. Our own minister is travelling up by car. The arrangements and route were changed hastily once that admin chap went AWOL and the connection established by you guys.

"I don't suppose you know who they are targeting, if anyone specific, or is the thinking that it's the conference as a whole?" Nat asked.

"We really don't know. It doesn't appear logical to target a conference if they're focusing on an individual, but I agree we can't rule that out. From your short time here, have you even an inkling for the most likely tactic for any attack?"

"That's the six million–dollar question and really depends upon the objective or target. If it's an individual, I'd vote for a sniper from the overlooking hills as whoever arrives or departs. But why wait for a conference to take a shot at someone? It doesn't make sense. It's generally far easier to penetrate the security detail of daily life because at some point either the target or a member of the protection squad will slip up, whereas security at an event like this is always scrutinised. Anyhow, just in case, the current patrols over those hills and amongst the trees will become a permanent presence tomorrow, from early until after departure. That said, a couple of high-powered sniper rifles were found during the Leicester raid. Whether that disrupts or changes anything, only time will tell.

"That aside, assuming that this is the target, I'm expecting a greater level of attack, but I really cannot conceive how it will be executed. Everywhere and everything has been swept for explosives. Divers have checked out the lake, and we've even been through the sand in the bunkers over at the pitch and putt. Manchester airport have an extra body on duty solely to monitor all aircraft and report anything potentially suspicious from miles out, at which point the RAF will be scrambled. An air strike does seem improbable, however. That would leave a rocket attack, which is plausible but unreliable.

"The one area of concern that has not yet been fully closed off is the staff here and a suicide attack, poisoning, or some other type of individual level of atrocity. There simply has not been the time to complete the vetting for all employees. I've frustrated the hotel's manager and those of the caterer by insisting that no temporary person or contractor be used who has not been engaged and worked here for at least three years."

"I can see why that didn't go down well, but good call," commented Laura thoughtfully. "But if the attack were to come from someone on site, how would they get the necessary weapons in? I'm sure you're frustrating everyone with searches."

"Sure am," Nat said with feeling. "Their cars as well, all of which I'm requiring to be parked well away from the building and behind trees. I have also insisted that all deliveries are made prior to the arrival of any delegate and that all vehicles have departed by that time as well.

"I suspect that the manager has changed his view of governmental conferences being easy and 'money for old rope.' This certainly started out that way, but he's had a rude awakening," Nat said with a chuckle and wicked grin.

"Well, not much more we can do for now, so best you get some sleep. I'll just go do my final rounds. Hopefully you've been shown where you're staying?"

"I have, yes, thank you. Good night. See you around six?"

"I'll be there." With that, Nat headed off, leaving Laura to find the way to her room.

21

Nat, carrying a plate piled high with scrambled eggs, bacon, sausages, mushrooms, tomatoes, and toast, joined Laura at the breakfast table where she was seated, studying the day's agenda again.

"I'm pleasantly surprised to see that they have to work for their pay at this one," she said wryly as Nat sat down. "No element of a jolly at all. It appears as all business."

"That's the positive influence of senior business folks being present, coupled with the severity of the matter at hand," commented Nat. "A brief and to-the-point conference. I understand that this was the only day they could all accommodate. That said, apparently the chip and putt, as well as the driving range, attracted some attention from the delegates, many of whom are keen golfers. Hence the choice of this venue, as it provides a short respite over lunch. Well, at least that's what the manager said."

As they finished their breakfast, Nat asked, "Care to join me on my rounds? I'll focus upon the golfing area on the basis that that presents one of the two external opportunities for attack."

"And the other?" encouraged Laura.

"Oh, the inevitable conference photo, which will be taken on the steps at the rear of the hotel. Both elements are overlooked by the hills, so they provide a good opportunity for a sniper or rocket attack." Shortly afterwards they headed off around the grounds, stopping to chat with the patrols as they passed.

◀──

Rob had also risen early, as was his way, and went for a run around Walpole Park in Ealing, followed by an out-of-breath protection squad. After a hearty breakfast of muesli and a plate of cheese, mushroom and tomato omelette, washed down with a strong coffee, Rob headed off to his new office. In between his engagements and activities in Leicester, he had maintained contact with his newly recruited team, all of whom had enthusiastically accepted the terms offered to join the newly founded firm, Zouches. As matters came to a head and approached a conclusion in Leicester, Rob had contacted them once again, proposing a meeting at the nearly completed new office.

At 8:30 a.m. they congregated in the bright and tastefully colourful reception, clearly the inspiration of a high-end interior designer seeking to create a modern, young, and professional working environment whilst also somehow appealing to traditionalists. Rob marvelled at how so much could be accomplished with such simplicity. The builders and decorators had disappeared, leaving the technology folks to their work. As the team looked on, drinking coffee, the workmen were setting up the comms room, the desktop computers, and the all-important multimedia gadgets. There was video conferencing and collaborative projection whiteboards with associated computer and printer. There were also various other toys that the technology folks of MI5 had conjured up for the group's pleasure. There were also the inevitable large flat-screen TVs hanging on the walls of the reception to display a variety of news channels and market data information. Each desk had at least two computer screens, and some had four.

Rob dinged a teaspoon against his cup for silence, feeling incredibly self-conscious and ill-suited for the role that he was now embarking on. However, he was determined to portray the confidence and assurance he was known for.

"Welcome, everyone, to our new head office. I've arranged that we can have access to the board room essentially from now, and afterwards we can wander around the office as we want, although please be considerate of those folks still working through the office setup. Expectations are that we will have a live environment within two weeks, although for many of you, because of existing commitments, it won't be possible to join until after that date. Well, shall we go through?"

Rob guided everyone through some impressive light-coloured wooden double doors with glass visibility panels into an expansive and well-equipped boardroom. At the far end was a large-scale plan of the office, showing a number of smaller meeting rooms, also directly off reception, and a large open-plan office area behind accommodating twenty stand-alone desks and two pods of four linked desks for the administrative and support teams. These were placed near the windows, as they would be permanently in the office, with all of the other desks arranged in an arc around them so they were reasonably central to act as a focal point within the workspace. Against the inner wall were a series of small meeting or quiet rooms. The reception and waiting area, boardroom, and most of the other formal meeting rooms had excellent views over the River Thames, which was running at near high tide, with gusts of wind whipping the dark water into sporadic bursts of small, white-topped waves.

"Welcome again all," Rob said as they settled down in their seats. "The agenda for today is short and simple: Explain some more about this setup—about Zouches, including its ownership. Explain the need for confidentiality and why both a firm confidentiality agreement and the signing of the 'Official Secrets Act' have been necessary and the consequential obvious link between Zouches and the government. Then I will cover the objectives for Zouches, and finally, there will be time for everyone to mingle and start to get to know each other. I'll keep the chat as short as possible to provide the most time for Q and A and time to mingle.

"So first, Zouches. You were, I am sure, enticed to join by the words 'a start-up private equity firm' and that Sir William is involved." At that Rob gestured to Sir William, who was sitting amongst the group. "So why am I standing here instead of Sir William? Simply because I own Zouches and am the primary beneficiary of the revenue generated. Well, that's after paying off some fairly hefty debts, that is!"

Upon that announcement, there were startled expressions from all those who had known Rob previously. He smiled before continuing. "And no, I have not always had the wealth to establish such an enterprise. How I came to effectively inherit the wealth that justifies a private equity firm also leads on to explain why it's been necessary to sign two sets of confidentiality agreements and the seriousness with which you need to treat the knowledge that you will gain.

"Essentially, I saved the life of Burak Demir and that of his young daughter. The name may be familiar as being the secretive multi-billionaire who walked from court in Paris a free man a while back because alleged links to criminality were not made. Well, the reality is that he was a master criminal and as part of saving both his life and of his daughter's, it was agreed that he would both hand over his entire empire to me and also accept coming to Britain to face justice. However, before facing justice publicly, he will assist the efforts to bring his criminal network to its knees. This is the essence of the need for confidentiality. We must not let the authorities down by letting it become known that Burak is helping us. This affects many countries, not only the UK. Until such a time as the network has been dismantled, he will continue to be at the forefront of all communication with those elements that have not been transferred into Zouches. This may take quite some time.

"Burak has a network of both legitimate and criminal business. You can split the legitimate businesses in two. First, there are those businesses that have absolutely no connection to any criminality. Unfortunately, there aren't very many of those. These businesses will transfer immediately to Zouches.

"Then there are other legitimate businesses through which Burak channels criminal activities without the operating managers knowing. In some instances, Burak would plant people into those businesses to run the criminal aspects. In other instances, the criminal activity is simply pushed through as though legitimate. These businesses will only transfer as and when the criminal elements and activities have been expunged. This is where the combined expertise of this group will come into its own and leads to our objectives.

"Put very simply, we will help those business managers rebuild and expand what has been disrupted, potentially severely, and we will maintain and create employment. If it weren't for this arrangement, once the networks are shut down, many hundreds of innocent people's livelihoods would be destroyed.

"We must remember, these businesses will have been disrupted, possibly decimated, and there will be damaged reputations, both to the business and most likely also to those caught up in the mess. They will be in shock, having been completely hoodwinked and let down by Burak as the owner or major shareholder when the manager also has a stake. In all cases, Burak has remained anonymous and worked either by phone or more frequently, through a Power of Attorney given to one of his henchmen. It is highly likely that those affected, once they realise, will lose confidence, and almost certainly their willingness to trust anyone will have evaporated.

"I'm sure you read in the papers or watched the TV coverage about a raid two days ago in Leicester that disrupted a major drug-smuggling operation. Well, I was there because those two premises are examples of legitimate businesses being abused by Burak for his criminal activities. However, in this case, and there are very possibly many more like this, unbeknownst to Burak, his sidekicks had expanded their operations and embraced the support of terrorism. There were not only drugs found at those premises. There were also weapons and explosives, giving a real example for the need of extreme confidentiality. Nothing gleaned within these four walls or during the course of your work is to go anywhere. Nothing." With that, Rob paused briefly for effect before continuing. Whether the silence was from respect to let him finish speaking or because they were too stunned, Rob had no idea, but he had noticed a few of them wriggling in their chairs. *I hope no one is getting cold feet,* Rob thought to himself.

"I spoke to the managers of the Leicester businesses afterwards, and they were thoroughly dejected, were in shock, and really are unsure who they can trust. We need to gain their trust and those like them and keep successful businesses successful."

"Rob, sorry for interrupting, but isn't this therefore potentially dangerous for us as well?" asked Huw Thomas.

"Fair question, Huw, and thank you for jumping in; I was getting concerned that everyone had lost their tongues!" Fortunately, everyone laughed a little at that, lightening the atmosphere.

"Anyway, to answer your question, no, I don't believe so, provided we respect the confidentiality and mind our part of the equation and not involve ourselves until businesses are transferred to us. At that point, the businesses should be post-criminal and should hold no interest for those groups. I must emphasise the confidentiality once again because we will sometimes have access to information prior to the authorities acting. That won't be frequent, for obvious reasons; the fewer people who know, the better. But sometimes it may be necessary. Much of the time I will know and help the authorities with the judgement call on whether to share or not."

"Ever the one for the excitement of danger, eh, Rob!" Julian Smith called out, raising some more laughter throughout the room.

"Rob," jumped in Yves Aussourd.

"Yes, Yves."

"So there are all these businesses out there and the boss has disappeared because he is in custody. So how does that work? Surely they'll go native or someone else will move in?"

"Ah, that's the beauty of the arrangements, whilst also being difficult to stomach. As briefly intimated, Burak will continue to manage them until the authorities are able to close down the criminal element. One of the reasons he was able to walk free from the Parisian court was that no links could be found. He has always managed his networks anonymously and by inference remotely, as well as with the aid of a small army of heavies. Personally, I find it tough to swallow that criminality is being permitted to continue, but having followed the preparation for the Leicester operation seen the outcome and now knowing that links to other criminal activity have been established, I can understand why it's necessary. Those links would not have been identified if the authorities had gone straight in and closed the operations down, thereby leaving other activities unidentified and able to continue unabated.

"So in essence, I am working hand-in-glove with the security services. Our combined intervention is absolutely essential to first close down a huge international criminal network that also has links to terrorist activity and bring those responsible to justice. The extent of the links to terrorism is unknown but is thought to be considerable. Second, our aim is to provide support to the affected businesses and help them to grow and not fail as a result of the loss of revenue provided by the criminal activities and keep people employed.

"A pack listing the legitimate businesses ready for immediate transfer will be circulated shortly. The managers are still unaware of the imminent transfer, and one of our first tasks will be to determine a strategy for on-boarding them and bringing some structure, cohesion, and good, but not burdensome, reporting.

"Before taking any more questions—I can see a few itching hands—there is one final objective that I have for Zouches." At that point Rob could see the raising of some eyebrows, particularly from

Sir William, who he knew was there both from a business perspective, as well as to keep a wary eye on proceedings. Thus far Rob had not shared his final objective with anyone.

"The extent of wealth to be managed by us far exceeds the requirements of any single individual, even should I marry a lady with expensive tastes and have a large, demanding family!" Rob paused as his friends of old had a good laugh at his latest witticism. "Therefore, I also intend to establish a philanthropic trust through Zouches to make the best social use of much of the wealth that has found its way to me. I am still drafting my intended focus for that trust, but much of it will focus around children and a reasonable proportion for the elderly. Right, any further questions?"

As he had spoken about the trust, Rob could see Sir William's relief and apparent support by way of a gentle nodding of his head.

"Rob, can you give us an idea of the types of business coming our way?" Timothy Havering, the CEO-to-be, asked.

"Absolutely. It's a mixed bag. In Leicester, for example, there is a carwash and a money-exchange business. There are also real estate and construction companies, farms, florists, travel agencies, and logistics businesses, including couriers and transportation businesses, the latter comprising cars, planes, helicopters, and boats. Those are the ones I can mention. I haven't totalled up the number of countries covered yet, but it's quite a lot."

There was a moment's silence as the extent and magnitude of what had been said and discussed was absorbed before Julian Smith aptly commented, "We'll have our work cut out then!" raising a good few chuckles.

"Rob, a question for curiosity purposes as much as anything," said Karen Ayles, who was to be the CFO. "Why have you chosen Zouches as the name for your firm?"

"I was wondering if anyone would ask," he said, partly laughing. "I came across the word as the name of a farm during my research for a university project focused in the Luton area. I liked the sound of the word and thought it would make a great and unusual name for a business and have harboured that thought ever since. According to an amateur historian, the word originates from a similar-sounding old French word meaning 'tree stump' and may also derive from the French place name La Souche. The name Zouche without the S is also an old aristocratic English name with a long lineage. As I say, I just liked the sound of it!"

With that, the meeting broke up, and folks milled around, initially gravitating to Rob, probing him with questions about how he came to save Burak and cut the deal with the government, during which he explained that much of the costs of the many forthcoming operations would have to be covered by Zouches.

22

Sarah Puddleford was understandably nervous as she sat in her ministerial car heading towards a conference she knew was important. Ordinarily, as the host, she would have felt the tingling nerves of expectation ahead of her required speeches. Now, however, the nervousness was for her life and that of all the other conference delegates. The presence of the unmarked police Range Rover escort did little to comfort her. If anything, its proximity simply served to exacerbate her nerves.

She had been badly let down by Nazim Omar and was disappointed beyond words. She had offered Nazim a job just over a year earlier after visiting his college on results day and had been impressed by his alertness, questions, and above all, determination to excel, which shone through. He had apparently turned his back on working at his parents' back-street café in the east end of London so he could pursue his studies, much to his parents' disappointment and familial pressure. She had wanted to encourage both him and the many others who knew his story.

Mrs Puddleford felt she had also been let down by the personnel vetting procedures. As Nazim had progressed and subsequently joined her administrative team, his proximity to her and his access to confidential information had necessitated additional background checks, all of which had been clear. That had been only five months ago. Somehow, whatever it was he was mixed up in had escaped the vetting team's attention. He had no political, ideological, or religious allegiances of note. Some serious questions about this failure were being asked even now as she made her way up north to face goodness knows what.

Now, as she sat in her car being driven north, she thought of her family back at their constituency and family home. Mrs Puddleford pulled out a notepad from her case, wrote two letters, and folded them away into separate envelopes. Turning to the bodyguard assigned to her for the day, she asked in as confident a voice as she could muster, "Dylan, if anything terrible happens, please make sure my family receive this and my parents receive this."

"Certainly, ma'am, although I will look forward to giving them back to you later today on the journey home."

"Thank you." Mrs Puddleford settled back into her seat again, thinking about Dylan's lifestyle and his complete lack of surprise at her request. *Do many of his charges make similar requests,* she wondered but did not dare ask. She wanted to put on a show of strength from now on.

The first of Mrs Puddleford's European counterparts' aircraft touched down at Manchester International Airport and taxied to the private terminal, where a series of smart limousines and escort vehicles awaited their arrival. The officials and other ground crew had been gossiping all morning about the suddenly imposed heavy security for various European ministers and some important businessmen. Flights from France, Germany, Italy, the Netherlands, Spain, and Switzerland were expected, with businessmen accompanying the relevant country's minister where appropriate.

The plan was that there would be a precise fifteen minutes between each transfer, and regular communication between the respective convoys would ensure that gap be maintained. Nat's intention was that there would be no grouping of the participants, other than at the conference venue. Assuming that any terrorist attack was intended to target multiple people for maximum damage and effect, he wanted to limit the potential locations to make maximum use of the resources available to him.

As the airplanes were landing and their respective convoys set off, it became busy at the hotel entrance as the staff and deliveries started to arrive. Every delivery was logged and compared against the list of what was expected. Nat wanted to review the log shortly before the arrival of the first delegates.

Each vehicle and individual was searched whilst each member of the staff was quizzed, and the required original form of identification was carefully scrutinised. Many of the staff were nervous and uncomfortable at such close attention, and a few failed to turn up. Their names and addresses were noted, ready to be passed on to Immigration for their residency status, to the Inland Revenue to ensure they were paying the correct taxes, and finally to Social Security to ensure there was no benefit fraud going on, as well as to the police for criminal checks.

Together with one of the roving patrols, Nat and Laura reviewed the grounds. At the chip and putt course and driving range, they stood and surveyed the surrounding landscape and hills with their powerful binoculars. Nat pointed out where he would position himself as a member of the Special Forces on a covert op to take out an enemy position. Radio in hand, he gave directions to the patrols on the wooded hillsides to make sure those spots were thoroughly checked out.

Next up was the rear of the hotel, where the obligatory conference photo would be taken. As they were walking there, Nat called each of the police checkpoints scattered throughout the surrounding area for a status update. They were positioned on the roads leading to the surrounding hills, the roads leading directly to the hotel, and the quiet back roads within striking distance of the hotel grounds. The reports came in satisfactorily, confirming there were no unaccounted for vehicles and no suspicious traffic.

Finally, they meandered through the woodland at the edge of the hotel grounds, Nat and the accompanying patrol using their training to seek any traces of recent human passage. It was a tough task, and as they finished, they could not be absolutely certain but were reasonably confident no one had been in the woods since the previous day. That said, Nat appointed a team of six to split into pairs and constantly patrol the woods just in case.

Nat's radio burst into life. "Ten minutes, sir, and the Minister for Business will arrive."

"On our way."

Immediately they turned and headed back to the hotel. Nat wanted to be present when the delegates arrived, particularly Mrs Puddleford. He expected she would want both an update and an assurance. Her bodyguard had sent a text a little earlier stating her evident and understandable nervousness.

415

By the time the Minister's car glided to a halt in front of the hotel's elegant façade, the small welcoming committee was lined up. The hotel manager welcomed her first and then introduced her to the in-house event coordinator, who would be at her beck and call for the day. If she wanted anything at all, she just had to press the call button on the small gadget he presented her with. Hesitantly she took hold of it, the tension in her face clear for all to see. Politely, as required, she thanked him whilst giving her bodyguard a look saying, "Is this safe?" Dylan glanced at Nat, who nodded. It had been pre-cleared, and Nat had held on to it after all of the checks until handing the gadget back to the manager just as the Minister arrived. The manager had also been searched just prior to arrival. There was no chance of a swap.

As Laura looked on, she wondered how any productive work could be accomplished whilst the possibility of a terrorist attack hung over the place like a dark storm cloud, echoing the weather above. When she had woken up Laura had been convinced it was going to rain. Even now distant rumbles of thunder threatened to prove the weather forecasters wrong again. It was supposed to be overcast but dry for the entire day. Could it last?

The manager had by now introduced Nat, who quickly briefed Mrs Puddleford on the current status and arrangements for the day prior to turning and introducing Laura. The Minister then uncharacteristically hurried into the relative safety of the hotel's interior. She had decided that future welcoming committees would be indoors, using the weather as an excuse.

The Dutch would be the next to arrive. The Italians would be last. Those businessmen not accompanying a Minister would arrive whenever in their own chauffeur-driven cars. They were not considered suitable individual targets.

In between arrivals, Laura called Simon Jones at the GCHQ research and development facility for an update. He sounded stressed as he described the influx of security personnel and the fact that there had been another breach the previous night. This time there were evident marks of an attempted break-in on the front doors to three of the campus buildings. One door had been left hanging open, but the intruders had been disturbed by a patrol. However, the perpetrators had given them the slip.

The news made Laura anxious. Had they focused on the wrong place? Should she relocate? Both locations were equally vulnerable and equally attractive for terrorists. She didn't like knee-jerk reactions and tried to think rationally. Gurning would have the same information as she did and would call immediately should he require a change of emphasis. Simon handed his phone to the day's head of security, who updated her on their arrangements, giving her some but little comfort.

Amidst her troubled thoughts, Nat had studied the log of deliveries and was muttering curses that barely registered about the golf pro from the nearby golf course bringing an unannounced stack of new boxed golf balls and collections of the latest clubs, bags, and other goods he hoped to sell. Otherwise, everything else was in order.

Laura mumbled her response, caught slightly by surprise. "Typical that someone would try to buck the system. Presumably everything checked out?"

"Yes. The manager assured me that he's well known and the search and sniffer dogs came up with nothing, so he got away simply with a good ear-full! I can't blame the guy for trying to be entrepreneurial, but everyone was told very clearly not to bring anything that has not been pre-cleared."

———

François Maranville was bored. "Why do the British have to be overdramatic with everything? First the conference and now the security arrangements. Mind you, it is almost like being the president," he said to Nadia Trivette, his attractive assistant who was, as always and as he preferred, showing rather a lot of her shapely, slim legs, which were stretched out in the long wheel-base limo.

She had been looking out of the window when he spoke, which had enabled him to yet again admire her feminine curves. She turned as he spoke, flicking her long blonde hair as she did so, releasing into the air an invisible plume of her alluring perfume. François breathed in deeply as she did. He longed for those moments of her scent.

They were on the M67 motorway near a place called Hyde. The silence in the car was tedious and the quiet thrum of the speeding tyres barely audible.

"It is, isn't it?" Nadia replied sweetly, flashing a beaming smile of perfect, gleaming white teeth. "It's a shame we can't stay over. The write-up for the hotel is very good, and I hear that the Peak District is beautiful, despite the gloomy English weather."

François was just starting to imagine an overnight stay with Nadia when their car swerved sharply, the driver cussing loudly as he slammed on the brakes. As he did so, there was a second, more jarring jolt, accompanied by the sound of squealing tyres and grinding metal as a car slammed into their rear. It was not one of their convoy. As Nadia screamed, François instinctively reached out to protect her. As he did, he saw that another car had come in between them and their escort in front.

Horrified, he looked on as two men jumped out carrying guns in a menacing manner. Shots rang out, and behind him the rear windshield glazed upon the impact of the bullets but withstood the impacts. The police response was rapid and incredibly efficient in its ruthlessness. Even before their vehicles were stationary, the armed men in the rear of each escort car were out and rolling on the tarmac, raising their handguns and firing rapidly at the attackers with great accuracy.

Moments later the attackers from the rear car were lying dead on the road, as was one of those from the other car, which, facing overwhelming and superior firepower, sped off, tyres squealing, adding the smell of burning rubber to the cordite from the guns. It was all over in such a short space of time that François wondered if the attack had really happened.

The police allowed the perpetrators to flee, their near-suicidal behaviour a cause for concern that if they were pursued, the French Minister would be left with a lesser extent of protection and therefore more vulnerable to a second attack, should one be planned, which, considering the circumstances, was very possible.

François quickly consulted the driver, who gave his consent for a brief sortie to inspect the scene prior to continuing the journey to the conference. The standard motorway police quickly closed the motorway to perform the necessary search of the area for evidence and to clear away the bodies. Other patrols gave chase to the fleeing gunmen, but it proved fruitless.

Nat quickly coordinated that the other arrivals each take a different route to the venue and liaised with Mrs Puddleford as to her intentions. Should the conference be cancelled or would they continue? Her response surprised him. Whilst clearly tense, she replied that the decision should be left to François Maranville when he arrived.

"Wow, she has more guts than I gave her credit for," he confessed to Laura as soon as they were alone.

"Agreed. It also says a lot about the importance of this conference. But why did they have to target the French minister in Britain? Why couldn't they just do it in France?"

"Good and fair questions but only answerable in time. For now, we have to concentrate on the safety of our charges. I'd like to think that attack settles it—that the threat is over and that we can relax a bit—but it's still early. I'm also with you. Why the French Minister and why here as opposed to anywhere else? That said, multiple terrorist attacks in the same area are incredibly rare and then are of massive scale—think 9/11."

"I'm with you, but even if he wants the conference to continue, we need to consider the implications to his mental capacity. Should we allow the conference to proceed?"

"Let's play it by ear when we are able to speak to him. We need to keep our options and minds open."

◆

Tense minutes passed as they waited for the battered limo to arrive at the hotel and an ashen-faced François Maranville to emerge, supporting his more-troubled assistant. Some hotel staff took her off to a quiet area, ready for some counselling that had been urgently ordered, as had medical support to check both of them. Maranville meanwhile was escorted to a second room, where Laura and Nat sat him down and first tried to determine his frame of mind and intentions and second began to quiz him gently on whether he had any ideas to why he had been attacked.

Laura took the lead. "Monsieur Maranville, we are from the security services. We can assure you that the hotel is safe. You are safe now. Are you happy to talk for a few minutes? Any information we can get at this stage could be very helpful."

"Absolutely, mademoiselle. I am of course happy to talk and help you in any way I can." His thick French accent had been made deeper, thicker through his habit of smoking fifteen Gauloises cigarettes a day.

"Thank you, Monsieur. First, how do you feel about the conference continuing?"

"It must, of course, continue. We don't come a long way to resolve a crisis of profound magnitude and cancel because of personal scares. We must look to history and learn from past heroes to know how we too must respond."

As he finished, François Maranville started to fumble inside his jacket pocket and fish out a packet of cigarettes. He extracted one and lit it.

Neither Laura nor Nat was going to challenge him on the legality of smoking inside a public building, but both noted that his hands were as steady as a rock. Nat simply hoped that any smoke alarm in the room would not be sufficiently sensitive to send the hotel into evacuation mode and send everyone's stress levels off the Richter scale.

At a loss as to how to respond to such courageous words, Laura could simply say the same words yet again. "Thank you, monsieur. As you'd expect, we've received a good account of what happened from our colleagues. What we would like to know is if you know of any reason why you would be specifically targeted, whether at home in France or here in Britain and particularly here in Britain? We wish to determine whether this is more likely to have been a random one-off attack or if there is an imminent risk that further attacks on your person could occur."

"Ah, mademoiselle, a good, a deep, and searching yet difficult question. My profession will inherently place people in one of three camps for how other people regard us: They don't care who I am or what I do. They approve of, maybe adore me and my philosophies, or they loathe and possibly hate me." At this he gave a very French and resigned shrug of not knowing. "Would anyone want to kill me in such a fashion? I should think not. Why? I am a minor minister. *Pas importante!*" he finished off with flair.

"We understand. That's very helpful." As Laura spoke again, both she and Nat exchanged their agreed signal of twisting their pens to signify their perception that he was not only willing but also capable of continuing with the conference. "Please, just a couple more questions. I understand that you asked to exit the safety of your vehicle and review the scene before continuing the journey. Why was that?"

"That is simple, mademoiselle. I wished to look into the eyes of those who wished me harm and who wish to disrupt the work I hold most dear. To see the persons who would try this. That is all."

"And what did you see? Did you recognise anyone?"

"Oof! *Non, mademoiselle.* I did not recognise anyone. What I saw was young men with no hope and probably brainwashed by those without the courage to stand up in public and discuss their points of view because they know their perspectives hold no substance!"

"Monsieur, that has been very helpful. Thank you. We will let you join the conference now and can assure you that your safety and that of all the delegates here is of paramount importance to us and will be protected with our lives if necessary."

"You are both very gracious, but let us pray it does not come to that, *n'est pas?*" he replied as he stood, straight backed, and shook hands with them, his double-breasted dark blue suit still looking immaculate, off-setting the crisp white shirt and pale blue tie.

As the door closed behind him, Nat whistled air between his lips to show his appreciation of what he had just heard. "There goes one cool customer and a tough cookie!"

"Now look who's talking," Laura said, smiling. "That said, my sentiments entirely, Nat. But I don't think this is over yet."

"Agreed. I'll take a swing around the guys shortly to emphasise that we remain on alert, at a higher level of threat than before, if that's possible. But I can't make heads or tails of this. If that was a diversionary attack or one to tempt us to drop our guard, it was first, a suicide mission for those who went and second, a pretty lousy attempt. It just doesn't make sense."

"I'm with you on that. Anyway, you need to rally your guys while I make some phone calls. The media will be braying for information, and the French authorities will want assurances."

23

The conference got off to a late, hesitant, and tense start, but eventually the doors were closed and the proceedings got underway. Every delegate was very aware that the reason or reasons for the interruption to the distribution of critical medicines throughout Europe had to be determined and a solution for fixing the problems found. They had also openly discussed over pre-conference coffee whether the disruption and the morning's presumed terrorist attack on François Maranville's car were connected.

Were there previously unrecognised built-in failures to the organisations and processes? If so, what fixes were required, and who was best placed to action those remedies? Alternatively, was something more sinister at play? To date, this had not really been contemplated, although it was not taken off the agenda. Now it was to be taken far more seriously.

By the mid-morning coffee break, it was clear to everyone else at the venue that the focus had not been lost, despite the morning's dramatic distractions. The delegates were talking with great fervour as they moved into the rooms set up ready for drinks and biscuits, and Mrs Puddleford's expression had changed from one of bordering upon a startled hare caught in a car's headlights to one of her usual professional gravity and seriousness as she contemplated what lay before them to resolve the crisis. She even managed to smile as Nat approached her to very quickly provide her with the assurance she wanted. Everything was quiet in the vicinity, and others were taking care of the enquiries from the world's press about the morning's events. All in all, she had nothing to worry about.

Mrs Puddleford even curtailed the length of the break to get everyone back around the table, so great was her desire not to lose the momentum gained from the previous session and to make up on time lost. She even sent the kitchen staff into a complete spin as lunch approached by agreeing with everyone that it should be a working lunch instead of the planned more formal affair in the dining room. The intended waiter- and waitress-served meal had to be rapidly rearranged to become a serve-yourself buffet in the conference room.

"Well hopefully such zeal will put pay to the golf," Nat commented to Laura when the hotel manager informed them amidst running around to coordinate the request. "That should make matters easier for us, at least."

The additional stress caused by the request was tangible throughout the hotel as people scurried around and exchanged conversations kept as quiet as possible, although the language used became more colourful.

However, by half past two, Nat's hopes were dashed. Everyone required a break and fresh air. Mrs Puddleford announced that they would first have the obligatory conference photo call. Then those who wished to could hit a few golf balls for fifteen minutes whilst the others could either simply relax or wander the gardens, which, she announced, had been designed by some famous gardener of ages past. She proceeded to speak eloquently about some chap Nat had never heard of and how he had incorporated some rare plants.

Now it was Nat's turn to stress. No one had said anything about garden walks! How could Mrs Puddleford's love of gardens not have been noted and associated with one of the venue's key attractions?

He and Laura had walked through the garden. He recalled thinking, *Not bad. Nice if you have the space and money,* but he had not been overwhelmed. Now he had to split and thin down a couple of patrols to cover this activity. He was fuming but refused to let it show as he rallied his teams.

"Base to all, delegates are emerging for their photo, followed by fifteen, I repeat fifteen minutes of recreation. Both golf and walking the gardens. I need someone to cover the gardens pronto. Hill patrols one and two, report in."

"All very quiet, Nat. Pass through traffic only. Hill one out."

"Same for hill two, Nat."

The responses were the same for the perimeter patrols and those spread throughout the grounds.

Both Nat and Laura stood behind the photographer, their backs to the delegates as they scanned the surrounding area.

"Grounds patrol four!" barked Nat suddenly, sharply, but quietly. "Movement in the woods, at least two persons unidentified. Move!"

Nat continued his search in greater earnest through his powerful binoculars but could not locate the movement he had seen again. The photographer was happily snapping away, and the conversation between shots amongst the delegates was lighthearted, so Nat really did not want to alarm people by bundling them all back inside if it wasn't necessary.

A few tense minutes later, they received a reply. "Just a couple of kids out for a bit of loving stuff, sir. All okay." Nat and Laura just looked at each other. There was no need for words; their faces articulated the relief that they felt.

"Good, but make sure we know how they got so far in without being traced. That's an unacceptable hole."

"Sir!" came the reply.

Then, turning to Laura, he added, "Someone's going to feel the toe of my boot on their behind for this one!"

By this time, the delegates were starting to disperse, some heading off to the gardens and others to the golf, carrying their clubs as well as the freebies of balls, tees, and cleaning clothes that had been left for them in the coffee room.

Laura and Nat trailed those delegates who fancied a swing at the golf in the direction of the driving range and chip and putt. As they let the delegates walk on ahead, they listened to the banter and challenges being levelled to see who could drive the furthest with the new balls they had just picked up and how they should all hit the balls simultaneously. Not particularly interested, Laura and Nat turned off towards the gardens via the pro's shop.

"Well, at least it appears that the conference is going well and that the earlier fracas has been put behind us," Laura commented.

Nat merely nodded and made an affirmative noise as he continued to scan the horizon.

As Laura strolled about the shop, fingering the clothes and other items for sale, Nat chatted to the pro, taking an interest in the new balls he was giving away. "So why give all these balls away?

What's wrong with them?" he asked in a half-teasing, half-serious tone.

"They're the latest and the best, or so I'm told. But as with all new things to enter a traditional game, it is difficult to get take-up. So what better way to get something established than to have a promotional giveaway, particularly to influential people who will hopefully like them and tell others?"

"Yeah, I guess that makes sense," Nat replied, unconvinced, his mind trying to fathom how another attack could be perpetrated, if at all.

"Would you like some, sir?" the pro was asking.

"Huh, oh, yes, thanks." Nat was looking out of the windows towards the distance, searching for anything at all that could be out of place. The pro handed him three boxes, each containing three balls. Without really looking, Nat flipped a packet open and rolled a ball into his palm, toying with it as he watched the delegates approach the range.

"Hmm, an odd feeling to them. Different somehow."

"Exactly, sir. It's as you'd expect from something revolutionary."

"I suppose. Hey, Laura, you play golf?"

"A little, why?"

"Take a look at these new balls." With that he tossed one over to her. "They feel real different." Then, turning back to the pro, he said, "So, tell me the sales talk on why these are supposed to be so good."

432

Laura caught the ball adeptly and fingered it thoughtfully for no more than two seconds before exclaiming, "Shit!" She carefully placed the ball on top of the golf sweaters beside where she was standing and charged out of the shop, shouting to Nat to put everything down. Then, as she approached the delegates, she yelled, "Stop! Stop! No one do anything! Stand still!"

"What the...!" exclaimed Nat, taken aback by her language and action. He partly moved to follow and partly reviewed the ball in his hand and the one Laura had laid on the sweaters. He then stared intently at the pro, examining his face properly for the first time, and he noticed that it was covered in sweat and he had large sweat marks beneath his arms. "What—" he started, but the pro placed a finger to his own lips.

"Maybe, sir, you need to follow your colleague," he uttered whilst holding up a piece of paper upon which was scribbled, "I can't talk," and he pointed to his lapel.

"You're right. I'll be right back for the balls—anything to help my game," Nat replied, and then he opened and closed the door but without leaving. He quietly walked back over to the pro, who was scribbling on a piece of paper, muttering, "Crazy people. A dozen balls and two sweaters—a good start. That's been worth my time." However, he had written, "*They have my family. I had to bring the balls but don't know why.*"

433

Nat nodded and wrote on another sheet, "*OK. Stay here. We can help. What's the address?*"

Armed with the address, he quietly left the shop, breaking into a sprint to follow hot on Laura's heels the moment the door was closed.

When he arrived, Laura was nearly bent double, trying to catch her breath whilst continuing to say, "Don't touch anything, don't do anything," to a lot of bemused and very concerned people.

"Okay, Laura," started Nat. "Take it slow and explain what it is about these balls. Presumably it is the balls, right?"

Laura nodded, breathless after her sprint and barely able to talk. Then between deep breaths she replied, "I don't know what it is about the balls, but they're new and you say they feel different. That's what some of the guys reported about the hundreds of golf balls found and confiscated during the Leicester raid. Too much of a coincidence."

Nat had no hesitation in agreeing. "Okay, everyone, sorry about this, but no golf today. All balls received today, whether free or bought, are to be handed to me immediately please."

Addressing everyone in a very authoritarian voice, François Maranville declared, "I think, messieurs, mesdames, that if the good lady and gentleman here consider that golfing holds potential danger, we should adjourn back to the hotel. More excitement will unduly detract from our intended purposes here today, and it does appear that the challenges ahead of us are of another's purposeful and menacing makings."

The murmurs of assent were unanimous. There was just one voice expressing a level of curiosity. "So just what could be the danger posed by a golf ball? The security services say that they have had sniffer dogs and thorough searches throughout the hotel and grounds, so I'm curious."

"A fair question, sir, because we also checked these balls," replied Nat, looking directly at the speaker, whose name he did not know. He recognised him as being one of the business leaders attending the conference. "Quite frankly, I don't know what risk could be posed by these things, but they feel different from a normal golf ball and only arrived today with the golf pro, who says he has been obliged to bring the balls here today by way of a direct threat against his family. Clearly, I trust that what I've just said goes no further because I have a team racing to his home address as we speak, and we don't want more trouble than we already have.

"That said, I too am curious, so since we have a couple of minutes, may I ask you all to head back to the hotel and I will then try to find out. You will be able to watch from the steps."

Once Nat was confident everyone had both handed in all of the golf balls and was well away, he picked one ball from the pile and walked forty metres towards the fifty-metre marker, a reasonable-sized concrete pillar in the ground.

Taking aim, he hurled the ball with all his strength at the pillar, confident he would be able to hit the target, which he did with ease. The explosion, whilst not huge, obliterated the pillar and would have comfortably killed anyone within the vicinity. However, a second, far larger explosion occurred almost instantaneously as the pile of balls Nat had left behind erupted, sending shreds of balls in all directions.

Laura, watching Nat closely through her binoculars, saw him spin around, mouthing expletives as he saw what had happened. Somehow the explosion of one had caused the detonation of the others within a certain distance. Fortunately, the pro's shop must have been beyond that critical distance as it remained standing, although she did see both the pro and the two security men watching over him emerge from the shop in a great hurry, mouths open in speechless shock.

François Maranville broke the silence of the onlookers. "This is too much. Mademoiselle," he continued, addressing Laura, "there are many questions and so far, no answers. I am sure you will inform everyone present of the conclusions you reach when you do. I am grateful to you for preventing our deaths. But I do suspect that your services will be required at the end of today to assist in unravelling what we think may be happening to critical European medicines."

"You have my word, Monsieur, that everyone will be kept informed. This is most disturbing. We are fortunate that no one has died here today, and let's hope the golf pro's family can be released safely as well. If there are links to what you have been discussing here today, then, most certainly, we will be ready to assist in whatever way necessary."

As everyone trooped back into the main conference room, Laura held back, waiting for Nat. "Now I wasn't expecting that!" he announced as he drew near. "Bloody impressive though, I must say. Each ball individually is a phenomenal weapon, but being somehow linked to others within a certain distance is sheer, evil genius. However it got past the sniffer dogs is beyond me.

"At least assuming the pro is telling the truth about being bugged, those listening in at the other end will assume the dirty deed has been done and was a success. Hopefully, therefore, his family may be safe."

"Ah, so that was your game. I was very surprised by your actions, I must say, but that does explain things."

Nat smiled. "Always sense in my madness."

"Glad to hear it. My concern now is the stockpile in Leicester. We need to find out where they came from and if they are being distributed elsewhere. Imagine this going off at clubs around the country!"

"Just don't go there. I don't want to contemplate the potential, but of course you are right."

Half an hour later, Laura and Nat were in a meeting room busy making and taking phone calls and briefing people about the golf ball situation when Nat's ferocious temper blew.

"Shit, the bastards!" he exclaimed viciously as he slammed the phone down. Looking over at Laura, he elaborated, "Sorry for the language, but the team have just entered the pro's home and found his wife and two children dead, tied up and shot through the heads at close range. The neighbours heard and saw nothing. We need to find these guys and just let me know where and when. Then me and my teams will want to participate and give them some of their own medicine. Now I have to go and tell that poor man. Shit!" With that, he stormed off.

Laura sat there shell-shocked. She knew Nat would be the consummate professional by the time he arrived at the pro's shop. She also knew she felt exactly the same.

Both were relieved when the conference finished and all the delegates had departed. Laura agreed to keep Nat updated on seeking the distributors of the golf balls and left, pleased that she had a driver, and she was soon asleep in the passenger seat as they headed back south to London.

24

As soon as the full details of the events at the conference and the pro's family were relayed to them, Steven Gurning and Rob paid an urgent visit to Burak at his place of incarceration, a farmhouse that was a heavily secured safe house.

Gurning wasted no time in briefing Burak and getting to the point. "Do you have any idea where these golf balls could be made and/or distributed from? Saturday is nearly upon us and will be a typically huge day for people to play golf!"

Burak merely sat there, silent, a look of profound horror on his face.

"Burak!" Rob chimed in. "Innocent people have died today. It had nothing do with the nature of the businesses you built up but was because of terrorism. They were needless deaths, which I know you also abhor. You have to help us.

Think of Evelyne and what she meant to you and your change of heart for the sake of both her and for Anja. That will be how the golf pro feels right now, if not more so because his entire family has just been wiped out!"

Burak looked at Rob through sad, defeated eyes. He had become a shadow of his former self in recent weeks.

"Burak, this is not like you! Where has your spirit gone? Is this how you want Anja to remember you? Come on. You have a great role to play here. I know Emilio's use of your network and links with terrorism have been hard on you, but let's *take him and them down*! Let's *take them down*!"

Gurning left Rob to it, aware that a relationship and level of respect had grown between the two men that he could not hope to emulate, which he was certain would have a far greater effect than his own entreaties.

Burak regarded Rob thoughtfully. "Of course you're right, Rob. It's just having lost Evelyne and effectively lost Anja as well as my freedom, coupled with the realisation that what I created—however dreadful it was—has been hijacked for terrorism is worse than hard."

"Burak, you know you don't deserve freedom! What you have is far more than most in your position. You have access to far more than others and are not incarcerated in prison. Look at you! You're living in relative luxury to enable you to see Anja from time to time, purely and simply on the basis that you agreed to help me and the authorities. This arrangement also provides you with your life which, I am sure you are all too aware, would not be long if Emilio and others were aware of your current arrangements!"

"Okay, okay, I get it. I need to stop moping, snap to it, and regain my zeal. I would love to see Emilio and that lot suffer. To answer your question, the most likely place is Kiln Farm in Milton Keynes and a pair of adjoining warehouses. One is a legitimate distribution business that belongs to Tracy Bond. She's a tough lady who takes no nonsense. Emilio persuaded me to let him use the other since it was sitting empty. Said he wanted it for preparation of materials. The only time I went there, without Emilio's knowledge, the place was decked out big time. At least a quarter of the warehouse space was set aside as a clean room, with a lot of scientific-type equipment in there. I didn't hang around for long; I didn't have the time. Nor did I have the inclination to ask any questions.

"I do know Emilio, under an alias, has struck a lucrative deal with Tracy to distribute his wares all over the place. She, of course, only sees a legitimate business and a profitable contract."

"Sounds worthy of a try," Rob suggested to Gurning.

"I agree, but we don't have time for potshots. That's my concern," Gurning replied.

Turning back to Burak, Rob asked, "What's your business relationship with this Tracy Bond?

Since you are still pulling the levers, would you be able to ask her what orders she has and what shipments she has made in recent days?"

"I guess I could, yes."

Without hesitation, Gurning handed Burak a secure phone one that could not be reverse traced. Burak gave him a hard stare but took the phone and walked over to the corner of the room, where he made the call, speaking in soft tones, disguising his voice in a way that neither Rob, nor Gurning had heard before. They could not hear the conversation clearly, but it was evident that the early minutes were exchanging courtesies and pleasantries. After a while, however, the tone took on a serious, business-like note. Finally, the tone changed again to the typical concluding pleasantries.

Burak leant back against the wall with a deep sigh and stared out of the window. The silence weighed heavily on the three men, none wanting to break those precious moments of private thought. The room was quite small, but the light colours of both the walls and the furniture made it feel more spacious. There were five lounge-type fabric chairs with a small coffee table beside each. A bookcase stood either side of the only door, each one stuffed with dog-eared paperbacks.

Eventually Burak broke the silence, aware of the two pairs of eyes fixed firmly on him. "Yes, she confirmed that her firm has delivered large numbers of golf balls across the country and has an order to pick up many more boxes tomorrow from the neighbouring unit for further same-day deliveries. She's got a pile herself and intends to share them with her friends when they go golfing on Saturday. I didn't have the courage to tell her not to use them. I will trust you to do that and save the goodness only knows how many souls who will otherwise be killed, maimed, or injured. Tracy's a good girl. Go softly on her."

With that Burak walked out without saying anything further to his visitors; he merely muttered, "What have I done?" over and over to himself. As he left, he dropped a piece of paper with the exact address and Tracy Bond's contact details onto Steven's lap as well as Steven's mobile phone. He had done his bit for now. Much more would be demanded of him in time.

"Come on, Rob, let's go. We've got work to do."

They walked out of the farmhouse to the car, ready for the return journey to London. Gurning's mobile phone was already firmly held against his ear, and he was talking earnestly by the time they settled back into the leather seats and the driver set off.

"Rob, I will leave the communication with Tracy Bond to you," Gurning said. "We will go in as soon as Emilio's building appears to be full of people. Your empire is growing, and from what I hear, you're doing pretty well as both owner and ambassador to soothe the transition."

"No problem, will do. It was a shame that Burak left as he did. I was hoping to ask after Anja and how she is doing."

There was a momentary hesitation from Gurning before he said, "I'm glad you didn't. It would have been a little awkward."

To answer Rob's questioning glance, Gurning continued, "Katherine and I have adopted Anja. Burak would have expected you to know, but it was decided to keep this as low key as possible. She needs a home and ideally one that can understand the complexities of her situation and provide the required security. She also needs to go to school. Katherine is a linguist; that's how we met. She also has a degree in psychology, so she should be able to appreciate what Anja is going through. Apologies—I should have let you know. It was clear that you'd grown fond of her and she of you. However, for her sake, opinion is that it's best that connections with the Services are minimised. Unfortunately, that includes you. I hope you understand."

"Yes, I guess I do, and I probably would not be the most reliable contact for her, which likewise would not help in her progression."

◆

Laura knocked on Rob's bedroom door at the Ealing safe house and popped her head round at 5:00 the next morning. Rob was still in bed. "Wakey, wakey," she said brightly.

"Oh, how can you? Surely you're not ready yet?"

Laughing, she entered, still wearing her nightwear of extra-long T-shirt. "No chance. Just wanted to make sure you'll be ready to leave in forty-five. Coffee's brewing downstairs. See you soon."

"Laura."

"Yes?"

"I heard yesterday was rather hairy. I'm glad you're okay."

"Thanks. I'll fill you in on the way to Milton Keynes. We need to get through today as well." With that she withdrew and left Rob to get ready.

Two and a bit hours later they were sipping the day's second cup of coffee at a command centre set up on the forecourt of a vacant warehouse two kilometres away from the target premises. They had driven up in a services-issue saloon and laughed frequently as Laura activated the wipers, making them swish and judder over a dry windscreen, instead of operating the indicator lights.

Rob was in a light grey suit with open-neck blue shirt. "So, are you ready for your meeting with Tracy Bond?" the day's commander asked. "She's expecting you any time after eight o'clock, aware that you may be caught in traffic. She said her diary is clear, and she has not arrived yet. I will let you know when to go. We want you there shortly after she arrives so that she does not take any calls or in-person meetings from the golf ball folks, so you must keep her talking. I suspect that will be easy enough considering your message and the implications for her business.

"It will be only when the other unit appears to be fully operational that we will strike, but no later than nine-thirty. You are not to tell her about the strike until it happens. At that point, a liaison team will come in to evacuate all employees from the side fire escape. A coach will be there to whisk them away to a safe distance. I sincerely hope the explosives won't be used, but we can't be sure. Everything clear?"

"Yes, but I think it's the wrong approach. An hour and a half is too long for me to keep her talking without coming clean about the raid. In her place, she may well ask me to leave after the first five minutes so she can at the very least seek confirmation of what I'm saying and very possibly seek legal advice. My arrival with an unannounced message of this nature will be like a bombshell. This is not the usual way of communicating a corporate change of ownership!"

"Okay then, we will have to play everything by ear and let you go in say fifteen minutes before we strike. That means you will have to wait until the target premises are fully operational. We are monitoring all phones into Bond Distribution, so if she receives a call from next door, if it's at all concerning, we will have to cut the line, in which case we strike immediately and you will follow afterwards, as you did in Leicester. How does that sound?"

"I still think it's the wrong approach, but I am happy to run with it if that's how you want it played."

"Excuse me, sir," a policewoman said as she turned around from her monitoring position. "Prime Zulu has turned up with two others, one of which is Delta from the London op. Delta was held by the third person and appeared both unwilling and possibly beaten."

"Just so I'm clear and that code names have not changed," interrupted Laura immediately, "Prime Zulu is Khartoum?"

"That's correct," confirmed the commander.

"In that case, there is no way that Rob goes in ahead of us. We think Prime Zulu is aware of who he is, possibly even has seen photographs. If he saw Rob going in next door, this operation would be blown, as would the potential for many others! Let me see the third person. If Prime Zulu is here, I'm willing to bet the other is Sharif Al Rashid."

Laura leant over the woman's console to review a replay. "Yes, that's Rashid all right. If both Khartoum and Rashid are here, we should go in now and not risk them leaving."

The policewoman interrupted, adding, "There are still cars arriving at the site, though, and there's quite a lot of traffic on the estate roads."

"Okay," said Laura, turning to the commander. "If you agree, this is how we play it. Prime Zulu must be apprehended, as well as the golf ball operation being taken down. I know we are trying for low key, but if he's here, we must act. If someone mentions they've seen a police command centre in the vicinity, then he's gone, no hesitation. We should block the surrounding roads for incoming traffic now, allow existing estate traffic to dissipate and get to where they are going and then strike. Agreed?"

"Agreed."

Rob could see that the commander was uncomfortable at being given such explicit orders, but he sensibly recognised he had no choice and put everyone on standby to go. Then he set about making arrangements for the road blocks. A covert surveillance team moved in to cover all possible exits to ensure Khartoum did not get away.

A painfully slow twenty-three minutes slipped by before the commander gave the green light to the strike force. Laura accompanied Rob and the liaison team to Bond Distribution, walking through the front door moments after the strike force went in.

The force went in through the three visible people entrances: the front door and side and rear emergency exits. The vehicular roller shutter door was left closed but guarded. Their instructions were clear: no flash-bangs or any other sort of explosive device were to be used. They just did not know enough about how the golf balls worked to risk using anything of their own.

The strike team knocked the doors in using their handheld battering rams, with teams of eight charging in immediately once the doors were down. Half the team entering the front door headed for the stairs to cover the small first-floor office space.

The remainder all found their way into the warehouse space, guns pointed directly in front of them and shouting instructions to stop what they were doing and lie face down on the floor, creating pandemonium amongst all who were there. The space was mostly open, but as Burak had described, a quarter of the space was partitioned off, creating the equivalent of a single-storey large box room. There was a heavy door and viewing panel in one wall, complete with an electronic keypad to control access. Otherwise the walls were solid and blank.

Apart from that, the space provided adequate room for a large van to reverse in and allow the roller-shutter door to close whilst the remainder of the space was fitted out with work benches, some of which appeared to be used for packing and others with mounted vertical drills and polishing equipment for some sort of assembly. Boxes of golf balls were stacked up close to the loading area, and hundreds more balls were in large wire-mesh baskets with empty cardboard boxes waiting to be filled piled high on the work tops. There was no mistaking that they were in the right place.

Most people immediately obliged and fell flat to the floor, and a few hesitated only momentarily.

Four went for their own weapons, either on their belts or lying beside them on a worktop. The armed police wasted no time in killing them. Seeing their colleagues fall to the floor, their heads and chests caving in from the impact of the bullets, was the only incentive those who hesitated required before obliging and taking a prone position on the floor.

The police then cautiously worked their way through the area, cuffing those already lying on the floor and ensuring that no one was hiding in some unseen place. In time, they came to the secured box room. The lead man raised a mirror to see through the visibility panel without having to expose himself.

"Brief activity seen. Unknown number of occupants," he reported before trying the door handle, which did not budge.

However, as he did, a burst of gunfire pepper-potted the door, sending the men retreating behind some nearby workbenches. The gunfire continued sending bullets in wavy lines all around and through the walls.

"Okay, we treat this as a hostage situation and consolidate our positions until we know everyone else is safe and all explosive material and golf balls are removed," the team leader ordered over his radio.

◆

Meanwhile part of the team worked their way rapidly up the stairs, crouched and ready for action. The door at the top was helpfully, but illegally, propped open with a fire extinguisher, giving them a clear view of much of the open-plan office floor, with a meeting room and office at the far end. As they rounded the half landing on the stairs, shots rang out from the far end of the office, sending bullets slamming into the wall above the oncoming police, splattering them with dislodged plaster and dust. The police immediately returned fire to provide cover as they scampered up the remaining few stairs to gain access to the office space and shelter behind some filing cabinets.

A few more shots rang out before a small explosion occurred that sent smoke, dust, and debris flying into the office space.

"Brace!" called the team leader as they all expected the rest of the building to blow because of all the golf balls down in the warehouse. Precious seconds ticked by. "Must be clear. Hold! Activity heading our way!"

From out of the billowing smoke, a figure started to emerge carrying a machine gun. The police called for the person to drop his weapon, put his hands on his head, and lie on the floor. The still-shadowy figure raised his arms rapidly, gun still firmly held and swinging forward. Four shots rang out from the police, hurling the person backwards and onto the floor. The team of four worked their way forward cautiously but without experiencing any further resistance.

When they reached the downed hostile, the lead officer checked him for life signs before confirming he was dead. The officer then cursed, "Damn it, he was a decoy. There's no magazine in the gun, which is also taped to his hand! We were forced to shoot a potential innocent! Looks like Delta."

They continued to work their way forward until they reached the office and meeting room. Darting his head forward and back around the doorframe, the lead officer looked into the office. "Office and meeting room are connected. Someone's in a chair sitting in the doorway between the two rooms. Appears to be alive. You two, take the meeting room doorway, and Joe and myself will take this one," the team leader announced, pointing to two of the officers.

When they were in place, those at the meeting room door reported in, "Ready, guv. Note that a hole has also been blown through the wall into the neighbouring unit."

"Understood. Assumption, therefore, is that this person is another decoy, but be careful. You two watch that hole and cover us. We'll take the chair." They moved in, sweeping their machine guns around to cover the area, and crept around the desk to check for potential unpleasant surprises there. Having secured the room, they approached the chair.

The lead officer gingerly approached the seated figure, who turned slowly on the swivel chair to face the approaching officer. In the dim light, the officer was confronted with a pale and utterly expressionless face with blank, lifeless eyes, as though looking straight through him. There was not a flicker from the eyes nor a twitch from the mouth as the figure slowly moved his arms to open his jacket.

"Shit! Explosive belt!"

That was the last the command centre heard from those four officers as a large explosion ripped through the front of the building, blowing out the curtain walls, both internal and external, the roof, and the floor. A cloud of smoke and dust rose forty metres into the air and covered the officers in the warehouse area below with debris. But still the golf ball explosives did not blow.

The explosion provided the required distraction for some officers to storm the box room, shooting the lock off and rolling into the confined space, avoiding the reactive burst of fire from the two occupants, the bullets smashing and scattering jars, boxes, and other items on the worktops. One of the officers sprayed a long burst of bullets at just above ground level, catching both hostiles in the shins and sending them crashing to the floor, screaming in pain. Rapidly, the officers ran forward, kicking the hostiles' weapons out of reach before rolling them over roughly onto their bellies to cuff them. The lead officer then radioed in.

"Rear box room hostiles down, injured and secured. Assistance required. All other areas secured."

As they entered Bond Distribution, Laura showed the receptionist her identity badge and asked where Tracy Bond could be found before telling her to leave her position immediately and follow the instructions given by the uniformed police who had entered with Rob and herself. The receptionist was required to guide the police around the building to evacuate all occupants. Laura and Rob would cover the first floor as they made their way to find Tracy Bond.

Laura announced her arrival on the floor with style. "Police! Please evacuate the building immediately by the ground floor side emergency exit. You will find officers on the ground floor ready to support you. Go!"

Tracy Bond emerged from her office at the far end, clearly frustrated at the interruption. Her loose-fitting trouser suit was elegant and flattered her large build. She had a commanding presence, with a kind, open, and friendly face. As she emerged, the staff who had stood up and started to leave faltered, looking back at her for guidance.

"Folks, that's an order. Leave! Now!" yelled Laura, having seen the sudden hesitancy. By now she and Rob were two-thirds of the way across the floor to meet the boss lady. "Ms Bond? I'm Lisa Grahams, Security Services. This is Robert Krane, with whom you had an appointment. Unfortunately events have overtaken us, and we need to evacuate the building. Now! We will explain once we are safe."

There was no need to say more as the muffled sound of gunfire was heard from the neighbouring unit, sending the now-panicked staff scuttling towards the stairs.

Tracy Bond fixed Laura and Rob with an initially firm stare and then said pleasantly, "I'll be with you in a moment. I'll just gather my things."

She turned and ignored Laura's protestations not to return to her office. A long minute dragged by before Laura popped her head in the door to insist that they get moving.

Laura and Rob became impatient as they walked slowly through the office, Tracy Bond pushing chairs under the desks as they passed. "Ms Bond, this really is unnecessary. We need to speed up and get you to safety. There are explosives next door!"

Tracy Bond looked at them blankly and as if they were stupid. "I know," she calmly replied, leaving them stunned, momentarily speechless, and totally off guard. With that, Tracy Bond produced a handgun from her oversized handbag and pointed it at them both. "Now, shall we start this conversation again?"

Rob judged the distance between them and sadly realised he was too far away for any action.

"Let's return to my office, where we can discuss my safe passage. I would like my friends from next door to join me, assuming you haven't killed them yet. If you haven't, then all hostilities next door are to halt immediately. While we wait, you can also enlighten me as to how exactly you traced the golf balls here. That idiot of a golf pro didn't know anything, and he was the only outsider I can think of. If you fail to answer satisfactorily and in a timely manner, I will have to use non-lethal parts of your bodies as target practice."

Laura was quick to respond, aware that Rob was trying to get close. She realised that her response would divert Tracy Bond's attention towards herself and potentially help him. "I'm not sure what you mean about golf balls or of your involvement in anything, but it certainly sounds like something we should know about. We were merely following some known criminals and tracked them to next door. You could have walked free without our knowing, had it not been for this." Laura waved a hand casually at the handgun.

It was now Tracy Bond's turn to look slightly surprised. "Uh-uh," she said quickly to both Laura's hand and Rob's proximity.

She then squeezed off two shots at a uniformed and unarmed police officer who had appeared at the top of the stairs, sending him toppling backwards down the stairs with an agonising scream. "Now that'll be a useful message to say that I mean business! Now come on, let's go to my office."

She moved to face them, placing herself equidistant between them, the gun also steadily alternating between them. "Turn round and move!" she ordered again as Laura and Rob, who had their backs towards the office, realised that their opportunity to hesitate further was gone.

Just then an ear-splitting explosion tore through the space from the office, sending fragments of concrete block, stud partition, and glass flying and smacking into them like blunt shrapnel pounding their bodies. Instinctively all three bowed their heads, and Tracy Bond shielded her eyes with her free arm. Rob took the opportunity to kick out and disarm Ms Bond, sending her gun flying off beneath a nearby desk. Laura pulled her own handgun from her bag, but a chilling voice cut her short.

"Drop that pathetic piece of metal, Ms Grahams. I thought I saw you and your boyfriend here as your colleagues broke the peace and quiet."

She turned to see Khartoum standing in the billowing dust with a machine gun pointed at all three. "Ah, Tracy, so pleased you weren't next to the wall when I pressed the button. The mess would have been so much worse. Since you're still alive and didn't leave with everyone else, perhaps you'd be so good as to help keep these two under control.

"Ms Grahams has proven to be a frustrating nuisance in the past, and now that I get a good look at your boyfriend, I would like to know whether it was him who caused Emilio so many problems in Slovenia. His appearance is very similar to the description I heard. I thought it could be but wasn't sure. Emilio will be so pleased. It's a shame I didn't let him know my suspicions as he'd have given me greater resource. He is one seriously annoyed man at the moment."

Laura and Rob looked at each other in a combined mix of horror that Rob had been identified and of relief that Emilio did not yet know.

Tracy looked around unsuccessfully for her gun. "Take Ms Grahams' gun, you stupid woman!"

"Mustafa!" Tracy said, sounding hurt. "Don't be like that, I thought…"

"Exactly your problem, thinking too much whilst flouncing around as some successful businesswoman instead of obeying me or staying at home where you belong!" Khartoum spat his criticism of her out. "Now let's see if you can be useful, and I will consider taking you with me." Then, turning to Laura, he said, "I presume you have a radio. Give it to me."

With the barrel of his gun thrust into her face, there was little choice but to comply. She reached with her left hand into her jacket pocket. "Careful!" exclaimed Khartoum, thrusting the gun at her once again. Laura extracted her radio, carefully pressing the emergency alert and system wipe buttons as she did. *At least the command centre will now know for sure that we're in trouble*, she thought, *even though it should be self-evident.*

"Good," said Khartoum. "Now, to the meeting room over there. We can wait there."

They started to pick their way through the rubble, Rob tripping almost immediately, putting his hands out as he landed and hit the floor. Tracy kicked him in the ribs. "Get up! And keep your hands open and where I can see them."

Khartoum's attention was on him as well, although his gun never moved from Laura. Rob shuffled his hands beneath him to get into a good position and slowly pushed himself up, opening his hands and moving them wide as he did so.

A few minutes later, Rob and Laura were bunched together in a corner of the meeting room on the floor while Khartoum and Tracy sat in a couple of dusty chairs. Khartoum was banging the radio, trying to get it to work when unexpectedly a voice called out from a loud hailer. "Mustafa Khartoum! This is Commander Peeves. Let me speak to your hostages."

Khartoum slammed the radio down onto the table and wriggled through the debris beneath the eye line of the windowsill, the blind swaying gently in the breeze. "You are in no position to give me orders!" he yelled. "I want an Audi RS4, fully fuelled, outside in thirty minutes and a clear passage to wherever I choose to drive. Otherwise I'll start throwing pieces of your woman out this window! And I'll take pleasure in doing so!" he added as an afterthought.

With that he started to work his way back to the meeting room. As he did, Tracy turned her head momentarily to say, "That was fabulous, Mustafa," even before he got to the room.

As soon as she turned her head away, Rob leaned in even closer to Laura and slipped Tracy's gun beneath Laura's now-ruffled and untucked blouse and into her waistband, whispering as he did, "Picked this up when I fell." Then he resumed his initial position again. Laura didn't flinch.

When Khartoum reached the meeting room once more and stood up, he kicked a chair across the room. He didn't like being cornered and trapped. Turning to Laura and Rob once more, he flicked, with a flamboyant wave of the arm, the dirt and debris off the meeting table at their faces, making them flinch and duck.

"You!" he yelled at Laura, thrusting his machine gun at her again once again. "Move over to the other side. I don't like you being together." Laura stumbled up, hunched and flinching, apparently in pain, cradling her right arm to keep the gun hidden. "Enjoy your pain whilst you can feel it!" Khartoum jeered, letting his gun dip towards the floor.

Laura spun suddenly, the dirt scrunching under her feet, her right arm stretching straight out steadily in front of her as she squeezed two shots from Tracy Bond's handgun into Khartoum's chest. He stumbled back, gurgling with a look of startled shock on his face. His involuntary reactions squeezed off a burst from his machine gun into the floor as Laura then shot him through the head before he could wreak further havoc and injure or kill someone.

As that was going on, Tracy Bond swung around, turning her gun on Laura. Whilst she was still rotating, she fired once, too quickly, just missing Laura's head. Seeing that, Rob kicked out and shoved the meeting table into Tracy Bond, catching her at the base of the ribs and toppling her over on the chair with a screech. Both leapt up and raced at each other. Tracy, screaming with rage, raised the handgun, trying to shoot Rob at near point-blank range.

Having despatched Khartoum, Laura turned her attention upon the raging Tracy, and registering the danger, she yelled "Rob!" The call distracted Tracy Bond, making her both hesitate and not focus upon her shooting, leaving herself off balance and shooting wildly. She missed Rob by a wide margin. That gave Laura the precious few moments she required to shoot Tracy Bond in the head and save Rob from harm.

Laura and Rob sagged into each other's arms with immense relief, aware that each had saved the other.

"Strange place to be romantic!" came a familiar voice announcing company as an armed policeman crept into the room. Nat's smiling face materialised from under the goggles as he raised them above his Kevlar helmet. "Come on, you two.

Let's get you out of here for a well-deserved drink and a brush-up."

"Nat! What are you doing here?" Laura exclaimed.

"I couldn't let you handle all these golf balls alone, now could I? Not after all of that useful experience I gained up north!"

As Nat led them back outside, members of the medical team wrapped blankets around them and guided them to one of the nearby ambulances to cleanse their wounds. "Numerous but all superficial, thankfully," they were informed as the dirt was washed from their faces. "You've been lucky. The layers of clothing protected you from the worst of the blasted debris."

Once they had been released from the medical crew and had moved away from the ambulances to make room for more needy folks, Nat wandered over to the nearby perimeter wall on which they were perched.

"No sign of Al Rashid. We'll review the footage from our team's head cameras shortly, but we assume it was Al Rashid wearing the explosive belt. Whether willingly or not, I doubt that we'll ever know. That was four good men we lost today. I'm glad you guys are okay. Rob, it's a privilege to meet you. I've heard quite a bit about you from this young lady and have also followed your competitive career. I'm too old, so I wouldn't stand a chance against you," he said with a wink and a smile. "Catch you both later."

Emergency services people were milling around, tending to the minor abrasions or other ailments suffered by others from the strike team, while police led the arrested folks away from the golf ball bomb factory to waiting vans. The two men from the box room were stretchered out to waiting ambulances. The ambulance doors closed and drove away under police escort. The assumption was that the men had knowledge of both the devices and the source of the materials, so they were important for interrogation by the authorities and also were vulnerable to possible assassination by those with something to protect.

As Laura and Rob continued to survey the scene, the forensics teams arrived in their vans and cars to sift through the debris and collect all of the computers and paper files. The expression on their faces said everything. They were under extreme time pressure to identify where all of the golf ball shipments had been dispatched. Gone was their hope that Tracy Bond would help them with that task. Only after they had found out where the shipments had gone would they start to piece together whatever other information could be gleaned from the two premises. They would start questioning the other employees as soon as possible as well, in case they could shed light on the locations of their recent deliveries.

Meanwhile, the commander was briefing the media at a hastily arranged live news conference. "Ladies and gentlemen, as you can see, there has been great devastation here today, sadly leading to the loss of life of four heroes from our security forces. They died in the line of duty and in the process of saving many lives around the country. Our thoughts are with their families and friends at this time.

"I now implore all golfers and all golf clubs throughout the UK to call a special crisis hotline immediately if you have received free golf balls in recent weeks or have received a shipment of new-style balls ready for promotional activities starting tomorrow. The hotline number should appear on your screens now.

"It is not possible to over-emphasise the dangers posed by these golf balls. If these balls are used, people will die. It is as simple as that. We do know that shipments were dispatched throughout the country, and we are currently trying to identify where they were sent to, but that will take time and we require your help. Call the hotline or your local police immediately. Do nothing with any shipment you have received. You will receive instructions from those on the phone. That is all for now. There will be a more detailed briefing in two hours. Thank you."

"Excuse me, Ms Harding, Mr Krane?" They looked up to see a smartly dressed young man standing in front of them and in the process of producing his MI5 identification. "Mr Gurning asked me to come and drive you home. He added that with the demise of the hostiles, there is no requirement to return to the safe house, other than to collect your belongings."

"Perfect," they said in unison. They staggered to their feet and followed the service driver.

25

Three weeks later, Rob was sitting in the office at Zouches, his injuries sustained in Milton Keynes now barely visible. He had become comfortable in the new surroundings during the weeks since the office had been formally handed over and all of the contractors had left, despite the somewhat eerie feeling of being alone in the vast space. Rob was pleased with the result. It was light and very pleasant. There was colour and the space felt modern but would not be off-putting to traditionalists. Importantly, it felt professional, it had style, and he loved the views and the wide-open vistas across the Thames and London, something that was lacking where he lived, although he did not really spend sufficient time at home to worry about that. In any case, he loved his apartment for its quirkiness.

The administration team had joined him two weeks earlier to familiarise themselves with the systems that had been installed and set up the filing. They also discussed and then established office processes and systems and the contracts for the smooth daily running of the place and generally organised themselves to be ready for this day.

The excitement was tangible between them all when Rob had taken the eight-person team—five women and three men—out for lunch. The chatter was all about the arrival that afternoon of everyone else and the formal opening of Zouches. Shortly after lunch Steven Gurning, Graeme Spreachley, Jed Milligan, and Laura would arrive to meet with Rob and discuss how and when the next phase of dismantling Burak's network would commence, including a discussion about how much should be divulged to everyone else. They would stay on to join that initial briefing before the early evening fun started with an opening party. Unfortunately, because of their business, there could be no guests, but between the twenty of them, the administration team were confident of and determined to create a good time.

Rob was waiting in the boardroom, enjoying the view over the Thames, when Gurning, Spreachley, Jed, and Laura arrived. He was lost in thoughts of distant lands and pleasant weather thanks to a couple of sightseeing boats gently gliding by and a small, white pleasure cruiser that bobbed about on the resultant bow waves. Snapping out of his reverie, he welcomed his visitors and gave Laura a polite kiss on the cheek.

As they took their seats, commenting about the weather and their fortune that the break in the rain had provided a dry walk over to the office, Rob poured coffees and water for everyone. Once everybody was settled, Gurning got straight to the point, in typical fashion.

"The last series of ops were an overall success and certainly will have disrupted matters for this Emilio chap. It's a shame we haven't worked out yet why they targeted that conference, but hey, we saved the day. Even more satisfactory was the taking out of Khartoum and his UK terrorist cell, even though at a high price. We've also picked up a whole load of others from the information found in Khartoum's car.

"The issue with that operation was the lack of time to plan properly. Sometimes that can't be avoided, but I would like to try. I would also like some additional expertise in our ranks and skills to advise on the approach we take when raiding these places. With your agreement, therefore, I will invite Nat McCall to join us. I know you've worked well with him, Laura, and Rob, he has incredible respect for you, which I believe is reciprocated."

"Yes, it is reciprocated, and I will be delighted to work with him," Rob replied, with Laura providing an assenting nod as well.

"Good. For him to really help, we need the plans of all the buildings under Burak's control. Rob, you and I will pay Burak another visit and get the intro to his real estate businesses. He is still sufficiently horrified at what we uncovered through Leicester, Bradford, London, and Milton Keynes that with your persuasive skills, we may just be able to get him to open up."

"I'll brief you on the structure of that organisation at a later date," commented Jed. "Not surprisingly, there are multiple entities but thankfully, in large part, a common group of people. My concern at present is that we have certainty that once we approach these guys, we have visibility of everything. Your own past dealings in real estate matters will greatly assist those conversations. We still need to separate the locations into categories, legitimate and untainted, legitimate but implicated, and straight downright criminal. Of those criminal locations, we need to understand which could be of interest to us and which we should pass on to the police or other national authorities."

"What all this tells me," continued Gurning, "is that while Burak shifted focus to his legitimate businesses, Emilio and possibly others solidified their grasp on their portions of the network, subtly changing emphasis without Burak's knowledge, hence his being blindsided with respect to the links to terrorism.

"Therefore, the intel that Burak is able to provide remains invaluable, but we have to accept there are distinct limitations to that intel—Tracy Bond's involvement with Khartoum being a prime example and no doubt engineered by Emilio. Frustratingly, however, Burak still remains reticent to share everything he has and knows. Why he thinks playing such games benefits him is unclear. That said, what is clear from discussing matters with him, reviewing what he is currently prepared to share, and considering our own intel, one of the hubs of activity appears to revolve around the Black Sea.

"Consequently, going forward for now, I want to split our investigations between activities at home and across the Black Sea region, moving west and northwest throughout Europe. Of course, I also expect that we all keep our ears open for this W person, whoever Doc is, and of course, Emilio and the other leaders of the network. At all times we are to be alert for links to terrorism and other threats to UK interests, whether at home or abroad. To that end, Laura, I have agreed an unusual pact with Graeme and his management in that you will have joint responsibilities across both Services. This will ensure that any links, any commonality, however small, will not be missed. We were lucky this time, and we must continue to generate that luck.

"Rob, you will continue to be central for both the UK and international matters. I suspect you will enjoy at least part of the next element because Burak has informed me that he has a yacht under construction in Istanbul and that it should be ready for handover quite soon. Depending upon suitability, you could use it to cruise the Black Sea and follow any links through into the Mediterranean. Burak has shared that there are locations in many of the ports throughout both seas, as well as throughout the Aegean and Ionian Seas.

"Here's a list of both the UK and international locations I want you to both focus on; yes, I know, there are rather a lot, and you will need to settle on a strategy and order in which to approach this."

Jed re-entered the discussion. "I will continue to assist with the transfer of legal ownership of Burak's assets. I have established contact with a global firm of lawyers to provide the cover through which the transfers can occur. Burak's principal lawyer in Vienna will play ball as and when Burak signs the paperwork. Money has already started to transfer, and assets, including the ownership of companies and the title of buildings, will start soon. From what I hear, there will be no problem about covering the many ports you have to visit from the yacht Steven refers to. It sounds really rather impressive, so I'd like some photos please!" he said with a smile. "And an invite on board, should you ever head this way."

"If it's that grand, we can have a firm's party on board!" Rob suggested, smiling.

"Right, let's have a review of some of the detail within this document," Gurning said, lifting his copy of the previously handed out file.

As they pored over the information in the file and began to discuss the details, the chink and clunk of glasses, plates, and cutlery could be heard in the reception area, together with the rattling of trolley wheels going through into the office area. Soon afterwards the delectable aromas of quality party food eased into the boardroom.

An hour after they had started their meeting, the receptionist knocked on the door to announce that the others had started to arrive.

"Any other business before we close?" asked Steven.

"Just a quick one," asked Rob. "What eventually happened at the GCHQ facility with all those mysterious break-ins?"

"Ah, good point," Steven replied. "It was as the local police suspected, small time criminals trying to get at computers and such like. Some were caught red-handed not long after Laura's visit. They had rather a shock as they looked up the wrong end of six assault rifles!"

"I bet!"

"And as a result, the cover for the place has been blown wide open so they are currently in the process of installing state of the art security measures."

"As they should have from the word go." concluded Laura.

473

Fifteen minutes later, they had joined the small group, and Rob raised his glass.

"Welcome, and I am delighted to announce that Zouches is now open for business."

Everyone cheered and clapped. "My final comment before we party is let's now toast our collaboration with the authorities to smash international crime and terrorism!"

A chorus of hurrahs and cheers rang out across the office as everyone started to sip their champagne and enjoy the canapés whilst admiring the blistering red-orange sunset shimmering on the Thames.

The End

If you enjoyed this book, please take a few minutes to review it on-line.
Also, look out for the next in the series Intervention: The Eavesdroppers by following the Author on Facebook.

James Hanford drew upon his imagination and varied experiences from extensive travels to write this book. He lives in London with his wife and two sons. James started writing as a hobby whilst working as a corporate real estate specialist, which enabled him to travel broadly and meet a great many wonderful and interesting people, sometimes in places he would not naturally visit for leisure, and he is grateful for the privilege of such experiences.